Flying
Between
Heaven
and
Earth

Flying Between Heaven and Earth

Gina E. Jones

Library of Congress Control Number:		2006907516
ISBN 10:	Hardcover	1-4257-3057-4
	Softcover	1-4257-3056-6
ISBN 13:	Hardcover	978-1-4257-3057-4
	Softcover	978-1-4257-3056-7

This book was printed in the United States of America.

McCarty, James Allen and Elkins, Don, and Rueckert, Carla, *The RA Material: The Law of One.* Books I-V, Whitford Press, Atglen, PA (1984)

Mac, Andi, *5 Astonishing Revelations Found in the Mayan Calendar Code,* (an e-book) Mayan Calendar Code/FreshAir Enterprises (2006)

Perala, Robert and Stubbs, Tony, *The Divine Blueprint: Roadmap for the New Millennium,* United Light Publishing, Campbell, CA (1998)

———————*The Divine Architect: The Art of Living and Beyond,* United Light Publishing, Scotts Valley, CA (2002)

To order additional copies of this book, contact:
Xlibris Corporation
1-888-795-4274
www.Xlibris.com
Orders@Xlibris.com
35636

For my daughter, the angel in my life,

And to all the flight attendant angels in the sky.

Preface

Have you noticed how the events of the last few years have caused people to start asking some serious questions? Recently I have had many questions of my own. Questions like: *Who are we really? Why are we here? Is humanity's consciousness shifting? Is time moving faster and faster and if so, why? Is the world at a breaking point because of terrorism, environmental damage, wars, and nuclear weapons? Are we, as human beings, truly capable of experiencing the higher consciousness of unconditional love? What does the end of the Mayan Sacred Calendar in 2012 really mean? Are these, in fact, the apocalyptic, end-of-time days prophesied in the Bible?*

If best-selling novels such as Dan Brown's *The Da Vinci Code* and James Redfield's *The Celestine Prophesy* are any indication, people are searching for clearer answers. My own search inspired me to write *Flying Between Heaven and Earth*. I truly believe this life-changing book has the power to help replace fear with love as it sheds light on answers to these questions and more in a very entertaining yet compelling story for those who desire a deeper understanding of life.

During my study of angels, ancient civilizations, and metaphysics, this story has taken flight. It is a blending of highly spiritual information with my everyday life on board an airplane. As a flight attendant with a major airline for twenty-seven years, I noticed the similarities between flight attendants and angels. Like angels, we're always there, every hour of every day—to guide and protect our passengers, to serve them without judgment. We are there to warn them and help them escape in the event of danger—to show them the way. This story is intended to do the same for the days ahead. It is a story ready to soar and to help show the way for those who are seeking.

Message to the Readers

Twenty-eight years ago, I found myself in Atlanta, Georgia, sitting in the hallway of the personnel office for a major airline. I was looking for an exciting career of travel and glamour. Like so many other applicants waiting for their interview, I wanted to be a stewardess. I knew I was at the right place at the right time. This was going to be a great job with a great company. Good pay with good benefits complemented by lots of time off—this was definitely the job for me.

Becoming a flight attendant, stewardess, or whatever term you like to use—I prefer the name, *Sky Goddess*—was a dream come true. There is nothing in this world like it. And I wouldn't trade my job for anything. I have learned about people, places, things about life, and myself that I would have never discovered in the regular, everyday work world. There is something special about flying and being of Service To Others that is hard to describe. For me, it was my calling and my destiny. Throughout the years, I have had innumerable good times and lots of laughs, made many friends, met amazing people from all around the world, saw the most fabulous places, and found the love of my life sitting in 5D on a flight to Orange County, California. But somewhere along the journey, the turbulence started to get a little rough, disrupting the ride not only for myself, but for everyone who flies.

Unfortunately what was once an exciting time in a world of tourists and businesspeople flying from here to there has turned into a war zone. Every passenger now is considered a possible threat to the very security of our lives and to those of the passengers flying on board with us each day. One minute we are serving you with a cheerful smile, hoping to make your ride most enjoyable, while at the same time we have to wonder, *Are you the one that may try to blow up our plane?* Every time a plane takes off, every time a passenger stands up and walks toward the cockpit door, every time a passenger disappears out of sight behind the seatback to get something from their carryon baggage, and every time there is strange smell or sound, your flight attendants are on high alert.

Although you may never have thought about it before, whenever you fly, the flight attendants on board are the first line of defense while the plane is in the air. While we may be busy serving pretzels and drinks, or even selling sandwiches, we are constantly on guard from the time we board the aircraft until touchdown at your destination. Prior to your arrival on board the plane, the flight attendants have briefed with the pilots regarding the flight and weather en route, searched the galleys, checked their emergency equipment, and ensured that every seat has been inspected for your safety. Today, flight attendants are stressed with what amounts to nonstop battle fatigue from an unidentified, unpredictable, and clandestine enemy.

As flight attendants, we are faced with potential danger every time we go to work. We say goodbye to our families, our children, our friends, and our pets, wondering some days if we will ever see them again. When most of us were hired, our main purpose was to provide assistance in rare event of an emergency or aircraft evacuation. Seldom have we ever had to use the skills that we were trained for. Because of the incredible safety record in aviation, most of us have worked for years and years, never encountering a single emergency situation. In reality, the most dangerous part of our job was driving to the airport. But that has all changed. Our new reality is much more nerve-wracking.

Airline flight attendants are the country's unsung heroes in the current "War on Terrorism" campaign. After the events of September 11, 2001, I found it fascinating how the media was filled with stories about the real heroes—referring to the rescuers, police, and firefighters—who risked their lives to save workers in those buildings. Please don't misunderstand what I'm saying here. The firefighters and police deserve the praise they received. But they are trained for danger. When firefighters and the police arrive, they can basically see what they are facing. They do it every day.

As these dangers in aviation continue, the FBI, the FAA, and other government organizations will never announce publicly where, when, or how a future attack may take place. Airport security alerts vary from week to week. As I write, we remain at Homeland Security Advisory System threat level orange. This means a high risk of terrorist attacks for all domestic and international flights. A ban on liquids and gels in carryon baggage is in full effect. Will we ever see green, blue or even yellow again? I seriously doubt it. Meanwhile, our pilots are now barricaded inside the cockpits behind bulletproof doors, many of them carrying firearms. What do flight attendants have? Nothing. Our captains now regretfully have to tell their flight attendant crews before they lock themselves in the cockpit, "Sorry, you're on your own."

As passengers, you may grumble about the inconvenience of waiting in long security lines and having your luggage searched and your bodies probed. I know there are many who have decided to give up air travel completely. However, flight attendants don't have that option. We have to go to work. While there are some who have no other options but to show up for their trips, I would say that most of us are on board the planes because we choose to be. Every day we choose not to go into the fear perpetuated by the media and the government agencies. Each and every day, we choose to rise above all the so-called warnings to do what we are called to do—to fly and serve others.

In the subsequent years that have followed 9/11, the only public reward for our efforts has been a series of furloughs, pay cuts, and reductions in benefits. Somehow the glamour has disappeared. Yet we continue to accommodate demanding passengers, whose rudeness extends beyond the wingspan of most of our airplanes, complaining about everything—from airplane food, to weather delays, to noisy children, to changing frequent flyer programs. Flight attendants have become the recipients of everyone's frustration. Yet we continue to smile, continue to serve you, continue to come to work 24 hours a day, 365 days a year, flying weekends and holidays—whether it is Homeland Security Advisory System threat level red, orange, pink, or even purple. We are there for you, responding to your requests, constantly providing, and comforting you along your journey. Flight attendants truly are the guardian angels in the sky.

For years, you have heard—and maybe even listened to—our flight attendant mantra, "We are here for your safety." These words ring true more so now than ever. And safety on the airplane, today, means far more than securing the overhead compartments, checking your seat belts, helping with oxygen masks, and opening emergency exits. It means that on each and every flight, we are willing to lay down our lives to protect you.

So next time you are on a flight, thank your flight attendants for being there. Thank them for what they do, because one day it may be one of them who saves your life. And don't forget to thank your own angels too.

This book is proudly dedicated to the unsung heroes—to all the angels in the sky.

 *Chapter 1*

"Dad, I'm really sorry, but I won't be able to get there in time for the funeral," a woman cries in distress at London's Heathrow Airport. Tears drop off the end of the telephone receiver as she wipes her swollen, blood-shot eyes with her last tissue. "Look, I'm doing the best I can! You have no idea what I've gone through to get this far. Here in London they made me check my cell phone, my purse, my books, my camera with all my pictures from the tour and even my carryon bag. I was felt up, patted down, and practically stripped searched at security, and now flight after flight is canceling. And to make matters worse, I had to stand in line for over three hours just to use this damn phone! This is the most frustrating experience I have ever had in my life! Yes, of course I've talked to the ticketing agents, Dad. And reservations and the gate agents. Like I said before, no one is going anywhere—especially New York City!"

The exhausted fifty-three-year-old American slumps against the terminal wall. One of the busiest airports in the world—where over 90 different airlines normally fly to more than 160 destinations worldwide—is at a virtual stand-still. In the last seventy-two hours the MI6, Britain's Secret Intelligence Service, has raised the security threat level to the United Kingdom to *critical*—their highest rating. Heightened security measures are now in effect at England's principal airport and all other UK airports.

In her quiet desperation, the dowdy, vacationing high school teacher feels the burning, agitated breath of other inconvenienced passengers panting down the back of her neck. She feels the intensity of the impatient glare of everyone standing in the long queue behind her. News broadcasts of the terrorist attack, foiled by British authorities, aimed at blowing up airplanes on transatlantic flights between England and the United States, blast through the international terminal as she tries to talk long distance on the coveted airport public telephone. She cringes and then hurriedly covers her other ear when another loud clap of lightening reverberates through the passenger terminal.

She takes a deep, long breath as she tries to explain her predicament once more to her distraught eighty-six-year-old father who has Alzheimer's. Earlier that morning she flew in from Rome—having to leave a ten-day tour of Italy—to catch a connecting flight back home to New York City for a family emergency.

"Dad, I know the funeral has been scheduled for tomorrow. But now I'm on standby. You don't seem to understand—no matter how many times I try to explain it to you—almost every flight on practically every airline is cancelled or indefinitely delayed. The last few flights have cancelled because entire flight crews are walking off the job. Even they're too afraid to fly!

"Just turn on the news, Dad. Now there are reports about terrorist threats being made against the Vatican and the Papacy in Italy because of the asinine things the Pope said in his speech. My God, I was just there! The rest of the history teachers aren't scheduled to leave for another four days. Yes, Rome, Italy! Dad, I said, *Turn on the news*, and you'll see what I'm talking about, dammit!" She slams the black receiver back into its cradle. The distraught woman sobs uncontrollably into her security-issued, clear plastic bag containing the few items that she will be permitted to take on board the plane whenever her rescheduled flight is released for departure. The normally calm and collected, prim and proper spinster turns to the man standing right behind her and, in anguished frustration, screams aloud, "I can't get a flight home for my own mother's funeral? My God, what in the hell is going on?"

The flight-status monitors and public announcements in a multitude of languages at various airports worldwide update weary passengers of flight cancellations and delays. Everywhere, flight operations are strained due to the news of terrorist plots to explode airplanes in flight. Airlines desperately struggle to cover their published flight schedules because of flight crew shortages, severe weather and escalating fuel prices. Meanwhile bizarre weather in London continues to wreak havoc on the already challenged airport operations at Heathrow and Gatwick with strong thunderstorms, lightning and high winds. To passengers all around the world who can't get to where they want to go, it seems as if all hell is breaking loose.

Armed military forces begin to turn passengers in the long, snaking queues at security screening areas away as more and more flights cancel, overloading the departure gates with anxious and disgruntled passengers. Those passengers who are allowed to remain in line watch as special airport trash bins bulge with everything from mouthwash, shaving cream, and hair spray, to bottled water, perfume, and fine wine. The foiled terrorist plot involved chemical and possible gel explosive compounds that were to be brought on planes separately and mixed in flight.

Police K-9 units with their highly skilled, explosive-sniffing Alsatian dogs are checking passenger belongings for anything suspicious. Stringent security measures now preclude anyone from carrying any electronic devices on board like cell phones, laptops, video games and iPods that could spark and ignite such explosives. Only prescription medicine, glasses, passports, keys and small wallets are allowed in the passenger cabins. Since security experts firmly believe the plot is to detonate liquid explosives on the planes, the only liquid allowed to travel with passengers is baby formula, which has to be tasted in front of inspectors by the accompanying parents.

In the United States, Homeland Security Advisory System is now level red for all commercial flights from the United Kingdom to the United States. With a severe risk of a terrorist attack, travel in and out of American airports has been and will continue to be next to impossible for those stuck at Heathrow. The stark vision of the future of air travel is not only seen by those stranded in the airports, but by businesses and corporations watching the unfolding of world events. They can easily foresee the impact that flying will have on their traveling employees and on business in general. Rumors quickly fly around the globe as it becomes glaringly obvious that these restrictions will become permanent.

The fear induced by the thwarted terror plot causes people everywhere to dial airline reservation numbers to cancel their future travel plans. Others frantically call friends and family to say they are too afraid to fly. And the ones who do want to fly are stuck without their personal belongings with nothing to do as they wait indefinitely for delayed flights in overcrowded gates at the departure terminals. Many sit in dismay as crew after crew walk off the planes, refusing to fly under such precarious, stressful, and dangerous conditions.

In every nation, airports broadcast the latest media coverage of the intensifying world events. The school teacher and others—international travelers from a myriad of countries, cultures, races, and religions—cram together into an airport lounge to watch the latest news. Reporters recite officials as saying that the plotters had hoped to bring the commercial passenger planes down in a cascade of horror over the Atlantic Ocean. Twenty-four-hour news coverage with televised atrocities continues to echo in Heathrow and around the globe with up-to-the-minute reports of the investigations into the threats promising the death of Catholics everywhere and irreparable destruction at the Vatican. Unnamed sources try to finger specific radical extremist groups that may be involved.

The teacher of world history sits in dismay as she studies first hand another time in humanity's existence when humans cannot get along. *Despite all the historical events available for study and review, why does humanity want to turn a blind eye to the mistakes of the past? Why does mankind choose to be so helpless, so unwilling to make the necessary changes in their ways.* She shakes her head along with the others as they watch the television broadcasts of senseless wars more closely. Many ask silently in remorse, *When will we ever learn? When will we ever get along and stop killing each other?*

Meanwhile weather forecasters everywhere describe the devastating, climatic, and catastrophic Earth changes that are occurring. The most powerful typhoon to hit China in five decades rages across its southeastern coast, capsizing ships and destroying homes after 1.5 million people are evacuated. The first recorded snow falls on the tropical lands of Somalia. Another earthquake sends a tsunami crashing into beach resorts causing death and destruction in Indonesia. Eruptions from a dormant volcano in Ecuador obliterate surrounding villages. Meanwhile researchers in the Philippines and Italy closely watch their active volcanoes for more activity. In Washington DC more than twelve inches of rain falls in less than twenty-four hours, while New York City receives over fourteen inches in the same period of time. In the United Kingdom, torrential rains continue to cause massive flooding and evacuations in low-lying areas.

Anxious passengers sitting throughout the various airport restaurants, bars, and gates remain glued to the airport news monitors where they watch in horror as death and destruction continue as a result of the ever-increasing freakish storms, massive earthquakes, droughts, record temperatures, raging fires, devastating tornadoes, flooding from erratic hurricanes, and tsunamis. Stranded passengers—with nothing else to do but wait—watch for hours on end, the graphic reports of catastrophic storms that hit South Africa causing a deluge that sweeps across the drought-ravaged southern Cape, flooding towns, cutting power supplies, and washing away roads. Record high temperatures are set in New Zealand while thousands of lightning strikes hit Australia. Europe shivers in a bizarre cold snap during the middle of summer, and unprecedented rains hit Kenya. Elsewhere, a severe Asian drought leaves millions struggling. And off the northwest coast of the United States, over three thousand minor earthquakes occur within seventy-two hours.

More and more stressed-out passengers—confined to the airport terminals with lengthy flight departure delays—gather to watch news commentaries of the global conflicts that are spiraling out of control as more and more countries develop nuclear weapons. Even though the reports have not been confirmed or denied, several third world countries are now strongly suspected to have arsenals of nuclear weapons as they attempt to develop uranium-enrichment technology. Many have successfully detonated nuclear weapons. Meanwhile, in an effort to show their own superiority, other countries publicly declare that they too possess nuclear weapons though they have not conducted any confirmed tests.

Intensely heated debates among politicians, governments, religions, and civilians about the latest events of terrorism, war, and civil unrest play out internationally on CNN broadcasts. Marooned passengers watch in dismay as Al Qaeda militants in Iraq vow war on *worshippers of the cross.* Viewers everywhere can feel the heat and hatred rising worldwide as protesters burn a papal effigy reflecting their anger over Pope Benedict's comments on Islam and the Prophet Muhammad.

As tensions continue to rise, leaders in every religion predict apocalyptic events, strengthening their position of control over their followers through fear of the unknown. At the same time, the Catholic Church appears to be trembling under the siege of the recent terrorist threats, shootings, and death threats to the Papacy. In the airport newsstands, newspaper and magazine headlines everywhere summarize the mood of world. Humanity begs to understand the bigger picture—to understand the *Why?* as well as the *Who?* behind the events. Meanwhile, more and more freedom is readily relinquished by people everywhere as governments promise to increase safety and protection for their citizens.

Heavy rain, lightning, high winds, and ominously threatening clouds continue to hang over Heathrow Airport. In a packed gate area in Terminal 4 where the British Airways flight to New York is experiencing yet another extended delay, bewildered passengers suddenly look out to the empty taxiways and runways where a lone white jetliner waits for clearance to takeoff. The grieving teacher, clutching her plastic bag to her chest, glances out the terminal window with a multitude of other stranded travelers. She gasps and holds her breath then silently says a prayer. The Infinity Airways I-888 jet—fully loaded with four hundred passengers and their extremely heavy karmic and emotional baggage—uses every bit of the long runway to take off into the dark skies above. While everyone observes the airplane lifting off in the pouring rain, the American teacher notices a perfectly dry, fluffy white feather dancing and twirling in front of the glass window. Her spirits lift as she wonders if it's sign—some kind of omen—that things will get better. She looks high above. *Maybe it's heaven-sent!*

Announcements and warnings inside the terminal seemingly grow louder and louder, while the volume of ominous communications all around the world increases in the background of everyday life.

As the soaring jet breaks through the top layer of turbulent clouds and levels off there is absolute silence. A collective sigh of relief is heard among the passengers on board when the seat belt light is turned off. As the airplane heads toward the setting sun in the west en route to Los Angeles, we continue to travel quietly upward into the infinite vastness of space, past the redness of Mars and the immensity of Jupiter where the radiant ringed planet of Saturn looms ahead. In the vast inky black sky, a spectacular shooting star crosses our path. The golden planet with fifty-six moons is the sixth planet from the Sun and the second largest in the solar system. Saturn was so named by the ancients to honor the god of time.

Chapter 2

Between the swirling rings of dust, rock, and ice, an enormously majestic crystalline city sparkles in the distance. In the Eighth Dimension of Consciousness within Saturn's magnificent rings lies the brilliant, sparkling Celestial City. At the main entrance of the divine sanctuary, a heavenly mist escapes into the ethers as angels fly away in swift succession, one after another with gloriously outstretched wings. Just behind the gates that reflect the lustrous white sheen of pearls, more angels wait patiently in line while Eve Matrona, a beautiful yet matronly-looking woman, holds a clipboard to check off their names. She stands proper and erect in her white flight attendant uniform with her long dark hair pulled back tightly, twisted perfectly in a bun.

"Nicole," announces Eve. The waiting angels look around and shrug their shoulders. "Nicole?" Eve impatiently rechecks the departure roster.

A very tall, handsome, and ruggedly masculine man, Archangel Michael, in a white airline pilot uniform suddenly appears next to Eve. His shoulder-length hair is woven with strands of gold while his appearance exudes confidence, splendor, and faith.

"Are we fully staffed, Eve?" he asks. His blue eyes sparkle like diamonds as if they were stars in the midnight sky of the cosmos. His lips are set with the strength of one who only knows wisdom and compassion. "We cannot have any more flight cancellations."

"Everyone is accounted for except Nicole. Who is she, Michael? I don't remember interviewing anyone named Nicole," Eve inquires as she looks to him for an answer.

"Ah, Nicole. I interviewed her myself," he says with a high-and-almighty smile.

Eve glances back at her roster, agitated and slightly resentful of Michael's intervention.

"I thought interviewing was my job. I am . . ." Eve responds sharply.

Lost in silent reflection, Michael doesn't hear her protestation. After a moment, he interrupts, "There's something very special about her, Eve. Seems to be a sort of a free spirit. Wait till you see her—she is full of energy and life as well as sweet, innocent, and quite beautiful. Apparently she's never been considered for an assignment before." A twinkle dances in his eyes.

"So you mean she has no experience at all? Don't you think this assignment is too important?" Eve quickly retorts in disbelief.

"She'll be fine—" Michael begins.

"Time is of the essence, Michael. I'll be departing shortly with the other trainees. I can't stay here waiting for her. We do have an airline to run," Eve interrupts defensively.

Beyond the pearly gates of the Celestial City, more exquisite than the human mind can imagine, massive, pillared crystal buildings, and temples of classic Greco-Roman style surround the city center with graceful yet understated grandeur. At the heart of the divine sanctuary, bathed in radiant light, stands the timeless Council Hall, with towering crystal columns and a kaleidoscopic dome that soars above the surrounding pathways. White marble meditation benches grace the sacred serenity within its gardens of breathtaking beauty. Unnamed flowers scent the air with a pleasant, soothing fragrance. Flawless, perpetual waterfalls of divinity eternally cascade down the walls of the sovereign intergalactic meeting place while the eloquent sounds of angelic choirs echo from every shimmering crystalline surface. A feeling of warmth and well-being welcomes all who enter the heavens of everlasting tranquility.

Dozens of intergalactic beings murmur as they walk up the white marble staircase into the building's main entrance. Many of them point to an enormously tall door just inside the Grand Foyer. They are amused by the handmade "CLOSED!" sign hanging in front of the larger plaque that reads "Hall of Records."

Behind the door, the wings of two angels, Nicole and Alexis, flutter overhead as they search feverishly from shelf to shelf. All around them—aisle after endless aisle, row after endless row—shelves overflow with ancient books, scrolls, and string-bound stacks of old parchment letters.

Alexis exclaims, "Nicole, it has to be here somewhere!"

"I'm looking, I'm looking," Nicole replies casually as she gently slides a pile of ancient journals to the other side of the shelf. She drops down one level and pensively studies the contents of the bookshelf. An ancient Athenian hourglass lies across a short stack of Sumerian clay tablets. Nicole turns the antique timepiece upright, watching closely as the sand begins to pour in a thin constant stream into the lower receptacle. The ever-increasing pile at the bottom changes shape as little avalanches of sand fall away from its heightening sides. The reminder of time prompts Nicole to glance back over at the door. "I really think I should leave for my assignment—"

"You can't! I need your help, Nicole," begs Alexis as she flies with her wings fully extended, halting Nicole before she starts to leave. "This book is extremely important. If I don't find it, I'll be reassigned to only God knows where!"

They descend together toward the floor to look through stacks of old Bibles and parchment scrolls on a large marble table. Alexis appears proper and very intellectual. Nicole is younger with long flowing blonde hair cascading around her beautiful face, radiating naïveté and innocence.

"I'll stay and help you, my dear friend." Nicole hums an angelic melody while she wanders around, curiously scanning through the shelves. Meandering through the vast storehouse of knowledge, she glances questioningly over to Alexis. "What is all this stuff anyway?" asks Nicole, flipping through the worn pages of an archaic manuscript. Casually she strolls over to a golden concert harp sitting near an enormous window, overlooking the city center. She plucks the wires of gold as she continues to hum.

Alexis answers impatiently as she anxiously searches through another table filled with the original Ancient Aramaic Scriptures from Earth. "I told you before—these are the *Akashic Records* known as *The Book of Life*. Inside this vast hall is every word ever written, every thought ever conceived, and every emotion ever felt." Waving her arm around the room, Alexis explains further, "These are the records of everyone and everything in every dimension that has ever existed."

Intently focused on locating the misplaced *Akashic Records*, Alexis continues to sort zealously through parchment texts and stone commandments stacked neatly on the table. Nicole looks around in amazement and then briefly glances out a window where she sees two beautiful white doves sitting on the crystalline window ledge. In the distance, more angels, deliverers of divine messages, continue to depart from the city's main gate. With magnificently beautiful white wings fully extended, they fly away commissioned to execute a task that has been assigned to them. Nicole observes numerous groups of intergalactic, interdimensional beings entering through the city's surrounding gates, walking quickly and quietly on the crystalline pathways toward the hallowed Council Hall.

"What's going on, Alexis? Where are all these beings—" Nicole starts to ask.

Alexis interrupts incredulously, "The emergency meeting of The Council? Everyone in the entire cosmos is invited. Don't you ever read the news, Nicole?" She shakes her head in disbelief. "That's why we have to find that book!"

Nicole looks back at the doves as they flap their wings. "Yes, my little feathered friends, soon I'll be ready to fly somewhere special too. But first, I want to help my friend, Alexis. She needs me too." She gazes longingly out the window into the breathtaking heavens above the Celestial City, wondering what the universe has to offer. Lost in thought, she absentmindedly backs away from the window and turns around, walking full face into a pile of oversized books stacked sky-high on the floor, scattering them everywhere.

"Watch where you're going, Nicole! I just—" begins Alexis as she turns to chastise her young friend for her clumsiness. Alexis's eyes widen in disbelief as she raises them to meet the more bewildered gaze of Nicole. The two of them look over just in time to see another stacked pile suddenly begin to fall, followed by another and yet another, virtually starting a domino effect—a celestial chain reaction inside the Hall of Records. Alexis and Nicole watch in utter horror as the destruction continues. Some of the oldest and most precious books and scriptures of all time begin to tear and crumble before Alexis's eyes. She looks painfully and reluctantly to her friend.

Nicole cringes inwardly, quietly standing with her head hanging down in total sorrow. Both angels stand silently, each for different reasons. To Alexis, it feels as though her long-awaited assignment as an assistant in the Hall of Records will be terminated forever. To Nicole, it feels as if the entire cosmos is staring at the infinite devastation she has caused—the knowledge, the wisdom, the understanding of millions of intergalactic cultures and civilizations now lost for all eternity. In her moment of reflection and repentance, she steals a glance to either side of her. Out of the blue through the settling dust, one of the dislodged volumes catches her eye. She looks up at Alexis with a smile of satisfaction, speechless with joy.

Chapter 3

"We clearly have a quorum. Can't we start this absurd council meeting now?" demands Semyaza, speaking impatiently from behind a newspaper. The endarkened angel with slicked-back thick black hair is sporting a very stylish long black leather coat. "I'm sure that I must have something, somewhere, more important to do," he states arrogantly.

Council of Saturn members Immanuel, Lord Buddha, Goddess Tara, the Prophet Muhammad, Mother Mary, Lord Pacal Votan, Ra, Kuan Yin, Quetzalcoatl, Lord Sanat Kumara, and Archangel Metatron all smile knowingly and exchange nods at the crystalline table where one of the thirteen council seats remains vacant.

Archangel Metatron, one of the most beautiful of all the angels, directs his attention to the impatient angel seated next to him. With glowing wings and a purple hue that surrounds him, Metatron responds calmly, "Semyaza, when will you ever learn to have patience, my friend? You know very well that we shouldn't start without Archangel Michael since this is his presentation."

"That's right, Archangel Metatron," Immanuel adds, his voice pleasant and resonant. Seated on the other side of Semyaza, he looks around at his fellow council members with eyes bright blue and serene. "I can't wait to hear it. Muhammad believes that this may very well help the humans evolve to the next level."

Muhammad, dressed in elegant Bedouin robes and keffiyeh, nods affirmatively to Immanuel. During his mission to Earth 570-632 C.E., Muhammad initially adopted the occupation of a merchant and was a charismatic person who was known for his integrity. In his youth, his nickname was *Al-Amin*, a common Arab name meaning *faithful, trustworthy*, and was sought out as an impartial arbitrator. He united the tribes of the Arabian Peninsula into a federation of allied tribes with its capital at Medina. During the holy month of Ramadan, Muhammad would retreat to a cave located at the summit of Mount Hira, just outside Mecca. There he fasted and prayed, and would often reflect on the troubles of the Arab society that seemed to affect him so profoundly. While receiving the verses of the Qur'an, Muhammad expanded his mission to be a prophet who spoke publicly preaching strict monotheism, preaching against the social evils of his day, and warning of a day of judgment when humanity shall be held responsible for their deeds. The Prophet of Islam did not wholly reject Judaism and Christianity, two other monotheistic faiths that were known to the Arabs, but was sent by The Creator to complete and perfect those teachings. His mission was one of restoring the original monotheistic faith of Adam, Abraham and other prophets whose messages had become misinterpreted and corrupted by people over time. Muhammad's mission continues today as he serves faithfully on The Council of Saturn.

Known for speaking only when necessary, for keeping his feelings under firm control, Muhammad, whose Arabic name etymologically means *The Praised One*, remains direct and to the point as the meeting continues. Seated between Mother Mary and Goddess Tara, the Prophet joins in. "My brother, I am hopeful, even though you have been preaching unconditional love and nonviolence to them for over two thousand years now. They do seem a little slow on the uptake, don't you think?" Muhammad's pleasant smile reveals his fairly large mouth. His broad and prominent forehead is graced with big black eyes, which accentuate his long and thick eyelashes. His sloping nose, his black beard, and his fair complexion further enhance his handsome looks.

"Sadly, yes," Immanuel agrees, stroking his thick beard that reaches below his chin. His ageless face reflects his majesty and mildness. Waves of chestnut-colored hair fall around his shoulders as he leans over to pat Semyaza, his fellow council member, on the back. Given the gift of a gentle hand and a kind heart, Immanuel smiles compassionately at the Lord of Darkness. With his strength of heart to be kind, Immanuel also extends his strength of spirit to forgive his old friend. "But if they would finally embrace nonjudgment, the rest would follow. Right, Semyaza?"

Mother Mary, Goddess Tara, and Kuan Yin smile knowingly and then speak in unison, their voices joining together, harmonizing like music. "Humans are still learning. They won't understand nonjudgment until they know compassion."

Semyaza, impatient and agitated, rustles his newspaper loudly in frustration. "Yeah, yeah, we all know how incredibly self-absorbed they are. They don't care about anyone but themselves. 'What's in it for me? Me, me, me!' Isn't that true?" demands Semyaza. Pausing momentarily, he stares at The Council with a loathing look. Slowly his features ease into a faint smile, then into a fully self-satisfied grin.

Mother Mary replies emphatically while a beautifully beneficent radiance exudes from her entire being. "Thank goodness that's not entirely true, Semyaza, and you know it."

"No? Then why don't they listen to that old worn-out message delivered by every one of you saints, holy people, masters, avatars, adepts, prophets, yogis, and saviors or whatever else you call yourselves? You keep on saying, 'We are all one, originally separated from The Creator, and we lost our way. It's time for humanity to come home.' Blah, blah, blah! Come on, friends, it's obviously not working!"

A light-skinned, bearded Mesoamerican deity seated at the council table between Kuan Yin and Lord Sanat Kumara stands in his colorful ceremonial Mayan regalia. He clears his throat and promptly addresses the assembly. "I am Quetzalcoatl. On behalf of The Council of Saturn, we greet you in the Love and the Light of our Infinite Creator. It is the highest truth that we present to you today. Humanity on Earth is literally running out of time as they know it. The Mayan Sacred Calendar is complete in the year 2012 for that exact reason. That leaves little time to help our friends advance to the Fourth Dimension."

Semyaza rustles a page in his newspaper and gives a loud *humph*. "Coming from a deity that encouraged human sacrifice—that's pretty rich!"

"Now, Semyaza, let's be honest," replies Quetzalcoatl, appearing old and wise in his feathered, conical headdress. His penetrating eyes hold the quiet challenge of Semyaza's words. "If you will remember, I was the one who abolished human sacrifice, transcending the local traditions and beliefs, offering compassion for all humanity, even if it was only temporarily observed by the people. Don't forget, it was your Forces of Darkness working through the local priests that ensured my demise."

"Oh, come on, Mr. Plumed Serpent! Can't you do better than that?" jabs Semyaza, grandstanding before everyone at the council table. "With your so-called prophetic prominence, couldn't you do any better than being one of those feeble little deities for the Aztecs, Toltecs, and those other pathetic Middle American peasants?"

Quetzalcoatl looks respectfully to The Council for permission to continue while everyone in the gallery watches Semyaza, who seems determined to corrupt any information offered by the Aztec god of light. The name *Quetzalcoatl* unites *Quetzal,* a bird of Mexico renowned for its brilliantly colorful plumage, with *coatl,* a serpent. The Resplendent

Quetzal, reputed to be the most beautiful bird that exists in the American continents, was sacred to the Mayans and figures prominently in their artwork and legends. This famous bird has a history as long as its tail since it was considered to be the spiritual protector of the Mayan chiefs. The iridescent color of its plumage appears green or blue, according to the changes of daylight. Integrating what soars brightly in the air and what slithers on its belly on the earth, the mythical symbol of Quetzalcoatl unites perceived opposites like Spirit and Matter, Heaven and Earth, and Light and Dark. And even in the Eighth Dimension of Consciousness, challenged by the Lord of Darkness himself, Quetzalcoatl continues in his efforts to help unite humanity with its highest destiny.

Lord Pacal Votan, in decorative-silk royal Mayan robes, stirs in his seat as he sits directly across from Semyaza. He hears Semyaza's sardonic tone and frowns. Agitated with Semyaza's attacks, Pacal Votan comes to Quetzalcoatl's defense. As he speaks directly to the Lord of Darkness, his manner becomes more authoritative while sharply clipping his words. "As far as those *pathetic peasants* are concerned, Semyaza, it is the Mayan civilization that may very well save our human friends, despite your efforts to do otherwise."

Semyaza yawns loudly to annoy Lord Votan further. He stretches his upper torso across the council table while strumming his thick dark fingernails in front of Pacal. The two lords exchange an unnervingly intense look. Semyaza slowly folds his arms on the table's crystalline surface and rests his head on top, pretending to take a nap.

Pacal continues, his annoyance firmly leashed as he ignores Semyaza's obnoxious antics. "Beyond their towering stepped pyramids and ceremonial centers, it may be the Mayan calendars, mathematics, and astronomy that will assist our awakened friends on the planet as to what lies ahead. Without metals, wheels, or beasts of burden, the Maya built astonishing cities and temples. As a Galactic Master of Time, I was assigned by The Confederation to alert humanity to the closing of this cycle of cosmic amnesia and the dawning of a new creation. This mission was quite successful due to Quetzalcoatl. Inscribing stone monuments with precise astronomical and astrological information to save humanity is not too shabby for *pathetic peasant* work, Mr. Lord of Darkness! And pretty powerful work for two *feeble little deities*, wouldn't you say?" Pacal's exasperation creeps through giving an unwanted edge to his voice. His generally easygoing demeanor loses its pleasant smile, becoming quite firm and forbidding. He looks to the overflowing gallery of guests. "The Mayan Calendar is real and is pointing to the coming cataclysms. It has a schedule. The schedule had a beginning 16.4 billion years ago. The schedule has an end, coming in less than five years during the Galactic

Alignment when the Earth's Sun, on the winter solstice, moves to the heart of the Milky Way Galaxy. This schedule for the divine evolution of consciousness was encoded in this calendar."

Pacal turns his attention back to the Lord of Darkness. "Can you think of anywhere better to put a timeline than in a calendar, Semyaza?"

Long ago, The Infinite Creator chose Lord Pacal Votan to come to Earth to be a teacher, much like a brilliant sun, to illuminate the native Mayan people. Bringing into his earthly incarnation the unknown sciences, the powers of healing, and the secrets of chakras and the kundalini, Pacal also brought forth his knowledge of the tunnels of time. Arriving into the world as an enlightened being, he shared his wisdom and the history of time. Pacal fulfilled the mission of guiding the Mayan civilization toward the cosmic light of wisdom. It is evident that these ancient people were intuitively aware of the basic rhythm of divine creation. Now the hallowed human race draws on that shared wisdom to complete its destiny of enlightenment into the higher dimensions.

Placing his palms together in front of his chest, Semyaza respectfully bows to apologize to Quetzalcoatl. However, Semyaza continues to arrogantly mock Pacal in front of everyone present by completely ignoring him and his comments. Pacal turns an angry glare on his fellow council member.

Immanuel laughs heartily, empathizing with Pacal and Quetzalcoatl having such aspersions, slanderous and defamatory remarks cast in their direction. "Indeed, my brothers, just ask me if you want to know about being misrepresented!"

"Despite our efforts, humans have forgotten The Law of One—that All are Part of The One—losing all sense of freedom, balance, and peace for everyone," adds Gautama Buddha, seated to the left of Immanuel.

Siddhartha Gautama, known as the Buddha, went to Earth in the sixth century B.C. in what is now modern Nepal. His human birth father, Suddhodana, was the ruler of the Sakya people and Siddhartha grew up living the extravagant life of a young prince. According to the local customs, he married at the young age of sixteen. Subsequently his father ordered that he live a life of total seclusion from local peoples, but one day, at the age of twenty-nine, Siddhartha ventured out into the world and was confronted with the reality of the inevitable suffering of life. The next day he left his family and kingdom to lead an ascetic life and determine a way to relieve universal suffering.

For six years, Siddhartha submitted himself to rigorous ascetic practices, studying and following different methods of meditation with various religious teachers. But he was never fully satisfied. One day, however, he was offered a bowl of rice from a young girl and he accepted it. In that moment, he realized that physical austerities were not the means to achieve liberation. From then on, he encouraged people to follow a path of balance rather than extremism. He called this The Middle Way. That night Siddhartha sat under the Bodhi tree, and meditated until dawn. He purified his mind and attained enlightenment at the age of thirty-five, thus earning the title Buddha, or *Enlightened One*. For the remainder of his eighty years, Buddha preached the eternal truths in an effort to help other sentient beings reach enlightenment. Now, serving on The Council of Saturn, his efforts continue.

The universal emperor's face shines with divine splendor and effulgence, smiling gently with clear wide-open brown eyes. He sits in monastic saffron robes, crossed-legged in his favorite yogic position. "Every living being has the same basic wish—to be happy and to avoid suffering. Humans have spent much time and energy improving external conditions in their search for happiness. What has been the result?" asks the Awakened One, gifted with great celestial discernment. "Instead of fulfillment, human suffering continues to increase while the experience of happiness and peace is decreasing. This clearly shows the need for them to find their true path before 2012 and the . . ."

Nicole and Alexis stand quietly at the entrance doors to the interdimensional, intergalactic meeting hall, gazing in awe at the numerous angels, archangels, diplomats, ambassadors, and shimmering light beings present. In the center of the vast circular crystalline chamber sits The Council of Saturn where the clash of temperaments and convictions continues.

"I've never seen so many angels and ascended masters in one place," whispers Alexis. "They say that each ascended master on The Council of Saturn has gone through the karmic wheel, learning all their lessons while transmuting their karma. It is collectively known throughout the heavens that they are no longer compelled to experience being reborn into a physical body in any universe if they do not choose to. Their scope and measure in the infinite cosmos is beyond comprehension."

Nicole whispers back, "Well, something universally compelling in these heavens must be happening to bring Immanuel, Lord Buddha, Goddess Tara, the Prophet Muhammad, and Mother Mary together."

"It's Earth, because there's Lord Pacal Votan, Ra, Kuan Yin, Quetzalcoatl, Lord Sanat Kumara and—" Alexis pauses momentarily to get a closer look. She points enthusiastically. "Look over there, Nicole. That's my boss,

Archangel Metatron. He's on The Council too!" exclaims Alexis excitedly yet quietly. "Wow, look at that! Right next to him is Semyaza. Who would have ever guessed that he would be here? You do know that he is one of the leaders of the evil angels who fell, right? And that he now serves as the Lord of Darkness between Heaven and Earth."

Distracted by the magnificence that surrounds them, Nicole replies weakly, "Really?"

"C'mon, the meeting has already begun," encourages Alexis.

Chapter 4

"Pardon the interruption, Lord Buddha," asks a flustered giant green alien with glowing purple eyes. In the front of the gallery of guests, he stands tall and erect, wearing a purple tunic, towering over those seated around him. The sound of irritation echoes in his words and around the chamber. "Can you please tell me why I have been summoned to a meeting about this Earth and its uncivilized inhabitants when my planet is evolving perfectly in another part of the galaxy into a higher dimension?"

An avalanche of small conversations ensues with clusters of beings murmuring and nodding to each other in agreement. The cacophony of dialogue is suddenly interrupted by The Creator's brilliant pure white radiance that envelops the entire assemblage in the Council Chamber. The room is swathed in flowing, iridescent Light as the omniscient voice speaks. It resounds clearly from every surface as a divine, unified chord of male and female voices blended together in perfect harmony.

"Beloved hosts of ascended masters, cosmic beings, ladies and lords, intergalactic friends, universal ambassadors, archangels, angels, and honorable guests of the Confederation of Planets in the Service of The Infinite Creator, We welcome you to The Council of Saturn on behalf of The United Stellar Alliances and The Greater Interdimensional Federation of Light. We have asked Ra, our devoted servant from the Sixth Dimension of Venus, to explain our urgent agenda for this meeting and give those beings from parallel and alternate universes some understanding of what we are facing here and the opportunity to participate in this most extraordinary intergalactic event. Ra, please chair the meeting until Archangel Michael arrives."

"Yes, my Lord," Ra responds in a most reverent tone. "I am Ra, a humble messenger of The Law of One. I greet you in the Love and Light of The Infinite Creator," he proclaims. Tall and perfectly proportioned as a god, Ra stands proudly before The Council and its guests. Robed in his ancient white Egyptian ceremonial tunic of fine-woven linen elaborately decorated with feathers and sequins, Ra addresses everyone, thanking them for their attendance. With his striking appearance and distinguished blue eyes, the powerful force for good begins to explain to those beings not familiar with Earth's progress that the time for the planet's ascension is at hand.

"Earth, as many of you know, has already begun her dimensional shift, raising her vibrational frequency. Humanity does not fully understand or acknowledge their Mother Earth as a living consciousness or that her frequency is increasing. Those of the Dark Side, operating within the human population behind the veils of their media, governments, religions, and multinational corporations, have intentionally for their own gain withheld this information from the masses. Therefore, humanity has no basis for knowing . . ."

Alexis and Nicole scurry to the council table struggling to hold on to an immense and very heavy ancient book. They look around in awe and wonder at the luminous ivory chamber with neither ceilings nor walls and only the faintest suggestion of a floor covered by a heavenly mist. Alexis looks to Archangel Metatron for further instruction.

"My liege," Alexis speaks softly then bows reverently. Nicole, unsure of what to say or do, nervously tries to curtsy then gives a friendly wave to him, all the while trying not to drop her end of the book. Archangel Metatron raises a knowing eye toward Nicole in his amusement. Moments later, he nods granting the young angels his permission.

Upon receiving his approval, Alexis and Nicole proceed carefully. As they cautiously fly overhead to place the colossal volume of the *Akashic Records* carefully in the center of the table, Nicole looks to Metatron for confirmation. Still hovering above, she cannot help but notice Semyaza seated next to him. Semyaza smiles at her with a smile more frightening than his intensely malevolent glare. Unable to maintain control, Nicole drops the book, and it lands on the crystalline table with a loud thud. Nicole shrugs her shoulders apologetically to Alexis, then to Metatron as he looks their way.

Across the old worn covering, the golden inscription reads, *The Book of Life: Planet Earth—Third Dimension*. The two angels glance at each other nervously and then rise. Alexis and Nicole fly expeditiously back toward the entryway and out of the meeting hall, relieved that they were finally able to locate the records for the historic intergalactic-interdimensional assembly.

"What a job that was! I still can't believe that I misfiled that book, Nicole. This new assignment in the Hall of Records is so exciting, yet I have so much to learn. I'm glad Archangel Metatron is in charge of *The Book of Life* and not me," muses Alexis as they fly joyfully together down the hallway. "Thank you, again, for stumbling into it—literally!"

"I'm so delighted that you received such an important assignment, Alexis, and such a great boss," Nicole heartens happily. They fly in silence for a moment when Nicole ventures to find out more about her friend's supervising angel. "I did not realize he was so . . . so tall and . . . so powerful. Your boss seems to wear power and authority as another would wear a mere cloak. Is it really true that he was once a mortal man who walked upon the planet Earth?"

Alexis smiles proudly as she boasts, "Yes! And because of the work he did as an honest and skilled scribe writing *The Book of Enoch,* he was escorted directly to the Seventh Heaven by The Creator and given a similar assignment here in the Celestial City. It is his primary task within the heavenly court to maintain the eternal archives for our One Infinite Creator, recording each and every event that transpires in all of Creation. Can you imagine the responsibility he has, Nicole? He also holds the highest power of abundance."

"Wow, now that's an assignment!" exclaims Nicole as they reach the main entrance to the Hall of Records and land gently on the gold-veined white marble floor.

"I see him work tirelessly to help Earth's inhabitants," Alexis explains further as the two angels converse quietly at the entryway. "He acts like an intermediary between Heaven and Earth, since he's had extensive experience as both a human and an angel. As such, he helps other angels to really understand the human perspective."

"Now that's something I would like to do," Nicole reflects. "But I guess that couldn't happen to someone like me who has never had an assignment before."

"Speaking of assignments, Nicole, you better hurry!" prompts Alexis.

Chapter 5

Two slender humanoid beings in long belted silver tunics watch momentarily as hundreds of heavenly angels leave the Celestial City through the main gateway. The two Plejarens are there to attend The Council of Saturn meeting. They walk quickly toward the Council Hall, having just arrived at one of the other city gates. Pleija and her father, Ptaah, had difficulty locating a parking space for their spacecraft on the outer rings. She looks back over her shoulder to admire all the beautiful departing angels.

"I wonder where they are going, Father," comments Pleija. "Looks like they are on some kind of mission, doesn't it?"

Ptaah nods in agreement. "Earth, I hope. Humanity needs more help and loving guidance now than in any other time in their history, Pleija."

Quickly they merge with others who are walking quietly toward the heart of the city. A sense of urgency permeates the air as more and more beings arrive through the gates surrounding the Celestial City. Pleija and Ptaah pause briefly, looking up at the magnificent heavenly entrance to the Council Hall.

"What an honor to be here, Pleija. Our invitation is truly a tribute to the work we are doing, my daughter," reflects Ptaah as he looks back to the skies above. "Strange that home seems so far away right now. Look!" he says elatedly. "There's our star system, Pleiades, over there in the constellation Taurus."

"Well, I'm certainly glad I did the navigating today," Pleija teases, pointing in the opposite direction. "Our planet, Erra, is about five hundred light-years from here. Please don't tell me you're homesick already, Father. We just arrived!"

He lets out a loud sigh, stroking his graying reddish moustache and full beard as they look out into space. "I do have to admit, as commander of the Plejaren spacecraft fleet and presiding over three different planets, a little time off at home would be nice. However, our work on Earth is definitely not over."

The two Plejarens are from a well-known family whose souls previously lived on Earth and evolved, surpassing human beings. Existing in a higher evolutionary pattern, they now function in the Fourth and Fifth Dimensions of Consciousness. Their desire is to oversee, not interfere—to intervene only when absolutely necessary to help stabilize Earth. It is common knowledge among their people that humanity is truly struggling, sending out a discordant vibration that is not in rhythm with the harmony of the rest of the solar system. The reason Ptaah and his youngest daughter have traveled so far to come to the meeting is to further assist their human friends and to help balance the energy of Earth. They recognize humanity's need to generate a flow of higher consciousness toward manifesting oneness on the planet by the Earth's year 2012.

Ptaah gently nudges Pleija to continue as he sees even more arrivals following behind them. He observes a daunting group of Reptilians moving quickly in their direction. Pleija looks back over her shoulder to see what has captured her father's attention as she notices his furrowed brow.

"Indeed, it does seem as though everyone in the entire cosmos has been invited," remarks Pleija, noticing the commanding Reptilian as he militantly marches forward with his minions following closely in his wake. His size and demeanor are anything but friendly. Crocodilian skin with coffee-colored scales outlined in dark green covers his firm yet lean, erect nine-foot-tall body.

Moving ever closer behind them, Ptaah queries his slender five-and-a-half-foot-tall young offspring about the Celestial City. Like her mother, Pleija's very long and somewhat forward-placed earlobes form a special distinguishing feature accentuating the fair complexion of her pretty face. Her straight light blonde hair rests gently on her shoulders, and her blue eyes sparkle with excitement as her father and she continue.

"The Celestial City is a neutral ground, right? No weapons, right?" asks Ptaah.

"This *is* the Eighth Dimension, Father," confirms Pleija knowingly. "Although I understand that they have lowered the dimensional vibrations for this meeting so all may attend."

"Then everyone in attendance is to be respectful—withholding any aggressive action. Right?" asks Ptaah, observing the Reptilians' powerful legs and arms as they all walk up the tiered marble staircase. "You know, Pleija, even though our friends over there have large brains and are possibly more advanced, I don't necessarily sense a compassionate intellect among this particular group." Ptaah feels very uneasy as one of the Reptilians glares at him intently.

Pleija turns her head slowly as she begins to sense the same thing as her father. She looks twice as the commanding Reptilian flares his broad snakelike nostrils.

"I know this is supposed to be neutral ground, Pleija, but I really don't trust these cold-blooded shape-shifters from the Orion constellation," he mumbles quietly, not wanting to be overheard. "They have done so much on Earth to interfere with the assistance we have offered our human friends. The Orion Group's only calling is conquest, dominance, and enslaving the *un*elite—those innocent beings who are not of the self-serving Orion vibration. The Orion Group is of a very dark negative polarity, indeed. I must say I am truly shocked any of them actually showed up for this most benevolent meeting since they regard humans as a totally inferior race."

"And I guess it shouldn't be any more surprising that a faction of Grays is right behind our Reptilian friends, Father. I guess they just arrived from the star systems of Orion and Zeta Reticulum," whispers Pleija.

Ptaah looks back to see the Grays Pleija is talking about. Dozens of small thin-built beings, with tough grayish white skin, large and rounded rear skull areas of an inverted triangular shape, follow the Reptilians closely. Resembling a praying mantis, the Grays' arms reach to their knees. Although absent of ears and noses, the cloned beings with large oval, tear-shaped opaque black eyes with vertical slit pupils seem to be focusing intently on Pleija and Ptaah.

"They do continue to heartlessly abduct and traumatize the humans without consent. And that certainly makes our job more difficult as humanity now considers all intergalactic citizens their enemy." Ptaah shakes his head incredulously. "It's interesting that after all this time the Grays are not masters of their own fate, rather they're still subservient to the Reptilian race."

While entering the resplendent crystalline structure, the Reptilians abruptly push Pleija and Ptaah out of the way when they march through the Council Hall doors at the same time.

"Hey there, fellows, watch it! Look where you are going—" starts Ptaah as he puts his arm around Pleija to protect her. The Reptilian Commander marches onward invoking fear in all those who cross his path, creating terror wherever he goes. Meanwhile his minions slam full force against Ptaah's midsection. As Ptaah begins to double over, they collide forcefully into him again, knocking him and Pleija toward the entrance door to the Hall of Records where Alexis is hugging Nicole goodbye. The tremendous impact of the last blow sends Ptaah stumbling to the floor sideways, knocking Pleija off her feet.

"Goodbye, Alexis. I hope to be back soon!" exclaims Nicole cheerfully as she spreads her wings to leave the Council Hall.

"Nicole, I'm going to—" Alexis suddenly looks down when out of nowhere, Pleija rolls into her shin. Seconds later, Ptaah barrels into Nicole, throwing her against the door causing the side of her outstretched wing to break over.

"We're so sorry," exclaims Ptaah apologetically. The Plejaren Commander, who took the full brunt of the blow, struggles to help his dazed daughter from the floor.

"What in the heavens!" Alexis cries out as she finds herself standing face-to-face with Pleija and Ptaah.

Nicole gazes longingly toward the entrance door. "It's time to fly, my friend," says Nicole as she looks back to Alexis then over to her injured wing and ruffled feathers. "Or maybe I should just walk," chuckles Nicole, trying to make light of the situation as she notices the repentant look on Ptaah's face.

"Yes. You have to go now, Nicole. It's time!" says Alexis reassuringly. "Go! I can take care of everything here." Alexis tosses a glance back to the Hall of Records and then looks curiously with upraised brows over to Pleija and Ptaah. "Remember, Nicole, trust your heavenly instincts—and trust your wings of divinity—as they will always guide you where you need to go!"

Pleija watches in awe as Nicole spreads her graceful wings outward, glowing pure white. She notices the sharp arcs at the upper arches of the angel's wings that turn inward and the long primary feathers that sweep down and outward, visible manifestations of their aptitude for swift flight. Ptaah, impressed with Nicole's wingspan, stands quietly in wonder. Alexis smiles proudly at her angelic friend and then hurriedly directs the two Plejarens toward the meeting.

Ptaah and Pleija hasten down the hallowed hallway through the massive crystal double doors. They stand in awe as the Council Chamber's gallery is overflowing beyond capacity with prominent angels, evolved souls, and a variety of intergalactic, interdimensional beings. Crystal pillars and sculptures glisten everywhere throughout the vast circular amphitheater. At the very center stands the magnificent crystal council table that radiates golden waves of white light from its center out to infinite distances.

"Have you ever seen so many prominent beings in one place before?" Pleija asks faintly, bewildered by the sheer magnitude of the gathering.

Ptaah shakes his head, enveloped with a sense of profoundness.

"Look over there, Father," Pleija whispers. "Look at The Council. Something of a supreme magnitude must be happening somewhere in the cosmos to bring this group together!" The Plejaren daughter and father observe numerous ascended masters bedecked in their traditional regalia, some in more contemporary Earth apparel, while others are in fashions that suit their extraterrestrial bodies.

Ptaah's expression becomes somber and stern when he sees the Lord of Darkness seated on The Council. "Look over there, Pleija. It's Semyaza, sitting right next to Immanuel. It is said that Semyaza now hangs between Heaven and Earth, head down. Legend has it that he, in fact, is the constellation of Orion. My sense is Semyaza is up to something, Pleija, and it can't be good."

"Well, that certainly explains the Grays and Reptilians being here. I can only imagine what other factions of the Orion Group that Semyaza may have summoned to this event," Pleija whispers. "By the way, Father, have you noticed that all of the council seats are filled but one? I wonder who that one is for."

"Well, certainly not me!" Ptaah chuckles. "Pleija, I think this emergency Council of Saturn meeting has already begun." He extends his arm prompting her to begin looking for a place to sit.

Chapter 6

Inside the crystalline Council Chamber, Ra continues to chair the meeting for The Council and its guests.

"The main cause of recent events on Earth lies not only within humanity itself but beyond their planet into the reaches of the galactic level."

The Book of Life opens by itself to the very last chapter. Murmurs are heard as vivid scenes of humanity's behavioral history, provided by a holographic display, are emitted from Earth's *Akashic Records* at the center of the council table. Everyone sees, hears, touches, smells, and senses emotionally what is being presented.

Ra begins the presentation, the hologram matching his words. "I invite everyone to observe and experience these Earthly scenes where the Spanish Inquisition seeks out non-Christians and persecutes them relentlessly. These audacious conquerors literally built their Catholic faith atop the remains of the older religions. Here we have the Salem Witch Trials trying to eliminate the threat of gifted and psychic people. Christian missionaries spread the word of sins, punishment, retribution, and the fear of God as their friars and priests burn holy scriptures and texts of various faiths. There's the Muslim jihad working to rid the world of infidels. See how the Hindu caste system defines the roles of individuals for life, relegating some to the caste of *untouchables* so they can never challenge the hierarchy or structure of their society. Observe Adolph Hitler as he unmercifully persecutes the Jews."

Members of the council and gallery begin to stir in their seats. Ra strolls slowly around the council table. Several ambassadors from higher-dimensional galactic systems in another faraway sector of the cosmos stare in disbelief and anguish.

"You can see the relentless suppression of information and inspiration throughout the ages with the near annihilation of indigenous populations and their cultures. In Mesoamerica, Spanish bishops burn all the Mayan books they can find. Conquistadors and friars forbid all forms of the local traditional religions, forcing the native ways of life to go underground. Mass killings of people based on their ethnic, political, or religious backgrounds continue even today." The hologram closes as he walks reflectively near the gallery as a desperate silence overtakes the assembly.

Ra adds, "Fear permeates the very core of humanity. Because of their pervasive fears, their levels of consciousness and their energetic vibrations are not keeping pace with that of their planet. Nevertheless, according to the divine cosmic plan, all planetary life is already being prepared for this shift. This birthing process is in the final phases of delivering Earth from a third-dimensional to a fourth-dimensional planet, reflecting the transformation of the physical dimension into the higher spiritual vibrations of consciousness."

Semyaza tosses his newspaper on the table with a disgusted flourish. "Yeah, yeah. C'mon, people, don't we all know this already? Anyway, why does Ra have to chair the meeting? You all know that old *falcon head* has delusions of grandeur, referring to himself as *The Sun God* for Christ's sake!"

Semyaza casually turns to Immanuel. "Oh, sorry, Immanuel—slip of the tongue." Semyaza slyly strokes his jet-black moustache and goatee. A long forked black tongue slides past his blood-red lips and flicks back and forth at the tip. Immanuel smiles in amusement and shakes his head.

Quetzalcoatl stands to help defend Ra in response to Semyaza's pompous outburst. He politely acknowledges the giant alien as he walks in front of the gallery with his outstretched arm. "This is a courtesy to our visiting guests who have not been involved with Earth." He directs everyone's attention to his Egyptian friend. "Ra, like many of us here, has chosen to pledge himself to humanity as an expression of charity and compassion," states Quetzalcoatl as his amber eyes narrow, his tone heavy with authority.

"During his Egyptian incarnation in 10,500 BCE of Earth's years, Ra became trapped in the heavy density of the planet and the Veil of Forgetting that causes those on Earth to lose touch with their true nature. I believe most of us here remember what that feels like." The Ascended Masters nod their heads somberly in agreement. Semyaza nods as well, mimicking the others, smiling all the while.

"Ra was deified into legend and became known as the Sun God because he had the ability to prophesy, perform miracles, and heal—influencing the destiny of an entire world. However, like all of us here," explains

Quetzalcoatl as he points to The Council, "he never intended to be worshipped as a god. He was always focused on The Law of One—that all entities are manifestations of The Infinite Creator and that no entity is above or below any other, regardless of their origin or destiny. We all know what a hard time our friend, Immanuel, had communicating this."

Immanuel sighs heavily. "Yes, well, let's not dwell on that. I don't think anyone else doubts the authority of Ra to speak on the subject of Earth's evolution and dimensional shift. Ra, please do continue."

Quetzalcoatl returns to his council seat as Ra looks closely at the members of the gallery. Ra's determination reasserts itself in his gaze and stance. "Thank you, Immanuel. If I may, I would like to expound a little further for our guests about my dedication of service to humanity," he conveys as he moves even closer to the gallery. His smooth, alabaster-skin face and perfectly proportioned, hairless body exude physical and spiritual beauty. Focusing intently on the assembly of guests with his keen and piercing eyes, there seems to be a sense of regret, of deep sorrow, within. He elucidates further, "I have walked upon the Earth. I have seen the faces of her people. I have looked deeply into their eyes. I have experienced their pain and their suffering. I have served with varying degrees of success in transmitting The Law of One, of unity, to her people. However, I now feel the great responsibility of removing the distortions and misuse of powers associated with my incarnations, especially the abuses caused by my building the Great Pyramid of Giza. I will continue in faithful service until this third cycle is appropriately ended. And if not this one, then the next." Ra motions to the center of the table where a hologram of the Mayan Sacred Calendar appears from Earth's *Book of Life*. Significant wave patterns emerge, visible to all, as the winds of history continue to follow an exact evolutionary schedule.

"This Mayan Sacred Calendar, authored by Quetzalcoatl, is an unambiguously accurate measurement system illustrating the cosmic plan for this planet. The calendar—clearly a divine blueprint—is a true and exact description of the evolution of consciousness. Due to the benevolent influences of The Confederation of Planets, four of these calendars still remain in existence, escaping destruction during the book burnings. They were sent to Europe, where they have been recently discovered in various libraries and museums. Conveying a unique and crucial message, the timeline in the calendars gives humanity the understanding that there is, indeed, a deadline for their creation. The end of time, as they understand it, is near. Everyone will participate in this transition, consciously or unconsciously."

Ra continues to enlighten the assembly of interstellar, intergalactic visitors in the chamber. "Unfortunately, most of the inhabitants of Earth use astronomically based calendars founded on the mechanical year of their planet and its endless revolution around their Sun. And with that, humanity continues to see their history as a series of chaotic, random events. The Gregorian calendar, for example, conveys the view of a creation that is not going anywhere. Life is perceived as an endless merry-go-round, and people view their lives and purpose in a similar way. The way of counting years according to the timeline of this calendar fosters a worldview where life seems to have no higher purpose. As a consequence, human beings are not aware of their participation in the divine plan and, in as much, regard their planet as just dead matter to be exploited." A strident gasp is heard throughout the chamber and the rest of infinity.

Pleija, Ptaah, and other members of the gallery nod in quiet agreement that the idea of a fixed calendar lacks any basis in reality. Suddenly their attention is drawn to Semyaza, who once again disrupts the meeting with his boorish and disrespectful behavior by imitating Ra's hand gestures. "I told you he is up to no good," Ptaah whispers to Pleija.

"Now, as you can see, the infinite cosmos is made up of spiraling intelligent light energy. This energy of consciousness is the building block for everything from subatomic particles, to human DNA, to planets, and to everything in between." As Ra continues, the projected images of spiraling DNA strands, the movement of atomic structure, weather systems, tornadoes, orbiting planets, and expanding galaxies are shown.

"In this sector of the cosmos, when this particular galaxy was created, Earth was designed with eight dimensions of existence. All life moves through these dimensions as part of their evolutionary process to return to The One Infinite Creator." Ra perseveres as the slowly spinning hologram displays fleeting scenes of wild animals. "As most of you know, in this universe, the Second Dimension animal kingdom operates on a more instinctive group consciousness, where the Third Dimension represents the beginning of the self-aware humanoid form—the sentient being." Evolutionary scenes of half-animal and half-human beings are displayed, including satyrs, centaurs, and mermaids.

Leaning back in his chair, Semyaza places his dirty scuffed black leather boots on the shimmering white crystalline conference table next to Immanuel. Tossing his newspaper aside, he lets out a loud yawn that can be heard throughout the Council Chamber. Ra smiles graciously and then continues with his presentation.

"This third-dimensional experience for any planet occurs in approximately three twenty-five-thousand-year cycles as their time is measured. At the end of each of cycle, as the highest possible vibration is reached, entities going through their reincarnational process can graduate into higher dimensions, as long as they have attained a sufficient grade of loving vibrations within themselves and when they are ready and willing to give up any attachment to their third-dimensional experience. One must not be attached to anything or anyone in their world. They must be willing to let go of everything at a moment's notice. When their calling comes—and it will come to everyone in their own time—the process will be blocked if they go into fear.

"To enter the Fourth Dimension, one must achieve an above 50 percent desire toward Service To Others, what we call the positive path, as opposed to Service To Self, which is known as the negative path." Everyone at the table smiles nodding in agreement. "The Confederation of Planets with over fifty-three civilizations, comprised of approximately five hundred planetary consciousness complexes, allied in service according to The Law of One, understands that very shortly a choice is to be made by every human being."

"Oh, this should be good!" Semyaza smirks, nodding his head as he cheerfully interrupts once more.

"It would be preferable if all of the people of this planet understood the choice that is to be made. It will be difficult for many to understand what this choice is, because it is a choice they have not considered. They have been shrouded in fear. They are too involved in their daily activities, their confusion, and their desires of a very trivial nature," says Ra, as he nods his head toward Semyaza, "to be concerned with an understanding of the choice that they are very shortly to make. Whether they wish to or not, whether they understand it or not, regardless of any influence, each and every one of the people who dwell upon the Earth will shortly have to make a choice—a choice that will affect them for all eternity. Service To Self or Service To Others—there will be no middle area."

"Excuse me! We all know this *choice* stuff, Mr. Sun God. Certainly everyone in this group knows about it," shouts Semyaza, defiance creeps through his tone. He points to the giant alien. "You are really wasting my time and that of everyone here. Can't you get on with it? I mean really—what is your point here, Ra?" he demands, exasperated with the pace of the meeting.

"Well, Semyaza, it is quite clear to everyone here what choice you made," Lord Sanat Kumara retorts as his agitation with Semyaza's continual interruptions grows. Mother Mary nods in agreement with the always-youthful great guru—a savior of Earth. Sanat's garment is white as snow, and the hair of his head like the pure wool. The Hierarch of Venus continues, "As the lord charged to be the source of human consciousness and faithfully devoted to ridding humanity and their Earth of negative entities and lower energies, I would like to clearly convey to everyone here the supreme significance of this emergency Council of Saturn meeting. Indeed, it is my charge from The Creator through my unwavering dedication to ensure that human evolution on Earth continues. With that being said, I ask that everyone please excuse Semyaza's discourteousness. Ra, please carry on." Lord Kumara's commitment to serve mankind was never more evident.

Semyaza imitates Lord Kumara by mouthing his last words, "Ra, please, carry on," when Sanat turns his back to return to his council seat.

"There will be those who choose to follow the path of love and service and those who choose otherwise," begins Ra as he walks around behind the council members looking out into the gallery. "The negative path, the one promoted by the Forces of Darkness, is a path of fear, a path of separation, a path which denies compassion; it is a path which denies universal love. This choice will not be made by merely saying, 'I choose the path of love and service,' or 'I do not choose it.' The verbal choice will mean nothing. It is measured by the individual's actual demonstration—"

"Excuse me!" interrupts Semyaza. "Should someone send out a search party for Michael? I mean, really! Where is the supposed leader of archangels? I do have important work do to somewhere. Like inciting a few wars, abducting some children, perpetuating more lust, crime, and drug use—you know, the usual stuff." Semyaza prolongs his flagrant disruption with his ironic wit. "Is this basically very boring lesson in Planetary Evolution 101 really necessary, Ra?"

"Yes, Semyaza, it is," retorts Ra. As he stands behind Semyaza's chair, Ra speaks over the top of his head toward the gallery of intergalactic diplomats and universal ambassadors. The Egyptian deity slaps Semyaza heartily on the shoulder. "We all know how much you enjoy misinformation, miscommunication, and misunderstandings. Right, my friend?"

"Ah, hello!" exclaims Semyaza with an Oxford English accent as he lunges out of his chair and begins to walk around the council table, imitating Ra's gait and posture. "Speaking of misinformation, aren't you forgetting something here, Ra baby?" Before waiting for an answer, he continues with his shenanigans. "Now tell me if I have this right . . . right . . . oh, how I hate that word! As I was saying, before I rudely interrupted myself!" roars Semyaza with laughter. He decides to make the council meeting lively with drama more like that of one in a courtroom. To keep the wheels of justice turning, Semyaza suddenly appears in a stately powdered white wig and black robes acting like a barrister in a British court.

"Emblazoned across all eternity, the truth must be sought! I come forth with my argument to set the record straight for the jury," Semyaza boldly announces, continuing as he walks past members of the gallery. Ra steps aside when Semyaza's fallen angels in the gallery applaud loudly.

"I would like to set the record straight about these so-called choices. We have Service To Self, my all-time personal favorite, versus the pathetic

Service To Others. Please let me explain. Our Creator was originally a single entity." Semyaza continues his grandstanding by audaciously enlarging his physical size. "If only The Creator existed, then the only concept of service would have to be Service To Self, am I correct? Yes, of course, I am!" he muses as he wraps his elongated arms around himself. "However, since The Creator subdivided Itself to experience Itself more fully, the concept of service of one of Its parts to another of Its parts was born."

Semyaza divides himself into smaller Semyazas to illustrate his point. Two small Semyazas happily shake hands. Two other smaller Semyazas pat each other on the back as more and more small Semyazas emerge.

Semyaza pauses to make sure his audience is following his demonstration. He begins to drawl out each word. "From that comes the equality of Service To Self with Service To Others. Are you keeping up with me, Pacal, ol' buddy?" Semyaza scoffs with a glare. "As The Creator subdivides, each of Its parts gets to choose what orientation It wants to be, you know, because of that Free Will thing."

As everyone watches intently, two small Semyazas begin to fistfight, two more slap each other's face, two more kiss passionately, and while one viciously kills another.

"Therefore, each part, each choice, is equal—Service To Self or Service To Others." During his declaration, Semyaza demonstratively waves his hand in a sweeping motion to include the entire chamber. "So there you have it—the positive path is equal to the negative path!" Everyone whispers as the smaller Semyazas merge back into the larger one then the larger Semyaza reduces down to his normal size.

"Ladies and gentlemen, members of the jury, you have now heard all the evidence. As you may recall, by the perfectly clear argument provided to you today, Service To Self is, therefore, unequivocally equal to Service To Others. And if you look to those beings on Earth, you'll see that they too rather enjoy Service To Self than that other lame option, Service To Others. That's it—plain and simple. I rest my case," states Semyaza abruptly.

Observing Semyaza's outrageous performance near the gallery, Ra stands silently as Semyaza's robe and wig disappear. While clasping both hands together, swinging them side to side over his shoulders like a champion, members of the Dark Side in the gallery jump to their feet cheering as the Lord of Darkness finishes his devious diversions. They stand enthusiastically clapping in ovation to their master. Ra waits patiently as Semyaza, dressed back in his shin-length tailored black leather coat, returns to his seat at The Council of Saturn with a smirk on his face.

# Chapter 7

Beyond the main entrance of the Celestial City, a flock of white doves surround a lone angel with her extraordinarily beautiful ivory wings spread wide. The messenger from Heaven hovers motionlessly, feeling very small in the spacious celestial courtyard of infinite space and infinite time. After focusing her gaze intently on a distant place over thirteen hundred million kilometers away in the vast midnight blue sky stretching before her, the angel explodes with a spectacular burst of light into a spiral of shimmering particles with wispy arms extending outward. In the brief moment following, the surrounding doves explode into brilliant orbs of light to illuminate her path as she flies toward her destination.

"It's time to fly, my feathered friends!" Nicole exclaims with great anticipation.

Although angels can slice through galaxies at immeasurable speeds, Nicole decides to take her time, to make hers a more leisurely flight. To make the most of her experience outside of the Celestial City, she decides to joyride the universe, planet-hopping along the way. First, she navigates closely around the intriguing yellow planet of Jupiter, where dark streaks cross its mostly gaseous surface. Its daunting size, the largest in the solar system, closely matches that of Saturn. As Nicole passes by, she spins herself faster and faster, imitating a small pale white spot above the surface—a fierce atmospheric storm with winds over 400 miles an hour. Nicole giggles as it shrinks slightly and quickly changes color, now matching that of its larger sibling spot, the Great Red Spot. In fun and jest, she bows respectfully to the larger, more noticeable spot with its reddish hue, which is three times the size of Earth.

Dancing and twirling through various stellar clusters along Jupiter's orbit, Nicole decides to catch an adventurous ride on the tail on an emerging comet before passing through the Asteroid Belt between Jupiter and Mars. Inside the orbiting ring of dust and asteroids, she playfully dodges the remnants of the destroyed planet of Maldek.

Looking straight ahead beyond her destination, Nicole notices the immense Sun, an enormous star relegated to the status of a yellow dwarf by humans. Its prominence in the sky is most glorious. As she flies closer, her energy glows brighter, absorbing the Sun's loving warmth. Mesmerized by its dramatic flares, she pauses once more to take in its glowing beauty. While slowly resuming flight, still distracted by the Sun's brilliance, Nicole nearly flies into the planet of Mars as it speeds away to her right. The Red Planet was so named by the ancients to honor the god of war. She smiles back cheerfully when the Face on Mars catches her eye. Emerging from a large, planet-wide dust storm on its cratered surface, the monument in Cydonia moves quickly from her view as Mars spins along its orbit. Suddenly she sees in the distance before her a planet of vibrant swirling colors looming ahead.

While admiring the glory and power of everything around her, and the dynamic changes that are occurring on all the planets for the upcoming ascension into the higher dimensions, the angel from above sighs a sigh of celestial satisfaction, knowing it is all heaven-sent. As Nicole excitedly follows the flight path toward her assigned final destination, she decides to veer off course momentarily to pause reflectively once more. In an instant, everything becomes still in the perpetual twilight as she marvels at the inky backdrop surrounding the heavenly jewel. From her perspective in space near its moon, the aquamarine oceans, swirling clouds, lush green lands, and statuesque mountains on Earth are positively breathtaking.

Still traveling as a spiral of light, Nicole dodges a few artificial orbiting satellites. Penetrating their communication signals from Earth with her vision and hearing, Nicole is startled by the faint clamor of frantic lives. The shocking reality of humanity's current level of consciousness begins to sink in, assaulting her delicate spirit. Nicole begins to question her ability to assist humanity in such treacherous times as she overhears radio waves of their news. Academics, clerics, and political leaders perpetuate divisiveness and fear in open exchanges about terrorism. Announcers convey accounts of rapes, school shootings, robberies, falling stock markets, political and corporate takeovers, dishonesty and embezzlement of pension funds, pollution, global warming, and reports of increasing climatic catastrophes.

Remembering that she has been summoned for a most important assignment, she continues her flight with more haste. The seriousness of her mission's challenges becomes more clear as she approaches her destination. The riveting aerial display of vengeful threats of nations, cultures, religions, and individuals reverberate off the planet's surface. From a distance so far away, she can see the explosions and killing of war as rockets of death and destruction are launched across invisible borders to annihilate one's perceived enemies.

Once more anxiety and trepidation begin to take over. Nicole drifts in a long reflective silence. She feels at a loss yet knows there is no victory in turning around. Truly committed to the call of service, Nicole shakes off her feelings of overwhelm and insecurity to go forth, to serve. She prays for the opportunity to be part of the great global healing that is to take place in days before Earth's year 2012. The messenger of love surrounded by her celestial escorts descends quickly through the Earth's atmosphere, now bound by its Law of Time and Space. Yet angst and apprehension sink in as Nicole hovers high over one of its oceans. The Earth-bound angel zeros in on the city where she is to reside. Beautiful beaches, valleys, canyons, and mountains grace the place to be called home albeit temporarily. Yet despite its awe-inspiring landscape, pain, anger, and confusion seem to plague the members of its community.

"I wonder if everyone feels this way when they come to LA," Nicole asks of her escorts.

The din of despair and broken lives, the hopelessness of the homeless, screams off its shores. Like toxic tides that ebb and flow, she can hear the stifled desires of those stuck in day-to-day ruts, while others hide behind alcohol and drugs to diminish their disappointments and heartaches. And yet others repeatedly chose the wrong path out of fear, out of their ignorance of the universal truths. She covers her tender ears when she hears others using the name of The Infinite Creator to create power over others in their insatiable quest for adoration, dominance, and wealth.

Now Nicole begins to understand how humanity's separation from The Creator—how humanity's collective wound—is festering out of control. She senses that humanity's collective disengagement—its divorce from Source—has not been acknowledged; its accumulated sorrow of severance has not been grieved. She feels the intensity of humanity's perceived heritage of estrangement from All That Is and wonders if healing the original split between Spirit and matter, masculine and feminine, and Heaven and Earth, can purge the infection of disconnection from so many. From her angelic vantage point, Nicole sees that everyone has trouble of one sort or another in balancing their lives.

Nicole looks mournfully to the orbs of light that faithfully illuminate her flight path. *It seems happiness here is the exception, not the rule. In deed, can*

these humans become fully present and embrace the full spectrum of the emotions they
have been given to taste, from their deepest sorrow to their greatest joy?

Out of the blue, a wondrous ray of light breaks through the surrounding clouds. She hears the faint yet familiar voice of her friend, Alexis, speak to her. *Remember, Nicole, trust your heavenly instincts—and trust your wings of divinity—as they will always guide you where you need to go.* The ineffable reminder of boundless faith eases her apprehension. The amazing opportunity for her to bring The Creator's Love to humanity calms her fears. An eternal knowing of her purpose to help others, her compelling desire to serve, echoes loudly. Her God-given traits of spunk and optimism return. Nicole chooses to faithfully fly into the face of adversity, overriding any limiting beliefs of what lies ahead, ignoring the uncertainty of what the future may hold for her.

Looking ahead, Nicole takes a deep breath, hesitates momentarily, then plunges into the gloomy pool of heavy smog that hangs over the city. Emerging safely on the underside, she quickly glances around at the tall steel structures surrounded by concrete that jut into the skyline. Her luminosity, her brilliance of light, now tinged with a brownish substance, begins to fade to yellow as she continues. Choking on the polluted air, she looks back to see where she came from—looking for the pristine Celestial City, looking for something of the shimmering clarity of the heavens above. She sees nothing.

Chapter 8

Ra proceeds with the information to be presented by The Council of Saturn to its guests. "Unfortunately, after the first twenty-five-thousand-year cycle on Earth, not one human was ready to graduate, and after the second cycle only one hundred twenty were ready," explains Ra. "And all of those souls lovingly elected to stay behind in the Third Dimension to continue their Service To Others. Reincarnating on Earth once more in dedication and service, these benevolent souls, including our friends—Saint Francis of Assisi, Saint Augustine, and Saint Therese—were able to help others move forward." Ra bows, acknowledging their presence in the front of the gallery of esteemed guests.

"However, after the third major cycle, which is where Earth is now, the planet automatically shifts to the Fourth Dimension, whether the inhabitants are ready or not. Their evolution of consciousness is directly related to the heartbeat of Mother Earth. As this dimensional shift proceeds, there is a quickening in the perception of time and an increasing anxiety for those souls who have not yet moved forward spiritually."

Holographic images of September 11 in New York, the Iraq War, and the bombings in Mumbai, Madrid, London, and Bali follow. The assembled guests in the gallery look quite moved and some shocked. Ra takes a deep breath to collect his thoughts before the hologram comes to a close. He looks around the table at the council of ascended masters and archangels and out into the gallery that extends into the infinite.

"How many?" A voice from the gallery echoes around the Council Chamber. "How many are projected for this third and final cycle?"

Whisperings suddenly turn into murmurs, then into private conversations, then even more loudly, erupting into all-out discussions.

"Please, please, may I have your attention? I would like to answer that question," replies Ra, pausing momentarily to respond. "In spite of the presence of all of our ascended masters throughout their various incarnations, along with angelic and intergalactic assistance upon the planet, only six thousand out of approximately six and a half billion are ready to graduate . . . to make the dimensional shift or ascension. That's only one millionth of 1 percent. Normally, we see about a 60 percent graduation rate on other third-dimensional planets," Ra answers. A unified gasp is heard throughout the Celestial City.

"Although the time is near, our current estimations are meaningless," he continues with clarity and emphasis. "The choices of the humans will determine the course of events, and they may choose to express themselves during this transition in many different ways. Whether their world will end up a paradise or a catastrophe does not depend completely on the cosmic plan but increasingly upon themselves and the choices they make. It is up to humanity to change the ending of this cosmic story!"

A sudden silence of understanding floods the room.

"Excuse me. If I may, I have a question for The Council," states the giant alien, his size ever looming over the others. "How can humanity change this so-called cosmic story when apparently they don't even know there is a story even going on?" The majority in attendance nod in an unspoken agreement with his question. "What is going to happen between now and their year 2012 on their planet that would possibly increase the number of beings to be of Service To Others? It would seem to me that nothing much is going to change in the way they perceive the reality of their existence. If anything, based on what we have been shown here, it looks as though it will only get worse."

Semyaza smiles pompously and looks sanctimoniously to his fellow council members. Immanuel is quick to interject. "Please allow me to answer that question, Ra."

During his mission on Earth, Immanuel was a Jewish teacher who was also regarded as a healer. His name signifies "he who is to save his people from their sins." The theme of his preachings was that of grace, repentance, forgiveness of sins, and the coming of the kingdom of God. Immanuel extensively trained disciples who, after his death, interpreted and spread his teachings. He was accused of sedition and on the orders of Roman government was sentenced to death by crucifixion. With a higher knowing of All That Is, the teacher is ready once more to offer his understanding of the way out of the present predicament for humanity to those in the assembly who are ready to hear.

"Please, be my guest." Ra graciously yields the floor to Immanuel and returns to his seat at The Council.

"Thank you, my brother," begins Immanuel as he walks toward the gallery. His most perfect body, extraordinary beauty, and divine proportions are revealed by his simple white cotton robe, belted by a coarse brown rope. His bare feet are cloaked by the heavenly mists that cover the chamber floor.

"As you have been shown, many inconveniences are occurring on Earth's surface in the way of hurricanes, earthquakes, and such. These catastrophes, as the humans call them, exist for two reasons. Although a portion of Earth's changes are a natural result of the physical evolution of the planet herself, they are also opportunities for humans to experience Service To Others."

Scenes of damage and destruction from recent Hurricanes Katrina and Rita are shown holographically. "Strangers assisting strangers, families helping families. Communities come together as abundant opportunities to serve others are provided on all levels. Amidst the stench of rising swamp waters in the back bayous of Louisiana, one soul reaches out to another. As gale force winds tear the doors and roofs off houses and businesses in the hurricane-ravaged towns that line the coast of Florida, people are torn out of their comfort zones to lend a helping hand to neighbors they've never taken time to meet. Opportunities for benevolent service abound."

Immanuel explains further, "Before incarnating on the planet, the so-called victims of these events chose how they would experience their physical deaths. By voluntarily sacrificing themselves, like this woman drowning in the floodwaters in New Orleans, they provide others in their families, in their communities, the opportunity to serve. Please observe as the woman's husband now has to care for their three young children." Holographic displays of the scenes that Immanuel describes appear for all to experience.

"These sacrifices potentially increase the number of beings that can evolve through service to the higher vibrations of the Fourth Dimension. It's not who they believe in." Immanuel turns abruptly and waves his arm with a powerful, lashing force to the ascended masters at the council table and in the gallery. "They don't need prescribed intermediaries like priests, rabbis, bishops, or even me to ascend!" Immanuel looks at Semyaza with disgust and then winks. "They don't need any of us saints, holy people, masters, avatars, adepts, prophets, yogis, or saviors or whatever else humanity calls us. They don't need any of the thousands upon thousands of holy scriptures that they read. Their future is not determined by their strict adherence to rules punishable by excommunication, death, and eternal damnation. Their destiny lies in Service To Others, not in religious leaders or the various manipulated scriptures they espouse." His voice grows louder and louder, powerfully emphasizing his point of truth with each word. "It's not who they believe in—one can believe in nothing and still ascend with Mother Earth into the next dimension. It's all about Love and Service To Others!"

Council members and their guests of the higher dimensions of consciousness nod in agreement, smiling brightly as they approvingly applaud Immanuel's dramatic and unambiguous explanation. A hush quietly falls over the Council Chamber when Immanuel continues.

"It's obvious to us here, but obviously not obvious to humanity that these massive weather events do not recognize which religion or faith that its *victims* proclaim. A tsunami, for example, this violent onrushing tidal wave of turbulent water, doesn't care if they have been *saved* by me or any one of us at this gathering. It does not distinguish the *believers* from the *non-believers*. It does not know whether the humans on the shores of destruction are Buddhist, Christian, Hindu, Jewish, Islamic, Sikh or even Atheist. It doesn't notice if the are black, white, yellow, purple or even green." Immanuel points respectfully to the green Goddess Tara and to the green giant alien. "It doesn't recognize the difference between young and old, male and female, or even the rich and the poor. The *victims* are all equal in these events . . . just as they are in every day life. There is no one that is greater or lesser than—"

"Oh, Jesus, here we go again!" Semyaza explodes from his council seat. "Don't any of you get it? Humans will never pass the test! Come on, carpenter boy, let's show everyone here the bigger picture of what's actually going on down there!" Holographic displays shows looters in homes and stores, people stockpiling goods only for themselves, price gouging at local businesses, and politicians stalling in their efforts to assist, while death and devastation continue to destroy families and communities. Semyaza revels in the fact that once again every one in attendance can experience the holograms of envy, greed, fear, lies, and deception—hallmarks of his great work.

Taking Semyaza's outburst all in stride, Immanuel respectfully waits for the hologram to close, then elucidates further, "My friends, let me make this perfectly clear. These events, and the humans' response to them, are not a test but an opportunity to elevate their consciousness. These climatic events are opportunities to draw people together—to share their love, wisdom, and knowledge with each other. They open the heart. Too few know how to do this, for most of their lives they have felt alone, separate from All That Is. In the days that lie ahead, individuals will have to choose to steal or be stolen from, to kill or be killed. As the frequency of Earth's changes increase, these events help prepare them for life in the higher dimensions where an open heart chakra is the essence of that existence. As humanity moves up from their third chakra to their fourth chakra, so too will they move up from the Third Dimension to the Fourth. In the Fourth Dimension, the ego falls away in favor of the heart. This will, indeed, be an adjustment for many and could be quite challenging for those who have not been on a spiritual path." Immanuel points to the hologram of looters.

Apart from Semyaza, everyone at the council table smiles, nodding in agreement.

"Thank you, Immanuel, you certainly are one who can speak in authority on the subject of sacrifice of self to help others," says the giant alien. "What, please, is the second reason for these so-called inconveniences?"

"Secondly, the frequency and intensity of earth changes are symptoms of a very difficult transition from this dimension to the next," Immanuel continues with his explanation. He walks slowly and pensively by the gallery, while his stature is dignified and manly. "The vibrational divergence—the energetic mismatch between humanity and their planet—is too great. It is actually putting a drag on spiritual evolution and in turn is stressing on the physical Earth. Earth is going into the higher, lighter vibrations of love and consciousness. That is a fact. It is her destiny in the cosmic plan to now evolve to the Fourth Dimension. Yet human consciousness remains low. This causes disruptions with Earth's vibration. Humanity has to keep pace with her, or they will experience more inconveniences—not only more frequently, but with more intensity—until they awaken to realize their connection to Mother Earth and their impact upon her and, hence, on themselves."

"Oh, please!" Semyaza blurts aloud as he picks up his newspaper again. "Spare me the dimensional drama!"

"I beg your pardon, my beloved Ra." Kuan Yin, a slender woman in flowing white robes adorned with pearls of illumination, speaks up. Her Asian features and long black hair highlight her delicate porcelain skin. Wearing a jeweled crown, several bracelets, and long dangling earrings, the female manifestation of the bodhisattva of compassion, sits in royal ease with her right leg up, her knee bent with her bare foot on the council seat. Kuan Yin's right arm rests casually on her upraised knee. The Goddess of Mercy gently balances herself with her other arm on the council table. "But is it not true that over sixty-five million beings, the Wanderers, from various realms, levels, planes, dimensions of all time and space, alternates and parallels, volunteered to assist with this dimensional shift by incarnating during this most glorious and significant time in the history of Earth and her inhabitants?"

"Yes, Kuan Yin, that is true," states Ra contemplatively.

Kuan Yin inquires solemnly, "Are they part of the projected six thousand that you mentioned earlier?" Her eyelids appear nearly closed as she holds her rosary of white crystal beads that reflect the reincarnational rounds of rebirth.

"The six thousand approximation includes everyone," announces Ra, "including the sixty-five million Wanderers who willingly chose in their wisdom to risk the forgetting that occurs in the Third Dimension. They are jeopardizing themselves selflessly be of Service To Others, assisting in humanity's evolutionary progress."

"What can we do, Ra, to assist in their return?" Mary interjects. Her beautiful round brown eyes reflect her motherly compassion and concern. "There must be something we can do to help these courageous and highly devoted entities from all reaches of creation that are bound together by their gallant desire to serve. There has to be something, Ra!"

During her mission to Earth, Mary was the mother of Immanuel, who at the time of his conception was the betrothed wife of Joseph. According to scriptures, Mary, being a virgin at time, learned from the divine messenger, Archangel Gabriel, who was sent by God, that she would conceive a child through a miracle of the Holy Spirit. She remains the subject of much veneration due to a passage from the Bible that says, "For, behold, from henceforth all generations shall call me blessed." Mary is highly revered in the Christian faith, particularly in the Roman Catholic Church and Orthodox Church, and is also highly regarded by Muslims worldwide. Presently she serves as a member of The Council of Saturn.

In an effort to assist with Ra's presentation, Sanat Kumara explains, "The Wanderers understood before incarnating on Earth that the challenge and inherent danger is that they will forget their mission, become karmically involved, and, thus, be swept into the maelstrom of which they had incarnated to avert. They went to Earth to lighten the vibration on the planet and to increase the numbers for this upcoming dimensional shift."

"As a celestial bodhisattva and an ascended master, assisting in the celestial spheres on the board with the Lord of Karma, I certainly understand." Kuan Yin sighs, reflectively stroking one of the lotus petals with her finger. "Thank you, Ra. Thank you, Lord Kumara."

Kuan Yin reflects momentarily on her own sacrifice for humanity. Remembering the time when she was about to enter Heaven and paused on the threshold as the desperate cries of the world reached her ears. The Goddess of Mercy is unique among the heavenly hierarchy in that she is so wholeheartedly free from pride or vengefulness—remaining hesitant to punish even those to whom a severe lesson might be appropriate. Kuan Yin responds to the heartfelt needs and anguish of the people of Earth regardless of their background or belief and especially those that are sick, lost, frightened, or simply in unfortunate circumstances.

"As one whose very name means 'she who harkens to the cries of the world' this must be difficult for you to accept, Kuan Yin," laments Mother Mary. "I emphasize with you completely. The numbers are discouraging. Like my son, Immanuel, and others in this celestial gathering, I am working relentlessly in awakening mankind through many forms—in all places, in all cultures, in all societies, in all lands. I come through forms of channels. I come through apparitions seen throughout their world such as those in Fatima, Lourdes, and Medjugorje. I come through the open, unbiased heart. I come through those one would least expect. I am igniting the world every moment of every day with my love. I too am calling our children—"

"Oh, there she goes again—whining about the damn children and those idiotic Wanderers—about bringing them home!" interrupts Semyaza. "If your children are really so special, Mary, then why in the Hell do they ignore you? Please tell us, *Mother*. Why are your apparitions during these perilous times to your little blessed humans kept quiet? Is there some sort of conspiracy of silence?" Semyaza presses his attack, not allowing her to answer. He relentlessly pushes her further. "Why aren't you on the nightly news? Just tell us, Mary—why aren't the people of Earth and your precious Wanderers on mountaintops spreading your messages that are supposed to be so damn important?"

Mother Mary studies Semyaza closely for a moment before responding to his questions. It pains her to acknowledge that humanity's position is a far cry from what she had envisioned for them had she been able to project their circumstances. She looks down at the table, unable to hold the intensity of his malevolent gaze any longer. "Because your Forces of Darkness, Semyaza, are working through their media, governments, and the churches to suppress not only my messages," Mary admits quietly with a tone of embarrassment as she extends her hand to the other council members, "but those of all of us here—"

Semyaza breaks in. "Now, don't feel so sorry for yourself, dear old Mom." He tosses out a final insult as his eye skims The Council. "You have proved to be just as inadequate as all the others!" Calming his tone, he replies, "Now, now, it's okay, Mary," he adds feigning sympathy, "we are only trying to help humanity too."

"It's true, blessed Mother Mary," Ra concedes in somewhat somber terms. A discernible sadness clings to his words. "Members of the Dark Side including those who are here with us today successfully continue to distort our messages of Love and The Law of One as we have assisted so many times throughout history on this planet, as you well know." Ra adds, "Members of The Confederation of Planets were there assisting the Lemurians fifty-three thousand years ago, the Atlantians thirty-one thousand years ago, and later those who escaped to Egypt and South America following the destruction of Atlantis. And we are still there today, along with those of the Dark Side."

Suddenly a loud applause erupts from the gallery. Abhorrent clapping along with distasteful cheering continues relentlessly. Members of The Council of Saturn look toward Semyaza who smiles proudly as his minions of Darkness, his endarkened angels, entities and spirits of denial, disrupt the unprecedented celestial call for assistance. The sovereign intergalactic meeting waits patiently so Ra may continue.

"Semyaza here can confirm the fact that the Wanderers are high-priority targets for his Forces of Darkness," Ra states simply and curtly, resting his hands on Semyaza's shoulders. "At the time of ascension in Earth's year of 2012, as time is measured, these Wanderers who have forgotten their mission will, indeed, be pulled into the lower planetary vibration and possibly repeat once more the entire cycle of the Third Dimension."

Semyaza leans back defiantly in his chair as he stretches his long legs out in front of him and crosses his arms across his chest, smiling arrogantly as he winks at the Reptilian factions in the gallery. He openly gives them a thumbs-up signal for a job well done, while the rest of The Council remains silent and observing. Many of the guests in attendance shake their heads solemnly. With each passing second, his grin stretches wider until it is thoroughly malevolent.

"However, some think we might have better results if we took a more hands-on approach; but as you all know, Earth, like all of Creation, is a free will planet. And as such, a quarantine has presently been placed around the planet, and everyone is asked to observe the quarantine," announces Ra. "Everyone is now being asked not to interfere during the remaining days of this last cycle on Earth. Right, Semyaza? All are to abide by the Universal Law of Allowance and Free Will, although we know there are certain groups who blatantly and habitually disregard such planetary quarantines."

Ra stares intently at a Reptilian congregation sitting in the middle of the gallery of guests. He notices their militant-looking leader with his broad, muscular shoulders and powerful arms. The Reptilian glares maliciously at Ra with large black eyes surrounding flame-colored vertical slit pupils. Ra knows the extent of the Commander's strength and fortitude as Semyaza always calls upon him when brute strength and Machiavellian intellect are required. Ra casually and confidently turns his back to the draconian leader as he addresses everyone in attendance.

"It has been decided by The Confederation of Planets and this Council that Archangel Michael's latest effort to assist the humans through Infinity Airways will be the last. There will no longer be any intergalactic interventions to balance the planet. The One Infinite Creator has encouraged us to take a hands-off approach from here on out."

Chapter 9

Nicole flies through the City of Angels where millions of city lights dominate the burnt orange edge of the sky as the Sun sets. A tingle of static shocks her system as the lights cut through the warm summer night charging the air over Los Angeles with electricity. Passing over the Los Angeles International Airport the celestial angel notices the unique parabolic arches and futuristic design of the Landmark Theme Building, home of the spectacular Encounter Restaurant. She detours momentarily from her flight path curiously peering into the windows. Nicole merrily encircles the space-age structure that resembles many of the visiting spacecraft she had left behind on the rings of Saturn.

Startled by the thunderous roar of an Air China Boeing 747 soaring above, she turns gracefully, gliding over to the control tower that now catches her attention. The letters L-A-X—the airport's city code—are uniquely incorporated in the tower's design. The impressive one-of-a-kind 277-foot-tall air traffic center rises above the central passenger terminal area, giving the air traffic controllers a panoramic view of the airport. Looking out their window toward the empty runways and taxiways, several tired controllers rub their eyes when the orbs of light that have accompanied Nicole suddenly explode into a flock of beautiful white doves. As a slow swirling spiral of light who is losing her momentum, she closely studies the tower's east face. Illuminated artwork on its surface captures her attention. Tilting from side to side, Nicole tries to understand the first rendition of a radarscope filled with various aircraft. Unable to appreciate the details of the work, she moves on to the second rendition of a blue butterfly. It brings forth a smile of hope.

An instantaneous telepathic communication from the doves returns her concentration to one building in the distance. They encourage her to hurry as quickly as possible as her light grows more and more dim. As Nicole approaches her final destination, two faithful doves break away from the rest to guide her safely to an open window.

Suddenly the twinkling and shimmering particles of light fade rapidly as the surrounding dense lower vibrations weigh heavily on the angel from above. With all the strength and energy within, Nicole pulls herself up, barely clearing the ledge outside the window. Exhausted from her long journey through multiple dimensions, space, and time, a few of her remaining particles are unable to fly any higher. In the distance, a red tinge lines the horizon where the Sun has dropped from view, announcing another day in the City of Angels is over. Soon the night's dark sheet will slowly pull up to whisper goodnight to all.

The two white doves bravely swoop in under the dwindling spiral to lift their precious messenger, to ensure that Nicole arrives at her final destination on schedule. Flying past the windowsill with the help of her feathered friends, the divine messenger makes it just in time and disappears underneath the sheets. The comforter rises slowly as she transforms into a female human with long blonde hair cascading across the white satin pillow. Her energy-formed body flows and ebbs as the vibrational particle fields now maintain her appearance of physical manifestation. Nothing remains of her angelic form save a single white feather, which slowly drifts down, settling atop the white satin comforter covering her. There she rests until the Sun rises in the eastern sky.

Chapter 10

As the meeting in the Council Chamber continues, members of the gallery genuinely desire to understand more fully what humanity is up against. "And why is this situation for a third-dimensional planet so different? How can the ascension projections for the humans be so far off?" shouts a guest from the back.

"I'll be glad to address that question, Ra!" declares Archangel Michael amidst the fluctuating waves and spiraling colors near the council table. He enters the chamber of The Council of Saturn through the Celestial Corridor, an interdimensional portal from the infinite, with his tawny golden hair flowing around his shoulders. Archangel Michael, one of the greatest of angels whose name means "who is like to God," approaches The Council dressed in his airline pilot uniform with his shining crystalline Sword of Light and Truth at his side and a handful of ancient parchment scrolls.

Michael steps before the gallery of guests. He looks closely at all those in attendance for what seems like an eternity. His eyes are filled with a remarkable blending of wonderment, awe, honoring, gratitude, and God only knows what else. Very few in the cosmos can capture an intergalactic-multidimensional congregation that way. The anticipation for his presentation heightens. Michael walks around the council table, silently acknowledging each member with a nod of gratitude and a sincere smile of appreciation for their presence.

"The difference is largely because this planet, as an experiment, was populated with souls from other various planets who also were unable to make the shift within in the allotted number of cycles," explains Michael responding to the question from the gallery. "As many of you know, that has never been done before. So the decision of populating Earth with cycle-repeaters has created a particularly recalcitrant group of souls that seem stuck in a very dense vibration indeed." He shoots a penetrating glare at Semyaza.

While continuing with his explanation, he pauses behind Semyaza. "We can only hope that they don't go the same apocalyptic way of the Red Planet, Mars, that troubled little warring planet, or like the complete planetary destruction of Maldek, which I'm sure many remember with great affection. After the demise of Atlantis—despite our continued efforts—the lessons of The Law of One seem to be lost once again. Nonetheless, like a timepiece used on Earth, these cycles move as precisely as a clock strikes an hour. Earth will shift with or without humanity. All cycles, great and small, come to an end eventually. Yet this particular ending is clearly not an ending as such but more of an invitation, an invitation for humanity to ascend to an even more glorious place, of raising their frequency to a higher expression of the Divine. Now, my friends, you are beginning to understand the urgency and why those of you from outside this realm have been summoned."

The striking archangel—his radiant presence, sparkling eyes, and exquisite golden hair—is an inspiration to all that lay eyes upon him. Michael appears as resplendent as his name, in a majestic display of Light and authority—an image chosen just for that purpose. He turns his back on Semyaza to acknowledge the assembly of beings with outstretched arms. Everyone watches closely as his purpose is revealed, engraved on his very soul and his desire for it all-consuming.

"I am Michael, the Archangel. Greetings to you, one and all! What a profound pleasure and a great honor to be with you. Sorry to keep you waiting, but the last interviewee was extremely late. Worth it, though. She may be the one we've been looking for. I'll explain shortly."

Semyaza shifts tumultuously in his chair, recrossing his legs. The Lord of Darkness strokes his moustache and goatee as he looks with upraised brows toward the harried archangel. "What's with the uniform, Michael? Looks a little absurd with the long hair and that ridiculous sword! Don't tell me they let you through airport security with that thing on your hip?" he laughs.

Michael smiles confidently. "All in good time, my friend. All in good time."

Chapter 11

Her heavy eyelids slowly flutter open as a brief glimmer of sunlight streams through the window and dances across her cheeks. A gentle summer wind rustles the muslin curtains. With slow and labored movements, Nicole struggles to move her long slender limbs. Lifting her new physical body into a sitting position, she begins to realize that her life will never be the same. Her head swings heavily down toward her chest, causing her long golden hair to cascade across her face. Nicole lifts her hands and runs her fingers through her silky hair, enjoying the way it feels as it slides across her new ivory skin.

Cautiously moving her hands to her face, Nicole slowly explores the curves of her lips, her nose, and her eyes. She blinks and then extends her hands in front of her, excitedly waving them back and forth, wiggling her slender fingers. Suddenly she giggles as she looks down at her chest. The divine beauty curiously cups her full breasts slowly in both hands, bouncing them gently in her palms. Sinking back into the pillows to look at her long shapely legs, lifting, and stretching them toward the heavens, Nicole yawns, feeling quite tired from her journey. Drifting off into peaceful sleep, the angel from above is startled by a tapping sound coming from the window.

"Where on Earth am I?" Nicole groggily asks herself. Her right hand flies up and covers her mouth. She giggles at the sound of her new voice. Throwing the plush white duvet aside, she scrambles out of bed, sending a myriad of pillows scattering everywhere. As her foot touches the floor, reverberations flowing out in waves from the planet begin to penetrate her body. Entangled in the satin sheets, Nicole trips—sprawling naked across the floor. The tapping at the window continues. Finally reaching the window and pushing aside the curtains, she sees that her view to the rest of the universe is clouded by the darkening overcast skies above.

Below Nicole finds two white doves sitting on the windowsill. "Oh yes! That's right. Thank God you are here to remind me!" she exclaims joyfully. "Yes, you are right. It's time to fly!" She laughs, flapping her arms, as she tries to disentangle herself. "But this time without wings." She kisses the windowpane and the doves coo while flapping their wings. In the distance, jets take off and land at Los Angeles International Airport.

Grabbing everything from the closet, Nicole sprawls her new belongings all over the bed. Awkwardly she manages to get dressed, after spending several minutes trying to figure out how to put on a strange and unfamiliar contrivance called a bra. Grabbing the white blazer, she notices a nametag. "Hmmm, N-I-C-O-L-E—Nicole." She runs her finger over the shiny engraved gold nametag. Glancing over at the clock on the nightstand, Nicole notices that she is going to be late. She frantically scoops everything up—including the long white plume that had drifted on the bed the night before—and stuffs everything into the white roll-aboard suitcase. Putting on her overcoat, Nicole lurches for the door, nearly falling face first in her white high-heeled pumps. Pulling herself together, Nicole clumsily dashes down the hall toward the elevator, commenting on the ridiculous nature of clothes and especially shoes.

Chapter 12

Pleased to finally have Archangel Michael at the celestial, intergalactic gathering, Ra formally announces the archangel's arrival. "Dear assembled masters and guests, it is my great honor and pleasure to turn our meeting over to our esteemed keynote speaker, Lord Archangel Michael." Ra starts the applause and is quickly joined by others.

As Michael, the archangel closest to The Creator, prepares for the meeting, he lays his sword and several scrolls on the table. At the same time that Michael starts to begin his presentation, another question comes forth from someone in the gallery. It is the Reptilian Commander. His top-ranking position in the Forces of Darkness—reflecting his eternal allegiance to Semyaza—is known to everyone in the cosmos.

"I want to know which third-dimensional planet the humans are going to be relocated to after 2012—the ones who are not going to ascend, the ones who are not going to make it." His cold, measured voice reeks of strict control and discipline. His unyielding features are unreadable, circumscribed, and structured. His authoritative stance is straight, more military than anyone else present.

An all-out discussion of grave concern begins among the council members and among the benevolent members in the gallery. Rumors of contention, of rebellion, begin as the oft-whispered plots and plans ranging from enslavement to complete annihilation resurface. His presence causes many to reconsider mankind's safety and status as the Reptilians' reputation of previously storming the gates of the Celestial City begins to circulate.

Disturbed by the commander's blatantly obvious intention to harm the humans, Pleija stands up boldly and addresses Archangel Michael before the infinite multitudes of beings with great strength and confidence. She straightens her stretchable, silver-plated tunic and robe as she looks proudly to her father before speaking. "Greetings, I am Pleija from planet Erra. My people share a common ancestry with our human friends, as you know, and we visit Earth frequently. Although we look very much like the people of Earth, we Plejarens do live for a thousand years. We also differ in that our consciousness and technology are much more highly developed than that of the Earthlings. Yet despite our differences, I would like to say on behalf of the Plejaren High Council and that of all Plejarens that we would be honored to have the humans placed near our planet where we could assist them further as they repeat another seventy-five-thousand-year third-dimensional cycle—if it pleases The Council."

The currents of uneasiness and discontent begin to swell. A stirring in the chamber occurs as many intergalactic, interdimensional ambassadors want to make a similar offer. Pleija feels a chill when she notices the Reptilian Commander glaring directly at her. Ptaah watches closely as his young daughter boldly ignores the reptilian leader's cold calculating look and militaristic facade. She continues with her impassioned invitation despite the restlessness that is occurring around her. "There is a beautiful uninhabited Earthlike planet in our star system in Pleiades that can easily support the more than six and a half billion cycle-repeaters coming from Earth. It is an ideal habitat for these beings. We could help them understand the divine cosmic plan, staying aligned with The Law of One, while encouraging them to listen to the voice in the universe that is calling them to remember their purpose—their reason for being. Please tell us, Archangel Michael, as Guardian Overlord of the Angelic Host and all of humanity, has a decision been made on where they will be placed next?"

As Michael speaks, an instant hush falls over the Council Chamber. Everyone is curious to hear what the archangel has to say. His manner is commanding and his expression stern. "No, Pleija, a decision had not been made. And on behalf of The Council of Saturn, may I say thank you for your most gracious and generous offer. I am touched and moved by your dedication, and that of the Plejarens, to further assist our human friends. However, it is our goal to have everyone on Earth graduate to the next level, where no third-dimensional transference will be necessary, especially for our sixty-five million volunteers, the Wanderers."

"What a preposterous notion, Michael. You have got to be joking!" blurts Semyaza, slamming his hand down on the table. The Lord of Darkness is abhorrently disgusted with what has just been implied. "One hundred percent? You must be suffering from too many pressurized airplanes, my pilot friend!"

Michael looks unswervingly at Semyaza. After a long silence, the archangel yet again announces more loudly and clearly, with a very reassuring tone, "One hundred percent, my friend!" Everyone at the council table smiles at each other, nodding in unspoken agreement. Semyaza and his forces of evil stare at Michael, shrewdly trying to deduce the rationale of his statement.

Chapter 13

Within moments, Nicole reaches the lobby. A friendly-looking doorman in a white suit and hat signals for her as he hails a taxi. While quickly loading her belongings inside the back seat, he comments casually, "You must be the last one. The others took a private employee bus to the airport earlier this morning." Nicole scrambles into the back seat and sinks into the worn upholstery.

Looking back to wave goodbye to the doorman as the taxi races away, she sees the huge high-rise white building towering behind him. A large gold sign over the entrance doors reads, "Infinity Airways Training Center."

"Where to, miss?" the heavy-set driver inquires.

"New York City," Nicole announces enthusiastically.

The driver scratches his head and chuckles. "That would be quite a long drive, miss. How's 'bout I drive you to the airport?"

"Yes, the airport please. Los Angeles International Airport—L-A-X," Nicole exclaims proudly. As the taxi pulls away from the curb, she clutches her purse and prays all the way to the airport that she will arrive in time to catch her flight.

The driver peers at Nicole in the rearview mirror, admiring her extraordinary beauty. Every model and actress he has ever seen in Los Angeles pales in comparison to the beauty that now sits praying in the back seat of his cab. "Running late, miss?"

"I have a ten thirty flight to New York City, the John F. Kennedy Airport." Nicole presses her face to the cab window as she watches an Infinity Airways I-888 plane takeoff into the gray morning sky. A ray of sunlight suddenly breaks through the heavy clouds glinting off the airplane's wings and undercarriage.

"New York? Better you than me, lady." The driver pulls up to the curb at Infinity Airways and glances again in the rearview mirror. "Better hurry up! This place is a mess—people been tryin' to get out of here for days," he exclaims as Nicole clamors to get out of the cab. "They're operating under security level orange today."

"Really?" Nicole smiles quizzically. "Orange is one of my favorite colors!"

"Better not have any liquids or gels in those bags of yours, miss. They're taking away everything. Today it's bottled water, tomorrow it will be our clothes!"

"Really? I don't care for clothes anyway!" exclaims Nicole as she wriggles around in her uniform. "They're so uncomfortable. Especially bras!" The driver raises a curious brow as he checks her out once more as she walks away.

Inside the main terminal, long lines of weary, frustrated travelers in the ticketing area startles the tardy trainee. Confused as to where to go and concerned that she might miss the flight, Nicole quickly gets into line where she too becomes increasingly restless and fidgety. After waiting for what seems like forever, the ticket agent calls, "Next, please." She teeters up with her suitcase and places her purse on the counter.

"Excuse me, sir, I'm new here and a little confused," Nicole apologizes. "Could you please show me where I need to go to get on flight 444 to New York City? To JFK?"

The agent carefully takes in Nicole's statuesque figure, flawless face, and gold-spun hair. He initially senses that there is something special yet very innocent about her. Patiently, he responds, "May I see your ticket, or do you have a reservation confirma—"

"Well, I don't have one of those." Nicole rummages through her purse. "Please, you have to help me. I have to be on that flight!"

The ticket agent smiles, amused by Nicole's disorganization. However, the passenger behind her does not find the situation so funny. "I have a flight to New York to catch," snaps the irritable traveler.

"I'm sorry, miss; but you won't be going anywhere without—" the ticket agent begins. Suddenly he peers over the ticket counter and notices Nicole's white uniform overcoat and her luggage, "Wait a minute. You are an—"

"Infinity Airways flight attendant trainee!" Nicole finishes his sentence and triumphantly produces her airline identification card.

"You should already be on the plane," he declares.

Nicole steps to the side as the irate passenger impatiently marches up to the counter with ticket in hand. She shoots Nicole a contemptuous glare of hostility. The agent promptly places a "POSITION CLOSED" sign on the counter. The irate woman is outraged and shakes her ticket in the air as he and Nicole walk away.

The ticket agent takes Nicole through the employee line at the congested airport security screening area. As they hurry through the concourse, Nicole rambles on about how she is new, how she overslept, and how she has never been in a taxi before. "In fact," she exclaims, "I've never even been in an airport or on an airplane!"

"Everything happens for a reason, Nicole," the agent says reassuringly. "The airline really does need your help. Now remember, gate 11. I'll say a prayer for you, Nicole—you're sure going to need it!" he shouts over his shoulder as he runs back toward the ticket counter.

Nicole scurries down the concourse, counting the gate numbers along the way. "Gate 5, gate 7. There it is—gate 11!" She looks nervously toward the gate area. "Okay, Nicole, stay calm," she mumbles to herself. "Smile and apologize. Remember what the ticket agent said, 'they need your help.'" She glances at the crowd of people waiting impatiently. Teenagers sleeping on the floor, children crying, business travelers checking their watches, and elderly people in wheelchairs lined up in front of the jetway door. Finally she spots the gate agent drowning amidst a sea of anxious travelers. *Wow, I wouldn't want that job! Those people are all talking at the same time—hanging all over the poor guy.*

The gate agent spots Nicole when he glances up from a demanding woman with flaming-red hair who is traveling with her cat. "This way, Nicole!" he calls across the counter as she attempts to wade through the sea of bodies. He signals for her to come around the desk. In rapid fire, Nicole begins to recount her morning drama. He chuckles, holding up his hands to reassure her. "Relax, Nicole, you can slow down. The flight has just been delayed due to the weather in New York. As you can see, we haven't started boarding yet."

Nicole glances back at the restless, agitated faces in the gate area. "Oh, thank God. Thank you. I'm so sorry; this will never happen again. I'm so relieved I'm not late—or even better, that I didn't miss the flight," she says nervously.

"Not the kind of impression you want to make on your first day of flight attendant training for Infinity Airways," jokes the friendly uniformed gate agent peering over his wire-rimmed glasses. "You must be very special to be assigned to this one." His bushy white brows rise as his golden-brown eyes widen slightly with wonderment.

Nicole smiles bashfully, unsure of the meaning of his comment. She notices the irate passenger from the ticket counter walking into the crowded gate area in a huff, heading straight for the gate agent's counter. As the frustrated middle-aged woman marches up, he places a "POSITION CLOSED" sign on the counter. The woman glares loathingly at Nicole as the gate agent helps her to the jetway door.

Chapter 14

Michael begins to enlighten everyone about the latest effort of the angelic realm to assist humanity in reaching higher vibrational levels of consciousness. "Infinity Airways was created shortly after the events of September 11 in the Earth year of 2001 as a counterbalance for all the fear that was emanating and perpetuated by the Dark Side during—"

"No applause is necessary!" Semyaza interjects smugly as he stands and bows to the gallery of guests. "Please, it was my pleasure—really!" A heavy silence descends over the chamber as everyone stares. Throughout the great city, the subliminal songs of praise and worship that have flowed eternally since the beginning of creation cease abruptly. Suddenly an uncertain applause can be heard. Everyone turns, looking at the various clusters of Semyaza's minions of Darkness seated in the gallery. A few more clap at the last minute in a feeble effort to honor their master.

Ignoring the outburst, Michael hastens to explain, "Infinity Airways, designed by our One Infinite Creator, is set up to operate on Earth in a way to assist humans in their spiritual journeys—helping to balance their karma, teaching them important life lessons that will aid them in preparing for their ascension. Its role is crucial as many have become immobilized, no longer flying, or even driving to the very people and places that they need to in order to reach their karmic destiny for this incarnation. Fear is gripping humanity so tightly that it is about to choke off the very life force they need to fulfill their preordained destinies.

"As Vice President of Flight Operations, and Chief Pilot, I have overseen the daily operations at Infinity Airways since its inception. All Infinity employees are angels who work within a vast infinite matrix to ensure that the right people are in the right seat, on the right flight, at the right time. This is most important as the majority of the passengers we transport are carrying tremendously heavy emotional and karmic baggage."

Scenes from the Infinity Airways reservations department are seen on the holographic display. "Seat assignments are never random or accidental. Everyone flying onboard Infinity will be given opportunities to gain in personal growth and understanding at some level from their seatmate or seatmates. Because Free Will is never to be infringed upon, these traveling souls are free to accept, reject, or ignore the very situations provided to them—situations that could quickly advance them into the higher vibrations of love and service. Thus far, our airline has been quite successful in helping our passengers process much of their karmic balancing and moving them toward their higher selves."

Michael points with his Sword of Light and Truth to one of his parchment scrolls sealed with his personal sigil. The scroll unrolls on its own as a holographic display of Infinity's latest custom-designed airplane comes to life. Michael points to each exalted feature of the aircraft and explains its function. "There is a great need for the expansion of our airline. The new Infinity I-888 is just the beginning of bigger and better things to come. Because the Infinity I-888 is the largest plane we have ever operated, we are experiencing an unprecedented demand for flight attendants." Michael now has everyone's undivided attention.

"Of course, in order to function on the planet, our angelic flight attendants have to lower their vibrations considerably to take on the appearance of the human form. If not, I suspect our passengers would lose it before the plane even leaves the ground!" Angels in the gallery join him for a good laugh. "So that means flying with no wings, my friends.

"Currently we are short staffed because almost a third of all the heavenly host have fallen, choosing to serve the Dark Side." Archangel Michael extends his arm toward Semyaza, who acknowledges the comment with a smile, raising his arms above his head to wave to everyone present. "Yet more angels than ever are needed because of the exponentially escalating rate of fear that is occurring on Earth. As I speak to you now, we are sending the next three classes of flight attendant angel trainees straight to the planes without prior classroom training." The idea of such a rushed training causes some consternation among a group of some of the more conservative angels in the gallery. Michael picks up on their wavering emotions and mentally notes each one that holds such cautious views. "Most will be receiving their training on the job."

"Now, this meeting is getting interesting—finally!" mumbles Semyaza, as he strokes his mustache and goatee, pondering the possibilities of challenging the efforts of the innocent untrained angels coming to Earth.

He laces his fingers together then rests his chin against them as he grins happily. He envisions the savoring pleasure of increasing the number of fallen angels to his ranks.

"Understanding the tremendous sacrifices to be made, we are nonetheless asking that as many angels as possible apply for these positions. You can find our ad in the employment section of *Celestial Clarion* if you feel called to help, or you can speak with me directly after the meeting. Because of terrorism and the current state of—" Michael stops mid-sentence when he notices Tara's desire to speak.

Tara, the Buddhist and Hindu savior-goddess, slowly extends her slender and graceful green hand. The beautiful woman of emerald complexion, long black hair, and the darkest brown eyes is richly adorned with jewels and a jeweled ornamental headdress. Tara's posture at the council table reflects her ease and readiness to act. While her left leg is folded in the contemplative position, her right leg is outstretched, ready to spring into action. In her hand, she holds a closed blue lotus, symbolizing purity. In a dignified and graceful manner, she adjusts her silk robes and scarves that leave her slender torso and rounded breasts uncovered. The marked contrast of her slender waist against her heavy breasts and hips reflects the ideal of feminine beauty. The goddess, representing chastity and virtue, is the very embodiment of love, compassion, and mercy.

Michael indicates for her to speak up. "Yes, Goddess Tara?"

"Pardon the interruption, Lord Michael. You mentioned earlier that you were looking for a certain person and that you think that you may have found her. Could you please tell us more?" asks the goddess of universal compassion whose devotion and compassion for human beings is stronger than a mother's love for her children.

"Of course, Tara," he replies, touching another scroll with the wand. "As I mentioned earlier, I have overseen all operations up until this point. However, with the rapid expansion of the airline, I need someone to work closely with me in a new position, overseeing the areas of flight attendant hiring and training and our company's inflight passenger service. We are conducting an unprecedented search for the most qualified angel to fill this position."

Tara nods reflectively.

The Chinese deity, Kuan Yin, speaks up, "Why not Eve Matrona? I've known her forever. She is far above the rest when it comes to service to humanity. Wouldn't she qualify for this new management position?"

Michael is quick to reply. "Yes, however, Eve is of greater service on board the airplane. Currently she is flying every day as the senior flight attendant on our most challenging flights between Los Angeles and New York City. And trust me, Kuan Yin, she and her dedicated staff of seven angel flight attendants are truly miracle workers on that run."

 *Chapter 15*

"Delta Air Lines flight 1842 to New York's John F. Kennedy Airport is in the final stages of boarding. Please report to gate 57B for an immediate departure." After the flight announcement, the airport public security message broadcasts once more, "Do not leave your bags unattended. They are subject to search. Maintain a close watch on all of your personal belongings. Do not accept anything from strangers. Report any suspicious activity to local authorities. Thank you and have a good flight."

Elizabeth Walters lays trembling on the cold tile of the restroom floor, listening with great trepidation to the streaming announcements coming over the airport public address system.

"Can't you shut up for one minute!" she screams feebly at the recorded voice. Her normally elegant hair twist has fallen out of place, mascara streaks her cheeks, and the color of her face now matches the white porcelain toilet she has been throwing up in.

"Look at yourself, Liz," she sighs. Staring at her reflection in the water inside the toilet bowl, she argues with herself once more, "You've been walking aimlessly through this airport, talking to yourself like some insane bag lady—"

Elizabeth suddenly slumps against the cold ceramic tile wall in resignation. She looks around in dismay while sitting inside the handicap stall at the far end of the ladies restroom. "Oh, God! I am a bag lady! I've been wandering around this damn airport from gate to gate with my bags all morning—again!

"Well, they are designer bags, Elizabeth," she states in her own defense.

"Oh, who am I kidding?" she confesses, closing her eyes while her mind races.

The stressed-out forty-two year old graphic designer missed seven flights the previous day and three so far that morning, wasting thousands of dollars on airfare and penalties because of her crippling fear of flying. With eyes still closed, she shakes her head. *I have got to get on the next flight to New York, or I can just kiss my career and everything I have worked so hard for goodbye. There is no way I can back out of this presentation. I'll be fired on the spot.* She gulps hard and shudders. "It's fly or die! Or maybe both," she chokes aloud.

For what seems like the millionth time that day, the public security announcement encouraging passengers to keep a close watch on their bags blares across the airport's public announcement system. The incessant recording is fraying on Elizabeth's last nerve.

"Easy for you to say, Mr. Announcer!" she screams out. "You're not going to New York City where there are terrorists, bombings, and airplanes flying into buildings. As a matter of fact, you're not going anywhere, are you? No, you're safe in some recording studio, unaffected by all these rising security levels. Today it's orange; yesterday it was red!" she sobs, collapsing against her luggage as her thin body trembles from head to toe. "Your constant security announcements, coupled with all of the horrific world news constantly broadcasting on those stupid airport TV monitors, make me feel anything but safe about flying.

"Maybe I just won't go to New York, Mr. Announcer!" she protests, caving into her fears. "Maybe I'll just make public security announcements for airports like you. Maybe I'll just continue to ruin all of my career aspirations because I'm too damn afraid to get on a plane!" she cries, slamming her shoulder against the stainless steel stall door. "What the hell. My fear of flying has already caused me to be fired from three jobs and cost me the broadcasting career of my dreams. So what's one more?" she sobs. "I know, I know—all that hard work, dedication, and years of psychotherapy have helped me to become a successful graphic designer; but if I don't get on the next flight to New York, I can just chalk this career up as another fear-induced failure!"

Several women walk in to use the facilities a few stalls away. Elizabeth sits quietly with her legs curled beneath her, her arms gripping herself and her purse protectively. Her head bows, sending wavy rivers of dark brown hair cascading over her face behind which she slowly tries to regain her composure. Her nerve endings crawl with uncertainty, and a hint of queasiness still churns in the bottom of her aching stomach.

Once again, the announcement blares over the PA, but this time the message seems to say something different. "Maintain control and keep watch of your personal *fears*. Do not accept any *fears* from strangers. Have a good flight. *Go to New York, Elizabeth, and have a good life!*"

"What the . . . where . . . who said that?" Elizabeth frantically peers around the toilet stall. "Oh, my God, I'm starting to hear voices. I'm really starting to lose it!" she cries hysterically. She rips madly through her purse, retrieves her cell phone, redials her therapist's number, and is promptly placed on hold, again.

"He's not available, Elizabeth, but I am," says a quiet little voice that seems to be coming from inside her.

"No!" she screams in her frustration, ignoring the voice within.

"Where are you when I need you?" Unable to reach her therapist, she flings the phone into her stylish Laura Wellington designer bag which is overloaded with numerous prescription bottles and toiletry items.

"I'm right here, Elizabeth—like always," the voice whispers reassuringly.

In the bathroom stall, sitting on the floor on the other side of the toilet with Elizabeth Walters is a magnificent guardian angel. This celestial messenger of love has been with her since the day she was born. Elizabeth, because of her limiting and constricting fears from the last twenty years, has choked off all communication and understandings from her angelic assistant. That is until today. With its beautiful ivory wings crushed up the tile walls in the last stall of the ladies' room, Elizabeth's guardian angel surrounds her continuously with unconditional love and support.

"Announcing Infinity Airways flight 444 to New York's John F. Kennedy Airport is now ready for passenger check in at gate 11," squawks the public address system.

"Oh, my God, that's it—that's the flight that I'm supposed to be on!" Elizabeth screams anxiously as panic rises inside her.

"That's right!" encourages the angel as they get off the floor.

"It's the last one to get me there in time for my presentation tomorrow morning!"

"That's just the way you planned it. Remember?" it muses. "Hmm. Of course, you don't," comes the quiet reply.

"What is Infinity Airways? Oh, God, I've never even heard of them before!" exclaims Elizabeth feeling unsettled and confused. Tremors of anxiety echo around inside her empty stomach.

"And soon you will never forget them. You are in for the ride of your life, Elizabeth. Now hurry up before you miss everything you have ever wanted." Invisibly the angel holds the stall door open for Liz, who struggles with her baggage.

Elizabeth tries to take a deep breath to calm her frazzled nerves. Gathering her belongings, she attempts to pull herself together. "Great, now it looks as if I'm booked on some fly-by-night, some kind of wing-and-a-prayer, start-up airline," she exclaims aloud as she continues to reprimand herself. "Way to go, Liz! You really did it this time."

Looking in the restroom mirror, Elizabeth haphazardly redoes her French twist. "Oh, you have no idea," muses the angel standing side-by-side next to Elizabeth, fluffing its ivory wings as it primps in front of the restroom mirror as well.

Chapter 16

"By the way, my name is Pete St. Hilaire," says the friendly uniformed gentleman with a long white beard as he unlocks the gatehouse door that leads to the airplane. Nicole notices the pair of oversized heavenly golden keys on his key ring. "I'm referred to as the gate agent here at Infinity Airways." As the agent walks her up to the airplane, he laughs heartily and winks, "Although I still prefer my old title of *gatekeeper*."

"Wait! Oh, my God . . . you're Saint Peter!" exclaims Nicole in her excitement as she recognizes his kind, caring face. "You're the heavenly saint who stands at the pearly gates. You're working here too?"

"Yes. Same type of job. You know, determining who can and cannot enter—just different surroundings." He winks again and returns her smile. "Now, this is going to be a full flight. I'll pray for you, Nicole. You're sure going to need it on this trip!"

Having difficulty walking and pulling her luggage behind her at the same time up the highly inclined jetway, Nicole teeters slowly on board the enormous Infinity I-888 aircraft behind Saint Pete. Once they enter the plane, he gives her a quick tour of the cabins.

"This newly custom-designed plane seats up to four hundred people—fifty in First Class and three hundred fifty in Coach Class. There are nine lavatories, and two galleys—one for first and one for coach." Saint Pete takes her inside the first class galley. "Carts are stored here," he explains as they look at all the various cabinets and drawers. "You will soon discover that this aircraft is like no other."

Nicole smiles, once again unsure of the meaning of his comment. Saint Pete continues to show her around the lavishly appointed aircraft. While gazing around at the beautifully designed cabin interior, Nicole accidentally walks into one of the flight attendants. As Nicole apologizes profusely, she looks into the most striking pair of blue sapphire eyes she has ever seen. There is profound wisdom and knowledge held within.

"Sorry. I . . . I—" starts Nicole.

"Nicole, this is Eve Matrona, the onboard leader for your flight. She'll show you everything you need to know . . . and maybe a little more," says Pete with a chuckle.

Eve Matrona looks over her paperwork for the flight. She gives Nicole a stern look as she takes a cursory scan to examine the young trainee's angelic qualities and flaws, her strengths and her weaknesses. "Nicole, we have been waiting for you."

"I can explain, Ms. Matrona." Nicole hastens to launch into the story of her hectic morning for the fourth time. "I—"

"Nicole, I know all about what happened. Let's see how you look in your new uniform," interupts Eve, ready for her quick head-to-toe inspection.

Nicole struggles out of the company-issued coat, knocking over her luggage and purse. Eve waits patiently with an uncompromising look. Without a word, the onboard leader leans over and repositions Nicole's nametag and buttons the top button on Nicole's blouse. Eve notices Nicole's wobbling ankles. "Although we have already started our flight preparations, we should have a quick briefing so everyone can meet you."

As if they appeared out of thin air, Nicole suddenly finds herself surrounded by eight flight attendants and one pilot. *Strange how everyone looks so familiar,* she reflects as she looks closely at the flight attendants. Glancing over to the man in a crisp white pilot uniform, she gasps. *It can't be . . . one of the most powerful archangels in Heaven!*

"Welcome, Nicole. We are glad that you could join us this morning," says the pilot. "While you may know me as Archangel Gabriel, on the plane I am referred to as First Officer Gabe Jones. I'm the copilot. We're glad you are flying with us. Please feel free to visit us in the cockpit if you have any questions or concerns or just need a break."

Just then, Archangel Michael boards the plane. Nicole inhales sharply, feeling as if she might float off the floor. Michael shakes hands with Gabriel and greets the rest of the crew. He smiles in Nicole's direction. "Good morning, everyone—and Nicole. Did I miss anything here?" With a twinkle in his eye, he winks and steps forth to shake her hand. He smiles at the new trainee and nods with approval at her mortal image. "You can call me Captain Mike Smith while we're on board, Nicole."

"Captain Smith?" Nicole repeats aloud with raised brows as she can't help but notice his shorter hair and clean-cut military-like appearance.

Michael points to himself and then to Gabriel. "Smith and Jones, get it?"

Everyone laughs but Nicole as she grapples to understand the humor of their names. Eve curiously watches the interaction between Nicole and Michael as she reviews her predeparture paperwork.

"So how do you like our newest bird?" Michael looks proudly around the cabin.

Nicole looks confused again as she tries to understand Michael's comment. "Bird?" she replies quizzically. The crew smiles at Nicole, whose mouth remains slightly agape as she stares at Michael. Nicole notices that his human form only augments and intensifies his perfection and spiritual purity.

Eve chuckles at the new trainee's bemused tone and expression. She steps up and places her hands on Nicole's shoulders. "He means the airplane. Now, let's continue with the introductions, shall we?" she prompts gently. "This is Sila, Achaiah, Itqal, Dina, Rochel, Sarakiel, and Tezalel." One by one, the flight attendants greet Nicole. "This very dedicated crew that has been chosen above all other angels to work with me on this run between LAX and JFK."

"Wow! I wonder why I have been chosen," Nicole whispers to herself.

Eve senses that Nicole is feeling a little overwhelmed. "Nicole, if you need assistance with anything, anything at all, please feel free to ask myself or any one of the crew at anytime. We want your experience on this flight to be as pleasant as possible." Eleven faces beam kindly at Nicole.

"I can't understand why Saint Pete said he would pray for me. So far everything seems perfect," she utters quietly as she smiles back at the crew.

Michael speaks up to make a brief announcement, "Since passenger boarding is about to commence, I will make this short. As expected, we are full today. As you know threats of terrorist attacks and the unpredictable weather forecasted in New York are first and foremost on the minds of our passengers. On top of that, this flight is also delayed. LAX along with the other airports today have dropped to security level orange. So we are all here to do whatever we can to influence our human friends in making better choices, helping them to lighten their heavy karmic and emotional baggage, especially during these stressful, perilous times. Nevertheless, we are not to interfere. Our passengers shall always have Free Will—no matter what. Now they all have their specific seat assignments, sitting next to the right person to assist in their life's toughest lessons. We will do our best to help everyone along in their journeys. So let's have a great flight!"

"Wow," Nicole mumbles, her voice awed. "They must have been really impressed with my interview to put me with this crew on the LA-to-New York run—on a brand-new I-888, no less!" She smiles proudly, still wobbling in her shoes.

 *Chapter 17*

Eve wastes no time in getting down to business. She puts Nicole's belongings in the closet by the boarding door. "Let's put up that long hair of yours, young lady," says Eve as Nicole's blonde tresses instantly go into a tight bun like hers. "Today you will be working in first class with Sila, Itqal, Achaiah, and me. On the return flight tomorrow, you will work in coach with Dina, Rochel, Sarakiel, and Tezalel." She gives everyone further instructions and motions for Nicole to assist her in greeting the boarding passengers.

"Good morning, welcome aboard. It's nice to have you with us," Eve says warmly to a very distinguished-looking man who points into the cabin with his boarding card, indicating that he knows exactly where his seat is. Next to board are several politicians in business suits. Leaving their security escorts in the jetway, they board the plane carrying on an intense conversation ignoring Nicole and Eve as they walk by.

Nicole quickly looks down at her new physical body. "Eve, are we somehow invisible again, back in our natural angelic forms?"

Eve shrugs her shoulders. "No, Nicole, we are still very physical. Most are too busy to notice us—physical or not. It's only when they want something that they wonder where we are—that applies to being a flight attendant and being an angel."

Nicole gives Eve a look of dismay while more passengers pour through the door.

"Good morning, welcome aboard," says Eve, continuing to greet the arriving first class passengers. Many of them simply avert their eyes and keep walking by. Few, if any, smile.

Eager for an opportunity to serve, Nicole jumps at the chance to greet a very tall and beautiful woman coming through the door. "Good morning, welcome aboard," Nicole says sweetly.

The six-foot-tall woman stops immediately and dumps her Gucci designer luggage at Nicole's feet then loads her overloaded shopping bag on Nicole's arm. The woman continues in removing her expensive, taupe leather coat, shoving it into Nicole's arms. After placing her hat on Nicole's head, the statuesque woman proceeds to her seat, talking on her cell phone the entire time. Not once does she speak to or acknowledge Nicole.

Nicole stares at the bags surrounding her feet. "Who in this world is that?"

"That's Brigitte Burton, one of the top models in this country," says Eve. "And it appears that she wants you to put her belongings into the overhead compartment for her."

Nicole stares back at the striking woman. "Well, it sure would have been nice if she told me that."

Eve senses the new trainee's frustration. "Don't worry, Nicole. I'll take care of Ms. Burton's belongings," smirks Eve, stifling a laugh as she collects the items scattered on and around Nicole. "Why don't you try assisting Itqal with the on-the-ground beverage service in first class?" Eve whispers in Nicole's ear, "He is the Angel of Affection who assists in situations of dissension among human beings."

In the departure gate, St. Pete announces boarding for the coach cabin. Hundreds of anxious travelers try to elbow their way to the front of the line, trying to get on board before the others. About halfway through general boarding while Eve continues to greet the passengers at the door, Nicole tries to walk up the aisle against the flow of passengers to speak with Eve. Standing in the aisle just inside the boarding door, with flared nostrils and a snarled look on her face, the irate passenger from the ticket counter sees Nicole in the aisle. Her eyes glare with absolute disgust and hatred for Nicole. Like a ferocious fighting bull, the heavy-set woman scratches her hooves in the carpet, then charges ahead intentionally slamming into Nicole as she tries to make her way forward toward the boarding door with a tray of drinks. Cocktail glasses, ice, and napkins fly everywhere. The surrounding first class passengers wipe their wet, stained clothes in disbelief as they stare at Nicole holding the empty serving tray in her hand.

"Did you see what she just did to me?" Nicole screams aloud as she wipes her uniform off. The ice on the carpet crunches under her feet as she rushes to the onboard leader. "I'm so scared, Eve. What is wrong with these people? I know they're stressed out, but they're all so mean and rude and demanding." Eve quickly motions for Nicole to lower her voice as more passengers continue to board. "Sorry, Eve," she whispers loudly. "I'm just so confused . . . these people in the back, well . . . this man at 7E keeps asking for someone named Mary, whom he wants to have all bloody! And then . . . and then he asked for a virgin for his wife. And then that passenger, that Mr. Tex Shepherd at 8A . . . he keeps treating me like I'm his own personal play thing, and he says he's so hungry he could eat a horse. Does Infinity Airways serve horse, Eve? And that model lady . . . well, I'm just not sure I'm cut out for this dimension!" declares Nicole in her exasperation.

"Never forget, Nicole, you are an angel," Eve says calmly and quietly. She turns and looks at Nicole face-to-face, then takes hold of her shoulders. "You are absolutely correct. They are rude, demanding, egotistical, obnoxious, and everything in between. And we are here to serve them. Remember who you are, Nicole—a messenger of The Creator who has come here to assist humanity to ascend to the Fourth Dimension. There is no greater assignment than that for an angel."

Nicole remains perplexed. "But—"

"Now, Nicole, Achaiah would like you to help him in the first class galley. Being the Angel of Patience and the discoverer of the secrets of nature, maybe he could show you a few things," instructs Eve with an upraised brow.

Chapter 18

As Nicole helps Itqal and Achaiah secure the cabin for departure, Senator Richard Stevens grabs Nicole's wrist as she passes by his row. "Bring me another scotch on the rocks." The distinguished-looking tall man in his mid-fifties with auburn hair and dark circles under his eyes turns to his seatmate. "How about another one, Jack?"

"Sure, Richard, sure. Sounds great." His colleague, Senator Jack Hughes, an overweight balding man in his mid-fifties, responds absentmindedly while looking over the latest senate bills piled on his lap.

"Here's to a successful outcome at tomorrow morning's conference." Richard toasts his colleague. "We certainly have these guys in our back pock—"

The ringing of Jack's cell phone interrupts their toast. "Hello . . . yes, this is Jack Hughes. Yes? . . . What? . . . What? . . . When? Oh, my God! Yes . . . yes! I will be there, right away!" Jack jumps from his seat, knocking over his drink. Frantically he stuffs the scattered papers into his old, worn leather briefcase and clamors to retrieve his garment bag from the overhead compartment.

"It's Dad; he's had a stroke. I have to get off this plane now. I have to get to Cedars-Sinai as soon as possible. I'm sorry, Richard, I have to go!"

"Oh, my God, Jack. I'm so sorry. Go! Go! I'll take care of everything. Thank God we haven't taken off yet," Richard exclaims reassuringly. He downs his drink as he watches Jack, his closest friend, rush off the plane.

"Son of a bitch!" yells Richard as he slams his fist on the center armrest. "Why did old man Hughes have to pick today of all days to have a damn stroke? Now I'm going to have to deal with those liberal bastards in New York by myself!" Overhearing his contemptuous remarks, several first class passengers in the immediate area stare at the senator with a disdainful glare.

Lost in thought, the senator stares blankly as Nicole carefully walks up with their drinks on a sterling silver serving tray. "Here are your—" starts Nicole as she looks over, seeing the unoccupied seat.

"Senator Hughes had to leave unfortunately—some asinine family emergency," Richard quips callously.

"Oh," replies Nicole noticing the condition of the empty seat cushion. "Here, please allow me to clean that up, sir. We will probably be using this seat as there are several people on standby for First Class. Please let me to take those newspapers for you." She leans over with the drink tray in hand to remove the rumpled, wet papers. Infuriated at the dramatic turn of events, Richard grabs the scotch on the rocks from the tray and downs it, then guzzles Jack's drink

 *Chapter 19*

Toward the end of passenger boarding, Nicole again scurries frantically to the forward aircraft door to speak with Eve. "I think these humans are beyond our help! I really don't see how on Earth we are supposed to accomplish so much down here in so little time. What is Archangel Michael, I mean, Captain Smith and our One Infinite Creator thinking? This just all seems so hopeless, Eve. I really don't know if I can help anyone down here. I can barely help myself." Nicole goes to the closet to retrieve her purse and luggage.

"Did I hear my name?" Archangel Michael suddenly appears beside Eve.

"I don't think this assignment is going to work out for her, Michael. She's having second thoughts about becoming a flight attendant." Out of the corner of her eye, Eve notices Michael smiling boyishly at Nicole. Sarcastically she adds, "The poor thing obviously can't handle the human emotions around her. She wants to go back to—"

Michael is quick to interrupt, "Let's not be so hasty, Eve. After all, this is her first experience on an airplane, let alone her first experience here on Earth. Naturally, Nicole is shaken—never having experienced anything like anger, frustration, and fear. Of course the poor innocent thing is overwhelmed."

Nicole stands quietly next to the cockpit door, clutching her purse and coat. She nods, affirming Michael's observations. While watching the discussion between the flight attendant in charge and the captain of her flight, Nicole notices that where Eve displays sternness, Michael shows lenience; where Eve wields a firm hand, Michael demonstrates affability;

and where Eve seems to find fault with her, Michael bestows flattery and encouragement.

"She'll be fine," Michael states firmly. "Do you remember how you felt on your first flight, Eve?" he asks with a wink.

Eve feigns a smile as she looks back at Nicole. "That seems like eons ago, Michael," laughs Eve flirtatiously as she steps closer to him and adjusts the gold epaulet on the shoulder of his uniform jacket.

Despite Eve's attempts to gain his attention, Michael remains focused on the new trainee. He walks over to the bewildered Nicole and directs her to the cockpit. "Come with me, Nicole." Eve watches jealously as the cockpit door closes.

Nicole looks carefully at the multitude of dials and gauges. The flight panels and instrumentation look technically complex. She notices the flight manuals, circuit breaker panels, emergency equipment, and curiously studies the oxygen masks hanging near the pilot seats. She turns very slowly when she realizes that Michael is touching her shoulder.

Nicole stands in awe and total disbelief. "I cannot believe that you, Archangel Michael, are speaking to me, one on one. You are one of the greatest of angels. And the Chief of Archangels and Chief of the Order of Virtues, as well as the Ruler of the Fourth Heaven, and much, much more that I can't seem to recall right now." Nicole's mind is spinning. Overwhelmed in his presence, she stands motionless basking in the energy of his extraordinary angelic vibrations.

"Nicole, let me say this first before I continue. You can leave right now or whenever you want. Like everyone else, angel or human, you have Free Will. Do whatever you feel that you are called to do; stay or quit, it will always be your choice. However, you are here because I believe in your ability to succeed, and because you too truly felt that you could help uplift humanity in their greatest time of need."

Michael speaks to Nicole with a voice and style that is celestially poetic and serene, filled with wisdom. As he continues, his words are warm and real yet universal and detached. Nicole nervously looks deep into his eyes, seeing the most beautiful sight ever. It is like endless love—love on wavelengths of light, colors, and hues beyond anything she has ever seen. There is ultraviolet and infrared and gradations of colors that heal, that love, that create. It is as if music, color, and love are all swirled into one and placed into the adoring eyes of an airline captain.

Nicole hears a voice from the center of her being that sounds like her friend, Alexis. *Listen, stay, and learn, Nicole. Someone of his stature in the spirit world with his omniscience, his enlightenment, and his knowing the mystery of divinity would not be dressed like an airline pilot if it wasn't really important.*

As the words echo within, Nicole looks at him with awe, smiles, then wordlessly says, "Thank you."

 *Chapter 20*

As the last few passengers continue to board, Archangels Michael and Gabriel are conversing in the cockpit preparing for departure. Eve enters, accompanied by an extremely frazzled Elizabeth Walters. "Excuse me, gentlemen, but Ms. Walters here has asked to speak with you. She is extremely afraid of flying," explains Eve.

"Ms. Walters, you have some concerns about flying with us today?" Gabriel asks, his voice smooth and steady, setting a calm tone for his conversation with yet another passenger afraid of flying.

"Well, yes! With pilots taking off on the wrong runway, understaffed control towers, exhausted air traffic controllers, and the near collision of that news helicopter and plane here at LAX earlier this morning, I'm very stressed about flying, sir! And what about the terrorist threats, exploding liquids and the red alert security level at the airports yesterday, and today it's orange . . . and the horrible weather in New York and the storms here? I just don't know if . . ." Elizabeth sputters in one breath before trailing off. Like everyone who enters, she is momentarily mesmerized by the high-tech appearance of the cockpit. Never before has she seen so many dials, circuit breakers, buttons, and gauges.

Her guardian angel smiles at the pilots while, in love and fun, it imitates Elizabeth's posture and exaggerates her hand gestures. Michael and Gabriel return the smile in amusement.

"Ms. Walters, I can certainly understand that all the things that you are speaking of may seem very disturbing. However, you cannot let these fears control you. You have to live your life," Gabriel says enthusiastically. "You cannot worry about everything you hear, read, eat, drink, think, wear, and do. You must learn to release your fears. Start by focusing on something that makes you happy—like your dog, Oliver; or your darling niece, Amelia. And how about that amazing presentation of yours early morning tomorrow."

Elizabeth remains frozen, not sure if she was still hearing things that are not really being said. She shakes her head and flutters her eyelids nervously. "How did you know about my—" she starts then stops.

Like a celestial clown, her guardian angel shrugs its shoulders and scratches its head while tapping its foot with a comical expression across its angelic face. Gabriel smiles, trying to contain himself.

"Here, I would like to show you something," Gabriel interrupts as he removes a quarter from his pocket. "Life is like this quarter. It has two sides—heads and tails, day and night, up and down, life and death, love and fear. Yet it's all life. You have just simply allowed the negative side of the coin—your fears, your negativity, your worrying, and that of everyone around you—to weigh you down so that you are lying flat. Please observe. When in balance, a coin can spin quickly on its own axis." Gabriel expertly rotates the coin on his fingertip. "You see, the very center of the quarter is calm and still, even though everything else is revolving around very quickly. When your life is in balance, you can operate from your center as well. When everything seems crazy and out of control, just go to your center, and there you'll find peace."

Elizabeth watches the spinning coin and feels the strength behind Gabriel's words. "But how do you do this every day—fly, I mean?" she asks fretfully.

Gabriel smiles reassuringly. His calming manner instills a feeling of confidence as he gestures to Michael sitting in the captain's jumpseat. "Miss Walters, we have been flying longer than you've been around. We love our job and take great pleasure in helping people get where they need to go. Even in the face of danger or when the flying gets really rough, we just stay focused and enjoy the ride. Indeed, it would become rather boring if every day were smooth sailing. It's the storms and turbulence along the journey that help to make us great pilots. So why not go to your seat, Ms. Walters, and enjoy the journey as well? Have faith, and we'll take care of the rest."

"Yeah, Elizabeth, let's get settled in and have some fun!" her angel joins in.

Gabriel smiles and tosses the quarter to Elizabeth. She catches it and turns it over in her hand. "I pay my therapist way too much," she murmurs as she leaves the cockpit. Her guardian angel nods in agreement.

Little does Elizabeth know that she has just been counseled by Saint Gabriel the Archangel, the bringer of news, and the one who heralds the revealing of answers. Known as one of the seven archangels who stand before The Creator, his name means "God is my strength." Gabriel is the angel of resurrection, mercy, vengeance, death, revelation, and hope. In 610-632 CE, it was Gabriel who delivered the Qur'an to Muhammad, sura by sura, chapter by chapter. During those twenty-two years, 114 chapters were dictated, which now comprise the Koran. It is the most-read book next to the Bible.

In many religious writings, Gabriel appeared as a messenger and deliverer of blessed events to humanity. Many call upon the Angel of Annunciation for guidance in their spiritual life, for revelation of their life plan and purpose. Many seek his guidance to release joy, happiness, and fulfillment from within. When called upon, he helps one to establish discipline and order in one's life. Little does the stressed-out graphics designer know that the angel who is the spirit of truth, the maker of changes, has given her the wisdom to do just that. Although he is the Ruling Prince of the First Heaven and is said to sit on the left-hand side of God, today he is the copilot of her flight.

Gabriel now has another announcement to make to everyone. "Ladies and gentlemen, we will be closing the boarding door momentarily and pushing back from the gate. Please turn off all cell phones, stow all your heavy baggage . . ." he continues over the airplane public address system.

# Chapter 21

Infinity Airways flight 444 is about ready for departure. Several standby passengers, two large men, and a foul-smelling teenager in baggy jeans with long sun-bleached blonde dreadlocks walk on at the last minute. Eve directs them to the last row in coach. Saint Pete walks on last to make an onboard announcement.

"Would passenger Mr. Stuart Patrick please come to the boarding door? Paging a Mr. Stuart Patrick to the boarding door please," Saint Pete announces clearly. Everyone onboard, including Senator Stevens, looks around curiously to see who responds to the page. A man in khaki slacks and a long-sleeved green cotton pullover shirt quickly bustles up to the door from the coach cabin with his luggage in hand.

"I'm Stuart Patrick," the fifty-four-year-old man says excitedly. His manner is affable and genuine. "Someone page me?" He breaks into a wide grin. "Did I get upgraded to First Class?"

"Yes, sir, you sure did!" Pete exclaims. "Nicole, our new flight attendant trainee, will be happy to assist you to your seat. You'll be at 4F, sir; that's a window seat, Mr. Patrick. Enjoy the flight."

"Oh, thank you. You're very kind!" Stuart zealously shakes the gate agent's hand. Visions of fabulous food, superior service, ample legroom, personal entertainment systems, and plush fully reclining seats dance in his head as he follows Nicole.

Pete hands Eve the passenger manifest and the final departure information with a wink and a smile and closes the boarding door.

After pushing back from the gate and taxiing for several minutes, Gabriel's voice comes over the intercom, "Ladies and gentlemen, this is

First Officer Jones. Due to more unexpected weather in the New York area, we have just been advised that we will be delayed for another fifty-five minutes. We ask that you please remain seated . . ."

Moans, sighs and expletives sound throughout the cabin before Gabriel's announcement is over. Nicole watches closely as Eve demonstrates the operation of the video equipment as she turns on the Infinity I-888 safety demonstration video for the passengers.

Nicole watches the safety demo on video monitors throughout the cabin and passenger screens in the seatbacks. "It's seems strange, Eve. Although there are four hundred people on board this newly designed aircraft, not flown by any other airline, I seem to be the only one really paying attention." The trainee looks around at all the passengers involved in eating fast food, reading their books, newspapers, and magazines. Others are talking and playing video games. "I guess they have faith that we'll take care of them—whether they notice us or not!"

Ding! Ding! Ding! Ding! Completely absorbed and intrigued by the information she is watching, Nicole is suddenly startled when a passenger call bell rings on the flight attendant call panel over her head. "Senator Stevens needs assistance." Eve nods her head encouragingly. "The other attendants are busy at the moment, Nicole."

Ding! Ding! Ding! Ding! Nicole covers her ears, irritated by the sound. "I'll do anything just to make him stop hitting that call button," she replies impatiently to herself. Senator Stevens is hanging over the armrest, waving his arm like a wild man. After nearly quitting her job, Nicole feels the need to somehow validate herself. She takes a deep breath and heads toward the senator, growing more irritated by his incessant ringing of the bell with every wobbly step.

"What can I do for you, Mr. Stevens?" she smiles and asks politely.

"It's *Senator* Stevens, and you have to do something about this situation! This man should not be sitting next me," he seethes pointing at a very calm and relaxed Stuart Patrick. "Is this some kind of sick joke!"

Unprepared for such an outburst, Nicole has no idea how to respond. She shifts nervously in her shoes as several passengers turn in their direction. "Give me a minute. I'll check with Ms. Matrona regarding your . . . uh . . . situation. I'll be right back!"

Eve is putting away supplies in the first class galley in preparation for takeoff when Nicole walks in. "Eve, Eve! Mr. Stevens has a problem with Mr. Patrick sitting next to him. Although I'm not sure why since Mr. Patrick seems to be minding his own business," Nicole whispers loudly. "I'll tell you, Eve, there is just something about that Mr. Stevens I seriously don't like."

Without looking back at Richard or Stuart to see what is happening, Eve says knowingly, "Those two have a long history, Nicole. It goes way back beyond this lifetime. But we'll have to discuss that later. Right now, we need to help prepare for takeoff. Pick up the beverage glasses, check seatbacks, and seatbelts while I attend to those two."

Relieved that she does not have to deal any further with the disgruntled senator, Nicole performs the final security checks down the opposite aisle with Achaiah.

Just before takeoff, Eve shows Nicole how to operate the flight attendant jumpseat. "Wait a minute, Eve. You mean we don't get to sit in actual seats? We have to sit on these . . . these boards?" Nicole warily eyes the seat. "I'm going to have to speak to someone at Infinity about these seats—if you can even call them that!" She looks back into first class at the plush oversized reclining passenger seats.

Eve sits Nicole down and teaches her how to fasten the harness and seat belt. "This will keep your body in place while the plane takes off. Just remember to relax and breathe deeply," advises Eve.

Nicole tilts her head back. "I don't feel as if I can breathe at all. Does it really need to be this tight?" she cries, tugging at the harness across her chest. "I feel so trapped."

"We'll be taking off soon," Eve says from across the aisle, fastening her safety harness. "Just stay there and try to relax, Nicole. We'll be airborne soon."

"Oh, don't worry. I don't think I could get out of this contraption if I tried!" Nicole yells, causing some concern among the already tense and anxious passengers who overhear her comment.

The airplane accelerates down the runway and lifts effortlessly into the air. Nicole leans back with her head against the headrest as she stares out the emergency exit door's window opposite her. "Seeing everything from this perspective feels natural. Yet I can't help but think that I am completely out of my element on this airplane," she murmurs to herself. "I really want to be an Infinity Airways flight attendant. I really want to help these passengers; but it seems the more I'm around them, the worse I feel. It's like I'm absorbing everything they are feeling or thinking like some kind of sponge." Nicole sighs deeply. *I'm definitely going to avoid passengers like Senator Stevens and Brigitte Burton, that rude model who had used me as a mannequin during boarding.* She closes her eyes momentarily and prays.

Chapter 22

Eve has instructed Nicole to take the first class meal preferences for the lunch service. The flight attendant angel trainee approaches a handsome, well-dressed couple seated on the front row as she continues her on-the-job training. "Hello, Mr. and Mrs. Theodore, my name is Nicole, and I will be serving you today. Have you decided what would you like for lunch today?"

"Yes, my wife would like to start with les escargots à la Bourguignon for an appetizer, and I will try le pâté de foie gras, s'il vous plaît," responds Mr. Theodore with his best French accent. The Theodores, a wealthy couple in their mid-sixties from Corona del Mar, California, are well traveled and enjoy the finer things in life, including the finest delicacies in French cuisine.

Nicole stands frozen before Mr. Theodore, unsure of how to react. "Okay, as an angel, I've never eaten and, I guess, never really bothered to pay much attention to what humans consume for sustenance. But surely, there has to be some kind of mistake. Would they really eat snails and the livers of geese that have been force-fed? I highly doubt it," she murmurs to herself quietly, as they look at their menus. "Excuse me, sir, but there must be some kind of mistake with your request. I really don't think you want snails that crawl or the liver of dead—"

"It's on the menu, young lady, and that's what we—" Mr. Theodore indignantly begins.

"I'm so sorry, Mr. and Mrs. Theodore," Eve interrupts, stepping quickly into the exchange. "This is Nicole's first flight and apparently she's . . . she's a vegetarian." Eve flashes a brilliant smile at the bewildered couple.

"We will have your meals out shortly. Please accept our sincere apologies." She promptly escorts Nicole back to the galley.

"Oh, Eve, I'm so embarrassed," pleads Nicole. "It just sounded so odd. I had no idea human ate things like that. What happened to fishes and loaves?" she jokes weakly.

Eve smiles and pats her on the back. "It's okay, Nicole. No harm done. You see, each passenger is going to see his or her all-time favorite dish on our menu. It's just one of the special things we do at Infinity. Here, I'll go through a brief list of some of these items so you can become more familiar with what our passengers will ask for." Most everything that Eve mentions sounds unappealing to Nicole, but she listens attentively anyway.

"Okay, I think I can handle this now," Nicole replies. "But if someone orders the frog legs in cream sauce." She grimaces.

"Just remember, we are not here to pass judgment, Nicole," says Eve. "What people choose to eat is their own prerogative. It may sound unappetizing, unappealing, or even unhealthy; but we are not to interfere with their choices."

"Should I continue taking orders for the other passengers?" Nicole asks sheepishly, hoping that Eve will assign her another task.

"Yes, that will be great. It will give you a chance to interact with our passengers," encourages Eve. "Go ahead and continue at the next row with the Steinbergs."

Nicole slowly approaches the middle-aged couple to her left. "Hello, Mr. and Mrs. Steinberg. May I take your lunch order?" she asks bravely.

"Well, we ordered kosher meals several weeks ago," responds Mrs. Steinberg.

"Kosher meal?" asks Nicole inquisitively. "What is a kosher? Is that some kind of dead animal?"

The Steinbergs laugh. "No, dear, kosher food has been specially prepared and blessed by a rabbi."

"Oh, yes, of course. All food is a blessing, but you don't need a rabbit for that," Nicole interjects innocently. Mrs. Steinberg opens her mouth to make a comment, but Nicole moves on to the next row.

"Hello, Dr. and Mrs. Westman. What would you like for lunch today?" Nicole asks confidently as she proceeds down the aisle.

"I'll have the pan-seared mahimahi with papaya and Asian noodles," Dr. Westman responds quickly.

Mrs. Westman looks over the menu then turns to her husband. "Dear, what do you think I should have?"

"Just get whatever you want, Nancy," he replies from behind the latest issue of the *New England Journal of Medicine*.

Mrs. Westman shuffles through the house plan magazines scattered across her tray table to find her menu. "Okay, well, let me have the Caesar salad. I want to look good in my new swimsuit. We're headed to New York for a cruise to Bermuda for a long overdue vacation," she tells Nicole, then turns back to her husband. "Right, honey?"

Dr. Westman ignores his wife's idle chitchat as he flips through his magazine.

"Oh, fine," she huffs. "Give me the pork tenderloin with sweet potatoes and whatever else comes with it. A salad won't really make a difference now as to how I'll look tomorrow, anyway. Bring me another glass of wine too!"

# *Chapter 23*

"Pardon me, Mr. Patrick, here is your salad. Which dressing would you like, sir?" Eve offers the various choices. "Would you care for any wine with your lunch?" she continues graciously. Stuart declines but takes his time in deciding which type of bread roll he would like. Richard squirms impatiently in his seat, becoming quite irritated by the fact that Stuart is being served first. It is simply standard procedure to serve the farthest person from the aisle first, but Richard is taking it as a personal affront.

Eve finally turns her attention to Richard. "Here you are, Senator Stevens. May I offer you a glass of wine to accompany your meal?" She displays the wide selection of bottles in the wine rack.

"Well, they all look very tempting, but I think I'll go with the Cabernet Sauvignon, since I am having beef." Richard raises his glass so that Eve can pour a sampling. "Ah, a lovely French wine. The color looks nice; the body ample, the bouquet inviting and," he takes a sip and then says, "the actual taste is well . . . okay." He shoots Stuart a look of superiority. Turning back, he accidentally bumps his glass into the wine bottle as Eve fills his glass, spilling Cabernet all over his salad, tray table, and shirt.

"Get out of my way, you imbecile!" Richard brusquely demands of Eve. He frantically tries to get out of his seat as red wine drips all over his clothes. She promptly removes his plates and turns up his table. He storms out of his seat toward the lavatory. Stuart smiles at her sympathetically as he helps clean the spill. Eve quickly grabs a bottle of white wine off the cart and hurries back toward the lavatory. She knocks quietly on the door. "Senator Stevens? Sir, I have something that will help." The door remains closed for a moment before he pokes his head out, attempting to draw as little attention to himself as possible.

Richard eyes the bottle of Chardonnay as she raises her hand. "More wine? What in the hell am I supposed to do with that, drink my stains away?" he screams, outraged by her suggestion. "What kind of service are you providing here, Ms. Matrona?"

"Senator, please, the white wine will take out the red wine," she explains quickly before he can close the door. "Here are some linen napkins. Just pour the white wine on the napkin and blot the stains. It should come right out." As quickly and discreetly as he can, Richard grabs the wine and the napkins then locks himself in the lavatory.

Eve returns to the galley where Nicole is getting more wine for Mrs. Westman. Nicole comments gratefully, "Thank you so much for placing me on the other side of the plane. What is that man's problem anyway?" Nicole replenishes the breadbasket for her cart. "I heard him yelling at you, Eve. Obviously, he has no idea who you really are. If only he did—he would surely be nicer. I don't know if I would have been able to handle that Senator Stevens as graciously as you. I guess that is why you are the Angel of the Lord and the Angel of Humanity and I'm not."

Chapter 24

"Here is your entree, Dr. Westman." Nicole leans over, ready to serve his meal.

"Excuse me, miss, but where are your magazines?" Lawrence asks as he rises from his seat seemingly oblivious to the fact that Nicole is attempting to set his lunch down on his tray table.

"Lawrence, won't you sit down!" Nancy starts to chastise her husband. "Can't you see the stewardess has your meal and mine too?"

"I've already finished all of the magazines that I brought with me," he replies defensively.

"I'm sure there must be some kind of airline magazine in the seat pocket in front of you. Sit down. I'm hungry; please let's just eat," Nancy groans to her husband.

She then summons Nicole, "Oh, miss, I'd love another glass of wine."

In her frustration to get the service over with, Nicole uses her angelic abilities to miraculously create several magazines based on the vibrational energies that she is picking up from Dr. Westman. Nicole knows she is not supposed to interfere, but she senses the magazines will somehow be of great service to the doctor.

"Oh, look! Someone must have left these from a previous flight," she says casually, handing the magazines to Dr. Westman. He flips through the pages, intrigued with what he sees. Dedicated to alternative and ancient Eastern healing modalities, the magazines are a far cry from what he usually finds in the typical airline magazine rack.

"Nancy, do you have a pen?" he asks abruptly as Nicole lays down his meal tray.

With a loud sigh, his wife retrieves her purse and sifts through it. "I'm sure there's one in here somewhere," she mumbles begrudgingly. Lawrence looks over just in time to see a pack of cigarettes tumble from her purse.

"How could you, Nancy? After all the discussions we've had. After all the promises you've made?" demands Lawrence. Totally outraged, he grabs the cigarette pack with the matches neatly tucked behind the cellophane sheath. "How many times have I told you that these things are an absolute guarantee to disease, cancer, and even worse, premature death? And furthermore, how did you get through security with those matches?"

"Give me those back, dammit!" She tries to snatch the cigarettes out of his hand. "You just don't understand! They help me to stay calm. I've got so much stress in my life. I sure as hell could use one right now. Too bad they don't let people smoke on the damn airplane anymore. I mean, really, what more stressful time is there than flying?"

"Stress!" he screams. His anger matches hers; his voice getting louder. "What in the hell are you talking about? You think you are stressed? You don't have a clue what stress is!" he yells, no longer able to contain himself. "You don't have to work. Both the girls are out of college. They're happy and healthy with great jobs. We have a live-in housekeeper and a fulltime gardener. All you have to do is get out of bed occasionally and figure out where you're going to have lunch with your girlfriends. Most of the time when I get home, you are out shopping—buying even more stuff for the house or for the next party you're going to throw!" exclaims Dr. Westman as he becomes more enraged.

"You want to know what stress is, Nancy? Try being told for years and years what to do and how to do it by the AMA, the pharmaceutical companies, and the goddamn insurance companies. Even my patients and my staff tell me what to do all day long."

Nancy in her horror notices that everyone seated around them is staring. Although she feels as though she would like to crawl under the plush first class carpeting to avoid being in the humiliating limelight that her husband has created, she reluctantly looks back at him, noticing the bulging veins on his neck.

Lawrence hands the pack of cigarettes and matches to Nicole. "Here, take these damn cancer sticks, please. And throw them away," he demands. "It seems that my wife is under a lot of stress. You know, she has to make so many decisions," he retorts sarcastically. "You know, like which expensive house to buy in a particular exclusive neighborhood!" Lawrence Westman is now erupting and the lava spewing. His stress has brought him to a boiling point.

"Just look at your husband, Nancy. These last few years of feeling tired, unappreciated, and stressed out has really taken a toll on me. I look like hell.

My body, mind, and spirit reflect my exhaustion. Look at my hair, Nance. It's turning gray, and my hairline is receding." Lawrence pulls back his hair from his forehead, then grabs his gut. "And my waistband is expanding. I no longer reflect the picture of health that I once exemplified. So don't talk to me about what stress is doing to you!"

Unsure of what to do or what to say, Nicole tries to smile and act nonchalant, unaware that she is picking up their intense emotions. She quickly shoves the cigarettes in her serving smock and fiddles with the cork from the wine bottle while the surrounding passengers look their way. Mrs. Westman sits still in a state of shock.

Lawrence sighs heavily. "All I have ever wanted from you, Nancy, is to take a real interest in what I do. I want to help people to be healthy, and yet my own wife is smoking cigarettes. It seems that the only thing you're really interested in is how much money I can make and what kind of social status I can afford you. And now you want me to expand my practice so that you can move into an even bigger house? Do you even care about what this job is doing to me?" He stares intently at his wife, his resentment emerging fully as he waits for a response.

Nancy sits mortified in a dead silence, completely humiliated by the scene her husband is causing. As Nicole starts to step away, Nancy grabs her wrist. Nicole's body recoils then begins to tremble slightly.

"Oh, did you care for some more wine, Mrs. Westman?" Nicole asks nervously.

"No," she replies quietly, avoiding the gaze of her husband, "I'd like a vodka martini. Make it a double."

Chapter 25

Stuart struggles to stifle a laugh when Richard returns from the lavatory in his wine-soaked clothes. "Well, Richard—may I call you Richard—or do you prefer that everyone call you *Senator Stevens?*" mocks Stuart, his quiet tone lacking respect.

"You can call me Senator Stevens for the rest of your damn life!" Richard responds vehemently. "Out of all the people that could be sitting next to me, why the hell must it be you? The odds must be a trillion to one and no comments about the way I smell." He settles back in his seat attempting to straighten his wet shirt and pants.

"Can we at least be civil?" Stuart asks. "We still have another three and a half hours before we reach New York."

"Civil? What is that, your favorite word? It's always civil this or civil that with you. If you really want to be civil, you can just shut the hell up and let me watch a movie!"

"Great," mumbles Richard as he quickly plugs his headphones into the entertainment system in the armrest. *A movie will be the perfect way for me to avoid any further conversation with Stuart.* He presses the video-channel selector repeatedly, unable to switch movies. He stares at the video monitor in total disbelief as the movie begins. "This day is only getting worse. How is it that *A Civil Action*—that asinine, environmentalist-whacko movie—is on all eight stations?"

Richard rings his flight attendant call bell repeatedly. *Ding! Ding! Ding! Ding!*

"You've got to be kidding me!" he screams, slamming his video monitor. He presses the flight attendant call button again. "This whole damn flight has been one huge practical joke." He angrily yanks his headphone jack from the armrest, leaving the headphones on in hopes that they will deter Stuart from any further conversation. Richard presses his call button again. *Ding! Ding! Ding! Ding!* Looking up and down the aisle for a flight attendant, he feels his wet shirt clinging to his bare chest and wants to check his carryon suitcase for a clean one, but the seat belt sign has just come on because of turbulence in the area. He twists and turns impatiently to look once more for a flight attendant to retrieve his baggage from the overhead compartment.

Stuart chuckles and ignores Richard's headphones. "So how are Jennifer and the children? Is she still playing tennis?"

"That's it—you're out of here!" Richard explodes as he jumps up from his seat.

Eve walks up. "May I be of service, Senator?"

"I will never fly this airline again!" Richard states emphatically.

"Yes, sir." Eve smiles knowingly and nods. "How can I help you?"

Nicole waits in the galley, peering past the curtain for Eve to return. "Okay, Eve, what's the story. I can't wait another minute!"

Eve smiles in amusement. "You may find this hard to believe; but at one time, Richard Stevens and Stuart Patrick were best friends."

"Really?"

"Grew up in the same town and went to the same schools. They were close until the summer following their senior year of high school. After graduation, they both received an internship with Mitchell Morgan & Associates law firm, which were highly sought-after positions. During their first week of interning for Mr. Morgan, Richard and Stuart met the attorney's wife and children. Jennifer, Mr. Morgan's oldest daughter, blew the boys away. She was beautiful, athletic, smart, and funny—everything that Stuart and Richard had ever wanted in a girl."

Eve waves her hand, and the dessert cart disappears instantly. Nicole is impressed as Eve explains the story while organizing the galley for the next service.

"Richard was awestruck," continues Eve. "He had had many girlfriends in high school, but none of them could compare with Jennifer. The chemistry and attraction between them was instant. Richard found himself in a dilemma since Jennifer was the boss's daughter. The internship would lead to many exciting opportunities related to his education and career aspirations but starting a relationship with Jennifer would only distract him from achieving his long-term goals. Richard's stern father pushed him to remain focused on his work and his political aspirations not girls. So did Mr. Morgan."

"Seeing how that senator behaves, I'd certainly go for Stuart; he's so nice and polite," interjects Nicole, leaning against the galley counter.

"Nicole." Eve gives Nicole a stern look.

"Oops, sorry, Eve."

"Stuart's desire to be with Jennifer far outweighed any academic or career goals. Although Jennifer was equally attracted to both Richard and Stuart, she was swept away by Stuart's love and devotion when he gave up his job at her father's office to spend as much time as he could with her. While Richard continued to work at the law firm, Stuart fostered his liberal views as an assistant editor for the local newspaper. His creative writing skills and passion for life, revolution, and innovation drew Jennifer even closer to him. Stuart constantly left her love poems—in her shoes, in her car glove box, in her books—anywhere that would surprise and delight her. With Stuart, Jennifer felt passionately alive as if she was living out a life from a romance novel."

"So that's where their animosity for each other began," states Nicole confidently.

Instantly a tray of cocktails appears in front of Eve. "Not exactly. There's more, but I'll have to explain the rest later. Right now, I need to go back and check on Elizabeth Walters again. Last time she was dozing, still grasping a bottle of sleeping pills in her white-knuckled hand. However, this time—because her fear of flying is so overwhelming—Elizabeth is awake again. What I'm picking up from her is that she is contemplating whether or not to take more pills in order to sleep her way to New York City." Eve says encouragingly, "Maybe I can help calm her fears."

"I better stay away from her," Nicole remarks weakly.

Eve smiles confidently as she hands the tray of drinks to Nicole. "Take these over to the Westmans. They'll be asking for them in a minute."

Chapter 26

"Are you just going to sit there the entire flight with your head in those damn magazines, Lawrence?" Nancy is perturbed and losing patience with her husband's relentless reading. "Don't forget, you're supposed to be on vacation—with your wife."

Lawrence barely hears her, as he is completely absorbed in a magazine that Nicole gave him about ayurvedic medicine. Mournfully he says, "I now realize that all these years as a medical doctor that I haven't healed anyone."

"What are you talking about, Lawrence?" his wife protests.

"I just know how to prescribe some kind of medication, guessing half the time, to mask the symptoms, not really healing the problem or even understanding why the problem arose in the first place. These doctors from India really have some fascinating techniques. You should read about these doctors who take what is called a pulse reading to diagnose any health issues or problems that a patient may have. By learning this technique—which has been used for thousands of years—these doctors can see over fifty patients a day and really heal people by improving their diet and lifestyle all by natural herbal remedies. Not just sending them to specialist after specialist trying to figure out—"

"You heal people all the time," interrupts Nancy, trying to engage herself with him in conversation. In an attempt to be the wife he said she wasn't, Nancy tries to lovingly refute his low self-assessment. "Look at all the people you helped this winter with all those flu shots you and your staff administered. I call that healing; they didn't need a specialist for that, Lawrence. They just needed you."

"Oh, Nancy. How many times have I told you that whole flu vaccine thing is just a scam? It may seem to the unsuspecting public that those flu shots really help; but with every injection into every man, woman and child, I know I'm putting more poison in their bodies and making their immune systems worse. For years, evidence is mounting linking flu vaccines to serious neurological side effects."

"What are you going on about, Lawrence? What do you mean poison?"

"I know you don't realize what's in those vaccines; but let me tell you, it isn't good, Nancy. Things like aluminum, which has recently been linked to Alzheimer's and fatigue and mental problems. There are phenol, ethylene glycol—a solution like antifreeze—benzethonium, and methylparaben just to name a few."

"I had no idea," she replies, halfheartedly taking an interest in what her husband is now explaining.

"This whole flu vaccination scheme is absurd. Year after year, the CDC and vaccine manufacturers try to guess what virus may come from foreign lands like China a year or two years in advance. They act as though they have some magical crystal ball. Well, I say that ball is cracked."

"Well, I say that someone else has cracked!" Nancy mumbles sarcastically under her breath. While the disparaging remark is directed to her husband, she casually directs her attention to the handsome corporate businessman seated across the aisle.

"And, if that isn't bad enough, as a disinfectant and preservative, they use thimerosal, a mercury-based substance. Mercury is the second most toxic substance on the planet. There's more, but I won't bore you with the details. Former Sen. Dan Burton, a Republican from Indiana, spearheaded a campaign to get mercury out of vaccinations after his granddaughter became autistic after receiving her MMR vaccinations when she was two years old." Lawrence shakes his head in solemn reflection, remembering all the inoculations that he himself had routinely performed over the years. "She was perfectly normal up until that time."

"That's just horrible. I'll be sure that Lindsey and Lacy know about this before they have children—our grandchildren. I just can't imagine how I would deal with having an autistic grandchild, Lawrence. What would people think?" Nancy peruses through her home décor magazines. "Poor Senator and Mrs. Burton."

"Well, I'm going to make some changes. I can no longer participate in a system that pedals poisons as medicine to innocent patients, all in the name of money. My new model of medicine is going to treat the patient's mind, emotions, soul, and their body. Looking back now, Nancy, I realize that I went into the healing field ostensibly to help people. But somewhere along the way while going through medical school, I forgot that people aren't just their bodies."

"Hmm, okay, now what do you think about this one, honey?" Nancy asks, leaning over the armrest to show him another house plan.

"Did you ever find that pen in your purse, Nancy?"

"Why?" she asks, noticing Nicole in the aisle with a bottle of wine.

Nicole smiles when she notices the Westmans talking quietly and respectfully to each other. She happens to overhear Lawrence saying, "If I can just figure out who the publisher is of these magazines, I'm going to order a subscription immediately." Nicole winces in disbelief as the doctor remains completely enamored with his new magazines. While writing some notes to himself, Lawrence mumbles aloud, "I'm going to thoroughly research this subject as soon as I can."

"How about a little research on this floor plan, darling?" Leaning even closer, Nancy intentionally pushes her magazine over his.

"Sure, Nance," Lawrence responds absentmindedly. "Just let me write down some of these web addresses."

Putting his magazine back over hers, he scans over another page. "Now this is interesting. Ayurvedic medicine deals with the balancing of five elements within the body: space, air, fire, water, and earth."

"Well, doesn't that just explain it all?" Nancy replies with her continuing sarcasm, now completely exasperated with her husband. "I must be lacking in the area of fire, because right now I would kill for a goddamn cigarette." Lawrence remains oblivious to her outburst. Nancy gulps the remainder of her martini, then brusquely grabs Nicole's hand. In defiance and total disregard of her husband, Nancy orders another drink before he can say anything.

Nancy and Lawrence are suddenly jolted back to the reality of their surroundings when they hear someone on the opposite side of the plane slamming luggage around in the overhead compartment. Nicole looks over to the other aisle as she walks away. She shakes her head, and rolls her eyes condescendingly as she sees the senator standing next to his seat at 4E. Richard continues to deliberately disturb everyone, especially Stuart, as he retrieves his baggage. The senator knows that such behavior on an airplane isn't just discourteous; it's downright disrespectful, especially in first class. With everyone's nerves fearfully on edge, loud, unexpected sounds are the last thing airborne passengers want to hear in flight. Yet in his anger and contentiousness toward Stuart, the flight attendants, and the airline for placing him there, Richard doesn't give a damn. In his continued disrespect, he triumphantly pulls a clean white shirt and a pair of slacks from his suitcase.

"How's Jennifer you ask?" he exclaims loudly, awakening Stuart who was trying to take a nap. "She's the best!" Richard throws him another superior smirk. "It's great having a wife who loves you. You should try it sometime, Stuart."

Stuart ignores Richard's not-so-subtle jab. The life-long bachelor begins to sift absentmindedly through a newspaper, pretending Richard's comment meant nothing. Yet the ever-present pain and heartache still linger as Richard's words weigh heavily on his mind. Startled from his thoughts, Stuart turns around when he hears a smoke detector blaring in first class.

Chapter 27

BEEP, BEEP, BEEP!   BEEP, BEEP, BEEP! The smoke alarm has activated the cabin warning system. Deafening chimes sound throughout the aircraft. Immediately, two of the male flight attendants, Itqal and Achaiah, run into the aisle equipped with fire extinguishers and portable breathing devices. They pound on the first class lavatory door to see who is inside. The indicator sign shows "OCCUPIED" yet there is no response. Some of the passengers start to panic when they smell smoke.

Eve asks everyone to remain calm until she and her crew can determine the cause. Several passengers begin dialing their loved ones from the aircraft phone service to give a detailed accounting of what is going on. Several large men in the cabin huddle in the aisle, planning their strategy to overpower the potential hijacker that is hold up in the lavatory. Like those passengers on United Airlines flight 93 on September 11, these men are ready to heroically give their lives to help save the flight and its passengers before anything else can happen. Together they scan the cabins looking for the missing passenger who may be the mercenary of death and destruction at 41,000 feet. They wonder who is locked inside mixing explosive gels and liquids in an attempt to blow up their flight.

Several other passengers point at a group of men seated nearby. They report to Eve about their suspicious behavior, their Middle Eastern looks, and foreign dialect—furthering the racial tensions strained by recent terrorist attacks throughout the world. Itqal and Achaiah try desperately to calm the passengers who are falsely accusing the others of racial profiling, but no one listens. Fear and anger spread like wildfire, blazing out of control in all directions, as passengers begin to push and shove and call each other offensive racist names. Each agonizing minute of uncertainty that passes, each moment of waiting and wondering who is in the lavatory, only fans the flames of hatred, fueling the rage, the violence, and the terrorism that is burning out of control in the world.

Unable to gain control of the rising tension in the cabin, Eve decides to ignore the passengers and focus her full attention on the potential fire hazard. Out of the corner of her eye, she sees Senator Stevens grab his briefcase and spinelessly hide in the other lavatory across the aisle. She shakes her head and then instructs Itqal and Achaiah to unlock the lavatory door while smoke continues to furl over the top into the cabin air. The lavatory smoke detector blares incessantly.

With hearts pounding harder, everyone cranes their necks to see which passenger, which potential terrorist, is in the lavatory. They want to know what clandestine plan has been directed toward their flight putting their lives, their very safety, at risk. They want to know what merciless act of terrorism is being perpetuated against them on their way to New York City. The gut-wrenching anticipation of what is to come is so overwhelming for some that they slink down in their seats and close their eyes tightly.

Passengers sitting nearest to the lavatory are the first to be distressed and stunned when they catch a glimpse of their first class flight attendant trainee, Nicole, sitting on the toilet lid—holding a flammable liquid in one hand and a source of ignition in the other. A cloud of grayish white smoke from the lavatory curls upward in thin wisps toward the ceiling while the smoke detector continues to blare loudly. Nicole sees all the bewildered faces staring at her as she's casually holding a martini glass while at the same time is attempting to light her second cigarette. Immediately she tosses the drink into the sink followed by the lighted cigarette, igniting a small fire in the basin. The intoxicated trainee tries desperately to put out the flames with a handful of paper towels, fueling the fire even further. Itqal and Achaiah stand at the lavatory entrance totally perplexed while Eve is quick to grab the H_2O fire extinguisher.

Achaiah whispers to his colleague, the Angel of Affection, "This is truly a first in the history of this airline. Itqal, we're witnessing an angel, one of our own—an angel trainee on her very first observation flight on her very first angelic assignment—smoking and drinking in the first class lavatory. Who would have ever guessed?"

"Yes, and has started a fire while we are in flight," adds Itqal, shaking his head as Eve quickly extinguishes the fire.

Nicole is startled when the overspray from the extinguisher hits her face and hair as she negotiates her way out of the lavatory. Reeking of smoke and alcohol, Nicole hurriedly squeezes past Itqal and Achaiah as she wipes her face. "I was, uh, testing the smoke detectors," she mumbles feebly, heading toward the galley with her head hanging down. Nicole feels the intensity of Eve's glare as her words belie her actions.

Noting the martini glass and the cigarette package, Lawrence looks gravely over to his wife and says, "Are you thinking what I'm thinking?" Nancy solemnly shakes her head in agreement.

The pot-bellied seventy-year-old oil millionaire, Tex Shepherd, who manhandled Nicole during boarding, lets out a Texas-sized laugh as she walks by. He takes off his light gray Diamante Stetson cowboy hat, places it on his chest and bows in respect. "Now that's my kinda girl!"

Chapter 28

Hiding in shame inside the first class galley, Nicole feels as though she is going to implode and explode at the same time. The incident with Dr. Westman and his wife is just one in a long series of intensely negative events that has played out before her. She sits in the jumpseat, her arms wrapped tightly around her body when Eve walks in.

Nicole begins her tirade, losing control quickly. "These people are insane, and they're driving me insane! Is Earth some kind of insane asylum for this galaxy? Talk about dimensional drama, I was feeling the feelings of both Dr. and Mrs. Westman—simultaneously. We are talking about some serious anger mixed together with lots of stress, insecurity, depression, and humiliation. That woman's addictions are so powerful that I had to lock myself in the lavatory. I mean, I was smoking, Eve! And drinking! What kind of an angel does that?"

"A fallen one," utters Eve matter-of-factly to herself as Nicole continues.

"That flight attendant application said nothing about verbal abuse, picking up filthy meal trays, sexual harassment, collecting trash, working long hours, and wearing high-heeled shoes!" exclaims Nicole. "I can not handle this lowly dimension any more, Eve. I quit!" Nicole throws her serving apron on the counter and her hands up in exasperation.

"Nicole, you need to take a break. Follow me," Eve says knowingly, while a tone of reluctance hangs in her voice.

Quickly and quietly, Nicole follows Eve to the flight deck. Nicole hangs her head as Eve opens the cockpit door. "I'm so ashamed at my inability to control these tumultuous emotions I'm feeling. Archangels Michael and

Gabriel are going to think I'm the worst angel flight attendant trainee ever," murmurs Nicole as she walks into the cockpit. "Who in this world is flying the plane? All the dials, instruments, gauges, flight panels, and even the pilot seats are gone!" shouts Nicole in disbelief.

"Shh." Eve tries to calm Nicole.

"Never have I seen anything so vibrant, so beautiful!" exclaims Nicole, watching curiously as Eve walks behind her. Nicole's attention returns to the two brilliant white lights glowing brightly inside the cockpit—pure in essence, form, and radiance. Nicole looks out the cockpit window only to see a silent shroud of white clouds.

Eve reverently whispers from behind Nicole's back, "Our pilots don't need dials and instruments. Michael and Gabriel are able to pilot this seven-hundred-thousand-pound machine flying over six hundred miles per hour at forty-one thousand feet above the Earth with nine angels and four hundred passengers on board all by the sheer power of love."

The glowing light on the left, which is Michael, circles around Nicole. Slowly she lifts off the floor as his light envelops her body. Eve observes Michael's energy field surging and pulsing as he intensifies his healing around Nicole.

"Eve!" begs Nicole.

"Everything is fine, Nicole," Michael conveys telepathically.

"Eve, I'll take care of her from here," instructs Michael, his voice peaceful and harmonic. She reluctantly leaves the cockpit, closing, and locking the cockpit door behind her.

Michael and Gabriel place their celestial hands upon Nicole. Her uniform immediately drops to the floor as her true angelic nature emerges as infinite waves of their love penetrate her energetically throughout every part of her being.

Their mental summons reaches the young angel. "Relax, Nicole. Allow the brilliant pulsating light to penetrate your being. Allow it to flow inside—to clear, to cleanse, and to rebalance your very essence." Michael and Gabriel wordlessly convey, "We are stabilizing the more serious internal breakdowns in your angelic energy fields."

With outstretched arms, Nicole glows brighter and brighter as she basks in their brilliant iridescent healing light. The energy swirls and sparkles around and through her as the two archangels coalesce into one essence of the most unfathomable love. "Oh, God, thank you, thank you, thank you," cries Nicole in the ecstasy of the most indescribable energy ever created. And there she remains suspended in mid-air for seemingly an eternity.

The gentle muted rhythm of healing continues. "The light is flowing through your entire being, Nicole, restoring your celestial energy. The anger, frustration, disappointment, impatience, and disrespect—among the many other human characteristics you have absorbed—are being replaced one by one with unconditional love, patience, and strength and also a wonderful sense of humor," communicate Michael and Gabriel with a smile of satisfaction.

"Oh, thank you," says Nicole joyfully as she shines in a glorious effulgence of purity, perfection, and beauty.

"Nicole," asks Gabriel lightly, "do you know how to transition into the slower denser vibration—"

Gabriel's question is interrupted when Nicole's feet abruptly land on the cockpit floor. Her glow diminishes rapidly when she quickly retorts, "Look, I demonstrated my abilities at that interview, and quite successfully, I might add!" Nicole's hand instantly flies up to cover her mouth, her eyes widen in disbelief. She waits for a minute, quickly trying to understand why she reacted that way. Her wide eyes dart back and forth nervously between Michael and Gabriel. "Oops! Sorry. Now, it looks like you have *an angel with an attitude* working for Infinity Airways."

Chapter 29

Nicole smiles from ear to ear feeling revived and refreshed as she steps from the cockpit into first class. Eve notices Nicole and walks up behind the reenergized angel as she looks into the cabin.

"What happened?" Nicole exclaims. Gasping in amazement, she is unsure of what exactly is before her.

"You're seeing the passengers for who they really are—beings of extraordinary lives and lessons."

"But their clothes, their faces and even their bodies are—"

"All from their past, present, and future lifetimes," explains Eve.

Nicole looks closely at the beautiful Indian saris, the exquisitely detailed Oriental gowns, and the vibrantly colored dashikis that several passengers are wearing. She observes several centurions in their tunics, armor, and helmets engaged in a zealous discussion, while just one row behind are two ancient Chinese armored warriors holding crossbows. Others passengers are wearing very plain and crude coverings—simple animal skins, rough rawhide sacks, and loincloths. Nicole stares at Dr. and Mrs. Westman. They are now interacting from a future lifetime as cloned bisexual brothers, both with hairless heads and faces. They communicate through their futuristic slick white spandex-type clothing with built-in computers and monitoring systems.

"Wow, they look so different," whispers Nicole as she slowly and carefully walks down the aisle, trying not to draw attention to herself by staring too long at all the passengers. She hears a great melody of foreign, exotic languages.

Suddenly, as if they are appearing out of thin air, Nicole is able to see the passengers' guardian angels traveling with them. She remembers Alexis telling her that each human being at conception is under the tutelage of a divinely chosen guardian angel. And that it is The Creator's Will that each of these angels is to be distinctly different from every other and to have complete knowledge of their charge, of their human, and their human's needs.

In awe and reverence, Nicole silently observes the numerous angels of guidance perched on the seatbacks of their traveling humans. They smile and wave enthusiastically as Nicole whispers back to Eve, "Where did they come from?"

"They've been traveling with us the whole time, ensuring that everyone is where they're supposed to be," explains Eve as they slowly walk down the aisle toward the coach cabin. The guardian angels nod, smile, and wave as Nicole passes each row.

"I knew the flight was full, but I had no idea it was this full! Everything is . . . is so perfect," whispers Nicole in a state of wonder and amazement.

"You are seeing our passengers the way we see them all the time. Presently you can see everything because you are operating in your higher frequency. Being with Michael . . . uh, I mean . . . uh, being with the pilots can do that," Eve stammers trying to correct herself. Nicole looks curiously back at Eve, aware of her omission of Gabriel's name.

Nicole returns her gaze toward the coach cabin and continues cautiously down the aisle by herself while Eve responds to Senator Stevens's call bell once again. Walking slowly and surely through the coach cabin, Nicole notices that even the fluffy white onboard cat is now flying in its past incarnation as a sleek and slender black Egyptian feline.

Abruptly Nicole's attention is drawn to a couple arguing. She watches as their hurtful words hit each other's auras—their surrounding energy fields—like tiny missiles that explode into gray areas. As more and more missiles of pain, anger, fear, and disappointment hit their target, their entire auras—what were previously vibrant blue and green—begin to turn gray and start to shrivel. The couple has no idea that the crew working their flight can observe them from a higher vantage point and a much deeper level. All that is inside them—their fear, their anxiety, their hatred, their glory, their depression—all those things are seen. The young trainee now understands that each flight attendant truly knows each passenger—knows their deepest fears, knows their highest hopes.

Nicole continues down the aisle in deep reflection about the human condition. *Strange how every thought humans have is a tangible energy, sacred, and significant. Thoughts—and every word used to express those thoughts—have a very real and powerful impact. I guess I should be careful how I use my thoughts and what I say as well.*

Walking past the lavatories, Nicole sees two high-ranking Roman soldiers from Caesar's army waiting in line to use the toilet. Dressed in their suits of armor, plumed helmets, holding their shields, and spears, they continue to discuss their plans of a hostile corporate takeover in New York while they wait. They casually glance at the woman wearing an Egyptian headdress over her elongated, angled skull when she opens the bi-fold door. Little do they realize that Nefertiti, wife of Akhenaton the pharaoh of Egypt, has just walked out of the coach lavatory.

Continuing down the aisle, Nicole smiles brightly as she observes hundreds and hundreds of guardian angels hovering around their human charges, surrounding them with unconditional love. As she passes by row after row, they smile, wave, and some even bow, graciously acknowledging her and her efforts to assist their humans. Without a sound, Nicole silently walks into the coach galley at the back of the airplane.

"Oh, Sarakiel, it's so beautiful," Nicole whispers loudly to one of the flight attendants working in the back.

Sarakiel smiles knowingly, her kind, warm expression embraces Nicole tenderly. "Earlier, because you were picking up on the passengers' emotions and lower energies, you were only able to see things as they see them. Once you learn how to keep your energies elevated, this is how you will see things all the time. It's heavenly, isn't it?"

"Yes, but what exactly is it that I am seeing?" Nicole is still transfixed on the passengers in the cabin. Sarakiel stands closely beside Nicole as they look up the aisle together.

"You are seeing just about every aspect of our passengers' souls—who they are, what they have been, and what they will be—simultaneously. You are also seeing all of their energy bodies as well—like their physical, etheric, emotional, mental, astral, and celestial bodies. Everything is energy, Nicole. Everything is consciousness. Now I am sure you must have noticed their guardian angels that are traveling with them as well. They are the ones that make sure that their people get on our flights."

"Oh, Sarakiel, if only the humans were able to see this, to feel this—to know that they are never alone—they would feel so much better," Nicole says, thinking of all the negative energy and emotion she has been experiencing throughout the flight. "Funny thing is then I would feel better too!"

Sarakiel nods in silent agreement. "As one of the seven holy angels set over the children of men whose spirits have sinned, I would have to say that would certainly make my assignment much easier. But I didn't sign up for easy, Nicole. I'm in for the long haul."

"But there are so many angels on Earth and more are on the way; don't you ever get a break?" asks Nicole naively.

"You're right, Nicole. Infinity has had angels working on this planet for a very long time," Sarakiel confirms. "Angels are working on airways, waterways, railways, tramways, highways, byways, alleyways, driveways, parkways, bikeways, trailways, passageways, pathways, doorways, hallways, stairways, sideways—pretty much every way!" She laughs joyfully. "We're everywhere, Nicole. And we are needed more now than ever."

Sarakiel takes Nicole's hand, gently leading her as they walk slowly together up the aisle. Nicole does a double take as she looks at the last row of passengers where the teenage boy and the two large men, who had boarded last, now sit together. Only moments before she had seen a beautiful woman and two adorable twin girls with corkscrew pig tails in the very same seats.

"Oh, Sarakiel, it's becoming harder for me to see them," Nicole cries quietly as she looks around the cabin. "I'm losing it! The passengers are taking on their previous outward appearances." Nicole runs back to the galley crying, bumping into several passengers, who have their feet and elbows in the aisle, along the way. Sarakiel quickly and quietly follows her.

"It's okay, my dear. You are just dropping back into the lower frequencies. It is strange how you seem to be very susceptible to the debilitating effects of the Third Dimension. But don't worry, Nicole. After your training you'll be able to see everything and everyone for what they truly are—uniquely individual expressions of The One Infinite Creator." Sarakiel gives her a warm smile and a hug.

A heavy disappointment weighs on Nicole as she stares back into the cabin, trying to see what she had seen before. "Why is this so hard for me? I doubt any other angel trainee experienced such difficulties when they first started flying for Infinity." She shakes her head sorrowfully. "I have to remember what I just experienced really does exist. I don't ever want to forget," pleads Nicole.

# Chapter 30

"I gotta take a leak, man," announces Tommy Wellington, the deeply suntanned, shabbily dressed teenager that was brought on the plane by two private detectives. Sitting on the back row of coach, Tommy stares at his escorts warily. "So who wants to watch me take a piss this time?" he asks, trying to elicit some kind of response. "Who's it gonna be? You, Ron, or Joe? Come on, man, I don't have all day."

"C'mon, kid." Ron, the forty-year-old Puerto Rican detective decides to take his turn watching Tommy. He clamps his hand on Tommy's shoulder and gives him a friendly smile. Joe sits in silence, smirking as he takes everything in that is going on around their seats, the lavatories, and the aisles to the galley behind their row.

"It's about time," Tommy replies sarcastically as he grabs his crotch. "You guys and your asinine procedures!" Tommy blurts out loud what has been racing through his mind since they went through airport security at LAX hours earlier. He shakes his head as he and Ron have about four feet to walk to the lavatories.

Elizabeth Walters drowsily stumbles out of the lavatory just as Ron and Tommy rise out of their seats. "Perfect timing," chuckles Ron. "Come on, Tommy, after all those years at the NYPD, I think I'm qualified to handle a little matter like bathroom patrol."

The five-foot-ten-inch-tall detective waits outside the lavatory door, just like the agency procedures require, while Tommy uses the lavatory. After the teenage runaway exits the lav, they both stretch and yawn for a moment before settling back into their seats. Joe, a short, heavy-set Italian from New York and Ron's partner for the last five years, starts a conversation to help pass the time.

"So what makes a young kid like you run away from home?" Joe asks in a heavy Brooklyn accent as he takes in the tattoos on the young man's forearms. "Seems to me you had everything, kid. What was so tough about your life?"

A twinge of uneasiness tries to take hold, but Tommy shoves it back into hiding as he shrugs his shoulders, not wanting to talk about his upbringing. It has been his area of expertise for years, avoiding intimate conversations, deflecting inquiring questions, and evading the authorities. "I'm not looking for any sympathy, fellas. I just needed to get away and to see if anyone would notice." Wanting to turn the topic of conversation off himself, he turns quickly to Joe and asks sarcastically, "What about you? Did you have a perfect childhood? You know, Mom and Dad and apple pie?"

"Mom, Dad, and apple pie?" Joe chuckles. "Not exactly. I grew up the middle child of seven kids—the oldest of the boys. My whole family worked, not just my mom and dad. We had to in order to make it, you know? Seven kids is a lot of mouths to feed, if you know what I mean? My parents are good people from the old country in Italy. Growin' up they always saw to it that we were never hungry or cold. They did the best with what they had," he pauses, thinking back to his early years, "my parents have been married for forty-seven years now. Not exactly *Ozzie and Harriet*, but it wasn't so bad. You know what I mean, kid?" Joe turns to his partner and snickers. "Uhh, what about you, Ron? You have *Ozzie and Harriet* in your house as a kid?"

"Yeah, right. Just like on TV, man!" Ron lays down his magazine on the tray table as he laughs. "It was more like *Divorce Court* in my house. My ol' man was always messin' around on my mom. She caught him a few times with the Argentinean lady down the hall. Every time she caught him, she would give him a real swift kick in the pants and then things would be back to normal—whatever that was." Ron rolls his eyes disapprovingly. "He was never really home, my dad. Always stayed out late drinking with his buddies. We knew when he was home though, because either he would be throwing stuff in the kitchen or Ma would be cussing him out for wasting his paycheck on drinking and gambling. It's amazing that they stayed together, both without killing the other too!" He laughs and shakes his head. "Ma could have kicked his ass if she wanted to. No kidding. Is that how Harriet was? I can't remember . . . been a long time since I saw that show."

Tommy, Ron, and Joe all laugh. "It'll be nice to get home," Joe reflects with a loud sigh. "Tomorrow is my youngest's birthday. She'll be three." He tries to think of what he can afford to buy her as he pulls his worn black leather wallet from his back pocket to show Ron and Tommy a picture. "Here she is trying to draw with the box of crayons I bought for her birthday last year. You should see the picture she tried to draw of me; it was hilarious! The nose takes up most of my face."

"She's beautiful," says Tommy handing the photograph over to Ron. "She's very lucky to have a dad care so much about her that he carries her picture around in his wallet," he adds in a melancholy voice.

"Here, here, let me show you my gang." Not wanting to be outdone, Ron retrieves his old, worn leather wallet. "Here's Maria, the oldest; then Matt, he's eight; then Sam, he's the trouble maker; and Anna, the baby. And this is Annemarie, my wife." He beams proudly at the pictures.

"Tommy," says Joe.

"Yeah, man."

"We shared about our families, what about yours?"

"Yeah, Tommy, it's only fair, man," Ron agrees. "Give us the story about your family. We've heard it all, kid. I can't imagine that your story would be so different." Joe leans his elbow on the tray table and nods in agreement.

"You wouldn't really understand my family," Tommy says, holding his temper and his words, withdrawing from the conversation. "Hell, I don't even understand them."

 # *Chapter 31*

Nicole sits quietly on the jumpseat in the coach galley while Dina and Sarakiel set up for the next beverage service. With the help of Rochel and Tezalel, the four small beverage carts are being prepared with everything that their 350 passengers will want.

"So how is our friend, Tommy Wellington, doing, Sarakiel?" asks Tezalel nonchalantly, his voice calm and peaceful.

"Everything is playing out beautifully, with the help of his guardian angel, of course," replies Sarakiel with a proud smile.

"Which one is Tommy?" interjects Nicole inquisitively.

"Are you feeling better now, Nicole?" asks Sarakiel with a questioning glance.

"My angelic vibrations are spiraling downward, sinking lower, and slower. I can't seem to control it; it's so frustrating! It seems I'm becoming more and more human every moment no matter who tries to help me." She hangs her head in disappointment.

"Everything works for a reason, Nicole, even for angels," says Tezalel encouragingly.

"That's what everyone keeps telling me. Knowing that doesn't seem to make me feel any better though," Nicole replies as she looks into the coach cabin again. "So who is Tommy?"

"He's the teenager on the last row, the one in custody. Sarakiel and I are assigned to him," explains Tezalel enthusiastically. "It's great that Tommy signed up for such a glorious lesson for this lifetime," he responds proudly. "Guess he understood that this would be the last lifetime for him in this dimension on this planet, so he made it a spectacular one—living a life surviving on the streets as a male prostitute, addicted to crack-cocaine. That young man, who is a very wise old soul, has been living a self-imposed exile for the past two years, wanting nothing to do with his parents or their money."

"Yes, that's right," Sarakiel adds proudly. "In refusing both, he found his way to Los Angeles, venturing as far away from home as he figured he could get at age fourteen. Tommy tried to put a lifetime of space between himself and everyone and everything he had ever known. Living in a violent combat zone of gang warfare, street racing, drive-by shootings, and prostitution, Tommy survived by shoplifting, petty theft, buying and selling drugs, selling himself, and whatever else presented itself. Using various aliases, Thomas Wellington, Jr. remained hidden behind the dark veil of a horrifying nightlife on the streets, living a hellish nightmare in the back alleys."

"And his guardian angel has been with him every step of the way," says Tezalel as he parks one of the beverage carts.

"Amazing," Nicole replies quizzically, her brows raised.

Tezalel continues with Tommy's story. "He chose his life. With the assistance of the Guardian Overlords for this planet, Tommy decided that in every possible situation he would have to pick the most dangerous and most outrageous of choices in order to advance his soul's progress. Soul growth accelerates more rapidly while in the Third Dimension than in between incarnations. To most human beings, it would look as though he was committing a very, very slow and deliberate suicide. In this earthly reality, most normal boys his age would have picked the opposite life than his. Although Tommy is not consciously aware of it, it is his empowered desire to accelerate his soul's growth that has determined his choices, nothing else."

"There is so much to know behind every one of these passengers. So I guess he's decided to go home now. Is that why he's on this flight?" asks Nicole, leaning against the galley counter, watching the other flight attendants stock their carts with supplies that appear out of thin air.

"Yes, today will be his homecoming," adds Sarakiel. "He is scheduled to meet with his parents after being on the run for over two years. His mother is Lauren Wellington, the world-renowned, high-end fashion designer. Her labels are on every item imaginable: bedding, cologne, clothes, purses, shoes, and even stationary. If you look around, you'll see that several of our passengers are wearing her line of sophisticated clothing and accessories. On the other hand, Tommy's father, Thomas Allen Wellington, Sr., is a famous and accomplished author. His brilliant knack for law and intrigue has produced numerous *New York Times* best sellers. Again, if you look around, you'll see several of our passengers reading his novels on this flight."

"Sounds like a good life to me," reflects Nicole.

"Yes, however, Thomas and Lauren Wellington live very different lives," says Tezalel. "Lauren is constantly caught up in a hectic whirlwind of fashion shows, models, consulting, designing, and travel. She wants to ensure that everything that bears her name is sophisticated, stylish, and perfect—including her son. Thomas's life consists of solitude and study. He spends days and days in his lavish mahogany study, researching, and writing. When he's not writing intensively, he retreats into his private home theater and turns on the television or watches movies, allowing his mind to go numb to everything and everyone else—including his son. So you can see, Tommy wasn't the focus of their lives—just a mere by-product."

"Feeling alone in the world doesn't feel very good—for anyone," Nicole adds empathetically. She tries to put herself in the teenager's position, to understand what must be going on inside him. Similar to her own brief experience of life, she understands the loneliness and isolation that was forced on Tommy by his circumstances. Yet she knows, as an angel, she would never truly understand or even begin to fathom what he, as a human being, has been through in this lifetime or any other.

"Now, years later because of all the chaotic events around the world, Tommy's parents have decided to find their son and bring him home," Sarakiel continues. "Tommy was aware that these detectives were on his trail, well before they apprehended him. At first, he had fun playing cat and mouse with them, but more and more he was feeling that it was time to go home. This morning, Ron and Joe were sitting in their rental car staring out the front window at a small park in LA that Tommy frequented for drug deals. To their surprise, the young man approached the car from behind, got into the back seat, and said 'Okay, let's go home.' And here they are, flying to New York City with us. Now we're taking Tommy home. The reunion with his parents will help lighten the vibrational load on the Earth, making the shift into the Fourth Dimension a lot easier for all."

Nicole looks around the galley wall to see which passenger they are referring to. Ducking quickly back into the galley she says, "Oh, him. Okay, I'm a little confused; you're talking about a teenage boy. Right? Yet earlier I saw him as a young woman and those two men were twin girls sitting on either side of him. What was that all about?"

Sarakiel smiles compassionately at the bewildered trainee. "You were seeing them as they were in a lifetime together during the seventeenth century. Tommy was and is Antoinette Bourignon, the supervisor of an orphanage in Belgium. Back then Ron and Joe were and, on the astral plane, still are twin sisters having been left by their parents at a very young age. Tommy was their teacher and caretaker. Currently the roles are reversed, for in that lifetime it was Tommy, then as Antoinette, who sought to find the family of the two young sisters to reunite them with their parents."

The other flight attendants join the conversation. "All time is now, Nicole. Outside of this third-dimensional experience on Earth is true timelessness. There is no past, present, or future. It's all happening in the now," adds Dina as he checks his beverage cart supplies. "It can seem confusing from the human perspective in the lower vibrations, Nicole, which you seem to be experiencing more and more. This forgetting that you are experiencing is similar to the condition that any soul who incarnates into a third-dimensional environment agrees to. It's called the Veil of Forgetting."

"Just like Tommy," Tezalel elucidates further, "everyone on the flight has done it hundreds, thousands, if not millions, of times—slip into a new body, live out a life full of experiences on the physical plane, and return home on the soul plane to digest those experiences."

"Why go to all this trouble?" begs Nicole. "Why don't they just play out their lives on the soul plane?"

"Because they would know two things, my dear." Sarakiel tenderly puts her arm around Nicole's shoulder. "First, they would know that they are just playing a game, and secondly, the goal of the game is to express unconditional love in every situation. Knowing all this, where's the challenge? Where's the growth? Just like an actor who *dies* in Act III of some stage play, they would get up, wash off the fake blood, and go home having learned nothing."

Rochel smiles warmly. "In your training, Nicole, you will learn that the Third Dimension and its Veil of Forgetting is a brilliant orchestration of creation. Incarnation is a tool to expand the soul's capabilities and potentials and to actualize their own identity. Here, one can learn everything about oneself, and one can only do that when one doesn't know that they are part of The Creator. It's easy to be loving in a loving environment. So like Tommy, to test one's understanding of love, one has to go where love is in short supply."

"These brave souls," Sarakiel waves her arm toward the passengers, "leave the warm, loving environment of the soul plane and undertake what many agree is the most arduous venture that any soul can tackle—a life here on planet Earth, acknowledged as the densest environment for learning and growth anywhere in this galaxy. With advice and counsel, each soul selects a plan with numerous lessons. Then the soul, with its ego, plays out everything beautifully over a lifetime—with no memory that there is a plan. And these souls do play it out down here ever so seriously. All souls have the potential for greatness and a life of joy and happiness, but how many really strive for that?"

Nicole shrugs her shoulders. "Not too many from what little I have seen. However, I do understand about the forgetting. Even now, everything I saw a few minutes ago in the cabin seems to be becoming more and more like a faint memory. It's all so confusing." She looks to Sarakiel for reassurance. "So you're saying that Tommy is a teenage boy who is also that young woman, Antoinette, at the same time?" smirks Nicole as she raises her eyebrows.

Sarakiel, Tezalel, Rochel, and Dina laugh with Nicole in her confusion. With everyone ready for the next beverage service in coach, Nicole reflectively returns to first class.

Chapter 32

"So what legislative sludge are you whipping up today, Senator?" Stuart, well versed in political debate, inquires tauntingly. "Some new law to take away more of our *potentially explosive* water bottles, liquids and gels, more of our *dangerous* toothpastes and baby formulas, more of our freedom and our rights—for our own good, of course, or that of the country or the economy or some other made-up excuse. Or are you just perpetuating more fear to gain even more power over the people?" he jeers.

"There should be a law that prevents someone like you from sitting next to someone like me," Richard replies matter-of-factly. "I'll make a note to draft that one right away."

"Seriously, Richard. Do you and all your crooked cronies really think that all this government control creates any kind of social harmony or happiness among the citizens of this country? Or do you even care? Seems like all you're interested in is business as usual with short-term profits over long-term consequences. It's obvious that you and your political buddies are focused on wars that destroy innocent people. I'm on to you, Richard. Not everyone has their head in the sand," Stuart pushes on before Richard can respond. His voice contains an unmistakable frustration, reflecting his growing irritation with the nation's political leadership. "It doesn't take a rocket scientist to figure out the hidden agendas of this administration and others abroad. Just look at their problem-reaction-solution policies. Do *they* create a problem so that *we* react and ask for an answer, then *they* offer their solution? When, in fact, it was the solution that *they* really wanted all along? Senator Stevens, this country is being led down a path of blind obedience, relinquished freedoms, inner deadness, addictive behaviors, chronic stress, and unadulterated economic and environmental exploitation. Is this truly the kind of world, my friend, you want to leave for our nation's children?"

Richard drops his pen. "Don't even go there, Stuart! Do you hear me, you son of a bitch? How dare you even speak to me about knowing what's best for the children. I'm doing a better job than you ever could." Richard heaves a stack of proposals from his briefcase, slamming them violently down onto his tray table. "I suggest you shut your damn liberal mouth right now and contemplate whether or not you'd like your jaw to remain in working order."

"Why is it that when someone challenges you on certain issues you can't discuss things calmly?" Stuart probes further. "Why does it become so personal for you? How in the world can we expect entire nations to get along, Richard, when you and I can't?"

Richard grabs Nicole's hand to order another drink as she walks by with a loaded tray of dirty cocktail glasses. His gaze is so intense that it causes a slight tremor to vibrate through her body. She struggles to avoid dropping the entire tray as he continues to hold her arm with his loathsome energy pulsing through her. Nicole stares back in equally loathsome disbelief when he places his empty glass on the full tray. The glasses clank and crash against each other as they start to slide to the edge. Quickly Nicole pulls away from his grip.

Eve watches the young trainee in the aisle as she carefully carries the overloaded tray of dirty glasses into the galley. "Haven't these people had enough?!" demands Nicole in her exasperation.

"Looks like you're back in your lower vibration again," comments Eve matter-of-factly. "Let's try something different. This may help you understand a little more about why your job at Infinity Airways is so important. And so things can go smoothly when we get to New York in a few hours." Eve quickly closes the galley curtains as an immense ancient book that looks as old as time itself materializes on the galley counter. On the front cover below the Infinity Airways logo is inscribed, *The Book of Flight.*

"I've seen these books in the Hall of Records. They're very sacred," Nicole declares confidently.

Eve nods as she slides the large book in front of Nicole. "Normally you would learn about its use in the third week of your training classes, but I think it will be good for you to have some hands-on practice." Eve slides the heavy book in front of Nicole. "Whenever a passenger makes a reservation, a record, referred to as a passenger name record or PNR for short, is made in our central computer system. All airlines use this terminology; however, at Infinity, the records are somewhat different." Eve turns some of the pages to show Nicole its contents.

"*The Book of Flight* contains the records of each passenger on board this plane. It tells us everywhere they have ever been, everything they have ever done, everything they have ever felt, everything they have ever said, or thought—not only in this lifetime but their past lives and their future lives as well. *The Book of Flight* is a very small portion of *The Book of Life*, which is like a mainframe computer housing information on everyone for the entire cosmos. Obviously, we don't need all that up here, so we are given *The Book of Flight*, containing information only on those people that are traveling with us today.

"Let me show you," Eve continues in her proper, schoolteacher manner. Sila comes into the gallery to fix several more beverage requests as Eve explains further, "For example, when a passenger is behaving in a particularly strange or baffling manner, we can look them up in *The Book of Flight* and learn what is happening to them past, present, and future. Any questions so far?"

Nicole is completely mesmerized and doesn't respond.

"*The Book of Flight* is here to assist us with the journeys of our passengers," Eve continues. "During the preflight briefing, each flight attendant is assigned a group of passengers. Prior to boarding, they can look up their passengers in *The Book of Flight*. However, the more experienced flight attendants, like the ones I have working with me, will know everything about their passengers just by looking at them."

"May I look in the PNRs?" asks Nicole inquisitively. She slowly flips through the beautiful pages.

"As you can see the pages are vibrationally alive, pulsing with conscious energy," explains Eve. "Whose record would you like to look at?"

"Senator Stevens. I bet his PNR is very, very interesting," Nicole comments sarcastically. "Oops—sorry!"

"Remember, Nicole, these records are not for judgment. Now concentrate all of your thoughts on love toward Richard Stevens," Eve explains. Nicole closes her eyes and extends her hands. A hologram reflecting Richard's life appears from the page. Scenes begin to materialize, playing out his life as if it were a movie in fast forward.

"I have it, Eve!" Nicole replies excitedly.

"In his last lifetime, during the mid-nineteenth century, Richard was an intellectual and financial genius. Stuart, then his older brother, was a very successful businessman, designing and manufacturing scientific lab equipment. However, by age twenty-eight, Richard had already achieved great financial success. Due to his wealth and his own interest in the sciences, Richard became a principal investor in the college of sciences that their father founded," explains Eve as the hologram reveals Richard's past life with Stuart.

"Both brothers shared their father's dream of creating an academy for scientific research and education, bringing together the greatest minds in the world. Stuart's extensive business background and knowledge of scientific tools and their use made him an extremely valuable advisor to this very unique academic community."

Nicole leans in closer, totally mesmerized by the hologram. Almost childlike, she puts her finger into the display to see what will happen. While Eve isn't looking, she pokes Richard's holographic image in the stomach. Nicole is oblivious of the fact that beyond the galley curtain, the senator is now double over holding his abdomen from a sudden and mysterious pain.

Eve continues to explain. "There was constant friction between the two, because Stuart felt that his brother, Richard, had too much control in the direction of the institution. Their joint interest in their father's work could have brought them closer together in that incarnation, but it didn't. Stuart truly believed that he had more wisdom and experience than his younger brother, even though Richard did have more money. Their father in that lifetime is now Richard's wife, Jennifer, in this lifetime."

"Wow," exclaims Nicole.

"Richard can't help but feel that Stuart is still criticizing and second-guessing his every move; it's a carryover from their past life. Conversely, Stuart has not been able to overcome the feeling that Richard doesn't really like him."

"Of course, Infinity brought them together to work out their karma. That's why Mr. Patrick got the last-minute upgrade!" Nicole is thrilled about her new understanding of the men sitting at 4E and 4F.

The hologram swirls backward to reveal another lifetime. "Their issue began when Stuart was Richard's mother in Atlantis. In that lifetime, Richard was involved with manipulating and misusing energy derived from power crystals. Stuart warned Richard of the destruction that would result, but he refused to listen. So the power to advance their souls' work once again lies in their own hands. It's simply a matter of their Free Will. If not in this lifetime, then perhaps in the next on another planet. All this is important for you to know, Nicole, because you will be working with them in New York."

"Why can't they get it together, Eve? Especially before 2012 and the Ascension," Nicole asks innocently.

"Growth of the soul does not depend on what someone knows; it depends on what they do with that knowledge," Eve reveals. "Contrary to what many humans believe about the reincarnational process, they are not on some endless treadmill or karmic wheel, returning to life to make amends for the previous life. They return to evolve beyond the cycle of lessons of the physical dimension, to move forward into the higher nonphysical dimensions. Since life is a progression, the wisdom gained from previous lifetimes is carried into the next. Although their future incarnations also carry back into the next as well."

"It's not so easy being human," Nicole says reflectively. "I'm beginning to understand the ramifications of every situation, of every relationship that is occurring on our flight. It's amazing . . . it's truly amazing."

"Any questions?" asks Eve.

"Just one," Nicole is quick to ask. "Are we able to see the past, present, and the future of the relationships that they have had or will have with the people traveling near them? You know, the ones that are to help them with their heavy baggage?" asks Nicole naively. She becomes flustered with her ability to express herself in the human language. "You know what I mean, Eve. The other passengers that are supposed to help them with their life's lessons, their seatmates? Is all that in *The Book of Flight* as well?"

Sila, who always works in first class, smiles at Nicole before leaving the galley with a tray of cocktails. As the Angel of Power, Sila inherently has the ability to handle anyone of any material, social, or political status on Earth. Sila gives Eve a quick wink as she holds the galley curtain back for her.

"Why, yes, Nicole. Good question. I'm impressed with your understanding of the PNRs," encourages Eve, as she closes the curtain by willing it closed. "Everything about our passengers is contained in the records. That is why they are sacred and to be used only for the highest good."

"Yes, Eve, I understand," Nicole responds confidently.

"Once you are fully trained, you will be able to review all the passengers you'll be assigned to on each flight. *The Book of Flight* will give you a better sense of what is happening during each flight and your role in those situations as well as the dynamics of the lives of our travelers. And the records reveal even more of what happens after we land, Nicole. I believe the layover is often the best part of our job."

The Book of Flight slowly disappears from the counter.

 *Chapter 33*

"They're all beautiful, Nancy," Lawrence comments dispassionately.

"Yes, but which one do you like best?" Before her husband can even open his mouth to respond, Nancy announces which one she likes. "I think this is the one."

"I'm going to watch the movie now, Nancy. I've been waiting to see this one for a long time. It's amazing that they have it on this flight." Lawrence dons his headphones to his wife's dismay.

"But what about the house plans?" begs Nancy.

"We'll talk later." Lawrence turns up the volume on his channel selector.

Brushed off again, Nancy huffs and shuffles around, then orders yet another drink and another dessert. She sulks, hoping to elicit some kind of response from her health-conscious husband. Ten minutes into the movie, Lawrence falls asleep. Nancy sighs and tries to concentrate on the house plans again but is unable to focus. She quietly reaches for her purse as he snoozes. She locates a prescription bottle of antidepressants stuffed under her wallet that bulges with credit cards. On the white pharmacy label the prescribing doctor's name is Lawrence E. Westman, MD. Little does the fatigued physician know that his wife has been forging his signature for years on prescription pads she has taken from his office. Nancy quickly downs two fluoxetine capsules with a gulp of her martini, then chases them with a big sigh.

Five minutes pass and Nancy cannot take it anymore. In her frustration, she reaches over to her sleeping husband. "Wake up, Lawrence. How can you just sit there when I am absolutely miserable here?" Lawrence slowly opens his eyes. "There are so many decisions to be made," she continues,

"I told the real estate agent that I would call her regarding our decision before we board the cruise ship. I need to know right now which house we're deciding on."

"Nancy."

"Now this one is really magnificent: an estate home with five bedrooms and five and a half baths, a two-story foyer with marble floors, and a winding staircase. Look, Lawrence, it has a pillared formal dining room with crystal chandeliers and a large master suite with cathedral ceilings—"

"Nancy," he repeats her name in an effort to stop her rambling.

"You pick out the one you want, Lawrence. However, I think with this one you could have a fabulously decorated office in the—"

"Nancy!" he calls out, finally catching her attention. A scowl covers his face, and bitterness creeps into his words. "I have been trying to say that you can pick out the house you want, but keep in mind, I won't be living in it." He reclines his seatback even farther, extends his footrest, and prepares to watch the rest of his movie. "I finally know what I need to do. Thanks for the vacation, Nancy; it really was a great idea."

For the first time since the flight has departed, Nancy Westman is completely speechless. "Are you saying what I think you're saying?" she asks gravely.

"Yes. And I'm not going to change my mind, so don't even try, Nancy. Let's just enjoy the rest of the flight."

"I don't know what to say. I mean, how can you?" she cries.

Lawrence sighs deeply and looks over at his sniveling wife. "Nancy, remember when we first met?" he asks. She barely nods her head. "I was drawn to you because I thought you had a real desire to help people—to help make a difference. I totally supported you when you quit nursing to raise the girls—that was important. But somehow over the years you've changed—changed drastically from the woman I married." He looks at her critically. Distain and resentment taint the hazel color of his eyes. "You have gone from being a supporting friend, a nurturing mother, a loving wife, and a dedicated nurse to a selfish, out-of-control, money-hungry socialite." He takes a shallow breath. "Where is the Nancy Jackson I met thirty years ago?" he asks sadly.

Nancy cannot respond; she has no idea how to respond. Her life appears to be crumbling before her very eyes.

"I've decided to go on to India after we get to New York, Nancy, to learn more about ayurvedic medicine. This healing modality makes complete sense. I think I've found a real calling here." He takes her hand. "You can go to Bermuda but without me. Pick out a house. Just keep in mind that I will not be living there, and I will not be there to pay all your bills. I'll be in India for some time."

Nancy slips into complete denial. Rather than taking her husband's words to heart, she maintains the socialite mind-set he has just condemned. Her drunkenness only intensifies her confusion and paranoia. *What am I going to tell my friends? What will they think of me when they find out that Lawrence is leaving me . . . and going to India of all places? Where am I going live? What will I do? He just can't leave me! There must be another woman—maybe it's that new young receptionist in his office! Why else would he leave me? Oh, maybe I should have had that salad.* Nancy discreetly sucks in her abdomen and thrusts her breasts toward her husband.

Chapter 34

"Infinity 4-4-4, you are cleared to climb to flight level 4-1-0, cleared direct to the Centralia VOR, then as filed," instructs air traffic control.

"Infinity 4-4-4, cleared to flight level 4-1-0, cleared to the Centralia VOR, then as filed," replies Michael as he sits in mid-air with Gabriel in their physical bodies wearing their pilot uniforms. "Sir, we are getting intermittent light chop. What are the rides like as we head east?"

"I've got constant light chop at all altitudes in my sector, Infinity, and occasional pockets of moderate turbulence," answers the controller.

"Thank you, sir," replies Michael respectfully to the air traffic controller. "Let us know if anything smooth becomes available."

"It's just as it is meant to be and right on schedule. Go ahead, Gabe, I'll let you make all the announcements," says Michael as he looks at the archangel that has served him faithfully and sound for thousands of centuries. "You've always had a knack for bringing messages to the people. Remember when you went to tell Joseph about Mary being pregnant? Oh, my God. I'll never forget the look on his face. I thought the poor guy was going to have a heart attack!"

"Yes, yes. That was an all-time classic," Gabriel cries hysterically.

"And who ever said that archangels don't know how to have fun?" Michael laughs uncontrollably.

"Hey, hey, where's my trumpet?" Gabriel reins in his laughter before making the announcement. "Okay, okay, here goes." There is a richness in his tone that even the intercom cannot suppress. "Ladies and gentlemen, we're currently cruising at 41,000 feet. The captain will be turning on the Fasten Seat Belt sign as we may encounter some rough air on our flight to

New York. For your own safety and comfort, we ask that you please return to your seats and remain seated with your seat belts fastened."

"Do you think any of them will listen?" asks Michael, a tone of agitation hangs on each word. "How many times do we, as angels—as divine messengers of The One Infinite Creator—warn our friends about pending danger, and then they just disregard what we tell them? Why do they choose to live their lives in a cloud of confusion, experiencing a lifetime of unnecessary turbulence? My friend, so many have fallen asleep at the wheel of life and live on autopilot. I know, I know about the Free Will thing, Gabriel, but something has to change and soon if these people are going to make it down here. How can we help them when so many are unwilling to help themselves?"

"Lord only knows," says Gabriel as he shakes his head.

"Well, you, my friend, have to work harder than ever in getting out the word about the Mayan Sacred Calendar," Michael beseeches. "The code within has finally been deciphered by humanity, and it is now without boundaries. You need to get the message out that it was and is meant for every living person existing on this planet—regardless of religion, race, culture, or creed—not just the Mayans. And you need to get the message out, more so now than ever. Semyaza continues to keep people in the dark about what lies ahead. It seems that many would prefer to remain adrift without direction rather than be informed as to where they are going."

"You know, Michael, my job isn't so easy when it comes to the likes of Semyaza," Gabriel begins to complain. "The schedule is so tight—"

Michael impatiently retorts, "Sorry, Gabe, the schedule of creation doesn't move according to our schedule. It's The Infinite Creator's schedule, and it moves according to The Creator's divine plan—a plan that is all-encompassing. And you and I, well . . . we're along for the ride. Everything imaginable has been planned for and is right on time. We must imagine with the same scope that The Creator imagines."

"I know there's a universal message in the Mayan Calendar that must not remain unspoken by today's voices," Gabriel confesses. "It can no longer be silenced from today's ears."

Michael reflectively looks out the window to the ground below before adding, "It's not the doom and gloom that some will profess. These intense times—when the cosmic energies are coming in, like compressed waves, like swift bursts of the Light and the Dark—humanity will experience enormous changes in a very short period of time. As we both know, these changes are not all pleasant. However, understanding the sequence and the nature of these waves can help our human friends to personally navigate these changes and help to create positive outcomes for themselves and their planet. Through the Mayan Sacred Calendar, humanity will be delighted to discover the sense of empowerment that this understanding creates—eliminating fear for all, eliminating fright, rage, hopelessness, and apathy for all."

Gabriel looks reverently to the leader of archangels. "Michael, I understand that in no uncertain terms this is the most powerful announcement I will ever make to this world for unifying humanity, once and for all." Michael smiles back in support of Gabriel's realized mission.

Michael warily acknowledges Gabriel's challenge. "In the last hundred years, Semyaza has packed in a multitude of end-of-the-world schemes coming from a wide variety of sources to confuse humanity. I know it will be very easy for them to think that this is just one more. Yet they will soon discover that this message is like no other."

Gabriel chuckles loudly. "Here's another announcement for you, Captain Smith. You forgot to turn the Fasten Seat Belt sign on."

"Damn!"

 *Chapter 35*

"Well, whose turn is it this time?" Tommy asks, hastily unbuckling his seat belt. "This is crazy; we're practically sitting right on top of the damn can."

"Didn't you just hear the pilot's announcement, Tommy?" begs Joe. "Come on, man, you can hold it for a little while."

"No, I really can't!" Tommy lies vehemently. His worn nerves, completely frayed like his torn baggy jeans, are making it impossible for him to sit still any longer. The stressed-out teenager wants to be alone for a couple of minutes. "Now, who is it gonna be?"

Joe sighs and reluctantly rises from his seat. "You better make this quick, kid." Tommy climbs over the seats and quickly goes inside, locking the door while Joe waits impatiently outside. Ron looks over to see what is going on as the flight gets bumpier. Joe shrugs his shoulders and rolls his eyes. Nervously Joe shifts his weight from one foot to the other as he does another visual sweep up the aisle and around the lavatories. He notices the flight attendants closing the cabinets, latching the drawers, and parking all the carts in the galley as he searches for anything out of place—a carryover from his days as a cop on the street.

"Sir, the Fasten Seat Belt sign is on. You'll have to take your seat now," Tezalel instructs with a tone of authority.

"I'm escorting a prisoner, and I cannot leave him unattended, even with the seat belt sign on," Joe responds firmly. The words no sooner leave his mouth than the plane begins to dip and shake violently.

"We'll look after Tommy," Tezalel and Sarakiel exclaim in unison as Joe anxiously returns to his seat.

Tommy sits on the toilet lid with his hands braced against the lavatory walls.

"You better hold on Tommy," says a voice beside him.

"What the fu—" says Tommy, his eyes widen in surprise as he looks behind himself. Figuring that the worst of the turbulence must be over, he stands up and leans against the sink, adjusting his low-riding, baggy denim jeans and dirty torn, stained tee shirt. "Mom is going to flip when she smells this," he laughs, looking at himself in the lavatory mirror. He takes another whiff of his underarms. "I'm sure I'll make a really big impression when I see my parents again."

"You better hold on again, Tommy," says the voice again. Unbeknown to Tommy, his guardian angel continues to guide him on the highs and lows of his turbulent journey through life.

Tommy takes his old, worn navy blue NY Yankees baseball cap out of his back pocket and places it over his matted dreadlocks. *Ron and Joe had great childhood families. Better than that so-called family I had,* Tommy reflects painfully. *Although, in some ways, I guess I'm ready to be home again but only if it's going to be like a real home, with a real family. I so want to feel connected to my parents; more than anything else I want to feel that I belong and that they truly love me.* He chuckles, "Maybe things have changed. After all, they have sent these two buffoons to find me."

"And there's only one way to find out, Tommy. Here we go!" exclaims the guardian angel, with its wings squashed up against the ceiling and walls inside the confines of the coach lavatory with his young teenage runaway.

WHAM! Suddenly, everything seems to turn upside down. The plane shutters then diminishes momentarily then shutters again, this time more violently. Tommy feels his feet fall out from underneath him as the plane hits a huge air pocket. His body is thrown upward like a rag doll. Coming down, he bangs the back of his head against the stainless steel hand basin and lands with his left foot crushed awkwardly beneath his right leg.

"Holy sh—" yells Tommy as he grasps his head tightly. Searing pain radiates across the back of Tommy's skull. His ankle throbs. Dazed and confused, he attempts to get up but is thrown back to the floor by another burst of turbulence. An adrenaline rush jumps his heartbeat into high gear. His eyes widen as shock jolts through his body, mixing with hints of excitement and thrills, while the turbulence continues.

"Perfect, Tommy! Just the way you wanted it!" cheers his constant celestial companion as it looks at the back of Tommy's head. "Good job, my friend."

"Tommy? Are you okay?" Tezalel asks from the other side of the door. "Listen, Tommy, you need to return to your seat right now."

"I . . . I think I'm going to need some help!" Tommy yells back with a slight hint of panic in his voice. He is powerless to twist or move his body from its contorted position as he leans against the bottom of the bifold door. Unable to open the door normally, Tezalel and Sarakiel quickly remove the lavatory door from its hinges. "And for my next act," Tommy jokes, as his upper torso falls to the floor. He tries to appear manly and humorously macho as if he isn't in any kind of pain.

Tommy's guardian angel winks at Tezalel and Sarakiel, while it sits on top of Tommy's chest, laughing at his present position. Ron and Joe storm into the galley to see what is happening. The two flight attendants motion to them that it's okay to assist Tommy. Everyone seems to be having a good laugh, including Tommy.

"Got the camera with you, Joe?" chuckles Ron as he looks down at Tommy sprawled across the floor.

"Oh, man, I wish I did. I packed it in the luggage." A crooked grin plays across Joe's mouth. "Looks like you sure got yourself into a jam here, Tommy."

Thoroughly embarrassed and not wanting to be humiliated any further, Tommy does his best to hide his injuries. He places his old navy Yankees cap back over his unkempt hair to hide the bump rising on the back of his head. However, there is nothing he can do to cover up his ankle injury. It appears to be broken or very badly sprained.

Ron and Joe reach into the lavatory to help pull Tommy to his feet.

"Oh, dude! That fucking hurts! I can't put any weight on it!" yells Tommy. He feels the blood drain from his face and his leg turn numb. He fights the feeling of utter helplessness that tries to overtake him.

"Let's page for a doctor," demands Joe. Slipping his arm around Tommy's waist, Joe sees Tommy's worried face as he helps him back to their row of seats.

"No, man. Don't be an asshole!" exclaims Tommy, forcing a casualness to his voice as if what has happened is no big deal. "I'll be fine, really." Tezalel, Sarakiel, Ron, and Joe help Tommy back into his seat. Ron and Joe sit next to each other with Tommy on the aisle seat with his leg propped across their laps. Sarakiel brings some ice bags, and Tezalel carefully wraps the ankle while Tommy's guardian angel sits on his lap sending loving, healing energy to his injuries.

"Now, now, don't you all look cozy?" Sarakiel teases, looking at everyone scrunched together. The teasing grin fades from her face when she sees the pain in Tommy's eyes. "Is there anything else we can get for you right now?"

"How about three more seats?" Joe shifts under the weight of Tommy's leg. "Just kidding, ma'am. We should be fine. Thanks for your help."

"Any time," Tezalel smiles, checking Tommy's ankle again before returning to the aft galley. "Just let us know if there is anything else we can do for you."

"Have you ever seen a flight crew so happy with their jobs and so happy to help?" Ron murmurs to Joe.

"Nope, can't say that I have," replies Joe with his thick bushy, upraised brows.

"Nope, can't say that I have," Tommy's angel, perched on his seatback, agrees as well.

Chapter 36

"Another hour and half to go. Hope I can make it there." Joe continues to squirm uncomfortably in his seat. "How's the leg, kid?"

"Leg's fine; it's the ankle that hurts like a mother," Tommy replies. "The ice packs seem to help."

Eve approaches Tommy, Ron, and Joe and introduces herself. "I'm sorry to hear about what happened to you, Tommy," she remarks sympathetically before directing her attention to his escorts.

"Detective Rodriguez and Detective Cappellino, I have spoken with the captain regarding Tommy's condition, and we are prepared to make an unscheduled landing in Cincinnati so Tommy can receive immediate medical attention. Because he is in your custody, gentlemen, we have to defer this decision over to you as Tommy's temporary guardians. We are prepared to land if you so choose."

"Tommy, do you want to stop in Cincinnati?" Ron asks reluctantly, thinking of the mountain of paperwork that he will have to fill out if their plans are altered.

"Oh no, I'm fine, really," exclaims Tommy reassuringly. "I can make it to New York. Please tell the captain not to stop. I just want to get home."

"Okay, Tommy," Eve replies. "But I will need to get some information from you so we can file a report regarding the incident. All standard legal stuff," she grins. "First, what is your complete legal name?"

"Thomas Allen Wellington, Jr.," he replies with an air of annoyance in his voice.

"What is your home address, Tommy?" Eve continues to fill in her report.

"Well, it used to be 1111 Park Avenue. I guess it's still the same."

Joe and Ron glance at each other. Joe leans over and whispers to his partner. "Knowin' who his parents are and what kind of background he comes from, I still wonder what in the hell would make a good-looking young kid who seems to have everything run away to live on the streets. Man, just think of the things we could do with that kind of money."

Eve continues with more questions for her onboard injury report. "What exactly took place during the turbulence?" Tommy reluctantly provides most of the details yet still chooses to withhold comment about his head injury. Eve asks repeatedly, "Is there is anything else that I can add to the report?"

Tommy says, "No, ma'am, there isn't." He pushes the crown of his cap down firmly over his head, the bill covering his eyes.

"Thank you, Tommy. Please let us know if there is anything else we can get for you. And again, we are very sorry about what happened."

"A Coke," Tommy says casually as she walks away.

"I'm sorry?" Eve looks back questioningly. His guardian angel, still perched on Tommy's lap, smiles and shrugs its shoulders.

"You asked if there was anything else you could get for me. I would really like a Coke . . . please." He rubs his leg, which is becoming stiffer by the minute.

"Yes, of course." Eve smiles and heads back to the galley.

"You seem mighty comfortable tellin' the woman in charge of this entire flight to get you a soda." Joe looks Tommy straight in the eye. "I guess you must be pretty used to orderin' people around and getting' what you want, huh?"

"Yeah, poor little Tommy with the hurt foot," mocks Ron.

"We've flown all the way to California to hunt down a spoiled little rich kid," adds Joe, irritated with the situation. "So get over it. Just how tough could your life have been anyway?"

"I told you that you wouldn't understand," Tommy replies defensively as his head continues to throb painfully. "No one would," he whispers.

"Come on, try us, kid. We're real understandin', ain't we, Ron?" Joe elbows his seatmate. His resentment and bitterness of being away from his family for so long in search of the runaway begin to flare up. The fact that Joe and Ron are getting paid very little by the agency that they work for doesn't help.

"Yeah, that's right. We're real suckers for a sob story," Ron says tauntingly.

"Okay, smart asses," Tommy responds sharply, an edge of anger slices into his voice. "In a nutshell, here's my life growing up. I am an only child, unwanted by two professional people so busy with their own fucking lives that they never even noticed me. I made straight 'A's; did everything they wanted me to; studied what they said and played the sports that they wanted me to play. I excelled in everything. I was the perfect child—one that begging for his parents' attention. Hell, it was three weeks before they even knew I had run away." Tears well up in his eyes as he laughs. "My mom had me right in the middle of her busy career—a real intrusion into her empire. First, I was handed off to nannies and then off to boarding school. My dad always had his head in some damn book. They never came to see me at school, not even during the holidays—too many deadlines, you know, too many book signings, and interviews. I figured they would never miss me; they never had before. Sure they may be famous and have a ton of money, but they never had time for family—never had time for me."

"Ouch!" replies Ron, the sting of Tommy's words catches him off guard. "Sorry, kid. I mean, my old man wasn't a saint, but at least he took the time to toss a ball around with us once in a while. Even gave us a few pointers for pickin' up girls." He attempts to lighten the mood.

"Well, we don't have to worry about you runnin' away anymore, do we kid?" Joe tries to cheer up their injured runaway. "But you were wrong about one thing, Tommy."

"Yeah, what's that?" he retorts defensively.

"We do kinda understand your situation, kid. We've heard a thousand stories from a thousand different people, and it always seems to come back to their childhood. Right, Ron?" Joe looks to his partner.

"Yeah, it's pretty amazin' really. Everyone's got their own personal drama goin' on." Ron looks around the cabin. "There's a story behind everyone here on this plane. You'd be amazed at some of the things we've heard. Just goes to show you, everyone's got problems even the ones with all the money in the world."

Tommy's guardian angel nods in agreement as he pats Tommy on the head.

Chapter 37

"Ladies and gentlemen, in preparation for landing we ask that you please return your seat back, tray table, and footrest to their upright and locked positions," instructs Eve over the speaker. "Please return any remaining cups and glasses to your flight attendants."

"Give it here, Senator!" barks a completely frazzled and exasperated Nicole. She stands impatiently in front of Richard, who is finishing off the last of his scotch. With one hand extended and the other on her hip, Nicole declares aloud, "We do have to clean up this place, you know. And I would like to be sitting down and strapped in when this huge flying contraption hits the ground."

Two of the first class flight attendants, Sila and Achaiah, are handing out the first class passenger coats from the closet. They overhear Nicole's barking command to Richard. Sila discreetly whispers to Achaiah, "Have you noticed that this seven-hour journey between Los Angeles and New York has nearly eliminated all of Nicole's angelic vibrations? It seems that no matter how hard she tries to resist the emotions around her, she's still tired, frustrated, anxious, irritated, excited, fearful, and relieved—like most of our passengers."

"Yes, however, Nicole is experiencing every emotion, all at once—overwhelming the devoted messenger of our Creator," adds Achaiah. "Feeling like most passengers on board, I know she can't wait to get off the plane." Sila and Achaiah nod in quiet agreement as they proceed to their jumpseats for landing.

Richard quirks a brow in amazement as Nicole impatiently continues to stand in front of him with her hand extended in front of his face. Her golden hair now hangs disheveled in her face, her uniform stained and wrinkled, and her serving apron pockets overflow with fashion magazines from Brigitte Burton. As Richard shifts his gaze briefly to look out the window, Stuart is there to catch it. Richard nudges Stuart and smirks, holding back a laugh as he turns very slowly to hand Nicole his glass.

"Sure, lady, whatever you say," Richard smiles at Stuart as he replies. His spontaneous choice of words triggers a memory that gives them both a pause. In an instant, they are back in their teenage years getting in trouble for trying to sneak out of the local diner without leaving a tip for the waitress.

"We'll be landing at New York's John F. Kennedy airport momentarily." As Eve's announcement over plane's public address system ends, Nicole victoriously turns away from Richard to return to the first class galley having triumphantly retrieved last of the remaining glasses in first class before landing.

Richard, Stuart and several other passengers in their seating area immediately bust out laughing.

 *Chapter 38*

"Hey, Tommy, wake up! We're finally landin'! You're home, kid!" Ron reaches over Joe to nudge Tommy. "Check his seat belt, Joe."

"He hasn't moved an inch," says Joe, nervously trying to clear his throat as he glances back at Ron. "Let's get the ice packs off him." Joe motions for Tezalel to come over and help.

"I think he may be unconscious," says Tezalel as he carefully checks Tommy's pulse. "He seems to be breathing fine, but we'll put him on oxygen, just in case." Tezalel calls for Rochel, the angel who finds lost objects, to locate an oxygen bottle.

"Unconscious?" Joe is startled. Swallowing his nervousness, he asks, "Is he goin' to be okay?"

Rochel hands the portable oxygen bottle to Tezalel and tells everyone, "I'll notify our pilots so that they can have paramedics waiting when the plane lands. We'll have everyone remain seated until they come on board and get Tommy out."

"Oh, man, Joe! We have one of the wealthiest kids in the country laying unconscious in our hands." Ron tries not to think of what possible repercussions can result from this whole incident. Yet a shiver of dread tickles across the back of his neck. "Keep tryin' to wake him up."

"Come on, Tommy, wake up," insists Joe, shaking the teenager firmly.

Gabriel's calm, soothing voice comes over the speaker. "Ladies and gentlemen, if I may have your attention for a few moments please. There is no cause for alarm. However, we have a medical emergency on board. Once we land, it will be necessary for everyone to remain seated so that the paramedics may board the aircraft and remove the injured passenger from the plane. I realize that we are arriving late, but this is a very critical situation; and your cooperation is greatly appreciated. Please remain seated until our flight attendant in charge, Ms. Matrona, has notified you when you may get up. Thank you for your cooperation in this matter. It has been a pleasure having you on Infinity Airways."

As the plane taxies up to the gate, Eve reminds everyone once again to stay seated so the paramedics can board. As soon as she opens the door, three paramedics rush on board with a stretcher and their emergency medical equipment. They follow Eve down the aisle to the back of the plane where Tommy is still lying unconscious.

Although everyone is advised to remain seated until Tommy has been removed from the plane, several people make a mad dash for their bags and bolt toward the open boarding door in first class. Realizing that the paramedics might be awhile, others quickly follow suit.

The paramedics attending to Tommy ask if anyone saw exactly what happened during the turbulence. Tezalel informs them that Tommy had been in the lavatory and, aside from his ankle, reported no other pain or discomfort. During the initial examination, the lead paramedic removes Tommy's hat and discovers a huge bloody contusion on the back of Tommy's head. "Let's get him out of here now!" he yells loudly.

Tommy starts to stir as they lift him up. "Joe? Ron?" he asks in a dazed voice.

"What is it, buddy?" Joe leans over Tommy on the stretcher. A half smile and a sigh of relief are all Joe can muster. Ron stands by, unable to shake off the most overwhelming feeling of trepidation tunneling its way into the pit of his stomach.

"It's not your fault; don't blame yourselves," Tommy mumbles. "You did your job, guys. I'm going home. Thanks . . . for bringing me back to New York." Tommy peacefully shuts his eyes and lapses back into unconsciousness. His guardian angel, sitting on Tommy's stomach, with its legs hanging over the side of the stretcher and crossed at the ankles, smiles at Ron and Joe in agreement with Tommy's last words.

The remaining passengers are no longer waiting. The weary, apathetic travelers and their carryon baggage block the aisles. "Move, people! This is an emergency!" The lead paramedic tries to order people out of the way, but no one will move.

Eve gets on the PA system once again and asks everyone to remain seated, but it is no use; no one is listening. The aisles are completely congested. She looks out the one of the aircraft windows and notices that the catering truck is arriving at the back door ready to service the plane for the next flight.

 *Chapter 39*

"These people are unbelievable!" exclaims Nicole as she and Itqal stand at the front boarding door and continue to watch passengers sneak off the aircraft before the paramedics have a chance to extricate Tommy. "Someone is hurt, and they don't even care." Nicole has been itching at the chance to get off the plane as well, but currently her compassion for the injured boy outweighs the selfish desires stirring inside her. "Isn't there anything we can do, Itqal?"

"As a crew, we can only encourage our passengers to make good choices. Remember, they always have Free Will," Itqal observes, as they stand side-by-side at the boarding door. "Those who are supposed to be here are. Those who are not aren't."

Ignoring what Itqal has just said regarding Free Will, Nicole approaches Richard, who is trying to discreetly leave the plane. She feels overwhelmingly compelled to get involved. Several passengers who are still seated near the door watch the crew closely, anxiously waiting for a signal as to when they can deplane.

"Okay, stop right there!" she demands loudly. With clenched fists on both her hips and feet spread apart, Nicole blocks the boarding door. She stands her ground as her scowl rivets directly on him. "Excuse me. It's *Senator* Stevens, right? I don't think anyone here," she points to everyone in first class, "will be impressed if you try to sneak off, just because you think you're some hotshot politician who should get special privileges!"

The remaining first class passengers applaud and whistle. Richard slinks back to his seat, highly embarrassed. Michael, exiting the cockpit, stands closely behind Nicole as she smiles, waving proudly to her new adoring audience. "Just remember, Nicole, everyone has Free Will, including Senator Stevens. Just relax. Soon you will see how this all fits together," he whispers to her quietly.

Stuart tries to refrain from laughing when Richard returns but loses it when Richard's eyes meet his. Instantly, the two men bust out laughing, taken back through another swirling vortex of time.

"Mrs. Blair! Do you remember? We were sneaking out of detention, and our fifth-grade math teacher caught us!" Richard and Stuart speak in unison as they laugh.

Richard recalls the event that awarded them the detention. "Oh my God, remember how we got little Donald, the dunce-head kid, to lay outside the classroom window two stories down and poured ketchup all over his head?"

"Yes! And how we handed Mrs. Blair his shoe when we told her that he had jumped while she was out of the classroom!" Stuarts finishes the story of days gone by with tears running down his face. "And how she fainted when she looked out the window!"

"Yes, Stuart, that's right. Oh, wait a minute; do you remember when we were in . . ." continues Richard as he settles back in his seat. Miraculously, a lifetime of hard feelings temporarily disappears as they reminisce about their old school days.

"Okay, everyone," instructs Eve, exercising her authority over the situation by opening the aft left service door in the back galley. "We're taking Tommy, the paramedics, and his escorts down on the catering truck. It will take you down to the ramp and drive you over to the ambulance long before you can make it down the aisles of this airplane!" She secures the aircraft door while notifying the surprised driver of the truck about the situation at hand. Within minutes, Tommy, his guardian angel, Ron, Joe, and the paramedics successfully leave the plane and are transferred to the waiting medical rescue vehicle. With sirens blaring and a police escort, the ambulance races across the rain-soaked airport tarmac to the hospital.

# Chapter 40

Sarakiel and Tezalel attempt to console Lauren and Thomas Wellington, as they explain what happened to their son during the flight. As the distraught parents try to comprehend the details of the incident, the two Infinity flight attendants, still in their uniforms, join Joe and Ron seated in the corner of the hospital waiting room.

"I have to admit, Thomas, I'm quite impressed that the flight attendants from Infinity Airways have come all the way to the hospital to check on Tommy," says Lauren cordially yet awkwardly to her estranged husband. "Especially since it sounds as though Tommy is the one at fault in this most bizarre situation."

"I would have to agree with you, Lauren," confirms Thomas. "As far as I'm concerned, after meeting Tezalel and Sarakiel and hearing the story of Tommy's injury, all thoughts of blaming or suing Infinity Airlines for the incident have been definitely been eliminated."

Joe walks thoughtfully over to Lauren with Tommy's cap in his hand.

"Here's Tommy's baseball cap, Mr. and Mrs. Wellington," says Joe apologetically. "Guess he didn't want anyone to know. He's a tough kid. Yet all he wanted to do is come home to be with you two again—to be a family."

Lauren breaks into tears. "I guess Tommy has become very good at hiding his pain. All those years we thought he was happy. He never said anything . . . or maybe we were just too busy to hear," says Lauren reflectively as Thomas tries to console her.

The distressed mother looks at the wear and tear on the bill of the cap. "Tommy always did love the Yankees. I guess he still does." Lauren attempts a weak smile. She suddenly begins to weep when she sees the large bloodstain inside the back of the cap. She holds it close to her heart, lamenting even more as Thomas consoles her once again.

Frozen in time, Lauren and Thomas look to each other, each recognizing their contributions to the present predicament of their son. They are indeed married—in name only. The last few years apart, the numerous affairs of infidelity, their obsession of fame and fortune have brought them to this very sobering moment of self-awareness.

Tezalel, the angel who regulates marital fidelity on Earth, walks over and invites them to sit with him and the others. The six of them—two parents, two private detectives, and two angel flight attendants—sit together, waiting quietly and patiently as Tommy's surgery continues.

# Chapter 41

"The best part of our layovers, Nicole, is assisting people to the Other Side," explains Eve as she sits next to the young trainee during the van ride to the hotel with the rest of the Infinity crew. A stack of fashion and glamour magazines, leftovers from the flight, rests on Nicole's lap.

"Don't they have their guardian angels to help do that?" mumbles Nicole looking out the van window, mesmerized by the advertising, billboards, and numerous stores along the way. "Traveling with people to their final destinations is all fine and good, but what about this city?" questions Nicole. "According to these magazines, this is the most incredible place for shopping, fine dining, and Broadway shows. After a flight like that, we should all have a little fun, don't you think?" Overcome with human emotions and compulsions, she looks excitedly at the rest of the crew for some kind of affirmation to her suggestion. They look back at their new trainee, a little perplexed with her unangelic attitude.

Nicole feels out of place with them, although none of them have ever given her cause to feel that way. Michael, though, is different; she always feels special and secure around him. She enjoys their conversations, albeit short and infrequent. Nicole never feels slighted or inadequate when she is with him. That only seems to happen when she is with Eve.

"Nicole, our job does not end when we land," retorts Eve. Her wide yet shapely brows rise at Nicole's refusal to accept her assignment. "On this layover, you are scheduled to assist me with Senator Stevens. Shopping is not part of your assignment."

"What?" exclaims Nicole in disbelief. "You mean to tell me that instead of getting to see one of the most amazing cities on this planet, I have to help some corrupt self-absorbed politician?" She is instantly flooded with the same anger and frustration that Senator Stevens himself had experienced on the plane earlier. Little does Nicole realize that she too is becoming quite self-absorbed.

As they drive into the city, Eve notices that Nicole is absorbing a multitude of energies, becoming more human each moment. The compulsion to shop completely overwhelms Nicole. Eve stares at Michael in the front passenger seat, bewildered by his decision to hire Nicole for the job.

"Remember, Nicole, we are not here to judge," Gabriel adds resolutely. "Senator Stevens has a purpose here, just like everyone else, corrupt or not. Everyone is created in perfection and is part of the divine cosmic blueprint for this planet during this phase in its evolution of consciousness."

The van pulls up to the hotel entrance where everyone gathers their belongings and heads into the lobby. The hotel manager at the taupe marble guest registration desk smiles at the returning airline crew. "Welcome back, Captain Smith. With all the craziness going on with the weather, heightened airport security, terrorist threats and the war stuff, we were starting to wonder if we were ever going to see an airline crew laying over here in New York City again. I must say we are honored to have you and your staff with us once more."

"Thank you, Harold. It is good to see you as well," Michael replies cordially as he completes the check-in form.

"Must have been a rough ride flying in here today with the bizarre storms we had earlier, huh, Captain? You guys certainly have your work cut out for you these days."

"Oh, nothing we can't handle, Harold." Michael laughs as he looks back to his crew. "As usual, several of our crew members will be checking in later. I'll leave their keys with you."

"Excellent, sir. Here is your crew layover expense money." The manager passes a sealed envelope to Michael. "If you will just sign here please."

"How much do I get?" Nicole asks eagerly, pushing her way through the crew and their luggage to the check-in counter. She looks impatiently to Michael. "Do you need all of yours, since you're not going shopping?" She turns abruptly and stares intensely at the rest of the crew. "And since you don't eat or drink, maybe I could have yours, too!"

Michael tips the waiting van driver and pockets the rest of the money. He smiles at Nicole. "You have much to learn," he tells her gently. "Since you have chosen not to cover your assignment, I will escort you to some of the stores and familiarize you with the way things work down here. Maybe this will give you a better understanding of humans and how their societies operate."

The other attendants look to Eve as she raises her brow. Her resentment of Nicole grows stronger as Michael, once again, goes above and beyond normal protocol to help the new trainee.

A teasing smile tickles Nicole's lips. "That's wonderful, Michael. Oh, thank you, thank you. So exactly how much money are you going to give me?" He hands Nicole her cash allowance for the layover. She screams excitedly as she leans over on her tiptoes to kiss him on the cheek. "You won't be sorry!"

Chapter 42

"Mr. and Mrs. Wellington?" asks a short balding man as he enters the waiting room. Everyone in the area turns in his direction and looks anxiously at the doctor wearing green surgical scrubs.

"Yes, right here!" Tommy's parents exclaim at the same time. They hurry over to speak privately with the spent surgeon.

"Hello, I'm Dr. Harrell. Tommy's condition appears to be stable right now. They've taken him to ICU. It will be some time yet before he comes out of the anesthesia." Dr. Harrell continues to discuss Tommy's injuries in detail and outline the measures that have been taken to treat him. He lowers his voice to say, "By the way, do you know that your son tests positive for HIV?"

"What!" demands Thomas, his mind reeling from the shock of what he just heard. The news cuts through to the very core of his heart.

"Tommy has tested positive for AIDS. We routinely check these things before any surgery takes place. I'm sure you understand our position, Mr. and Mrs. Wellington."

Lauren drops Tommy's bloodstained cap onto the floor. She and Thomas stare at each other in disbelief. Lauren sees the painful expression that covers her husband's face and the overwhelming sadness in his eyes. Taking charge like she does in her everyday business world—a world of image and illusion—Lauren instinctively conducts the present situation in the same manner. She raises her hand before Thomas can say anything else.

"Doctor, is Tommy in any pain?" Lauren tries to ask calmly, pretending as though the new earth-shattering announcement about her son having AIDS doesn't disturb her.

"No," says Tommy's guardian angel silently as it shakes its head from side to side. Standing next to the doctor, it lightheartedly mocks some of the doctor's gestures, acting as if they are all having a conversation together.

"No, ma'am," Dr. Harrell continues in his attempt to reassure them. "We have him on a continuous IV with medications to ensure that he is comfortable. If you have any other questions or concerns, the nurses or I will be happy to . . ."

Thomas picks up Tommy's cap. It instantly reels him back to the day Tommy came home excitedly with his new Yankees authentic game cap. Tommy had attended his first New York Yankees baseball game with a school friend and his father. Tommy had begged Thomas to join them for the opening game at Yankee Stadium, yet he declined because of a deadline he had to meet for his publisher. Tommy was heartbroken. He pleaded and begged repeatedly, yet Thomas remained unyielding in his answer, suggesting that they would be able to go another day. Yet another day never came as Thomas, time and time again, turned Tommy down for the rest of the season. The look of disappointment and devastation in his son's eyes now haunts Thomas's every thought as he looks at the very same baseball cap.

As guilt and pain of the past floods his senses, Thomas clears his throat. A discernible sadness clings to his words. "Dr. Harrell, if you need any specialists or experts from anywhere at anytime, my wife and I are prepared to spend whatever it takes to make sure that Tommy receives the best care possible. Of course, I don't mean to imply that you are not capable. I just want you to know that we will do anything to help our son—no matter what it costs."

"Thank you, Mr. Wellington," replies Dr. Harrell. "I'll let you know if we feel that Tommy's case requires any special assistance. But right now, he is stable. We have done all that we can for the time being. The rest is up to Tommy."

"That's right, Doc," mocks the angel. "The rest is up to Tommy."

"Thank you, Doctor; thank you for taking care of our son," says Lauren, struggling to hold back the next wave of tears. "Can we see him now?"

With great trepidation, Thomas and Lauren walk down the sterile hospital corridor to enter Tommy's room. Buried amidst a myriad of monitors and machines, they first see his ankle is wrapped and elevated. Looking closer, they see their son's head covered in bandages. Tommy's face looks tired and swollen. Immediately Lauren is reduced to tears at the sight of her son. She and Thomas are overwhelmed with feelings of guilt, pain, and remorse. In this very moment, everything they own and everything they have become mean absolutely nothing. The only thing that matters is their son. In their silence, they wonder how everything got so out of balance. They wonder how their young son could have AIDS?

Looking even closer at their child, they notice that his face is much different from the face of the boy that left home over two years ago. He appears more mature, not just physically but emotionally. There is a hardened look of experience and wisdom about him, replacing the innocence that once was. His body has grown much taller and leaner. Lauren pulls the chair up closer to his bedside and grasps Tommy's hand. Even in her state of anguish, she can't refrain from inspecting the tattooed designs and images that cover Tommy's arms. Thomas nervously paces the room back and forth. Quietly to themselves, they both pray for the same thing. They will change their lives completely—give up everything if Tommy's life is spared.

"Tommy has AIDS, Lauren. What are we going to do? What are we going to say?" Thomas asks delicately. "Is our son now a homosexual? Or did he get this through some kind of drug use? Or worst yet, both?" He shakes his head mournfully.

"I just want Tommy to get better so we can take him home," she says matter-of-factly, maintaining a detached yet restrained position to help her sort methodically through the details.

"I know, honey. I want the same," adds Thomas reflectively.

Surprised, Lauren eyes him closely. "Honey?" she laughs through her tears. "Do you know how long it's been since you called me that?"

"Too long," he whispers.

"Most definitely," replies Tommy's celestial companion.

"It's been too long for a lot of things, Lauren. We've got to make changes, starting with Tommy." Thomas looks over at his sleeping son. "Our lives have become so screwed up, so disconnected. We don't even know who he is; maybe we never knew. We only knew what we wanted him to be. And look what happened."

Lauren lays her head on the bed. "All he ever wanted was to be a family. Was that too much to ask? Doesn't every child want that?" she sobs. "Doesn't every child deserve that?"

The angel shakes its head up and down with eyebrows raised and a frown on its face.

"We lost ourselves before Tommy was born. Both of our careers had started to take off," admits Thomas remorsefully. "You know, Lauren, I think our happiest days were when we were living in that old rundown loft. Remember how the roof leaked?" Thomas and Lauren smile at each other through their tears, remembering the days when they were young and passionately in love, with the world and each other. "We didn't have much back then, but we had each other."

"I know we're not exactly the religious type, Thomas, but do you think that we could pray together for Tommy?" Lauren asks, extending her hand to his.

Tommy's angel, acting like a mime, begins to smile, nodding its head in agreement.

"Of course, of course." Thomas pulls a chair up to Tommy's bedside. They each grasp one of Tommy's hands and silently hang their heads in prayer. Hovering above, Tommy's guardian angel grasps the hands of Lauren and Thomas's guardian angels and prays too.

# Chapter 43

Eve waits in the dingy dark backstreet watching Richard and Stuart argue outside an old yellow taxi with missing hubcaps. She stands quietly in uniform yet fully an angel, invisible to humans.

"Will this day ever end!" Richard yells as Stuart takes all their baggage out in an effort to get the spare tire out of the trunk. The cabbie is on his radio asking his dispatcher to call for a tow truck. "There's a shortage of taxis, and I'm forced to share one with you!" He points to a flat tire. "And now this!"

"Look, Richard. Oh, excuse me, *Senator*, the poor guy got a flat because you insisted that he find a shortcut to your hotel!" Stuart retaliates in his frustration.

Richard replies defensively, his jaw clenched tightly. "You always blame me for everything!"

Eve patiently watches as the two men argue relentlessly, rehashing every fight they've ever had. Refusing to help change the flat, Richard leaves in a huff with his roll-a-board and leather briefcase in hand. In the dark, down the middle of the alley, he walks hurriedly through the wet rotting trash. Following a dim lamp-lit path, Richard looks nervously from side to side when the heels of his shoes begin to crunch on the glass from a nearby broken liquor bottle lying partially inside a brown paper bag. Richard's heart begins to pound harder when his heavy suitcase suddenly stops rolling; glass and debris block the wheels, preventing them from moving any further.

Even though the flat tire occurred just a few blocks from a main thoroughfare, the side street is deserted and the buildings dark. In spite of the driver's observation that the neighborhood seems safe, Stuart still feels very uneasy as danger permeates the damp summer air. The rank smell of urine only increases his uneasiness and puts him on full alert. He chases behind Richard asking him to stay with the taxi until help comes. Richard in his arrogance shrugs Stuart off and continues on his own.

Chapter 44

While the rest of the crew head out with their respective assignments, Michael escorts Nicole around the city. Advertisements lure her into high-end boutiques, where she caresses the fabric of beautiful, expensive garments. Nicole wants everything and can afford almost nothing. To Michael's amusement, she spends hours looking in the mirrors while trying on various hats, shoes, scarves, and gloves. As they walk down Fifth Avenue, Michael mentions that Filene's Basement is having a sale and that she will probably be able to afford something there. Without a second thought, Nicole agrees. Knowing that she is determined to buy something, Michael watches as she charges ahead, aware that with every block they walk, her angelic energy is diminishing.

"I said, 'Let go!'" screams Nicole, holding on tightly to the gorgeous aqua blue silk pants that she desperately wants. Her contender is not prepared to give up so easily as the Lauren Wellington designer pants are marked 70 percent off. Nicole, an angel of the Divine Order, is reduced to behaving like the frenzied shoppers around her. Throughout the store, women fight openly over clothing, each claiming that she had found the bargain before the other. Nicole stomps around to the other side of the table, attempting to intimidate the other woman with her height. Nicole gives the pants one final pull, stretching them at the seams. "Unless you're willing to pay the consequences, I suggest that you release these pants immediately," Nicole commands, glaring threateningly into the woman's eyes.

After several similar encounters with other frantic bargain-shopping customers, Nicole proudly emerges from the sales tables. She walks over to Michael with an armload of clothes. "Look, you were right!" she cries. "These bargains are great."

Waiting in line to check out, Nicole becomes increasingly impatient. She overhears several women standing around comment on Michael's good looks and charming magnetism. Picking up their envy and jealousy, Nicole hooks her arm through Michael's. She suggests loudly, "I'm going to model my new lingerie for you tonight, Michael." She hangs a red lace thong on her index finger in front of his face. While Michael remains stoically silent, he arches a brow as his eyes sparkle with amusement.

"That will be $317.23, ma'am," says the frazzled cashier at the check-out register.

"I only have one hundred and fifty dollars!" Nicole exclaims as she recounts her allowance. "Michael, I need these clothes. Just look how beautiful they are and how sexy they make me look," she begs sweetly. "Please."

"No, Nicole," Michael states clearly.

"What! Do you have any idea what I had to go through to get these? I mean there was this one woman who—" Nicole stops midway when she realizes that he is not going to change his mind.

"The answer is no. Your allowance for the layover is one hundred and fifty dollars, just like everyone else's."

"Decide, blondie!" barks the impatient shopper standing behind them. "You're holding up the whole damn line."

Nicole tearfully looks down at her hard-won items on the counter. "I want them all, Michael. It's my first time shopping." Suddenly she glares at him with absolute disgust. "But I guess I can't with only a miserable one hundred and fifty dollars!"

They hold up the line for quite some time while Nicole sorrowfully tries to decide which clothes she will keep and which ones she will leave behind. She becomes quite irritable and indignant when the store manager steps up. "Lady, the store will be closing soon. You need to make up your mind and quickly, or you'll be walking out with nothing."

Moments later Nicole is proudly carrying her shopping bags through the streets of New York City, looking excitedly in every window along the way. "Nicole, we should hurry back to the hotel as it seems your energetic level is diminishing," encourages Michael.

"Oh, please," replies Nicole with her face pushed against the glass window of yet another expensive fashion boutique. "Can't you see that I feel just fine?" Before they make it another block, Nicole collapses into Michael's arms. Gently he picks her and her shopping bags up, gallantly carrying her and her purchases for several blocks back to the hotel. The doorman holds the hotel door open for him and asks if she is okay.

Michael chuckles. "She shopped until she dropped." Together they have a good laugh. Declining any assistance, Michael maneuvers Nicole, the shopping bags, and himself through the hotel entrance. After reaching the eleventh floor, Michael wills her hotel door open and lays her exhausted body on the bed.

"Good night, Nicole, my dear sweet angel," whispers Michael, as he tenderly smoothes the hair back from her face and kisses her forehead. He looks down longingly at her full breasts, fighting back his gnawing attraction for her. As much as he wants to hold her in his arms again, to share the closeness of another, he knows it cannot happen. The Protector of Humanity knows he has to remain true to his mission. However, struggling with his own temptations within the lower vibrations of Third Dimension, he steals one more lingering look at her as he heads slowly for the door. Nicole turns over on her side and snuggles comfortably on the bedspread. His eyes follow the enticing curves of her voluptuous body. Thoughts of being one with Nicole, being one with her angelic beauty, enhanced by her feminine human form, and her endless passion for life, is more than he can fathom. Mustering all the celestial power inside, Michael forces himself to leave, disappearing into the ethers as he dare not risk staying one moment longer.

Chapter 45

A distant streetlamp suddenly begins to flicker and crackle. Eve turns her head as Michael unexpectedly appears next to her. "So how's everything going with Richard Stevens and Stuart Patrick?" he asks casually.

"After arguing about which way to go, they got into it again, rehashing every fight they've ever had. Instead of staying with Stuart and helping the driver, Richard has just left the cab in an arrogantly prideful attempt to find another one," explains Eve. Richard's guardian angel gets out of the back seat of the taxi and shrugs its shoulders toward Eve and Michael. Eve looks to her left as each of Richard's footsteps echo along the deserted alley. "There's Richard now. He's about to be shot by that drug-crazed addict. Nicole would have really enjoyed seeing this," she laments with a deep sigh. "So how was shopping?"

"I decided to assist you in her place—not that Infinity's number one flight attendant needs any help," he teases. Eve and Michael watch as Richard continues to walk toward a side alley, sidestepping large puddles along the way. "Nicole? Never in all eternity have I seen an angel quite like her. Have you?"

Eve doesn't respond. Michael senses her jealousy and resentment.

"She defies everything I've ever known," Michael continues. "She seems to be falling, Eve, and yet she's not consciously making that choice."

Eve smiles gently and nods in agreement. A smirk of satisfaction tugs at the corner of her mouth.

"So have you decided who is going to be Vice President of Inflight Service?" Eve inquires nonchalantly.

Michael shakes his head. The heavenly messengers of love continue to watch the scene being played out before them and the actors saying their lines right on cue.

Worried about Richard's safety, Stuart rounds the corner of the building just as Richard verbally threatens his assailant. The gunman panics and fires at the sound of the approaching footsteps.

The shot rings out. "Oh, please, God. No!" screams Stuart as the bullet enters Richard's body. Running frantically toward him, Stuart grabs Richard just as he collapses onto the rain-soaked pavement. Eve and Michael watch as the drug addict staggers off right in front of them with the senator's wallet and cell phone, disappearing into the shadows.

"Damn it, Richard!" cries Stuart. "You always have to have it your way, don't you? You always think you know what's best, and now look where it's gotten you!" He looks down at his bleeding friend. "Hang on now, damn it! Put some of that stubbornness of yours to good use." Tears stream down Stuart's face, and Richard stares back in disbelief. "When are you going to understand that I'm your friend, your best friend, not your enemy?" begs Stuart.

As the cabbie emerges around the corner, Stuart screams, "Call for an ambulance!"

"Stuart," Richard gasps painfully as his eyes open wide. "I need to tell you something about," he inhales sharply, desperately trying to get air, "it's about . . . Jer . . . Jeremy."

"Save your breath, Richard. I know that Jeremy is my son, I've always known," he cries, attempting to plug Richard's wounds with his jacket.

"Stu . . . please. Jeremy has—" begins Richard.

"What is it? What's wrong with Jeremy!" demands Stuart as he tries to keep Richard conscious.

"A rare con . . . condition . . . he needs a transplant . . . Jenn is the wrong blood type. I can't . . . maybe you can." Richard struggles for air as blood flows uncontrollably out of his mouth. "Take care of them, Stu . . ." he pleads, giving Stuart one last look as he grasps Stuart's shirt, pulling him closer. Tears pour out of his eyes and blood from his wound. "Take care of my daughter, Katie, too," he whispers painfully.

The air hangs thick with only the sound of the distant hum of traffic and honking horns in the distance. All the color drains from Richard's face. "No! Richard, no! Don't give up!" begs Stuart. "Why did you have to be so arrogant, so damned stubborn!"

Eve watches as Richard's glowing aura dwindles to a pinpoint of light. His guardian angel takes his hand and pulls him out of his physical body. Richard stares at Stuart, unaware of what is happening and starts to yell.

"Arrogant! Who in the hell do you think you are?" demands Richard looking at Stuart. Sensing that something is wrong, Richard anxiously looks around and sees Eve, Michael, and his guardian angel.

"Oh, my God!" exclaims Richard.

Michael looks over at Eve. "I think you can handle the rest."

Richard stares in disbelief as Michael disappears. He shakes his head in dismay as he looks at his angel and then at Eve.

# Chapter 46

"Mom?"

"Did you say something, Thomas?" asks Lauren while reclining in the bedside chair with her eyes closed.

"Mom . . . Dad?" comes a faint voice.

"No, I was just thinking about Tommy," replies Thomas as he lays Tommy's bloodstained Yankees cap on the windowsill.

"Mmmmooooommm . . . Daaaddd?"

"Tommy? Tommy! Yes, we're right here, son." Lauren springs forward from her chair. "Oh, my God, Tommy. Are you all right?"

"Oh, son, we've been so worried about you." Thomas rushes over to his side. "How are you feeling? Are you in pain?"

"I'm okay, Dad. It's great to see you and you, too, Mom. I've missed you guys." Tommy remains groggy from the anesthesia. "Where are we? What . . . what happened?"

Thrilled to hear the sound of his son's voice again Thomas explains, "Well, you're home in New York, Tommy, but in the hospital. Apparently, you never told anyone about hitting your head when you fell during the turbulence. The doctors had to operate to try and stop the internal bleeding and the swelling."

"Well, I'm just glad to be home." Tommy smiles awkwardly as the bandages pull his mouth to the side. "With my parents."

"Oh, my God, Tommy. We're so sorry for everything." Lauren sobs, "I owe you an explanation; I really do." She attempts to dry her eyes and squeezes Tommy's hand tightly as she rambles on with her apologetic confession. "I had been working hard and struggling to make it for a long time before my business took off, Tommy. Just when things were starting to come together, I found out I was pregnant with you. So I worked even harder. For some reason, I felt that if I took one day off, that somehow we would lose everything. I was haunted constantly by visions of my mother; she had also gotten pregnant at an early age, and it destroyed her. My parents were forever struggling to keep food on the table and clothes on our backs. I promised myself that I would never let that happen to me, that I would have a better life." Lauren begins to cry again.

"Mom, it's okay. I—" Tommy begins as he tries to console his mother. Yet she can no longer contain her herself or her guilt.

"Oh, Tommy, I am so sorry. I was so afraid of ending up like my mother that I failed to celebrate your life, to enjoy having a family, to enjoy being a family. I was so fearful of having everything taken away from me that I never stopped to consider all that you and your father had to give. Tommy, I love you so much. Can you ever forgive me?" she pleads. Her words are spoken with a softness that makes them almost inaudible. "My God, I am so sorry for what I did to you, to all of us."

"It's okay, Mom. Please don't cry." Tears of forgiveness well up in Tommy's eyes. "At least I understand now."

Thomas comes around the bed to hug his sobbing wife and hold his son's hand. Tommy is overjoyed to see his parents together.

"Sorry to intrude." A young nurse enters the room, followed by Dr. Harrell. "We just need to check Tommy's vital signs."

The doctor looks over Tommy's chart then glances over to his patient. "Well, Tommy, you are quite a determined young man." While examining Tommy's bandages Dr. Harrell remarks, "I've never seen someone conscious so quickly after such an operation. You must be on some kind of mission," he says jokingly.

"Well, that's Tommy for you!" Thomas beams proudly at his son. "Hardheaded kid. When he decides to do something, there's no stopping him."

"You're going to need some rest, Tommy. Let's say you can have visitors for about another fifteen minutes; then it's lights out," orders Dr. Harrell as he looks at the clock.

"Okay," Tommy agrees, feeling a little lightheaded from the anesthesia and medications. "Is Joe or Ron here?"

"Yes, son. Actually there are several people in the waiting room that would like to see you." Lauren asks, "Doctor, is it okay if they come in for a few minutes?"

"Yes, but just a few minutes. I don't want to have to throw anyone out on their head," he replies with laughter. He walks into the corridor, amused with his own humor.

Chapter 47

"I'm confused. What are you doing here?" Richard asks Eve inquisitively. "Look, I'm really sorry about the incident on the plane with the wine. Lately, I've been under a lot of stress, pressure, and deadlines. You know what I mean," rambles Richard as he looks at Stuart and the dead body again. "And who the hell is that?"

Without waiting for an answer, he looks to his old friend. "Hey, Stuart, it's okay. I'm right here, buddy! Can't you hear me?" Richard watches as the ambulance arrives to take his body to the hospital. "Hey, look down the street, Stuart! There's that thug who shot me for a lousy couple of bucks! Go get him! Lock that bastard away—forever!" he shouts unmercifully. Richard stretches his arm to point. "Wow, I feel amazing," he exclaims, rubbing his arm and shoulder.

"Richard, we're here to take you home." Eve points to a billowing mist nearby. To Richard's astonishment, his father emerges. He appears different from the man Richard remembers from his youth.

"Dad? Is that really you? You look so—"

"Kinder and gentler, even peaceful?" his father adds, fully emerging from the mist. Mr. Stevens looks back at Richard's dead physical body. "Isn't it wonderful to be free, to be rid of that old Rent-A-Wreck? Here you can go anywhere as fast as you can think it."

"Dad, how can this be? You died of a stroke fifteen years ago." Still somewhat confused, Richard looks back over at Eve and his guardian angel. "And what is she doing here, Dad?" he asks, referring to Eve.

"She's an angel, Richard. Angels are among the many, many beings and energies behind the curtain on the stage of your life—assisting, guiding you along your journey. Angels are always waiting in the wings, pardon the pun, waiting for you or any of us to ask for their assistance. It's just too bad that most people fail to recognize their angels and utilize their help," explains his father telepathically as love weaves through every word that is communicated. "Life would be so much easier if humans would wake up to what is going on around them."

"I'm sorry. I don't mean any disrespect, but a flight attendant as an angel? And who is that other one, Dad?" He suddenly becomes aware of the fact that he was speaking without words, only communicating with his mind.

"Flight attendants at Infinity Airways are really angels. They are helping to make sure everyone gets to where they are supposed to be going. And the other one that you unfortunately don't recognize is your own guardian angel. You've shut it out most of your life, yet it has been with you faithfully since the day your mother brought you into this world."

The tall angel with magnificent wings smiles, then moves next to Richard.

"That's right, Richard," his angel says proudly. "Angels are everywhere."

Eve waves her arm. Suddenly the buildings fade, and they see ghosts pushed against the ashen waste rising above the ground, remnants of the attacks of September 11. In an instant, Richard sees all the lingering spirits still bound to Earth, unwilling to release their own fears. He sees these souls being guided by their guardian angels and Infinity flight attendants, being encouraged to move upwards to the brilliant Light above.

"Our work is crucial, Richard," explains Eve, pointing to various entities floating around endlessly in circles. "Many souls are trapped by their misconceptions and fears, trying to transition to the Other Side in anger or a highly confused, emotional state. Experiencing horrific deaths, some are unaware that they have even died. Meanwhile, those that left the planet during the recent terrorist events are on schedule, so to speak, having learned what they needed to learn and accomplished many areas of their growth. But still there is anger. To release these lost souls from the Earth's field, we help the guardian angels to move their human charges forward, returning to The Creator. That is why I am with you now."

"Is this the part when you tell me that I'm going to Hell . . . for all of eternity? With all the crap and dirty deals I've done, I wouldn't think that this is going to be a trip to Heaven. Not for someone like me, anyway. Hell, I don't even believe in—" Richard stops mid-sentence, looks around repentantly, then corrects himself. "I guess if I had believed this stuff about an afterlife, I would have done things a little bit differently."

His guardian angel sees the concern creeping into Richard's face. "Don't worry about Jennifer and the children. Stuart will take great care of them. Jeremy gets the transplant he needs and later joins Stuart in his political efforts. Of course, Stuart and Jennifer marry and remain together throughout the remainder of their lives on this planet. Next year Katie finishes law school becomes an attorney just like you, Richard, except she goes into environmental law, successfully defending many of the country's natural reserves—the very ones you legislated for industrial development. Which you did, all for power and money, and very corruptly I might add," concludes Richard's angel.

"Bravo! You did a great job, Richard," his father interjects. "It's just as you planned. Your karma is balancing very well."

"My karma? What the hell is . . ." Richard is slow in comprehending what is being conveyed. Eve, his guardian angel, and father all smile lovingly at the disillusioned senator. "You mean to tell me that everything I've worked so hard was for nothing? That what I did for fifty-four years just goes to Stuart? My wife, Jeremy, my children—everything I did in Congress—that was the purpose of my life?" pleads Richard in his anger and confusion. Sarcasm clings to each word. "To be murdered by some desperate thug in some grungy backstreet in New York City—that was what my life amounted to?"

"It's all about growth and understanding," Richard's father explains compassionately. "You and Stuart agreed before you came down here that you would marry Jennifer after she got pregnant and be a father to Stuart's son, Jeremy. That way, Stuart could devote his time to improving the environment and working for civil rights. If he had been married to Jennifer up to this point in his career, he would not have achieved all that he has."

Richard's guardian angel glows brightly as it telepaths, "Your death here in New York City will result in an effort spearheaded by Stuart, Jennifer, Jeremy, and Katie to keep people off the streets through education and job opportunities, not by being locked up in prisons. All of this will lighten the emotional vibrations weighing heavily on this planet, helping to ensure a smoother transition for everyone in 2012. Jennifer and Stuart, who are true soul mates—actually twin flames—agreed to delay their time together so that you could lay the foundation for Katie's future. All of which will lead her to being elected to a major political office very soon."

Richard remains silent as more is revealed. Mr. Stevens further enlightens his bewildered son about karma. "Karma is how we receive the lessons that our souls need to evolve. Your karma is the situations you create for yourself to teach you your own lessons while in the physical. These lessons can come in many forms, Richard, some quite painful and some not. Yet many challenges in your life weren't karmic at all, but you choose them simply to speed your growth. Asking Stuart to take care of your daughter in the very last minute of your life did that."

"So you see, Richard, your life was not all about you; it wasn't all for nothing," his father admonishes gently. "It was about the good of everyone involved. Isn't it beautiful? And by the way, you and Stuart have been everything to each other throughout your existence. No matter what role you two play, you always like to pick ones where you annoy each other to death. Get it—to death!" His father chuckles, "Okay, okay. I'll be a comedian in my next life."

"Now seriously, Dad, was it like this for you when you . . . when you died?"

"It's different for everyone, son. You get whatever it is that you expect. It's that simple. Some people believe or are led to believe that they are going to Hell, which doesn't really exist—well, only in their thoughts. If Hell is what you expect, Richard, then Hell is what you get. The Infinite Creator is so wonderful to give you whatever it is you set your intention toward. And you are The Creator. Each of us is The Creator of our own life, so you give yourself whatever it is that you think about or believe you deserve. No one else makes that choice for you. There are no judges or jury, Richard. It's just you who judges yourself." His father jokes, "Tough news up here for us lawyers, isn't it, kid?"

"But why don't I . . . why don't we . . . remember any of this when we're alive? Why can't we see these angels?" Richard adamantly implores, "Why can't we remember what happened in our past lives?"

"If you came down here knowing everything from every incarnation you've ever had, then you could never learn the lessons you have set for yourself," his guardian angel explains. "It would be like taking the bar exam and already knowing all the answers. What good is the test if you know all the answers, and if you know that no matter what you do, you cannot fail?"

Richard begs to understand. "But, can't we just—" His father's sudden laughter interrupts his plea.

"That's a politician for you, always looking for a way to make things more complicated!" Mr. Stevens jokes heartily as he pats his exasperated son on the back. "Come on, Richard, everyone is waiting. The arrival area is very crowded. They all want to congratulate you. You did a great job, son. I'm so proud of you."

"Now that's really funny!" Richard retorts sarcastically. "I had to die to hear you finally say you're proud of me."

A tunnel of light appears before them. Eve's uniform disappears as her human form merges into shimmering light with that of his guardian angel. Wrapped in a choir of angels, they swirl into a symphony of color, tones, light, and sound, the likes of which have never been seen or heard before. Flying as one, the angels fly around Richard and his father as they walk together arm in arm. Richard turns, facing the tunnel of luminescent light descending from the heavens, then hesitates. He looks to his father for reassurance.

"You trusted me with your life, Richard." The father conveys to his son, "You should also trust me with your death." Together with the angels and his father, Richard steps forth in faith into the extraordinary essence of love that cascades all around. Mr. Stevens states with a heavenly assurance, "Death was never more glorious!"

 *Chapter 48*

"Hey, kid!" Joe leans over Tommy's bed. "I still wish I had my camera. From the toilet to the hospital, you are somethin' else, man!" He says jokingly, "Doc says you got quite a blow to that hard head of yours. Hope the john on the airplane is okay."

Tezalel steps up to Tommy's bedside with a big smile. "That's right. I'd better call the airport and tell maintenance to check the lavatory for any big holes."

"Tezalel! What are you doing here?" Tommy is surprised to see the two flight attendants in his room. "Sarakiel too! You guys are the greatest," he says excitedly then pauses momentarily. Tommy and everyone else present wonder how it is that he knows the flight attendants' names and very unusual names as well. In his excitement, Tommy quickly dismisses the matter. "Mom, Dad, they're the Infinity crew that brought me home."

"Yes, Tommy, we know. We had the opportunity to meet everyone while you were in surgery. Now, I think it's time for you to get some rest," his father encourages.

"Well, it's our job to make sure that you get to where you're going," Tezalel adds. "And you sure made it exciting for us. I must admit that's the first time I've ever seen the meal catering truck take a passenger off the plane, and an injured one on a stretcher, no less."

While holding Tommy's hand and squeezing it gently, Sarakiel leans over the bed railing toward Tommy and whispers in his ear. "We'll see you again real soon. Everything will be just fine, you'll see."

Tommy grins and squeezes her hand knowingly. "Thanks, Sarakiel. Hey, where's Ron?"

"I'm right here, buddy."

"Thanks for taking such good care of me, Ron. I guess if I would have listened to you guys in the first place, I would have never gotten into this mess."

"That's okay, Tommy." Ron chuckles. "I'm happy to bring you back to New York. Although I must admit that I am looking forward to a nice, boring car ride home. You take care now, kid."

"Okay, everyone, it's time for this young man to get some rest," instructs the nurse. "Mr. and Mrs. Wellington, you may have a few more minutes with Tommy, and then it's lights out."

"Take care, Tommy!" Joe yells as the group from the flight heads for the door.

"Thanks, everyone!" yells Tommy, struggling to see them before they leave the room. "Even though you would never guess it by looking at me right now, this is the best day of my life," Tommy says with grin of satisfaction. "My mom and dad are here together, and we're a family again. I guess all we need is some apple pie." Everyone has a good laugh as they each wave goodbye, leaving Tommy alone with his parents.

"Thank you, Tommy." Lauren holds her son's hand. "Thank you for bringing us together again. You know, if you had never run away, we may have never realized how important we all are to each other, and how unimportant everything else really is."

"It doesn't matter how much money, fame, or prestige you have," his father announces as he steps up to Tommy's bedside. "It means nothing if you don't have a family—if you don't have love. All that stuff can't love you back. It can't fill an empty heart. Only love can."

"Dad, that's the nicest thing you've ever said—or written!" Tommy laughs painfully.

Lauren strokes her son's swollen cheek. "Just try to get some sleep, dear. I promise we'll be here when you wake up. We'll always be here for you, Tommy."

His eyelids grow heavy. "Promise that you'll stay together as a family . . . no matter what?"

Tommy's father leans over his bed and says reassuringly, "We promise, Tommy, no matter what. Now try to get some rest, son."

"I love you, Mom, Dad. Everything's going to be fine, isn't it?" Tommy whispers as he drifts off.

Lauren wipes away her tears and kisses his cheek. "Yes, Tommy, everything is going to be fine. Sweet dreams, my sweet little boy."

Thomas and Lauren settle into the chairs next to Tommy's bed, holding his hands lovingly while he sleeps.

In the space of a heartbeat, Sarakiel and Tezalel rise from their seats in the hospital lobby. "Looks like Tommy's ready to go home," Tezalel announces as he straightens his uniform blazer and adjusts his white silk tie.

"Yes, it looks as though they won't have to do another surgery in the morning," Sarakiel announces proudly. "Tommy made his own plans about that, didn't he?"

"He sure did," his guardian angel agrees as he looks at the grains of sand passing through the miniature hourglass watch on his wrist. "It's time to fly!"

Chapter 49

Michael stands atop the Empire State Building in his Infinity Airways pilot uniform wearing his Sword of Light and Truth strapped firmly on his hip. He quietly watches as a multitude of angels and his staff of Infinity flight attendants help to move the lingering ghosts forward to the Light. Under the fully illuminated moon, a warm wind gently blows through his hair as Gabriel, holding his trumpet of gold, flies up to join him.

"How's it going up here tonight in the Big Apple, Gabriel?" asks Michael. The two archangels look out in wonderment at the manifestation that The Creator and Heaven have combined, forming the infinite aspects of the world-famous city that never sleeps. "What a magnificent place. It is wondrous to see that throughout these five boroughs, there are over eight million inhabitants worshipping twenty-four hours a day, displaying a multitude of their cultural, religious, and spiritual disciplines. New York City should inspire a worldwide audience that unity can exist in the heart of such diverse self-expression."

"Yes, indeed, it is most spectacular, Michael," replies Gabriel, holding his trumpet to his chest. He looks over the city, sending out messages of love. "There is prayer in the whisper of the night, prayer in the sound of traffic, prayer in the songs sung, prayer in the speech spoken, and gloriously, even prayer in workers working. Which is what our angels have been doing here relentlessly and unceasingly," he says with an irritated tone in his voice. He passes his arm across the vast night landscape of the city's skyline.

Michael looks to Gabriel in silent agreement. He understands Gabriel's frustration. Like his own, Gabriel's strength and power are formidable; his loyalty and faith are unwavering. As an archangel, Gabriel's sense of self runs deep and true, and his sense of The Infinite Creator is all-encompassing. Two of the greatest archangels ever created stand on the threshold of eternity as they look out, not only on New York City, but also the world.

"Have you noticed over there, Michael? It's getting bigger." Gabriel looks imploringly at his leader as he points to the jagged pitch-black tear in the sky, a virtual rip in the fabric of space and time.

Michael responds sharply as concern over his fellow angels and humanity is uppermost in his mind. He wastes no time in a prolonged explanation. "The forces separating the dimensional planes are weakening. The Ascension seems to be moving closer and closer, giving humanity less time. The disturbances on this planet caused by the scheming of the Dark Side are literally tearing away the very opportunities our human friends will need in the days and years ahead."

Gabriel nods and points beneath them with his shining trumpet. "Below are millions upon millions of angels working diligently in love, peace, and joy, healing this city and its people that was once again the target in the efforts of a few to put fear into the citizens of not only New York but the world," Gabriel adds. "Look how this city after all these years is still surrounded by a celestial band of angelic beings playing their golden harps with a heavenly harmonic resonance. The penetrating sound of healing is occurring on multiple levels for the souls that still have not crossed to the Other Side. Tremendous healing is continually being offered for their grieving friends and families. And even more angels are healing the victims of the more recent terrorist attacks, not only here in New York City, but everywhere in the world."

Michael's handsome features take on an ominous expression. The commander of archangels seethes with turbulence and unrest at the lack of more options. "These ghosts have to move forward, to help lighten the heavy vibrational load on this magnificent planet. These spirits are enmeshed in discord," Michael states emphatically as he pulls his crystalline sword from its golden scabbard. He waves the sword while observing the myriad of healing angels working below. Deep, luminescent rays flare into blue and pure white flames while arcs of fiery energy flow together and spin away like fireworks, exploding into the night air. "We have to cut the cords that bind these deceased peoples to their loved ones on Earth and allow these souls to rise to the eternal Love of The Creator."

"We are putting forth as much influence as we are allowed down there, Michael. Our messengers are working unceasingly to increase the human awareness and reception of the higher frequencies," Gabriel reports with more irritation than intended. "But the Dark Side is very successful in broadcasting the lower frequencies, in the slower, denser vibrations. All day and all night, humanity receives their evil signals, keeping them stuck in thinking that there is nothing else."

Gabriel notices that Michael is wavering precariously as he looks below. Michael rests his right hand on the hilt of his weapon and uses it like a walking cane to steady himself.

"Are you okay, Michael?" questions Gabriel as he edges closer to Michael. Gabriel notices the dark shadows under Michael's eyes. Looking weary and distressed, Michael's pursed lips confirm to Gabriel that his friend and leader is deep in thought.

"I'm so tired," Michael confesses to his brother archangel. The archangel commander gazes past Gabriel to the heavens. "My frustration with this situation is growing day after day, year after year, century after century, millennium after millennium. We have been putting out the messages in about every way imaginable, and they are just not getting it. How do we open their hearts, Gabriel? How do we open their eyes to the reality of their own existence?"

Michael gives a deep sigh and utters in disappointment. "Even the Wanderers, who came here for this anticipated shift—bringing in the higher dimensions—have entered the illusion. Knowingly they took on the limited human awareness as well as the human form, thinking that their advanced status would somehow permit them to swiftly resolve the distortions of the Veil. They were wrong, Gabriel, as few have succeeded in cleansing the sleep from their eyes. Like the humanity they came to serve, the majority of them are caught up in this dimensional drama on Earth—unable to remember who they are, where they come from, and what their mission is. Look all around—evidence of the shift is unmistakable yet so many are sound asleep."

"I agree. Our angels are here nonstop, Michael, speaking to every soul every moment of every day, broadcasting through the channel of love, sharing inspired revelations, and foretelling future events to guide them on their life's journey. These celestial messengers are shining Light through the Veil of Forgetting in an effort to awaken the knowledge and self-awareness that slumber in humanity's soul. Many awaken to hear their call, yet few truly listen for fear that they are not worthy to receive such divine guidance." Gabriel adds, "Or worse, some remain unaware that we even exist at all."

"Sounds like you guys are giving up here!" interjects Semyaza laughingly, as he swoops in behind Gabriel and Michael with outstretched black wings. "You boys know that New York is my kinda town."

"Don't get your hopes up, my friend," Michael retorts defensively.

"Well, you have to admit, things are looking quite dark around here!" he roars devilishly, shaking the windowpanes in the surrounding buildings.

Eve flies in over the cityscape to join the archangels. "Semyaza, how nice to see you again. I heard you were in town. Thought I should come by and give you my best."

"Ha! Looks like your best is passed out on the hotel bed from all the excitement. Isn't that right, Michael?" Semyaza winks at Michael and laughs. "She can't even handle a few hours of shopping. Do you really think that your pathetic little crew of flight attendants is a match for my minions of evil who have been digging deep into the trenches of this town for over three centuries?"

Suddenly they are surrounded by hundreds of endarkened angels, a shadowy mass of malevolence. Michael scans the area, but Semyaza's minions are so numerous, and so closely packed, that it is difficult to separate their individual forms from their demon master. Their features are indistinguishable; their murky forms blend with the night sky. With the moon high above, only the silhouette of their merged wings displays any definition.

Semyaza flexes his sleek black wings, extending them to their impressive full width and then folds them snugly against his back under his black leather cape. The Lord of Darkness suddenly signals for everyone to leave the rooftop. His angels, fearsome and strong and exuding pure evil, now hover around the perimeter of the building. Their powerful ebony wings effortlessly outmaneuver those of Eve and Gabriel, squeezing them out of the way. Gabriel and Eve retreat, letting them have free rein. Gabriel and Eve choose to fly higher to see what eminent revelations are about to unfold below between Michael and Semyaza.

Chapter 50

"Even with your recent events of terror, Semyaza, we see individuals taking time to honor their own spirit. Harmony prevails among hundreds of different faiths," observes Michael, as he quickly draws his sword and points below. "On just about every block there is a temple, a church, a mosque, an ashram, or other place of worship. Homes are filled with sacred images and statues, altars, and shrines from all sorts of religions."

"Yes, isn't religion empowering, Michael? Do you remember the good old days when just a few religions ruled the world? It was, in fact, called the Dark Ages. Hmm, I wonder where they came up with that term," Semyaza muses as he strokes his moustache and goatee. "And now today there are more than ten thousand religions worldwide. Hmm, I wonder what they will call that in the years ahead." As his leather cloak whips about his tall muscular frame, Semyaza responds sharply, "And isn't it wonderful how willfully so many of these religious, fanatical terrorist organizations faithfully perform my evil acts of aggression and war? Motivated by power and greed, hiding behind their feigned love of God, they make it so easy for me to further political turmoil, enslaving and controlling these feeble little humans even more—the very souls you and your impotent angels upon high try to defend against my diabolical plans. You know, Michael, I still cannot understand why you find it necessary to try to protect this godforsaken wasteland!"

Michael ignores Semyaza's disparaging remarks. "You know, my friend, a spectacular part of this layover is to watch the millions of prayers chanted toward the heavens. For every prayer, for every request, that is made, a white arrow of hope carries it to our Creator. What an amazing sight. Don't you agree, Semyaza? Seeing all these prayerful arrows of light like channeled lightning being directed upward to the celestial skies?" Michael smiles as an arrow, flying straight and true, suddenly pierces Semyaza's cloak while he isn't looking.

"What the hell!" exclaims Semyaza noticing the resulting hole.

Semyaza's sharp tone brings Michael back to the matter at hand. "This may not be the Eden it once was, but it is still my charge to protect for all of eternity the humanity that our Creator has placed here," says Michael, vowing his allegiance and obedience to The One Infinite Creator.

"Oh, please, Michael!" exclaims Semyaza in disbelief. "I know, you'll tell me that four and a half billion out of the six and a half billion people on this planet believe in a higher power among fifteen thousand different human cultures. But don't forget, my pilot friend, that in their twisted holy beliefs, they have killed over one hundred sixty million people in just the last hundred years—all in the name of God! God is known everywhere and anywhere on this third-dimensional existence on Earth. And these so-called believers all want to book a seat on the flight to Heaven—First Class, of course!" he jokes. "And they are willing to kill each other for it!"

The archangel's tone hardens as his foe's demonic laughter cuts through him. Michael lashes out, "Yes, thanks to you!"

"Oh, no thanks are necessary—really! It's child's play, actually. To be honest with you, Michael, it's become really quite boring, you know," remarks Semyaza as he buffs his dark clawlike nails on his chest. "I have my people everywhere, controlling just about everything. In a city like this, I have the advertising industry working overtime to make sure everyone is feeling that they don't have enough; seems it has worked rather well on your shopping-crazed little angel trainee, Nicole," brags Semyaza. "And then, of course, there are the major news networks, one of my favorites." He winks. "They don't call it television *programming* for nothing. And the so-called men of this world are so consumed with their twenty-four-hour coverage of sports that most of those supersized couch potatoes have no clue to what's really going on. The real winners of this game called life are about to be announced, Michael. And they are not it!" Semyaza howls louder. "They are all losers . . . just like you!"

"The game is not over, Semyaza, and you know it!" Michael retaliates defensively.

"Oh, really, Michael? Well, let's see, my little jet jockey friend! We can't forget my control over the financial, publishing, film, and entertainment industries and even the weary, bankrupt transportation industry belongs to me. And last but by far not least, the Illuminati. Oh, I do feel a close kindred connection with that insatiable power-hungry secret society," he howls laughingly as he refers to his pride and joy, the shadowy conspiratorial organization that controls world affairs behind the scenes. The windows of buildings within several miles of the Empire State Building ripple like waves of fluid glass as the sound of Semyaza's voice reverberates loudly through the towering high-rises.

"Yes, and all of them wanting to rip away humanity's ticket to the eternity promised to them through The Creator." Michael swings his sword, pointing the sharp tip of the twenty-five-inch sharpened crystal blade at Semyaza. The sword captures the purity and glory of the celestial hero. Michael grips the clear crystalline handle with its platinum guard and pommel even tighter as blue and white arcs of pure energy, attuned to his celestial essence, flare into the vast star-filled darkness above.

"Thanks to your relentless evil broadcasting, you and your legions of fallen angels, all your minions of darkness, have succeeded in closing the hearts of many. Our human friends are tuned in, and many even addicted, to your evil messages of lack, the messages of fear, and the messages of hopelessness. You have studied our human friends very well. Every weakness is known and being exploited," Michael concedes as his word and his sword slice deeply into the Truth and Light.

"Cleverly through your advertising and marketing—through what I prefer to call them, your deceptions and lies, your manipulation and seduction—you actually are inducing human cooperation. If humanity's trend of this ignorant and blinded cooperation continues, rather than resisting the evil you perpetuate, it will very soon be too late for them to even try to resist. So shackled to the world of materiality, they will never ascend into the Fourth Dimension. It's true, Semyaza, in your relentless efforts of evil, you have carefully and strategically laid plans to overwhelm our human friends, both physically and spiritually," continues Michael walking closer and closer, his shimmering sword cutting through the cool night breeze.

"Why, Mike, was that a compliment?" asks Semyaza sarcastically.

"Remember, all of you at Infinity Airways," continues the Angel of Evil as he shouts up to Gabriel and Eve, "if they can be held at the lowest level of their dimension, in fear and in lack, they cannot take advantage of the dimensional leap at the upcoming shift of the cycles. Soon I'll have everyone so afraid that every plane, train and automobile will be empty. Too afraid to go anywhere or do anything, these spineless beings will miss their opportunities to balance their karma for this lifetime. Soon they'll be stuck in the Third Dimension again where I can have my way with them for all of eternity!" Semyaza roars with pure malevolent evil. "Indeed, with little or no resistance from humanity, I have created a world where humanity's search for power and control over others is far greater than their pathetic little soul's desire to evolve."

Semyaza returns his attention to Michael's sword. An unfathomable glare of evil and hatred is delivered to the Defender of Mankind. "In their sojourn through space and time, humanity has forgotten their spiritual essence, Michael. They have forgotten their true relationship, their divine connection with The Infinite Creator. There is no Law of One practiced here!"

Semyaza pushes Michael to the very edge of the building, with his broad chest up against the blade's tip. "A sword, Michael? Your fire and flame, your symbol of justice and retribution?" Semyaza snickers darkly as spectacular blue bolts of lightning radiate from Michael's sword. The flames burn deep blue in Semyaza's eyes. Michael wavers as Semyaza pushes back harder, flexing the sword's rigid crystal blade. "You may be thought of as one who puts up with no bullshit. One who separates the wheat from the chaff, the Light from the Dark, the Truth from the Untruth. But down here, Michael, you're powerless. Even your mighty Sword of Light and Truth has lost its power!" Semyaza grates on Michael's nerves and his pride.

Michael argues, tenaciously holding to his sword and to his divine beliefs about humanity. He grips both firmly, taking an aggressive stance. "Our friends, walking in faith, must be willing to act upon what they are given, for they are never given more than they can handle. They need to understand that The Creator has done Its part. Now humanity is to do theirs. As co-creator of this planet in charge of spiritual evolution of humanity, I serve The One Infinite Creator. We will force no one to hear, to act, to live in the divine message of Infinite Love."

"Captain Mike Smith, please! You sound like a damn broken record. Let's cut to the chase now, old friend. When are you going to decide to get on the winning team? It's so bloody obvious that they aren't going to make it—again. Generation after generation, cycle after cycle, the following of their old ways gets these pathetically predictable souls nowhere. You will never win this one, Michael!" boasts Semyaza, radiating a glow of satisfaction.

Michael forces his sword further into Semyaza's chest, boldly daring to act outside the expectations of his hierarchal position, refusing to be a doormat to the evil forces of the Dark Side. "Only the sword of an archangel can destroy another angel," he announces. Although less in stature than others in the hierarchical world, Semyaza's physical appearance rivals the perfection of Michael. His demeanor holds confidence and command equal to that of Michael. Michael hesitates a moment longer, looking thoughtfully at the smooth crystalline surface of the sword's blade. The moonlight reflects on the razor-sharp edge as the archangel's own power and energy continue to flow through the sword.

With all eyes still on them, Semyaza's quiet tone carries to everyone present. "You can't be serious, Michael?" Michael nods thoughtfully and

186   GINA E. JONES

continues. Semyaza realizes that Michael is indeed very serious. The ability of the Lord of Darkness is about to be tested to its ultimate limits. Then everyone will know exactly how he measures up against the hallowed leader of the archangels.

Michael takes a defensive stance, ready to slay the dark evil that is devouring humanity's very soul. Semyaza moves to a more advantageous position, providing a better view for all his angels watching the confrontation between The Creator's greatest warriors. Michael's face is now more fully lit by the moon. The leader of the archangels lunges, his blade striking with enough force to dislodge planets from their orbits. Yet Semyaza stands firm, while at the same time unassuming and nonthreatening. As Gabriel watches below, along with the other angels, he gains a greater respect for Semyaza. For Semyaza not only deflects most of Michael's expertly aimed thrusts but actually drives him back a few steps—without a weapon. Then, to everyone's amazement, Michael falters, not following up on what is perceived to be a definite advantage.

With his sword raised once more, Michael takes another jab at the Lord of Darkness and misses as Semyaza's reflexes are quicker than lightning. Realizing his mistake a second too late, Michael flinches as Semyaza ferociously kicks his weapon out of his firm grip, sending it over the side of the Empire State Building. Crimson lightning bolts crackle, and red sparks now explode brightly as the weapon is now attuned to Semyaza's spirit instead of Michael's. Much to everyone's astonishment, the sword spins wildly, riding the current of destiny as it falls. Michael grimaces as his weapon hits to the concrete sidewalk more than a quarter of a mile below. The crystalline Sword of Light and Truth, the most famous sword in all of Creation, shatters on the pavement of Fifth Avenue, scattering minute splinters of Semyaza's energy everywhere. The ground-shaking impact is felt instantly throughout the Celestial City as Semyaza screams aloud, "Earth is my dominion!" The windows in the surrounding buildings start to shake and shatter. Suddenly, they all explode simultaneously, ever so violently—sending glass and debris throughout the city of old ghosts and frayed nerves.

Semyaza's rich deep-set green eyes gaze down at the kneeling archangel with the utmost look of authority. Semyaza laughs devilishly, brushing back his black hair resting on his broad shoulders, as he pulls Michael up with his strong muscled arms. Semyaza's sleek black wings fold primly against his back. "Why don't you come and work with me, Michael? We can have some great times together." In a friendly effort to recruit him, Semyaza throws a comradely arm around Michael's shoulder. His calm demeanor belies the sarcasm in his tone. "Call me anytime; we'll talk. You've got my number! I can even get you in touch with a fabulous tailor in Chinatown and get you out of that hideous pilot uniform."

Semyaza's majestic wings extend fully, and he casts himself forward into the steady night's breeze. The winds of change begin to swirl violently when his dark angels follow in his wake. Gabriel and Eve hover above as Michael staggers to sit down. Gabriel tries to hold Eve back so Michael can be alone as he looks pensively out over the cityscape. She defiantly ignores the archangel, pushing his arm aside, and descends to be with Michael. Gabriel normally embodies the essence of serenity; however, in this moment, it disconcerts him immensely to see his commander so distraught, so diminished, that he prefers not to remain in Michael's presence.

# Chapter 51

"What are you going to do, Michael?" whispers Eve as she lowers herself to sit by his side.

"Eve, I have always considered the possibilities of my victories, but now I must also consider the possibility of my defeat. Semyaza grows stronger every day. If I should fail—no longer able to defend Heaven and Earth—then there is none to fight in my stead. I may indeed have to embrace my own worst fear as there is no one prepared to take my place. This thought troubles me deeply, Eve."

Michael looks up at the silence his statement has caused. Eve stares at him with a heightened degree of concern. She struggles a half-smile.

Michael continues, "I loathe the thought of leaving them. However, I must if it is their choice. It is unfortunate that most of The Creator's creations are exerting their Right of Free Will against their Creator. But, again, it is their choice." A certain sadness and compassion in his eyes reveal his knowledge of the ills of the world and his desire to raise humanity to a higher dimension.

Unsure of how to react, Eve holds back her eternally suppressed desire to hug him, to be one with him. "Oh, Eve, don't they realize that it will be a true Hell for those who don't ascend? How I weep for those who do not know The Creator. For those—by the very nature of their behavior and their beliefs—are worshipping Semyaza, the Lord of Darkness."

Torn as to what to say, Eve affirms Michael's observations. "Indeed, Semyaza seems to have done a masterful job of manipulating everything and everyone down here. Through the power of fear, he skillfully continues to manipulate the fears of humanity with his timely orchestration of this world's conflicts and events." The heaviness of Michael's defeat weighs sullenly on her every word.

Michael pauses then hesitates, uncertain how to continue. Throughout his existence, he never needed to ask for anything—never needed what he is now searching so desperately for—something that no other archangel had ever asked for. Indeed, something no other heavenly host seemed to need—a companion who is his equal. An equal whose truth stands strong and firm against any temptation, not falling apart under the weight of the evil offered by Semyaza. Someone who has experienced similar trials and tribulations. He longs for a companion who is equal in courage, unafraid to question conventional wisdom. A partner that won't hold him in too much esteem to ever question or challenge him. Someone to help him save humanity.

Eve is torn, nevertheless unable to release her feelings inside. The usually stoic commander of the heavenly hosts allows a faint smile, understanding Eve's inability to ease his anguish and agony. During his continued silence, she watches as his brilliant radiance glows dimly.

Michael's eyes darken with disquiet as he lowers his head into Eve's lap and weeps. Eve remains stiff and immobilized, refraining from any kind of affection while Michael continues to cry in his darkest moment on Earth.

Chapter 52

BEEP! BEEP! BEEP! BEEP!

"Thomas! Something's happening to Tommy! Quick—get the doctor!" screams Lauren, awakened by the sound of the blaring heart monitor next to Tommy's bed. The screen indicates a flat line. "Somebody help! Tommy! Somebody, help us, please!"

Within seconds, Dr. Harrell and a team of technicians come running in, surrounding Tommy. The defibrillation paddles are applied. His bare chest lifts spastically off the bed as shock after shock is administered. Tommy's parents stand back in absolute horror as the doctor and his staff do what they can to save their son.

"This can't be happening! Don't take my son!" Lauren goes into complete denial. The scene seems surreal, as if she and her husband are watching a movie—unable to comprehend the drama involving their own child as it plays out before their very eyes.

"Mom? Mom, why are you crying?" says Tommy as he looks over at his parents. "Dad, please tell Mom I'm okay." The resuscitation team continues. "Look at all the nurses and doctors! What's happening?" yells the teenager confused by all the commotion as they repeatedly call his name. "Hey, man, I'm right here!"

"Tommy!" Sarakiel waves to him across the room.

"You came back. You said you would see me again. Uh, I didn't realize that it was going to be so soon. Don't you have another flight to catch?" asks Tommy innocently.

Sarakiel smiles. "Yes, that's why we're here. We have to make sure that you get home safely."

"You already got me home, though," Tommy states innocently as he looks around his hospital room. "See, there's my mother and father."

"Yes, but New York City is not really your home. Whenever you're ready, we'll take you there," Tezalel says with a smile.

"Tezalel! Dude, you look so different. Wait a minute; you guys aren't wearing your uniforms. And, hey, I'm not talking! Oh, man, that is very cool. Somehow I'm just thinking, and you can hear me; and I can hear you. This is so unbelievably rad! I can't wait to tell my parents—"

"Tommy, we would like to help you get home," conveys Tezalel. "There are so many people who are very anxious to see you."

"This is so cool. I've never felt so free of pain and full of love like this in my whole life. It's what I've always wanted. What's going on, Tezalel?" Tommy asks excitedly as he tries to grasp the nature of his present circumstances. "You and Sarakiel, are you angels? I mean, I thought you guys were flight attendants. And how can you be here if I'm dead?"

"We are here to assist you on your way home, Tommy. At Infinity Airways, *flight* is short for *flying to the Light*. Granted not everyone that flies with us passes on, but it is part of our job to help those that do." Tezalel smiles at him warmly.

"There's someone who wants to see you, Tommy," conveys Sarakiel, guiding an older woman out of a brilliant burst of light.

"Grandma Ruth! What are you doing here? Mom was just talking about you earlier." Tommy slowly realizes that something truly profound is happening.

"Yes, I know, Tommy. I heard her." His grandmother smiles a smile of compassion.

"Wait, didn't you die when I was like thirteen? Right before I ran away from home?" asks Tommy, his thoughts traveling faster than the speed of light. His grandmother nods as a look of empathy crosses her face. "You were the only one I could talk to, Grandma, the only one who really ever seemed to care about me. And then you died . . . you left me all alone in this screwed-up world!"

"It was what you wanted, what you asked me to do to help you fulfill your mission for this incarnation. You're right. I really did care about you, but I never left you, Tommy. I was with you during every minute of every day. I was with you through every high and every low. And I am with you now."

The room is silent. "I've died too, haven't I?" He looks down in confusion at the medical team. "But I'm not dead; I'm right here with you guys. But . . . but my body's down there. And by the looks of things, it doesn't look like it's going so well." He stares intently at the scene below as the doctor and nurses frantically perform CPR, trying to resuscitate his heart.

"I'm right here! Look up here guys!" he yells in an effort to get his parents attention. Lauren and Thomas watch in a state of shock.

"Tommy," his grandmother says without speaking. "I've come to take you home. You can try to talk to your parents, but they will not be able to hear you. You can put your arms around them if you like, so that they can feel your energy and your love." Tommy fretfully looks down at his parents, wishing they could see him.

"No, this can't be happening! This is my home. Please, I can't stand to see them so upset!" Tommy cries, "I have to go back and tell them that I'm all right. They don't need to be upset. I'm right here! I'm okay!"

Tezalel explains to Tommy what his life's purpose has been. "You came to this lifetime to bring your parents back together, to love each other as they did before they were rich and famous. In this lifetime you chose to show your parents how lost they have become."

"But there has to be a way to show them I'm okay. There just has to be!" insists Tommy as he looks around. He suddenly eyes his old, worn baseball cap sitting on the windowsill. "I've seen this in the movies! I know one of you or all of you can knock that cap onto the floor, right? Please tell me it's true. I just have to give them a sign, some kind of sign. Please, Grandma, won't you help me?"

"Your mission was very clear and has been executed in the most selfless way. By running away, becoming HIV positive, and returning seriously injured, you showed your parents how lost they have become. And you got your wish in the end, Tommy—to be a loving family. Even though it was for just one hour," Grandma Ruth conveys with great compassion.

His guardian angel continues proudly, "And in loving memory and honor to you, Tommy, your parents will devote much of their time and money into AIDS research and establishing shelters for runaway teens all across this country." Tommy looks at everyone in awed amazement. "In their pain and heartache over their loss of you, they will help thousands of teenagers to be reunited with their families. Your parents end up hiring Joe and Ron to train hundreds in locating and counseling runaways in this foundation that will be named in your honor, Tommy. Ron and Joe will finally have the income they need to support their families while they continue to help put other families back together."

"Wow, all 'cause of me?" asks Tommy, humbled by the impact that his life and his death will have on so many. "And my grandma, of course!" Tommy winks to her, proud in his new revelation.

Grandma Ruth returns the wink and pats him Tommy on the back. "Yes, you should be proud of yourself. Now it's time for you to go home." Sarakiel, Tezalel, Tommy's guardian angel, and Grandma Ruth fill themselves with a shimmering white light. "We're ready when you are, Tommy. You just let us know when," encourages his grandmother as her loving energy embraces his very essence. "The rest of your family is waiting for you."

"But wait!" begs Tommy. "What about the baseball cap? Please, they need some kind of sign!"

Chapter 53

As the brilliant swirling energy of Light and Love guides Tommy toward the closed hospital window, he passes slowly between his parents who are arm in arm. They stare out the window in absolute grief, distraught by the rapid turn of events. Suddenly, out of nowhere, Tommy's baseball cap miraculously falls off the sill to the floor as his parents each feel a cool tingling sensation brush by their cheeks. Thomas leans over to pick up his son's hat. An unusual quiver ripples across his skin as he eyes it nervously. Not only has the large bloodstain that he had seen only moments earlier disappeared, but it has returned to its original brand new condition. Lauren and Thomas Wellington both shiver unexpectedly when loving energy is sent to them while they look up into the brilliant sky over New York City. An unexpected peacefulness overcomes them.

Tommy looks out over the spectacular city, instinctively knowing he is, in fact, going home. As they move upward, a mass of incredible light forms a tunnel stretching into the infinite. Everyone stares up into the tunnel while suspended motionlessly. Grandma Ruth looks to Tommy. He smiles back confidently, "I'm ready."

Tommy's body begins to move forward. "Wow, I'm moving by my thoughts. Man, this is so cool! I could have used this when I was hitchhiking across the country." Everyone smiles at the intrigued teenager. "Look! No legs or arms. I'm flying like an angel, like you, but without wings."

Tezalel telepathically conveys, "Tommy, you can do what we do and even more."

Entering the tunnel, he hears a loud continuous *whooshing* noise all around. "That's the most beautiful sound ever; it's like chimes and crystals.

194

Sounds like none I've never heard before on Earth." Still being the curious young boy that he has always been, Tommy reaches out to touch the walls of the tunnel. They move like waves on the ocean. Crystal sparks explode into brilliant colors as they dance with the synchronistic crystal-like chimes when his fingers touch the surface. Tommy is overwhelmed at the beauty and magnificence of this unique form of transportation.

Love is continuously communicated as they proceed up the tunnel. Time, mass, and space seem to blend into one as they progress on their journey. Looking forward, in great anticipation of what is to come, Tommy sees a brilliant Light growing stronger and stronger. Continuing to scan all around, his eyes distinguish amazingly brilliant whites and gold. The teenage runaway is ready to enjoy all the wonders of Creation without the overshadowing pain and heartache that he had experienced his entire life on Earth.

Looking back at his angelic escorts, Tommy admires their airy wings like long feathered fingers of transparent white light. Wearing long robes, flowing and white, belted around their waists by golden cords, Tommy realizes that these radiant, luminous flight—*flying to the Light*—attendants are beyond human description. Hovering over their heads are rings of bright golden light. "You're more beautiful than any angel painting I've ever seen," he says to them wordlessly. As they continue to ascend, all communication is thought and emotion, enveloped with peace and unconditional love. "I feel your awesome strength and power; and yet, at the same time, you're so gentle and loving—beyond what can be experienced on Earth."

Traveling at an incredible speed through unfathomable distances in a brief moment in time, the tunnel suddenly ends; and they are suspended in a vast universe of universes comprised of the most amazing brilliant stars. Tommy watches the evolution of quasars, black holes, clusters of galaxies, planets, stars, and nebulas in an instant, as all time is now. As they begin to form and emerge from pure consciousness, he sees that everything is energy.

A calm peace overtakes Tommy, and suddenly there's nothing. Total stillness surrounds him. He begins to feel like *he* is a million tiny pieces of conscious energy spread across the cosmos, like vapor, as if he is part of everything. *So this is what death is.* Something unexpectedly catches Tommy's attention. He notices brilliant lights moving so rapidly that they appear as white streaks in space. "Where are all those spiraling white lights going so quickly?" asks Tommy as he tries to locate the planet he just left behind.

"Earth. Those are angels who have eagerly chosen to serve humanity," Sarakiel explains. "Just like Tezalel and me, they are working for Infinity to help bring humanity home."

"Where is Earth?" he asks breathlessly. Looking back, he notices that the tunnel is gone. "All I see are stars. My God, it is so beautiful!" The dome of Heaven sparkles with the fire of millions of stars that glow radiantly against a deep dark sapphire background.

"It's still down there, Tommy. It's just a speck of light now," communicates Sarakiel as she points, helping him to find it among the multitude of twinkling lights. "It's beyond the horizon of time in your visible universe." He stares as the stars beckon and entice him into their vastness of space, devoid of fear, remorse, and judgment.

Tommy resists the stars' incessant call, continuing instead toward the highest spire in Heaven. Before he can ask another question or think another thought, he is suddenly engulfed by a brilliant golden Light, brighter than the Sun, more radiant, more powerful. Tommy turns and looks at Sarakiel, Tezalel, his guardian angel, and his grandmother as he feels this magnificent energy throughout every part of his being. He savors its warmth and revels in the soothing Light without thought or consideration for anything else, truly living in the moment. At first, it is so peaceful, even intoxicating, and yet a little disquieting for Tommy. He has never known such freedom while on Earth. The freedom he now experiences is limited only by the boundaries of the infinite cosmos. And it is freedom that he is not completely sure he deserves.

"It is time for us to leave, Tommy. We have brought you home, your real home. Your flight is finished. It is time for you to become one, again, with The Light, with The Infinite Creator. We love you, Tommy. Enjoy your homecoming," convey the Infinity Airways angels. They no longer have any semblance of being human or an angel, as each one glows as pure celestial energy brighter than the brightest star.

"Thank you for taking such good care of me. And for bringing me home. Maybe you'll see me on another flight, guys." He laughs joyfully, "Do you have a frequent flier program?"

Grandma Ruth brags proudly, "Sarakiel, look how Tommy is so incredibly receptive to The Light."

"Yes, and as he opens himself up even further to receive, more golden Light of Love will flow in. He is experiencing Love like he could never have experienced on Earth. Even the last hour with his parents can't compare to what he is feeling now, what he is being now," adds Sarakiel.

For a period of infinite timelessness, Tommy remains suspended as The Light penetrates the top of his head, pulsating, and vibrating down through his spiritual being. Microscopic particles of The Light radiate throughout his astral body, transforming his very existence. "See, all the memories of sadness, isolation, pain, and sufferings are removed. He feels The Light cleansing his very soul," reflects his guardian angel as it watches

Tommy closely. The golden Light that permeates Tommy's being turns to pure whiteness. His soul now suffused with unconditional Love.

Tezalel conveys, "He knows his journey is over; his separation from The Light has been a learning experience, and now he is delighted to return to The Source—to The Creator."

As Tommy feels his being overflowing with the white Light, he sees his grandma Ruth. Behind her are Grandpa Norton and other family members. Even his favorite sixth-grade teacher is there. Although overwhelmed by the awesome sight before him, the feelings of love and joy conveyed by the spiritual beings are even more overwhelming. They are cheering for Tommy, showing encouragement and loving support. Welcome Home is the message emanating from this infinite place.

Tommy thinks to himself, *I'm in Heaven!*

"Indeed, you are, Tommy," conveys his guardian angel. "Indeed, you are."

Chapter 54

Nicole rubs her eyes as she looks around at the magnificence and luxury of the richly appointed room as she lies in the Louis XVI-style bed. High ceilings with crystal chandeliers, the silk wall coverings, and the deeply carved crown moldings and wainscoting bring a smile to her face. "Now this is the way to live!"

She springs out of bed, remembering the clothes she bought the evening before. Pouring the bags out all over the bed, Nicole surrounds herself with colorful garments of silk, wool, and linen. She stands before the full-length mirror, trying on each and every item several times, dancing and twirling around the spacious suite. As she smells the scents of the new fabrics as she watches herself in the mirror. Nicole exclaims excitedly, "How intoxicating and exciting it is to have the power to purchase things that I want."

Two white doves are cooing on the window's ledge as they peck each other gently. "Yes, my little friends, the Sun has risen on a brand-new day for me in ways that I can't quite understand, but I sense something wonderful in the air," exclaims Nicole as she looks out the window. She notices several cracks running through the glass panes. "Hmm, I wonder how that happened."

Turning on the television, Nicole becomes utterly engrossed in the programming. Skinny models slink down runways, showing off the latest fashion, jewelry and makeup. Slick new cars glide around beautiful mountains. Soap opera stars slap their two-timing lovers across the face. Nicole flips to the news channels and becomes extremely disturbed. She is barraged with scenes of terrorism, death, war, hate crimes, and bombings.

The local news stations report the bizarre occurrence of windows shattering in homes and businesses everywhere overnight; yet there is no evidence of an earthquake to cause such extensive damage. The weather reports show flooding, storms, and hurricane destruction with forecasts for more of the same. Unable to bear another minute, she turns it off, consumed with fear. She sits on the bed amidst her new clothes, shaking, and crying. "What in this world is happening? Can't there be just one day where everyone gets along?"

After a few minutes in silence, the fear and dread begin to subside. She looks through some hotel magazines to take her mind off what she has just seen. However, Nicole is overcome once again by a compelling desire to acquire new and stylish merchandise. Every glossy page promises the finest of everything and demands that she be as beautiful and fashionable as she can.

Looking through the newspaper that was delivered under the hotel door, Nicole becomes even weaker. "Lord, what is happening?" Page after page—reporting more terrorism, death and crime, rape, gang wars, car bombings—lowers her already diminished angelic energy even further. With the turn of every page, she glances at the photographs and news articles. "It's just too much for me!" she exclaims, tossing the paper aside. *The news of all this world's events is more than I can handle or even want to think about.*

Nicole notices the alarm clock on the nightstand. *There's three more hours left before crew pick up. I'm going shopping!* She leaves abruptly, heading for the main lobby.

The friendly doorman holds the brass and glass hotel door open for Nicole. She steps out into the bright mid-morning sunshine, taking in a deep breath of pleasure before she heads toward Fifth Avenue. "This time I'm going to get what I want. No one, I mean no one, not even Captain Smith, is going to tell me what to do or what to buy. And what does an airline pilot know about style, fashion, and the latest trends anyway?"

Chapter 55

"Blue . . . no, red. I love the red one. Oh, wait a minute. Let me try the black one on over there as well. Oh, yes! Yes! The black one is so divine!"

The sales clerk opens Nicole's dressing room door. "What about this very chic white silk dress? Isn't it beautiful?" The clerk hands the dress hanger to Nicole.

"What? White? I'm sick and tired of white. I want color—lots of magnificent color." Nicole shoves the dress back into the clerk's hand. "Go on . . . quickly now and don't forget the matching shoes!"

The sales assistant in Saks Fifth Avenue becomes increasingly flustered as Nicole demands to try on more and more clothes, shoes, and hats from the different departments. While in the fitting room, Nicole is completely oblivious to the prices on the clothing that she is feverishly trying on.

"Do you think this one makes me look fat?" Nicole asks, suddenly self-conscious of her body. "I mean my thighs, do they seem wide to you? Oh, by the way, what time is it?" She rambles on, "Am I too tall for this skirt?"

"No, miss, and it's eleven o'clock," the clerk responds politely.

Immediately Nicole pushes an armload of clothes to the exhausted clerk to take to the register. "Damn! If I hurry, I'll have just enough time to get back to my hotel room to change into that wretched-looking Infinity Airways uniform," Nicole exclaims as she hurriedly gets dressed. She stumbles in her new red sling-back sandals as she rushes to the check-out desk.

"That will be $6,446.66, including tax, miss."

"How much! That is absolutely ridiculous!" exclaims Nicole. The sales clerk is taken aback by Nicole's unexpected outburst. "Oh, I'm sorry. I didn't mean the clothes. I meant this pathetically minute amount of money that Infinity Airways gave me as an allowance for this incredible New York City layover. It's a long story, sorry. What is a girl to do when she—" Nicole starts to complain.

"You could apply for our credit card and save an instant 20 percent on today's purchases," the clerk exclaims enthusiastically. "We'll just charge everything to the card. Here's your application." Nicole stares curiously at the document.

"You mean to tell me that if I fill this out, I can have all these clothes?" questions Nicole.

"Yes, ma'am, and anything else you see!" She points to the strategically placed displays overflowing with colorful, eye-catching impulse items for shoppers to purchase while waiting in line.

Nicole grabs a handful of accessories off the racks near the register and brusquely hands them to the clerk. Then hastily she fills out the highlighted areas on the application. "Now this really makes me mad. Why didn't Michael tell me about getting a credit card when we were out last night?" she mumbles as she fills in the appropriate boxes. "Who does he think he is?"

Looking over at the stacks of new clothes on the counter, Nicole asks again, "All of it?"

"Yes, ma'am, it's that simple! Just fill out these few lines, sign at the bottom, and you'll be set to go with all these fabulously beautiful things you picked out. By the way, did I tell you just how gorgeous you looked in all those outfits?"

"Yes, you did," Nicole replies politely. "Like eighteen times." Nicole hands the credit card application to the sales clerk.

"Great! Another few commissions like this should cover it," the sales clerk mumbles to herself. *I can't believe I'm only thirty years old, and I'm on the verge of filing bankruptcy . . . again. Now, all I have to do is fill in a few more false social security numbers and credit card numbers on these applications, and I'll be out of this mess once and for all!*

With a blink of an eye, the purchases are approved. Both the salesclerk and Nicole are ecstatic. Noticing the time, Nicole becomes frustrated that she still has not shopped to her heart's content. She quickly leaves the store, and then decides to stroll leisurely through the crowded streets of New York City, with shopping bags in hand, back to the hotel.

# Chapter 56

The polished brass hotel elevator doors open slowly. Inside is Nicole—overly accessorized and fashionably dressed in her Infinity Airways flight attendant uniform. Her elegantly swept-up hair accentuates the heavily applied makeup over her flawless complexion. The hotel bellman standing next to her struggles with the luggage cart full of shopping bags. Wearing dark oversized Lauren Wellington designer sunglasses, Nicole steps out of the elevator acting like some kind of Hollywood celebrity. She strolls into the hotel lobby with an attitude of superiority and arrogance that does not befit an angel.

"Looks as though Nicole has had a very busy morning," Michael remarks casually to Eve.

"It is ten minutes past the scheduled pick-up time. Gabriel and the rest of the flight attendants are in the transportation van ready to go to the airport," Eve quips as Nicole slinks up as if she is on a fashion show runway.

"My, my, looks like you made the most of your layover, Nicole," smirks Eve, an air of cynicism surrounds her words. "You'll have to tell me how one can acquire so much with so little, especially in this city."

"Eve, would you go with—" starts Michael as he raises his eyebrow.

"With the bellman to the van so you can talk to Nicole, privately? Sure, no problem," says Eve as she finishes Michael's request. She looks back at Nicole and Michael with mounting frustration as she leaves the hotel.

"Michael, please be a dear and tip the bellman for me," instructs Nicole, pointing to the struggling young man walking behind her as she walks toward the hotel entrance. The young bellman frantically tries to keep the shopping bags from falling onto the floor.

Michael steps firmly in her path. "The Sun is outside, Nicole. You can take the glasses off if you want. Now, please tell me, where did you get the money to purchase—" Michael resolutely begins to inquire.

Nicole melodramatically raises her hand, cutting him off mid-sentence. "Don't even go there, Michael. I don't want to hear it!" declares Nicole with an air of defiance, similar to what she had seen earlier portrayed on the soap operas. "Now let's get going, or we are going to be late. You know, we've got a schedule to keep."

Michael holds her gaze. "I'm well aware of our schedule, Nicole."

She removes her sunglasses, propping them on top of her head. Detecting a hint of interrogation in his tone, more than simple curiosity, Nicole postures herself defensively.

"Where did you get the money to purchase all those things? At Saks Fifth Avenue, no less?" demands Michael, pointing to the bags on the luggage cart.

"I didn't need any money. I have a credit card! It is amazing all the things you can get with one of those cute, little plastic things."

"Great! An angel with a credit card," Michael remarks irreverently.

"Ask and ye shall receive; surely you remember that one, Michael," Nicole replies sarcastically, her impatience clinging to every word. "We really need to be going. I want to make sure that bellman puts all my things in the van properly. There's this fabulous little red dress that is just to die for—"

"Nicole! I'm *asking* for an answer, and so I shall *receive* one." Michael remains firm and undaunted by Nicole's glaring looks as he probes further. Nicole becomes annoyed at the invasion of privacy when he studies her more closely. She stares back defiantly, standing her ground.

"Okay, if you really need to know," Nicole concedes quickly, "I filled out a credit card application and saved 25 percent! Aren't you impressed? What does it matter anyway? I got what I wanted," Nicole rambles as she turns on her heel and starts walking out the door toward the waiting van. She pulls the glasses from her head and puts them on as she looks over her shoulder to Michael. "Remember we have passengers who need to get to their final destinations on time. You know, flying to the Light and all that stuff."

# Chapter 57

In the crew transportation van seated on the first row, Nicole tries to hold her hair from flying around. She leans over to the driver and indignantly taps his shoulder. "Close the window. My hair is going to be ruined!"

"I'm sorry, miss, but your perfume is giving me a migraine. What is that anyway?" chokes the driver. He waves his hand past his nose then sneezes.

"I call it *Nicole*. It's a little bit of everything. I mixed these cute, little samples together. You know, a little bit of Passion, a splash of Dare, with a drop of Glow, and a hint of Desire." She shakes her head and shrugs her shoulders. "I can't remember the rest."

"Wow, now I understand why I have a headache," the driver replies as he rubs his forehead.

Quickly changing the subject, Nicole turns excitedly to Eve who sits with her hands folded on her lap, rigid, and correct. "You should have come shopping with me, Eve," she exclaims. "You could have seen all the fabulous things they have coming out for fall. I can't wait to come back and try them all on. And I got a credit card too. They're great!" Nicole pats Eve on the knee. "You probably have quite a few, huh?"

Looking sternly at Michael, Eve replies, "No, Nicole, I don't have any credit cards. While you were shopping, the rest of us were quite busy during the layover. Let's see, I assisted Senator Stevens as he passed over to the Other Side. Sarakiel and Tezalel were with Tommy Wellington in the hospital when it was his time to go, then we all—"

"What about the Westmans?" interrupts Nicole, excited by the drama between the doctor and his wife that had unfolded before her during the flight. "Does she die of lung cancer or something?"

"Now that's an interesting one," Itqal interjects eagerly. "Because you gave those magazines on ayurvedic medicine to Dr. Westman, he will divorce his wife, sell his medical practice, and move to India."

"Oops!" says Nicole, slinking down in the seat. "I was only trying to help. He was just being so impatient when I—"

"Oh, it's perfect! Don't you see how much he loves his wife, Nicole?" asks Itqal.

"He does?" questions Nicole in disbelief.

Tezalel joins in excitedly. "Oh, yes. Thanks to you, Dr. Westman actually saves his wife's life. If they had stayed together, she would have continued smoking, drinking, and eventually would have overdosed on a bunch of antidepressants, leading to an early death. But now, Mrs. Westman will hit an all-time low once she spends all of the money from the divorce settlement. After a period of deep reflection and soul searching, she will return to nursing, where she can support herself as well as care for others. It will be a very positive change for her and the planet. Before they incarnated, Lawrence and Nancy planned that things would be this way. Unfortunately, most of their family and friends in this dimension will never know what a truly loving sacrifice Lawrence has made to save his wife from a life of drugs, alcoholism, and depression."

"Wow, I never knew a few magazines could do all that," reflects Nicole.

Gabriel further explains to Nicole, "The other side of this arrangement is that Nancy's behavior gives cause for his departure so he may truly find a way to heal people. When Dr. Westman arrives there tomorrow, he will immediately put all his money into building a hospital with several ayurvedic doctors that he'll meet to avoid paying out a lot of money to Nancy and her money-hungry attorneys during their upcoming divorce. Again by doing so, this speeds up her side of their plan for this incarnation. Dr. Westman will be known as the doctor from the West when he remains in India, using his skills to help heal many of the sick and destitute people of that country."

"Yes, it is amazing how everything worked out," Michael interjects as he looks over at Eve. "Nancy will join Lawrence in India several years from now, around late 2009. They will remarry and work together happily in Service to Others, to serve and care for others unselfishly, readying them for their ascension to the next dimension."

"Wow, I would have never figured that out," admits Nicole innocently. "It would be nice to have my angelic vibrations back so I could see all these things too. I could really help people, you know!" Michael smiles proudly at Nicole, then glances over at Eve.

"Yes, I'm sure you could," says Eve, forcing a tone of encouragement.

"I mean, seriously! I could help all the women in New York City. I could help them to find the latest fashions and greatest styles at the best boutiques! I could tell them in advance which stores are going to have the best sales so they could get the best prices on . . ." Nicole rambles on.

Eve glares scornfully at the captain of the crew as she begs to understand his motivations. *Why on Earth did you bring her here, Michael? With all the challenges you have with Semyaza and his Forces of Darkness, why do you waste your time on an inexperienced, insignificant angel like Nicole?* Eve turns her attention to Nicole and gives her a cold quelling look that conveys more emphatically than any words in any language that she has no time for such foolishness. There is hushed silence in the van as they drive toward John F. Kennedy International Airport. Realizing that she has not impressed anyone, Nicole stares out the side window. The overcast gray sky only serves to dampen her mood.

Chapter 58

Following the crew briefing on the plane, Nicole tries to prepare herself for boarding while assisting in the first class galley. The new trainee feels flustered and inadequate because her vibrations are too low to access the passenger records for the flight.

"Oh, great. I'm flying blind!" exclaims Nicole. In her frustration, she slams closed *The Book of Flight.* "Infinity carries the most challenging people on the planet, and I can't access their records."

"You'll have to trust your inner guidance, Nicole, to get through this flight. Just believe you'll make the right decisions," Eve says knowingly as she enters the galley, "and you will."

Nicole's attention suddenly lands on an ailing woman being seated in the first row of coach. "I don't remember hearing about any sick passengers during the briefing," says Nicole haughtily.

"Mrs. Bradley is with us because she was denied boarding on the other airlines. She's gravely ill, Nicole, apparently vomiting and needing oxygen during flight," Eve responds calmly as they prepare for passenger boarding.

"Vomiting?" Nicole becomes alarmed and nauseated at the same time. "Is this when humans disgorge the contents of the stomach through the mouth?"

"Yes. Since she could die during the flight, the other airlines do not want to have to make an unscheduled landing somewhere."

Nicole, still repulsed by the thought of vomit, cannot stop staring at the woman. She is afraid that at any moment, disaster will strike. "Oh. I can see where the other airlines are coming from. After all, we're the ones stuck with the—the mess!"

"Remember, Nicole, everyone is here for a reason," Eve says mindfully. "Even you, as an angel, have much to discover and learn from our passengers. I guarantee you that each one can bring you rewarding lessons."

Nicole looks back at the poorly woman and mumbles to herself. "Okay and just how can I experience anything positive from someone on the verge of physical death?"

Chapter 59

Martin Peterson, a distinguished-looking large man in a business suit, sits in the Infinity Airways gate area with his open briefcase on his lap. Speaking into the microphone on the headset of his Blackberry mobile phone, his voice conveys a toughness born of experience. "Look, Frank, I'll be in LA as soon as I can get there. I don't know what in the hell is going on today. It seems that everything is out of my control. I've been sitting in this damn airport since six this morning. Like I told you earlier, my flights on three other airlines were cancelled. I don't know how in the hell it happened. But three times? Yes, like I said, two were due to some damn unknown mechanical reasons and the third one—the whole damn flight crew walked off the plane!" He darts a glance at his platinum diamond bezel Rolex watch before thrusting his fingers through his graying black hair. His eyes look tired and his face frustrated. "And this is the damnedest weather I've ever seen."

Martin closes his customized black leather Henk briefcase and tucks it safely behind his calves before crossing his legs "Yeah, yeah, well, I'm stuck flying commercial this time since the company's private jet is scheduled to pick up several members of the board for the annual meeting tomorrow." Martin glances over at the gate agent. "Yeah, right, my friend. These cattle-car operators don't care that I'm the president and CEO of a national multibillion-dollar real-estate-development company," scoffs Martin sarcastically in his frustration.

"Look, Frank, I'm finally booked on Infinity Airways, having spent most of my day so far sitting in broken airplanes and waiting in long lines. Yeah, well, I did manage to talk them out of the last first class seat and had to pay full price for it, of course. Okay, okay, buddy, just make sure everything is ready for that meeting. I'll call you when I get to LA."

As a self-described overachiever, Martin is dynamic at what he does. Business comes easily to him, and he constantly looks for new challenges. He finds most of his days too predictable, too routine. However, he realizes that this day of all days is not turning out to be that way.

Five seats over, another man, Kent Phillips, is talking on his cell phone. "Hello, Gladys, it's Kent. Sorry to call so late, but I was called in at the last minute to make a presentation to a potential client, a major corporation in Los Angeles. I need to cancel our meeting for this afternoon," he says glancing at the marked-up calendar in his personal planner. The smooth dark green leather is worn on the corners. Kent pulls anxiously on the double row of light black stitching that has begun to fray while he looks at his overloaded schedule. The brass buckle-style snap closure no longer works as his papers and numerous memos bulge between the pages.

Kent explains further, "I don't know what happened, Gladys. Somehow Matthew got food poisoning last night, and now I'm in line to make the proposal. Yes, the clients do usually come to our office here in New York. However, Laine Electronics Corporation is weighing between Andrews Advertising and Duncan & Klein Advertising Group for a five-year worldwide advertising contract." Kent grabs his worn brown leather briefcase to look for his boarding pass. He notices the woman next to him is glaring as she tries to read the latest Thomas Wellington suspense novel, *Tampered Evidence.*

Lowering his voice, Kent continues the conversation with his business associate and long-time friend. "That's true, Gladys. But since I'm the top account exec at Andrews and very close to becoming a partner in the firm, I figure this presentation and signing with this international electronics conglomerate will secure my long-awaited partnership. Again, I'm sorry about today's meeting, but there isn't anything that's going to stop me from making this presentation. Even being six foot four inches and ending up with Matthew's center seat in coach for a six-hour flight to LA won't stop me." Kent rubs his outstretched knee. "Although I may be the last one to board the plane."

The gate agent, Pete St. Hilaire, makes an announcement in the gate area regarding the boarding procedures and gives an update on their estimated time of arrival in Los Angeles. The anxious travelers begin to storm toward the already crowded door as he announces that First Class is ready for boarding.

"Look, Gladys, I've got to go. Boarding is about to start, and there is no way that I'm going to miss this plane. It's truly a miracle that I even got a seat on this flight if you consider all the crazy weather and the terrorist crap going on around the world. The Infinity ticket agent was very understanding of my situation. I didn't get first class, but I'm happy to be leaving. You should see how crazy it is here at JFK; it's more than the normal insanity!" he jokes as he watches several tattooed and multipierced teenagers with blue and orange hair walk by. Behind the Gen Yers, two military personnel armed with submachine guns walk slowly through the concourse looking for any suspicious passengers, luggage, packages, or liquids. "It's always an adventure to fly between the Big Apple and LA," he remarks laughingly.

Kent glances over to the large window overlooking the ramp area where another thunderstorm seems to be approaching from the south. "Yes, I'll call you to reschedule when I get back in town. Thanks, Gladys, you too." Kent closes his cell phone and checks the time. He looks back to the gate area at the first class passengers queued up for boarding. He rubs his knee again, longing to be flying up front where he could stretch out his old college-football-injured leg.

Christopher Dunn and his two young children stand impatiently at the gate counter talking to the agent. The thirty-four-year-old man angrily pulls his confirmation number and flight itinerary out of his denim shirt pocket and slams it on the counter.

Once again the agent states firmly yet politely, "I'm sorry, sir. The flight is full. All I can offer you is two seats together and one directly across the aisle. May I suggest that the children sit together, and you sit across the aisle—"

"This is ridiculous!" exclaims Christopher in his outrage. "I just stood in line for over two and a half hours at security only to have my children's *dangerous* apple juice and their *explosive* Play-Doh thrown away while we were practically stripped searched. And now you're telling me that the seats I booked together over a month ago are not in your computer system?" He angrily shakes the itinerary in the agent's face. "Look, here's our reservation confirmation!"

Pete shakes his head regretfully. Several passengers turn in their direction to see what the commotion is all about. Suddenly a loud rumble of thunder is heard throughout the terminal. Christopher's children stand quietly while tears stream down their faces. His son, Ryan, buries his face in the leg of Christopher's jeans as more people in the gate area look their way.

"Listen here, Mr.—" Christopher glances at the agent's nametag, "Mr. Peter St. Hilaire, they are afraid to fly!" screams the frustrated father.

"Sir, I'm sorry—"

"This is not good enough, sir! I'll be writing to the president of Infinity about this situation!" While Christopher's face grows redder, his children cry harder.

Pete smiles respectfully and nods. "Yes, sir."

# Chapter 60

Jane Bradley is only forty years old and the very picture of death. Unable to sit upright, she slumps awkwardly over the armrest on the first row in the coach cabin. Her husband, Louis, leans over her frail thin ashen body, to set up her medical oxygen bottle. Nicole joins Eve to help store the remaining oxygen bottles in the overhead compartment for takeoff.

"Nicole, I'm so glad you're here," says Eve as she closes the compartment. "This is Mrs. Bradley, her husband, Louis, and their son, Briggs."

Eve looks to see if anything else needs to be stowed away as she tells the family, "This is Nicole, our flight attendant trainee. She'll be working in your cabin."

Another man walks up and joins the family. "Oh, Nicole, this is Father Simon Knorosov, their priest. He flew in late last night with the Bradleys from Germany," adds Eve as she prepares for first class boarding.

Father Knorosov smiles nervously at Nicole, completely disarmed by her beauty. The captivating blending of her angelic innocence combined with her physical nature of sensuality can cause grown men to act like fools. She smiles back in awe, unable to take her eyes off him. They both lapse into an awkward silence. Father Knorosov hesitates momentarily, his body stirring uncontrollably as he stares into the depths of her heavenly blue eyes. The tall, rather athletic-looking, man with perfectly chiseled features apprehensively reaches out to shake her hand. His shining gray eyes hold a look of caution. Bashfully placing her palm in his, she is stimulated by a surging course of electricity that rushes through her body. Nicole does not let go.

Father Knorosov feels a tightening in his chest as their hands remain clasped. The unexpected sensation immediately irritates him, but he covers the annoyance. The priest is an expert at hiding his true feelings. He can't afford the luxury of allowing himself to be tempted by an attractive woman—a flight attendant no less—no matter how much she causes his pulse to race. Yet the tightening in his chest, a sensation he has never experienced before, is his indication that there is, indeed, something very special about her. Again he tries to shove the unacceptable feeling aside as he steps back in an attempt to regain control. Requiring all his inner strength to maintain his composure, he turns, ever reluctantly so, to speak with the Bradley family.

Father Knorosov clears his throat. "Miraculously, the gate agent found a passenger that was willing to give up their seat in first class at 9B so that Jane may rest. Unfortunately, we'll have to move her again; but once settled in, she should rest more comfortably. I'm sure she will be better off up there as opposed to sitting in a coach seat with us," Father Knorosov addresses Louis, yet his thoughts and eyes are on Nicole. "That is, if you don't mind being away from her?"

Louis agrees. Immediately, he and his son lift Jane's gaunt body over to the plush oversized first class seat.

As the first class passengers begin to board, Martin Peterson, assigned to sit at the window seat at 9A, glances briefly at Mrs. Bradley, wondering how she got on the plane before him.

"Excuse me," says the priest, extending his hand to Martin. "My name is Father Simon Knorosov, and this is Mrs. Jane Bradley. She has terminal cancer and has traveled from Germany and now on to LA. Another passenger was kind enough to give up his seat in first class so that she might be more comfortable during the long flight to California. I was wondering—"

Martin ignores Father Knorosov's attempted handshake. "Look, Father, no offense. I want nothing more than to sit down, relax, and get some work done before my meeting." Martin retrieves a handful of papers, several folders, and a laptop computer from his briefcase.

"Sorry to disturb you again, sir," the priest begins hesitantly, "but we were wondering, Mr. Bradley and I, that is, if you would be so kind to switch seats with him?" Father Knorosov points to Louis's coach seat. "His seat is right here on the front row of coach and you can—"

Martin looks back at the Bradley family and smiles. "Coach? I don't think so," states Martin, abruptly ending the conversation.

Nicole stumbles up to the seats out of breath. "I'm so glad that you are here, Mr. . . . Mr. 9A!" she exclaims as she pats her hand on her chest. "Sorry.

I just ran up the aisle all the way from the back when I found out that we're boarding first class. I didn't realize that you came on so quickly . . . sir."

"The name is Peterson, young lady. Mr. Martin Peterson."

"Miss, I have already spoken with Mr. Peterson," explains Father Knorosov. "He does not want to switch seats."

Nicole looks at Martin in absolute disbelief. "What! I don't think you totally understand the magnitude of this situation." She excitedly waves her hand, directing Father Knorosov back toward his seat. "Let me speak to Mr. 9A for just a moment . . . privately."

At about eighty miles an hour and all in one breath, Nicole explains the situation in colorful graphic detail, especially the throwing up part to Mr. Peterson. During the final gleaming moment of her plea, Mrs. Bradley abruptly stirs in her seat, throwing the blankets back revealing her thin, wrinkled gray face and emaciated body with her arms flailing in the air. Looking much like a live corpse struggling from its grave, Jane's eyes pop open, and her hand flies to her mouth in an attempt to stop vomiting. Father Knorosov watches Jane closely while Nicole talks to Mr. Peterson and retrieves numerous airsickness bags from the seat pockets. He makes it just in time for Jane to heave into a bag. No further convincing to switch seats is needed as the sight, sound, and smell are enough to change Martin's mind.

Nicole notices Eve's disapproving glare when Martin moves his personal belongings back to Louis's seat in coach. Nicole says indignantly to herself, "What is her problem? The year 2012 and the end of time for these people is not that far away!"

Ignoring Eve's reprimanding stare, Nicole turns back to Father Knorosov. He reluctantly hands her a full bag of throw up for disposal. As they gaze into each other's eyes again, some of the vomit leaks out of the bags and drops on her white uniform shoe. Looking down, Nicole now feels as if she is going to heave. She starts to gag uncontrollably. While running down the aisle to the back of the plane, Nicole holds the bag out in front of her, desperately afraid of dropping it.

Louis apprehensively tells Eve, "Ms. Matrona, I'll need to administer some medication via an intramuscular injection for my wife before the flight takes off."

Eve immediately halts passenger boarding and summons several flight attendants, including Nicole, to the first class cabin. Within minutes, Nicole, Rochel, and Sila are holding up a curtain of blankets around Jane's seat while Louis rolls her over for the injection. He lifts up the syringe, squirting a small amount of the medication from its tip to ensure no air bubbles are present.

Suddenly filled with compassion for Jane, Nicole bends down to hold her hand while Louis administers the shot. Jane is extremely fearful of needles and hates the injections more than anything. While Jane squeezes her hand, Nicole is instantly overcome with the all-consuming feelings of anxiety, fear, dread, illness, and death. In one fell swoop, Nicole feels Jane's entire life, her hopes, her fears, the pain of her childhood abuse, and the abyss of her horror at abusing her only child, Briggs. Out of all the experiences in her life, her sense of inadequacy and desolation are most dominant. The overwhelming emotions from Jane are so excruciatingly intense that like a rubber band that is stretched beyond its capacity, Nicole passes out and collapses into a bundled heap on the floor.

Chapter 61

Nicole feels a warm, compassionate hand brushing her hair back from her face. Her eyes barely open, yet she can see Father Knorosov bending over her with a concerned look on his face. When her eyes fully open, he smiles then squeezes her hand reassuringly. Nicole longs to stay on the floor and gaze into his eyes forever, wanting him to touch her again and again. She aches in her desire to bring his face closer to hers.

His deep voice penetrates her lustful thoughts of desire. She looks up in time to catch the warming glow in his eyes. "I was worried about you, Nicole. I couldn't seem to find your pulse anywhere," he says. Again he is taken with her beauty and innocence, while at the same time disturbed by the feelings they are arousing inside of him.

Gazing back at the priest's face, Nicole is struck once more by its strength. The knowing eyes, the determined lips, and the beginnings of a five o'clock shadow on his manly square face bring a slight smile.

Father Knorosov becomes very concerned by her sudden pallor. "Are you okay?" he asks endearingly.

She inhales deeply then slowly releases the breath with a soft whispered yes. Nicole smiles back at Father Knorosov and faints again.

Eve is quick to intervene. "Nicole?"

"Please take care of Mrs. Bradley, everyone. Nicole will be fine," instructs Eve, kneeling on the floor next to Nicole. She encourages the priest to return his attention to Jane while she places both of her hands on Nicole in an effort to angelically revive her, but there's no response from Nicole. "Looks like she's fainted. Her first trip—probably too much excitement."

Michael suddenly appears out of nowhere. "Eve, I'll take care of Nicole. Looks as though Mrs. Bradley could use your help." He gently picks Nicole off the cabin floor. His strong arms tenderly embrace her firm long body as he carries her up the aisle through the first class cabin to the flight deck.

Eve and Father Knorosov watch with concern as the cockpit door closes, each for different reasons.

Chapter 62

Behind the closed cockpit door, Michael watches Nicole closely as she lays suspended in mid-air. He adjusts the translucent healing field that surrounds her supine form while her erratic energy continues to dim and ebb.

"Michael, what's happening?" Nicole murmurs weakly.

"Your vibrations are so unpredictable. One minute you're angelic; the next minute, you're human and sometimes even both." Michael lovingly sweeps Nicole's golden hair from her face. "You seem to absorb everything around you—especially the lower vibrations—in very concentrated levels. Never in all eternity have I ever encountered an angel like you, Nicole. And this is beyond any kind of training; you are very unique, indeed."

Nicole lays quietly, once more comforted by Michael's words.

Several minutes later he asks, "How are you feeling now?" His voice is a gentle reminder of his presence.

"I feel disorientated. It is difficult for me to think, to focus my thoughts." As her eyes begin to open slowly, she hears a roll of thunder rumbling in the distance.

"You need rest and more time to regain your strength," Michael says in a quiet, soothing tone. As he rises to his feet, the pilot jumpseats shimmer out of existence. He locks the cockpit door by looking at it while the suitcases and flight kits slide silently out of the way.

"You have shifted multiple dimensions, Nicole. This is a dimension outside of your normal existence in the Celestial City. When angels materialize, there is a sensation of displacement. This is normal. You will still be able to function but at a much different and reduced level—"

"I don't know. Mrs. Bradley—her pain, her fear—I felt them all!" interrupts Nicole, her voice somewhat faint. "The humans are dragging me down, aren't they?" Michael nods in agreement as he helps Nicole to sit upright.

"Yes, and the effects increase with proximity. Actual contact with our passengers can be completely debilitating but never fatal. Your strength and power can be incapacitated to a degree that could possibly leave you vulnerable."

"I know . . . Father Knorosov. I experienced sensations just by being near this man, a priest! I felt a flutter in my chest, a weakness in my knees, and an incredible warm sensation between my legs," Nicole cries as Michael sits by her side.

"Oh," Michael replies quietly in a curious tone.

"I don't think I'm going to make it as a flight attendant. I feel like such a freak! I'm not an angel. I'm not a human. I can't even control what I am or even when I am. It's so frustrating, Michael! Maybe I should get a ground job—"

"Nicole, it's all right." Michael holds her closely with his all-embracing wisdom and his face next to hers. Unintentionally his lips brush against hers as he seeks to console her in the moment of her sorrow. An uncomfortable shift of feelings course through Nicole, accompanied by an undercurrent of apprehension—slight but discernible to Michael as she seeks comfort in his arms. He hears her audible sigh.

With his arm reassuringly around Nicole's shoulder, he continues. His voice is gentle without negating the seriousness of his words. "For the meantime, Nicole, you are encapsulated in a body that resonates with water, with the Earth, with fire, and with air. Get to know these energies, Nicole. You now possess them. Become familiar with what you truly are, and all else will be given to you. Even answers will be given to you if you so desire them."

"I know the other flight attendants think I'm strange. I'm not like them. I'm not like anyone!" Nicole sobs uncontrollably into his shoulder. Tissues instantly appear in Michael's hand. He gently wipes away her tears as she looks in his eyes. "One minute I'm up, and the next minute I'm down—literally! I just don't think I'm going to make it as a flight attendant. I mean sure, flight attendants go up and down—with the airplane. However it seems I'm on a totally different flight path than the rest of this crew," sobs Nicole, as fear and insecurity overwhelm her thoughts.

Michael tries to reassure her. "Everyone in Creation has unique gifts and talents. And you, Nicole, are very special too."

"I am?" asks Nicole, bewildered by his kind assessment.

"Let me help," he says as she tries to stand up. As her left foot touches the cockpit floor, she feels faint but steady. The reverberations from holding Jane's hand are still flowing out in waves. Nicole stands up with the support of Michael's firm arms. With her hands resting on his forearms, she looks up into his blue eyes that seem to behold the past, present, and future. Although he is on Earth in a physical body, Nicole sees deep within beyond the boundaries. She sees the reflection of the ethereal world of his existence while the sound of rain dancing on the cockpit windows plays softly in the background.

After a long silence, Michael speaks. "You have come here to teach us something. Trust that, Nicole, and be the best you can be," Michael explains as he holds her hand. She looks to him to hear more. Her innocent smile softens the strong angular lines of his face. "You are a part of the totality of all that is. No one is a freak—just a portion of The Creator expressing Itself."

Nicole hears his words, but she hears something more. Something between the words. She hears love. She hears the concern, the compassion. She can feel him filling her essence with his soothing peace and never-ending love.

"You are focusing on your fears of imperfection, distress, and frustration. I, along with all the other angels, see this and acknowledge all of this—and also understand," adds Michael encouragingly. "I see the complex spectrum of who you are now and the potential of who you can become. Remember, Nicole, you exist outside of time and space. Choose the highest expression of yourself, always, remembering just how special you are to me and everyone at Infinity."

"You're right. I am special!" declares Nicole. "I can do this flight attendant job. I'm going to be the best flight attendant Infinity has ever had. Now if you will excuse me, Michael . . . Capt. Smith, sir . . . I've got a job to do!"

Chapter 63

"Oh, miss! Excuse me, could you please put my bag up there?" asks an elderly hunched-over woman with a walking cane. Nicole gladly helps her put the overstuffed bag into the overhead bin. "My doctor told me not to pick up anything heavy. Thank you, doll, you are such a sweetheart."

Nicole happily works in the coach cabin hoping for another opportunity to run into Father Knorosov. Eventually she loads over thirty suitcases of all shapes and sizes into the overhead compartments. "Hmm, that's interesting. No matter how much luggage I put into the overhead, there always seems to be room for more."

Nicole is unaware of the fact that the uniquely designed Infinity I-888 aircraft can hold an infinite amount of carryon baggage in the overhead compartments and an infinite amount in the cargo hold as well. Among the airplane's numerous distinctions, she has yet to notice that they never run out of supplies, that every passenger gets whatever they ask for and the flight attendant meal carts never run out of trays or choices.

When a passenger asks for a specific entrée, it just miraculously materializes on the next tray. The Infinite Creator decided that on their newest planes they would continue using the miracle of *loaves and fishes* from 2,000 years ago. Since Immanuel was able to feed over 5,000 people with only five loaves of bread and two fishes, Infinity Airways would use that same concept to feed everyone onboard while allowing more room for passenger comfort and all the passengers' heavy karmic and emotional baggage instead of the large galleys normally used to store all the meals.

"Oh, stewardess. May I have a little sip of water to take my pill?" asks yet another passenger. It is the twelfth such request that she has had in the last thirty minutes. It seems that every time Nicole returns from the galley with a cup of water for one passenger, someone else is waiting to make the same request.

As more and more passengers board the coach cabin, Nicole observes that passengers seem to come in all shapes, sizes, attitudes, and temperaments. And some come up with the most creative ways to secure their baggage. *The Creator must really love stupid people. It made so many!* She begins to see that people actually look like their bags. Passengers who are slim and trim, dressed nice and neat tend to carry bags are much the same. Overweight passengers who look sloppy with their shirts hanging out tend to have overstuffed bags with garments hanging out of the sides or clothes stuffed into torn paper shopping bags.

Determined not to let anything or anyone bother her, Nicole continues with a sense of joy to assist everyone the best she can even though another passenger impatiently pushes their way past her, banging her arm with their overloaded backpack.

Suddenly out of nowhere, a frazzled young mother traveling with an infant and twin three-year-old boys rushes up to Nicole, thrusting the diaper-clad baby into her arms. "I'll be right back!" The harried mother dashes off out of sight to the back of the plane.

"Uh, okay," says Nicole, not sure how she should respond. She looks curiously at the baby. "Well, hello, there, little one. What cute rosy red cheeks you have!" Nicole bounces the chubby child up and down in the air.

"Wait a minute, why isn't it smiling?" she mutters. His face is growing redder and redder as it seems the baby is not breathing. "Something is wrong with this baby!" Nicole cries frantically, looking for assistance of any kind.

"The baby is fine, stewardess." An older woman seated on the aisle motions for Nicole to come closer. With the baby propped on her shoulder, Nicole leans over and the passenger quietly begins to explain the situation. Suddenly, it becomes apparent to Nicole and everyone else seated in the immediate area what exactly is going on as the distinct odor gives it away. A warm brown substance begins to ooze out of the diaper and down Nicole's arm. Apparently, it wasn't only the mother that had to go to the bathroom.

The baby proceeds to spit up on Nicole's shoulder while the twins throw Cheerios at each other. Standing on their seats, they begin to scream, looking over the headrests frantically wanting to know where their mother is. Within seconds, Nicole's angelic vibration begins to drop dramatically. None of the surrounding passengers want to help. The bickering twins are screaming at each other and for Mom while throwing Cheerios at everyone within a six-foot radius.

"SIT DOWN NOW!" screams Nicole in exasperation. "These are the lessons I need? What in Heaven do I need to learn from this? Not to wear a white uniform?" she asks herself while holding the baby out away from her uniform. A wry, sardonic look disgraces her otherwise beautiful face. "Oh, my God, this is not what I signed up for! Where is that mother—"

"Excuse me!" An annoyed deep voice comes from a man standing directly behind Nicole as she waits in the aisle looking anxiously toward the aft lavatories.

"Just wait a min—" Nicole starts as she angrily spins around. Standing face-to-face with her is a young man completely covered in tattoos, sporting a spiked multicolored mohawk. Nicole gasps as she stares in horror at his multipierced face with eyebrows, nose, ears, ear lobes, chin, lips, and cheeks pierced in a randomly bizarre fashion, reflecting his exotic flavor of self-mutilation. Clad in black leather, wearing a spiked choker and chains, he pushes past Nicole, forcing her to hold the baby high over the head of the helpful older woman. Nicole's energy plunges immediately as his body brushes up against hers, taking all she has not to drop the crying baby.

"I'm taking matters into my own hands," Nicole exclaims in desperation.

Nicole begins to hum angelically. The children are instantly mesmerized by the beautiful celestial sounds, causing them and several passengers in the immediate area to fall asleep. She looks around quickly to the other flight attendants to see if they saw her angelic trick.

The young mother comes back thrilled to find her children sleeping, each and every one safely buckled in. She notices the baby is resting comfortably in a new, clean diaper. "My God, it's a miracle! Bless you!" The mother crosses her chest and looks up to thank the Lord above. Nicole smiles.

Chapter 64

"Miss Walters, what a pleasure it is to see you again!" remarks Eve standing at the boarding door as the last few passengers arrive. "How did your presentation go? A big success, I'm sure."

Her guardian angel gives Eve a thumbs up and hand-clapping gestures, indicating how proud of Elizabeth it is.

"Well, I'll find out next week. The real success is my flying on an airplane . . . again," mumbles Elizabeth nervously as she fumbles with her boarding card. "I just really want to get back home. By any chance, are the same pilots flying this plane today?"

Everyone in the plane looks around as the sound of heavy rain hits the aircraft fuselage. Passengers seated at the windows look outside to see the torrential downpour. The Infinity Airways ramp workers on the tarmac continue to load the baggage and service the plane in the driving rains. Marble-sized hail begins to pummel the airport and surrounding areas. Silence hangs in the air as passengers squelch their fears about traveling under such circumstances.

"Yes, they are," Eve speaks up. The onboard leader smiles reassuringly as she notices Elizabeth's trepidation about traveling. "Flying is what our pilots do best!" she announces loudly, hoping to reassure the surrounding passengers that can hear her voice.

"Really?" asks Elizabeth weakly as she walks slowly to her seat, clutching her prescription bottle in her jacket pocket. "That makes me feel better."

Eve notices a Portuguese family of nine who do not speak English coming up the jetway to the plane at the last minute. She summons Dina telepathically to assist. He arrives in time to see by their weary and frightened appearance that they have never flown before. Dina smiles at the man who appears to be the grandfather and the head of the family as he walks up to the boarding door.

"Boa tarde, Senore Ricardo. Como posso eu ajudar a lhe e a sua família hoje, senhor?" Dina inquires, speaking in pristine Portuguese.

The family is surprised and relieved to find a flight attendant who speaks their native tongue. Mr. Ricardo explains that they were detained at security and have been lost in the airport for several hours. They were originally booked on another airline to Ontario, California. The grandchildren are tired and hungry, and he is concerned for his elderly wife, who is very weak and upset about missing their earlier flight.

Dina reassures them. "Everything will be fine. Allow me to help you and your family to your seats. Although your seat assignments are not together, with a little encouragement, I'm sure the passengers seated in the area will switch their seats so your family can sit together." Mr. and Mrs. Ricardo thank Dina profusely, kissing his hand several times to demonstrate their humble appreciation before following him to the coach cabin.

Within minutes Dina returns to inform Eve that the Ricardo family has been seated together.

Eve smiles smugly at Dina. "I would hope so," she exclaims with a chuckle. "Unbeknownst to the Ricardo family, they have been helped by the Guardian Angel of the Law and Wisdom. Do you think that any of these passengers would ever believe that you, a flight attendant, are credited with having taught seventy languages to the souls created at the time of creation? And that you normally dwell in the Seventh Heaven?" Eve winks, patting Dina on the back before he leaves. "However, today you're flying with us today between New York and Los Angeles."

An exasperated Nicole joins Eve at the boarding door, trying to regain her composure from all the stress and strain of boarding four hundred passengers.

"Well, hey, hey girls" says a very handsome man who is boarding late for first class. "Are we really going to take off? I think I need another drink." The dashing Charles Hamilton reeks of alcohol and wealth too. Losing his balance, the thirty-eight-year-old drunk drops several boarding passes onto the floor. "Ish the plane moving already?" he asks, slurring his words.

Catherine Hamilton, a very fashionably dressed petite woman with perfectly styled hair and makeup, nonchalantly appears at the boarding door after him. "Where the hell are we sitting, Charles?" demands the thirty-six-year-old socialite of her intoxicated husband. Eve hands her the boarding passes.

"Mrs. Hamilton, it appears that you're sitting in seats 7E, 7F, 8—" Catherine grabs the passes from Eve's hand and storms down the aisle. "And seats 8E, 8F, 9E, and 9F," Eve continues as the stumbling husband, a young Hispanic nanny saddled down with blankets, bags, toys, and three boisterous children follow behind.

"Good afternoon, Mrs. Montgomery, we're so glad you could join us today," welcomes Eve as she helps steady the last-minute passenger over the threshold of the aircraft door. "Our new trainee, Nicole, will help you to your seat. Looks as though you made it just in time," adds Eve as she looks down the jetway. She sees Pete with the final paperwork in hand. "We are just about to close the boarding door."

Nicole helps the sprightly yet elderly woman, wearing a very old-fashioned lavender dress and a white hat, to her seat. Mrs. Montgomery wavers slightly as she and Nicole walk slowly through first class.

Rather than sitting down, the three Hamilton children decide to boisterously run around their tired nanny, playing hide and seek in her long skirt. When she does finally sit down—after putting away all the carryon baggage for the children and their parents—the Hamilton children resort to darting around the first class cabin. The youngest, Ashleigh, runs straight into the lady seated across the aisle, spilling the woman's Chardonnay all over. Mr. and Mrs. Hamilton sit comfortably in their seats ahead of the nanny and the children, seemingly oblivious to the raucous their young ones are creating.

Nicole and Mrs. Montgomery observe Mrs. Hamilton flipping passively through her society magazines while her husband hopelessly tries to don a pair of headphones in an attempt to listen to some music. "Children these days are certainly *different* than when I was growing up," comments Mrs. Montgomery as they pass the Hamilton's row. "The parents are certainly *different* today as well." Ashleigh runs right in front of Mrs. Montgomery causing her to stumble into one of the first class seatbacks. "Or maybe it's just that the parents are *indifferent*." The dawdling woman chuckles with an upraised brow.

"Yes, ma'am. I think you're right," Nicole says absentmindedly while smiling at Father Knorosov as they walk by his row.

"I've been counseling my granddaughter about the direction of her life since she was that little girl's age. I just wish I . . ." Mrs. Montgomery rambles on as they continue down the aisle to her seat.

"Yes, ma'am, that's nice." Nicole is oblivious to Mrs. Montgomery's story about her granddaughter. The infatuated flight attendant gazes at the back of Father Knorosov's head as she reaches across Christopher

Dunn, the gentleman sitting in the aisle seat next to Mrs. Montgomery, to help the elderly woman fasten her seat belt. After securing the talkative grandmother into the center seat, Nicole lingers around Father Knorosov's row helping other passengers to get settled before she returns to assist Eve.

With passengers, and their karmic and emotional baggage loaded and secured, and the boarding door finally closed, Infinity Airways flight 555 leaves the departure gate.

Ding! Ding! Ding! Ding!

"Nicole, would you mind responding to Mrs. Hamilton's call bell?" asks Eve.

"Sure, Eve, I'll do anything to stay in first class near Father Knorosov," Nicole says quietly to herself as she cautiously approaches Mrs. Hamilton's row.

"What kind of an airline is this!" scowls Mrs. Hamilton incredulously. "What are *those* children doing up here?" She points furiously at the Ricardo children, who are playing on the floor in the first class cabin with her children. Nicole, mesmerized by the size and brilliance of Mrs. Hamilton's diamond ring, stands quietly, unsure of how she should respond.

"Isn't there some kind of law about people from back *there* not being able to come up into first class?" she continues angrily. "We did not pay for these seats to be around people like . . . like *them*!" Mrs. Hamilton now has not only Nicole's attention but also the attention of every one in the surrounding area. Upon seeing how upset Mrs. Hamilton is, their nanny immediately attempts to get the Hamilton children back into their designated seats. Rosa feels hurt and embarrassed about the fact that her employer, Mrs. Hamilton, is behaving so rudely toward the Ricardo family, a family much like her own.

Nicole assists Rosa in picking up the children and their toys. "Don't worry, Mrs. Hamilton," Nicole says reassuringly. "We'll take care of everything." Nicole can't help but notice the socialite's expensive Dior designer scarf and purse. She makes a mental note to look for something similar on her next shopping trip.

After ensuring the Hamilton children are buckled in safely, Nicole helps the Ricardo children back to their seats. She grimaces as she notices Mrs. Ricardo's old, worn dress. *That dress is absolutely atrocious!* Nicole thinks to herself. *It looks like something she picked up three lifetimes ago.*

Nicole suddenly blushes when she catches Father Knorosov looking her way. Their eyes lock momentarily, and Nicole hesitates before sullenly returning to speak with the Hamiltons again.

"Mr. and Mrs. Hamilton, although everyone should have been in their seats during taxi, your children and the children of the other family were getting along peacefully. They were just having fun and enjoying each other's company. Maybe we should all be so fortunate to have everyone accept each of us for who we are," says Nicole, reflecting on her own situation. "People are just people, Mrs. Hamilton, no matter where they are from, what they do for a living, where they sit, or how much they want to spend for their ticket. We are all the same and All are Part of The One!" Nicole walks up the aisle to the galley, brushing Catherine off with apparent unconcern.

"How dare she say that to me!" exclaims Catherine to her husband. "I should—"

"Get her to bring me another cocktail," interrupts Charles, ignoring his wife's constant criticism. "Well, she's right, Catherine. You know, she's exactly right," he whispers loudly as he tries to hold her hand and nuzzle his face into her neck and shoulder. "Why don't you accept me for who I am, honey bunny? Maybe we can have some fun on the floor too."

"You're crazier than that stupid flight attendant. Talking about how we are all the same. Ha! Now get your filthy hands off of me, you miserable excuse for a man!" demands Catherine as she slaps her husband's hand, completely repulsed by his feeble and drunken attempts to get into her good graces.

"How did everything go back there?" inquires Eve as Nicole returns to the galley.

"Everything is wonderful," beams Nicole as she thinks about the priest. "But that Mrs. Hamilton sure has an attitude. She thinks that because she has a first class seat that she can tell everyone what to do. She certainly likes bossing everyone around," explains Nicole. Abruptly she asks Eve, "Did you happen to check out her adorable Dior purse and those gorgeous matching shoes? They look absolutely stunning with her outfit, don't you think?"

"We'll be taking off soon, so let's get the cabin and passengers ready," instructs Eve, ignoring Nicole's growing obsession with material wealth. "We need to pick up all the cups and glasses, check seatbacks, and seat belts. Make sure the luggage and all those *adorable* purses are out of the aisles." Eve chuckles as she secures the galley for takeoff.

Gabriel makes the takeoff announcement over the aircraft public address system. "Ladies and gentlemen, looks like the weather has cleared up, and air traffic control is moving things along smoothly and efficiently here at JFK. We are now third in line for takeoff. Flight attendants, please make your final cabin preparations."

Chapter 65

With the flight smoothly under way after flying through several areas of moderate to severe turbulence, the pilots turn off the seat belt sign. Quickly and efficiently, the beverage service in first class is finished, and the passengers begin to relax. Eve approaches Nicole, who is putting on more lipstick and blush, in the galley. "We have everything under control up here. I think it's time for you to help in coach, Nicole."

"I . . . I can't," Nicole stammers. "I mean, I prefer the passengers in first class." Nicole looks in Father Knorosov's direction as she unfastens three of the buttons on her uniform blouse. She will do anything to stay in first class, as he is seated nearby in the first row of coach with Briggs Bradley and Martin Peterson. "The people up here . . . uh . . . they're more attractive, and they have more class. They just seem to dress better, and they even smell better too. I mean, Eve, it's absolutely deplorable how some of those people in coach look." She reflects back on Mrs. Ricardo's dress. "Have you looked closely at what they are wearing?"

"We are here to give each and every passenger the best service possible," Eve says in an even tone. "Everyone—first class and coach."

"Well, I just don't think that I can handle it anymore back there, Eve." Determined not to work coach, Nicole begins to look for an excuse, any excuse, not to. "You know, with my whole energy thing and all. I just don't think that it would be a very good idea for me to go back there again. And my uniform would probably get all messed up again. Speaking of uniforms, Eve, do you think my skirt makes my thighs look big? I just don't understand why we have white uniforms anyway; they're so unflattering." Nicole continues to ramble, "Oh, Eve, did you see that fabulous navy blue uniform dress the flight attendant from Delta Air Lines had on at JFK? It was absolutely divine. Why don't we wear navy blue too?"

"Nicole!" Eve interrupts. "This *holier than thou* attitude is not flattering for an angel or a flight attendant. Your feelings of insecurity are being governed by fear. You are picking up on the illusions of beauty that are perpetuated through the media and marketing down here on Earth. I'm guessing that you were watching television in your hotel room and looking at too many fashion magazines on our layover."

"What are you talking about?" Nicole becomes very defensive. "I don't think or feel that anything has changed about me just because I watched a little television and looked at a few magazines. Oh, by the way, do you like my new hairstyle?" Nicole swings her long blonde hair around. "You didn't say anything about it in the van."

"Nicole, please listen to me," Eve interjects. "You need to be aware of the way in which television can negatively impact your energy, especially someone as sensitive as you. Television itself is not the problem; it can be a very powerful tool in distributing useful information. However, it is the content of its *programming* and its many messages that can be harmful. Commercials and make-over reality shows promote fear and insecurity—fear of what others may think of you and what they don't think of you. If you are in fear, Nicole, then you are controllable through their manipulations of all that you fear. Those advertisements and shows play to your fears of inadequacy and insecurity. Advertisers want you to feel and truly believe that everything you are and have is insufficient, that you need to have whatever they're offering in order to make you thinner, richer, healthier, hairier, sexier, or smarter. Need I go on?"

"Come on, Eve!" Nicole retorts defensively. "You're blowing everything out of proportion—"

Eve breaks in, her voice hard and insistent. "Am I?" demands Eve with an unyielding look on her face.

Nicole pauses reflectively, with her hands on her hips staring at Eve's hair. "You know, Eve, if you let your hair down and put a little blush on your cheeks, it will really make your face look thinner, more alive. Here let's try some lipstick too." Nicole proceeds to rifle through a huge array of cosmetics samples stuffed into her new designer purse.

"Excuse me!" says Eve incredulously, her lips tightening into a straight hard line.

"You might be able to meet the man of your dreams. A real man, like Martin Peterson. One that is successful and knows what he wants—one that can make you feel like a real woman. After all these years of flying, Eve, aren't you ready to meet someone who can make you feel really good about yourself?" Nicole winks, attempting to take Eve's hair bun down.

"Even Michael might begin to see you as a beautiful woman, which is what you really want. Right, Eve?"

"Nicole!" Eve exclaims, brushing Nicole's hand away. "I don't need a man or anyone or anything to make me feel better about myself, and I suggest that you don't either!" She takes Nicole by the shoulders and looks straight into her eyes. "The beauty of life, Nicole, is in you, in your very being. You are made in total perfection, just as you are, before you put on all that silly makeup and fancy jewelry. Everyone is perfect just as they are. There is nothing or no one that can make you feel better about yourself—that feeling has to come from within!"

"You don't believe all of that, do you?" Nicole nods and then raises her eyebrow. "Come on, Eve, live a little. I've seen the way you look at Michael."

Eve stiffens as Nicole walks out of the galley smiling.

Chapter 66

Another passenger call bell rings in the coach cabin. *Ding! Ding! Ding! Ding!*

"I'll get this one," Rochel announces to the other flight attendants in the galley before she walks up the aisle to where Kent Phillips is seated.

Under normal circumstances, the successful advertising account exec would never have been happy in a center seat in coach. But these are not normal circumstances.

"Excuse me, miss, but do you have any champagne?" he asks. "It's time to celebrate!" He squeezes Elizabeth Walter's hand.

"Yes, sir, we have a 2001 Perrier-Jouët Belle Epoque." Rochel displays the bottle and two glasses in her hands.

"Does that sound good to you, Liz?" Kent looks over at the woman he thought he had lost forever.

Elizabeth's mouth drops in amazement. "Kent, that's the champagne we had on our first date, the one we couldn't seem to get enough of. Remember?" She can't believe they have her favorite on the flight.

Kent stares at the bottle. "I guess that will have to do," he replies teasingly while he reaches for his wallet. "How much is it?"

"Oh, no charge, Mr. Phillips. Compliments of First Officer Gabe Jones." Rochel winks at Elizabeth.

Kent leans over and whispers in Elizabeth's ear, "Did you notice that she already had the champagne with her when she got to us? How did she know what we were going to order? And to have that particular one?"

"I don't know. But isn't this crew the greatest?" brags Elizabeth. "I told you, the pilots are the ones that got me on this plane yesterday." She raises her glass. "And thank God they did, because my presentation was a huge success, and now I'm sitting next to you."

"Finally we're together," he whispers, kissing her on the cheek before taking a sip. Kent cannot believe that he is seated next to Elizabeth. With all the unusual circumstances that brought him on board and of all the flights out of New York City to Los Angeles, the reality of what has transpired has yet to completely sink in.

"Oh, Kent, I cannot believe this is happening. Not one day goes by that I don't think of you, about what our future could have been." Tears well up in Elizabeth's eyes. "This is a dream come true," she chokes. "I never stopped loving you. Oh, I wish this flight would go on forever—you and I together, no phones, no deadlines."

He smiles at Elizabeth. "I wish this flight would go on forever too, but in some ways I can't wait for it to be over."

"What do you mean?" asks Elizabeth nervously, her heart suddenly diving in her chest.

"Because my legs and back are killing me!" He laughs, rubbing his knees pressed up against the back of the seat in front of him.

"Would you like to trade seats? You'd probably be more comfortable in mine since it's an aisle seat. It really is very roomy." She happily rises from her seat. They quickly switch with Elizabeth now in the center. "There. Now you can extend your leg into the aisle. Is that old football injury still bothering you?"

"Wow, this is great," says Kent curiously as he looks around the seating area. "This seat feels so spacious, even though it looks to be the same size as the one I was sitting in." Several moments of silence pass while he tries to comprehend the strange and unexpected chain of events.

"Liz—" Kent begins.

"Kent—" Elizabeth begins at the same time.

They both laugh nervously. Elizabeth asks Kent to start first.

"Liz, you seem so different," he commences. "Different yet the same." He takes a large gulp of the Perrier-Jouët champagne. "All I want to know—all I've ever needed to know—is why you broke up with me in college." He stares longingly into her eyes looking for answers, then chugs the rest of his champagne. "I believe that everything happens for a reason, Liz, like the fact that you and I are seated next to each other on this flight. But I have never felt like there was a reason for you to break up with me. Something changed dramatically during our last year of school to put out your spark and your passion for life . . . and for me. I have never been able to figure out what happened."

Kent refills his glass as Elizabeth stares deeply into hers.

"Was it something I did? Something I said?" Probing even deeper, Kent continues after taking another gulp. The emotion buried inside causes his voice to falter. "What could I have possibly done to create such a drastic change in you, Liz? I've been trying to figure it out for the past twenty years . . . and to no avail." He reaches for Elizabeth's hand as tears of pain, tears of joy stream down her face.

Although ecstatic to be reunited with Kent, Elizabeth is paralyzed by fear of having to finally reveal the reason behind their breakup. Once more the past crowds in. *What if I lose him again?* Elizabeth worries in anguished desperation. *But I know that it is not possible!* A battle inside her thoughts ensues. *I made a deal with God: If I ever see Kent again, Lord, I know it will be a sign that we are meant to be together, no matter what.*

Elizabeth begins to tremble. *Here he is—sitting on the same plane, on the same day that I'm flying—and is seated right next to me. Oh, God, help me! How am I to reveal the secret that I've had locked up inside myself all these years—never revealing the terrible events to anyone. Now I'm face-to-face with my greatest fear. Now I'm to disclose to the love of my life, the horrific events that took place during our last semester of college. Oh, God, please help me.*

"Liz . . . Liz, are you all right?" Kent notices that she suddenly looks very pale, her hands starting to shake violently. With memories of another time feeling so real, so present, so tangible, she abruptly excuses herself. Climbing frantically over Kent before he can get up, she heads to the lavatory.

Chapter 67

Christopher Dunn can't explain why he feels so comfortable talking with Mrs. Montgomery, the elderly woman sitting next to him. *There is just something about her that seems so familiar and caring. How can that be?* He shakes his head in disbelief as he wonders. *Before I realized it—after exchanging the normal pleasantries observations, and opinions regarding the weather, flying and New York—I was telling Mrs. Montgomery about Kim, and how I'm left to raise Rebecca and Ryan on my own.*

Christopher smiles wryly then continues with his story. "I'm sure you know how unpredictable kids can be, Mrs. Montgomery. Don't get me wrong, Rebecca and Ryan are wonderful, but an owner's manual would have been nice!" he says in jest. "But seriously, I was so clueless. Looking back, I realized that before Kim died, I had really only been partly involved as a father. I had no idea how much work she put into raising the kids." He looks proudly over at his daughter. "Thank God Rebecca paid enough attention to her mother's parenting that she was able to help me through the difficult parts."

"Did you put the children in day care while you were at work?" Mrs. Montgomery asks politely.

"Childcare was out of the question," Christopher replies definitively. "The first big decision I made as a single father was to stop working. Kim had been so dedicated to the family; she had even decided that we should homeschool the kids. And I wanted to support what she would have wanted." He looks over again at his sleeping children. "Every time I look at Rebecca and Ryan, I see Kim's beautiful face. I have no regrets about what I decided to do. It was crazy at times, sometimes pushing me to the very edge, but I wouldn't take any of it back."

"I must say that I'm extremely impressed with you dedication, Christopher." Mrs. Montgomery pats his hand. "Most men in your situation would have used day care or remarried, you know."

"Well, take this for example," he brags. "I remember when Rebecca lost her first tooth. Now, if Kim had still been alive, I probably would have come home from work, and she would have told me the news. And then I probably would have just said, 'That's great,' and continued on with whatever else I was doing. But being there to experience something like that for myself—it was priceless." He sighs while staring blankly up the aisle.

"And?" Mrs. Montgomery encourages.

"And I could really feel that Kim was there with me, you know?" he says softly. "I do believe in Jesus's promise that life is eternal, and I believe that she is still with me. But the pain of not being able to look at her, not being able to hold her, to run my hands over her soft beautiful skin, well, most days it's overwhelming," Christopher chokes on his emotions.

"I can only imagine what that must have been like for you," replies Mrs. Montgomery sympathetically. "But it's good that you can be open with your feelings, not like in days long past, when people were supposed to keep everything inside—especially men. Times have certainly changed and for the better I think."

"You know, Mrs. Montgomery, when she first passed on, I had a lot of guilt and shame," Christopher admits, folding the corners of the magazine in his lap. "All I could think about was all the times that I must have disappointed her or that maybe I didn't really love her as much as she needed. But ironically, it's Kim that relieves me of these feelings. I see her all the time in my heart, in my mind. And it's so comforting. I can't really begin to explain it. It's as if she is telling me that somehow everything is going to be all right."

"That is so gloriously touching, Christopher." Mrs. Montgomery dabs the corner of her eye with her lace handkerchief.

Christopher takes a deep breath as he reclines his seatback, continuing to tell Mrs. Montgomery about his late wife. "When she first passed, the grief was unbearable. I had lost my best friend, my wife, and the mother of my children. However, in retrospect, the grief has ultimately brought me a lot of insight. I've come to understand that everything happens for a reason," he carries on, oblivious to whether or not anyone seated around them is listening. Somehow it feels good, somewhat therapeutic, for Christopher to share his innermost feelings and even safer with a stranger. "Being able to accept that has brought me a certain peace and serenity."

Mrs. Montgomery remains silent as he continues. "Kim was such an inspiration, even on the verge of death. She was completely unafraid and at peace. I knew that I had to admit to her that my fear of pain had sometimes kept me closed to her love. And then she was gone, and that was it. I have never felt the presence of God so profoundly than at that very moment." Tears roll from his eyes as he sits quietly, reflecting momentarily. Slowly turning his head, Christopher looks to Mrs. Montgomery for some kind of comforting acknowledgement, for some kind words of wisdom, but she is sound asleep.

Chapter 68

Having exchanged seats with Martin, Louis now sits in first class with his ailing wife, lovingly holding her hand. As the plane heads west, he looks out the window. "What a blessing that two strangers have given up their seats so that Jane and I may travel more comfortably. Now, Lord, if only she can make it to Los Angeles." Louis looks down at his dying spouse, his sweetheart since high school.

In the first row of coach, Father Knorosov and Martin sit elbow to elbow next to the Bradleys' son, Briggs. Being as tall and as large as he is, Martin gives up trying to accomplish any work within the confines of such a small space. Closing his laptop and his briefcase, he reclines the seat in an attempt to get more comfortable. The usual conversation passes between himself, Father Knorosov, and Briggs before turning to the current situation with Jane. Martin is impressed by the priest's dedication to the family.

"She really should be in the hospital," Martin says delicately, wondering how she ever made it on board. "I'm really surprised that this airline agreed to take her."

Father Knorosov smiles graciously and nods in agreement. "Well, I think at this point, everyone is helping to grant her last wish, which is to pass away at home," the priest replies. "Jane doesn't have a single internal organ left that is not affected by her cancer. The disease, originating in her colon, has progressed rapidly through her body."

Martin leans over, directing his attention toward Briggs. "Sorry to ask, but why were you all flying to Germany as sick as your mother is?"

Briggs responds, "We went to Medjugorje, a small mountain village in Bosnia and Herzegovina where miracles of healing are performed by the

Virgin Mary. Mom was healed there in the past when she was wheelchair bound due to advanced multiple sclerosis. By the time we got home from her first trip, all signs of the disease had disappeared." Briggs looks mournfully to his mother. "Unfortunately, this time around, her condition has only become worse."

As Martin and Briggs talk, Father Knorosov gets up to stretch his legs with hopes of seeing Nicole. Walking around the bulkhead, he notices the man who appears strikingly familiar in the last row of first class seated across from the Bradleys.

"Sorry to disturb you, sir, but do I know you from somewhere?" he asks apologetically.

"Well, you don't look familiar to me, so I'm not sure." The dark-haired man in his mid-forties extends his hand to Father Knorosov. "I'm William Gladstone. Do you happen to live in Los Angeles, Father?"

"It's nice to meet you, William," says the priest, staring at the man a moment longer. "No, I live in Victorville, a small town east of LA," he continues, briefly explaining the situation with the Bradleys before returning to his seat.

Chapter 69

Elizabeth looks closely in the lavatory mirror, seeing the face of a twenty-two-year-old college cheerleader. Her guardian angel takes a closer look too.

"Okay, Elizabeth. I know you just overcame your paralyzing fear of flying yesterday, but today you're being propelled to deal with your greatest of fears. Locking yourself in the lavatory for nearly twenty minutes is well and good, I guess. A little cramped, but it seems to be the only place for you to calm your nerves," says the angel, squeezed within the small confines of the coach lavatory with Elizabeth.

"Why is this happening now?" begs Elizabeth. "And why on an airplane?"

"The horror, the pain, the heartache of that life-changing day twenty years ago is written all over your face, Elizabeth. The memory remains stored away in every cell of your being. You need to let it go; the karma is balanced," encourages her guardian angel. "You need to move forward. Talk to Kent . . . he really loves you, Liz."

Elizabeth continues to talk to her reflection. "How can this be? This is the best day of my life, being with Kent after all these years, my dream come true. And yet for my dream to be completely true, to become a reality, I have to tell him about the worst nightmare of my life!"

"The reality of your past is the missing piece of the puzzle for Kent," Elizabeth's angel explains. "It is understanding the past that he wants—what he needs to move forward with you." Her angel states emphatically, "Now get out there and talk to the man, Elizabeth!"

The answer that Elizabeth seeks is staring her in the face, almost yelling at her. An answer that her guardian angel has been giving her for so long. An answer to enable Elizabeth to finally fit together all the pieces of her life.

Sitting down on the toilet lid, Elizabeth breathes deeply, rehearsing the words over and over in her mind. *What will Kent say after I disclose everything? My God, every fear, every worry, every ounce of guilt has to be laid aside if I want to be able to move forward with Kent as part of my life.*

"That's right!" Her angel winks and smiles.

Elizabeth walks slowly down the aisle, trying to find the right words, in the right sequence. *Oh, God, can I really do this?*

Her guardian angel walks ahead, guiding, comforting, and encouraging. Like a plane being guided into its gate, her angel waves its wing directing Elizabeth to her row. Apprehensively, Elizabeth looks over at Kent.

"Are you okay?" asks Kent, quickly getting out of his seat to let her in.

"Yes, I mean, I will be," she says softy, not wanting to draw attention to herself from the surrounding passengers.

"You can wait to answer my question, Liz. It doesn't have to be right now, you know." He takes her hand in his and laces their fingers together, holding it reassuringly then places a gentle kiss on her lips. "No matter what happens, no matter what you say, I'll always be grateful that destiny has brought you back into my life, even if it's only for the length of this flight."

"No, I have to do this," she replies, her throat tightening. "You deserve to know."

Elizabeth stares at Kent, his eyes so full of compassion and love. Drawing a deep breath, she is suddenly hit again with an avalanche of pain, anger, guilt, frustration, and disappointment. The cabin air swirls with the stress and tension that Elizabeth is experiencing. Her lower lip begins to quiver.

Noticing her pain and anguish, Kent gently strokes her forearm. "Elizabeth, I will always love you. Trust that everything is going to be fine." He places his hand on top of hers for a moment, trying to offer a gesture of reassurance and understanding, even though he does not know what is causing her apparent sorrow and heartache. His words are spoken just as softly as hers, as if he is fearful of intruding into her private world.

Collecting herself while forcing the words out of her mouth, Elizabeth begins to speak very quietly, "Do you remember the day when we planned to have stir-fry at your apartment? When we were going to eat Japanese style on the floor with our shoes off, and I was going to bring the sake?"

"Yes, of course I do. I had everything ready. You never showed up, never called."

Elizabeth pauses as she tries to focus her train of thought, to pull together the proper words and the proper sequence of events. "Well, that afternoon while following some leads for an investigative report I was working on for my journalism class, I got an anonymous phone call.

Apparently, the people I was doing the report on were getting nervous because I was onto something really big."

"You should have called me. I mean, I know it was confidential and all that, but, Liz, maybe I could have helped," says Kent in his attempt to help resurrect the past.

"Some of the cheerleaders overheard something before one of the games. A rumor was going around that the football team was using steroids and other performance-enhancing drugs. Of course, if the head coach found out about it, there would be a huge scandal at the school and in the media, probably up to the national level. Anyway, I interviewed head coach Rollins regarding the rumor. And, of course, he discounted the whole thing. He was looking forward to retirement, and the school had one of its best teams ever that year." Elizabeth nervously takes a sip of water.

"Yeah, I remember; the stadium was packed every Saturday," adds Kent.

"That afternoon after football practice—the same day, the same evening that we were supposed to have dinner—I went to Coach Johnson, the assistant head coach, to challenge him about the steroid use. I went to his office and—" Elizabeth abruptly stops talking. Looking away from Kent, she covers her mouth momentarily as she begins to feel overwhelmingly nauseated. Elizabeth sits in silence for a moment then looks desperately into Kent's eyes, trying to compose her inner turmoil, trying desperately to find the courage to continue.

"Coach Johnson exploded when I pressed him about the rumor. He came around the desk to where I was sitting and threw my tape recorder against the wall." She shudders then looks nervously to see if the passenger sitting next to her is listening. "I was so scared, Kent. I tried to leave, but he locked the door and started screaming about how he was next in line for the head-coaching position and that no one was going to take that from him. He said that his team was going to remain the best and that he didn't care what it took to make that happen. I tried to remain calm, but he was going ballistic. I demanded that he let me out, and before I knew what was happening he had me up against the wall. Being the feisty, tenacious and very naïve reporter that I was, I threatened that I would call the police and tell them everything!"

"Liz, I had no idea. My God, how did you get out? Did he hurt you?" Kent clenches his fists as the knot in his stomach tightens. He feels the anger building inside him. "I'll kill that bastard!"

Elizabeth sees the change in Kent's behavior, feels his tension level increasing as she explains. She places her hand on his arm and looks into the distress that fills his eyes.

"Kent, that's exactly why I didn't tell you anything." Kent sees the pleading in her eyes and hears the heartfelt sincerity in her voice. "I knew that you would try to go after anyone who had tried to hurt me. But the situation was truly bigger than you or I or even the police would have been able to handle. In his crazed ranting, he practically told me the whole story—names, places, and people. The scandal went as far as the governor's mansion. Apparently, gambling and extortion were heavily involved in the whole situation. Coach Johnson was buckling under the pressure of his huge scheme. I mean, if anyone were to ever find out, he'd be sent to prison for a long time."

"But you, Liz, how did you get out of there?" Kent's voice is firm, but there is a slight edge of apprehension to it.

"After rambling on about what the steroids could do for the players, he got this really strange look on his face. He called a few of the linebackers into the office and—" Elizabeth stops again, focusing her attentions on the video monitor in front of her that tracks the airplane's flight path on a map. Although they have traveled far, it looks to Elizabeth that it will be forever before reaching LA. Every minute now seems like an eternity. She takes a deep breath trying to relax while knowing that Kent anxiously wants to hear the rest. A strange sense of inner calm momentarily settles over her nerves.

"Liz, would you like something to drink?" Kent asks patiently. Tezalel is standing next their seats with the beverage cart.

"Just another water, thank you," she whispers.

"Two bottled waters, please," Kent tells Tezalel. Taking the glass bottles, he opens them, handing one to Elizabeth.

She takes a small sip and fixates on the bottle, no longer able to look at Kent. "Oh, my God," she hesitates before continuing, "he called the biggest, toughest guys on the team into his office. He had them take off their shorts. He was making jokes, telling the players to flex and pump their muscles, to show me just what steroids did for them. He then closed all the blinds in the office. He told the players to show me what the drugs could do for me." Elizabeth trembles uncontrollably.

Kent is speechless, trying to visualize what happened yet not wanting to at the same time. He gulps all the water from his bottle in an effort to ease the tension and torment of his troubled thoughts.

Elizabeth is shaking. "I have to go. Please excuse me, Kent. I have to get up!"

"Liz? Right now?" asks Kent in disbelief.

"Yes, Kent. Please."

"Okay, let me just unbuckle my seat belt. Are you going to be okay? Do you want me to—" starts Kent as he stands up to let her out.

"Please! Excuse me," she demands frantically. Elizabeth rushes to the lavatory once more.

Chapter 70

Pushing an empty meal cart into the first class galley, Eve walks in on Nicole searching desperately through the cabinets, drawers, and carts as she cries out loud, "Where is it?"

"You're supposed to be in the back," Eve states firmly noticing that every drawer, every compartment, every carrier is open; and their contents scattered on the galley counter.

Nicole sees the look of disapproval in Eve's eyes. The desperate trainee turns away to rummage around in one of the supply cabinets. Her restlessness grows with each passing moment. Like that of the passengers, her nerves are on edge.

"Where is *The Book of Flight,* Eve?" demands Nicole. An anxious churning increases in intensity throughout her being. "I need to look up a PNR. Who is he, and where is he—"

Eve doesn't give Nicole the opportunity to finish her sentence. "Where is he going?" Eve asks tauntingly. "Father Knorosov, I might guess?"

In her frustration, Nicole glares loathingly at the onboard leader. "Give me *The Book of Life,* Eve!"

Eve hesitates for a moment, taken aback by the young trainee's rudeness and disrespect. "Seems you have lost much of your angelic vibrations—again," Eve says as she parks her cart. Her expression shifts, appearing more sympathetic but no less judgmental. "You won't be able to access his record or anyone else's. Sorry."

"Then you have to do it for me, Eve!" demands Nicole as she slams the cabinet door shut.

Eve furrows her brow for a moment. "No, Nicole. The PNRs don't work that way." She slides a trash cart directly in front of Nicole. "Take this through both aisles in coach and see what you can find back there! I expect that the 350 people back there may have something to give you. You can start at Row 10—Father Knorosov's row."

# Chapter 71

"So what brings you and the children to Los Angeles, Christopher?" Mrs. Montgomery asks delicately. "Did I miss that part?"

"Excuse me, would you care for anything to drink, Mrs. Montgomery?" Sarakiel parks the beverage cart next to her row.

"A cup of hot tea would be lovely, dear. No cream or sugar, thank you. Can't gain any weight on this flight." Mrs. Montgomery pats her large tummy.

"Anything for you, Mr. Dunn?" asks Sarakiel.

"Bottled water please, no ice. Since they confiscated the kids' juice boxes at security, just leave a couple of bottles of water here for the children for when they wake up." His annoyance with the whole travel experience that day edges through his words as he points to Rebecca and Ryan across the aisle. "Thank you, ma'am."

Christopher continues with his story. "Well, obviously, I needed to get back to work. Love is a powerful thing, but it can't pay the bills and feed your kids," admits Christopher as he chuckles. "I'm going back to California where my family lives. And my parents are just going to have to accept it." He sighs, looking at Rebecca and Ryan again. "You see, my parents were dead set against my marriage to Kim because she was Vietnamese. They had all these grand elitist notions regarding the type of woman I should or should not marry. After the wedding, they basically disowned me. We rarely talked, and they hardly acknowledged the fact that Ryan and Rebecca were even born. Because of their narrow and prejudice way of thinking, they wanted nothing to do with Kim, myself, or our children."

"Well, I have a feeling that everything will work out now," Mrs. Montgomery says in a knowing manner. "Your parents have obviously consented to your return. It's a huge step for them, no doubt. It will be a real blessing for you, the children, and your parents."

"Even though staying in New York would have felt like the safe thing to do, I knew that I needed to give the children more than I could offer them there," Christopher explains. "They need the love and support of a family. After all these years and Kim's passing, my parents said they would try. The situation in the city was totally draining me. It's like Abraham said in the Bible, 'Leave the land you know and go forth!'"

"That's exactly what I've been telling my granddaughter, Samantha." Mrs. Montgomery nods in agreement. "That she needs to learn, grow, and move on with her life. For years she had been involved with a young man that was just all wrong for her. She wasted too much time on that hopeless relationship. After talking with her day after day, she finally listened to me, got enough courage to end the relationship, and is moving to California—today as a matter of fact! She's actually sitting toward the back in 47E. We couldn't sit together either." Mrs. Montgomery cranes her neck toward the back of the plane. "Anyway, she's the reason I'm on this flight. I want to be sure she really goes through with the changes she promised to make."

Christopher raises his brow, giving her a questioning look. "I know, Christopher, I shouldn't meddle; but I feel responsible for her. I'll never be able to rest until I know she's taken care of and has her life on the right track.

"Samantha is a very gifted artist; you should see her work," brags Mrs. Montgomery. "She used to teach art in the public schools, but she found that she was doing more crowd control than teaching. I convinced her that she really ought to open her own art gallery, and that's what she's going to do. She'll be offering art classes for young aspiring artists during the summers. Doesn't that just sound wonderful, Christopher?"

"She sounds like a nice girl, Mrs. Montgomery, and certainly very lucky to have you as a grandmother." His voice and thoughts trail off. Christopher is only partially listening to his seatmate while still caught up in the emotions and the memories that surfaced while talking about Kim. He looks over at Mrs. Montgomery and realizes that she is waiting for him to respond to something that she has just said.

"I'm sorry. What did you say?" he asks politely. "I was somewhere else."

"I said that you should meet my granddaughter, Samantha," replies Mrs. Montgomery. "I know that you two would have a lot to talk about."

"She sounds like a wonderful person, Mrs. Montgomery; but really, I'm not in the frame of mind to meet anyone right now," Christopher apologizes. "I'm just focusing on my children and the move to California."

Chapter 72

Kneeling by her seat, Father Knorosov offers a silent prayer over Jane. Her breathing is shallow and her heartbeat slow. Briggs now sits with his mother holding her hand, needing reassurance that she has not died. She seems to respond ever so slightly.

In the first row of coach, Louis currently finds himself deep in conversation with Martin. "Surely she wasn't this sick when you traveled to Germany?" Martin asks delicately.

"Truth is that Jane has always been challenged with various medical problems." Louis looks painfully at his wife and son. "When she was delivering Briggs, the doctors discovered that she had developed ovarian cancer. It had never been detected before, so we were all shocked. It was advanced enough that they insisted on a hysterectomy. We'd always wanted a large family, so the news was especially devastating for Jane." He looks proudly at Briggs. "The doctors said that it was a miracle that he was even born.

"After the delivery and the surgery, I had to take care of Briggs and Jane. It was a challenge, but I had help from friends and family, so everything worked out. Jane took it very hard. For some reason, she blames herself for everything and carries around all this guilt. She just never understood how much I loved her. She is just so insecure."

"Oh." Martin responds with a faint smile.

"Later, when Briggs was much older, she was diagnosed with multiple sclerosis. Jane refused to accept being sick again and that there was really nothing that the doctors could do. So she started looking into alternative forms of healing, and that's when she heard about the miracles taking place in Medjugorje."

"Never heard of it before today," Martin interjects.

"I can't tell you what happened, Martin, except she was completely healed. Everyone was amazed—except for the people that live there. I guess they're used to seeing that kind of thing happen all the time." He chuckles nervously and takes a gulp of black coffee.

"So it came back?" asks Martin curiously.

Louis shakes his head and looks frankly at Martin. "This is a long story. Are you sure you really want to hear all this?" Louis asks doubtfully. "Don't you have your work to finish?"

"Right now, I have all the time in the world." Martin points to his broken tray table and shifts his large arms crossed awkwardly over his broad chest. "Please, continue."

"Well, Jane started having severe constipation; you know, that kind of thing. She was too embarrassed to mention any of it to me and chose to ignore the symptoms all together. Her life was exactly the way she had always dreamed of, and she didn't want to mess it up. She was afraid that she'd go to the doctor and that he'd find something wrong, and everything would come crashing back down on her again. She thought that if anything else happened to her that I would leave."

Louis shakes his head in disbelief and lets out a big sigh. "When the pain became too much, she finally did go see the doctor. He confirmed that she had colon cancer. Jane left his office with no intention of ever returning or telling me what was happening. Of course, it started to become pretty obvious that she was sick. I ended up taking her to the doctor myself one day, six months after her initial visit. That's when I discovered that she had already known about the disease." Louis hangs his head and slowly rubs his temples.

"I could not understand why she had not told me, or why she had refused to go back. She said she couldn't face the thought of another operation, of putting us both through another bout with cancer, of losing our savings again, and so on. Honestly, Martin, I was crushed that she couldn't realize how much I loved her and that she didn't trust me to be able to provide for our family. I couldn't take the fact that she was willing to abandon me and our son because she did not trust me to stay with her."

"Trust is very important," Martin agrees. Nodding his head, he reflects back on his own life. "It's everything, isn't it?"

"Well, her biggest fear came true; I left her. Not because she had cancer, but because she didn't trust or believe in my love. It was the hardest thing I'd ever done. However, I couldn't stand to be away from her, knowing that she needed me there. And that Briggs needed me there too."

"So you went back?"

"How could I not have?" Louis stares at over at Briggs while Father Knorosov prays over Jane. Louis sighs as tears run down his face. Unexpectedly he rises up from his seat, motioning for Father Knorosov to go back and rest. Martin watches painfully as Louis now stands vigil over Jane and tries to reassure his crying son.

Chapter 73

Elizabeth returns from the lavatory and squeezes back into her seat next to Kent, just five rows behind Father Knorosov, Martin Peterson, and the Bradley family. Kent takes her hand and holds it tightly. "Liz, I'm here for you, just remember that. Everything is going to be okay," he reassures her. Elizabeth cannot meet his eyes. She just nods quickly, sucking in her breath, praying that he is right. An expressionless mask forms across her face. Staring blankly at the seatback in front of her, she begins to speak in a very detached manner as she continues with her story.

"I was still trying to get out, screaming as loudly as I could when one of them grabbed me and pulled off my skirt and underwear. They pinned me down on top of the desk. They all took turns. When they were finished, Coach Johnson sent them back into the locker room. They all acted as if nothing had happened." Elizabeth drones on as if she is a robot. Attaching herself to the event made it much too traumatic to talk about.

"Coach Johnson told me that if I ever told anyone about what I knew or what had happened to me, I would be taken care of—permanently—and so would everyone else that I cared about. He remembered you from playing for the school the year before and referred to you by name." Tears stream from the corners of Elizabeth's eyes.

The initial outrage that Kent feels toward the men that had raped and threatened Elizabeth subsides into a deeper concern for her. "Liz, you could have told me, sweetheart. You knew that I loved you. I would have understood that it wasn't your fault. What happened to you could never change my love for you." He puts his arm around her.

"There is nothing more that I want to do than to hold you, to somehow protect the love of my life from something that has already happened. Things make more sense to me now, Liz, the way that you had changed overnight," he whispers in her ear. He begins to recognize that the signs of her confusion in the beginning are now coming together into a more cohesive understanding.

"Kent, that isn't the end." Anxiously she looks around to see if the man sitting on the other side of her is listening, then hangs her head, relieved that he is wearing his headphones.

"What do you mean?" he asks in a state of bewilderment. Kent starts to suffer as much from jangled nerves as Elizabeth. He cocks his head and studies her face, not quite sure what to do or what to say next. He twists awkwardly around in the seat until his eyes squarely face hers.

"God, please help me. Kent, several weeks later I realized . . . I realized that I was pregnant. Pregnant . . . I was pregnant, and I had no idea whose baby it was! The thought that I could have become pregnant by one of those monsters horrified me. I was too frightened to tell anyone."

Kent's stunned silence is unnerving as the shock of her words catches him totally off guard.

"I could not let anyone know what had happened. I couldn't put anyone at risk. I was repeatedly threatened into silence. They said they would kill you, my family, my friends. So I left you, I left the school paper, I left cheerleading, I left everything that I loved. I didn't want anything to happen to anyone I cared about. Leaving was the only way I could protect everyone involved," she cries as the pain of her past glistens in her tears. A hard knot twists endlessly in the pit of her stomach.

Sitting in his seat, next to the woman he has loved since their sophomore year of college, Kent finally has the answers to his questions, as horrendous as they are. His tries to quell the heartache that is controlling his thoughts.

"It explains everything." His voice can barely be heard, his thoughts racing through his mind, and his emotions in a state of turmoil. At that moment, Kent is not sure that he really wants to know any more. He is not really sure that he wants to understand what was going on in her head all those years ago.

Elizabeth searches Kent's face, then his eyes for any sign of his intentions about their future together. She does not see anger, just a tremendous amount of pain and uncertainty. "I was left with no choice but to have an abortion, Kent. I had to rid myself of that nightmare. I had never believed in abortions before, but I had never believed something so horrific would have ever happened to me either. I was so scared, Kent. I had to destroy any evidence of what had happened that day."

A question begins to gnaw at his insides. After several moments of anguished reflection, Kent asks gravely, "Liz, what if it had been our child?"

Elizabeth gasps for cabin air that now somehow seems thinner, less available. She finally finds her voice; the hard lump in her throat makes it difficult for her to breathe and to speak. "My God, Kent. That's what made the decision so hard. I have cried for years. That very question tortures me every minute of every day. I was so confused then, so scared, so alone. Losing you, losing the baby, losing everything that had ever mattered to me, it crushed me. I felt that God must be punishing me. And I asked God that if he would ever forgive me that he would allow us to be together again. And here we are." Elizabeth begins to sob uncontrollably. As she sees the anxiety come into his eyes, feeling the tremor of pain move through his hand, a torrent of emotion that has been pent up for the past twenty years spills from her heart. "Oh, Kent, will you ever forgive me?"

Chapter 74

"Good afternoon, ladies and gentleman. We are currently at forty thousand feet cruising approximately forty miles north of St. Louis. Air traffic control is going to vector us around a series of thunderstorms, so it may get a little bumpy. We're turning on the Fasten Seat Belt sign. Please remain seated with your seat belts fastened, and we will let you know when it is safe to move about the aircraft. And as always, thank you for flying Infinity Airways."

"Oh, that always seems to happen just when I need to go to the ladies room!" exclaims Mrs. Montgomery.

"But, Mrs. Montgomery, the pilot said it may get rough." Christopher points to the illuminated seat belt sign over their row.

"After that lovely cup of tea—"

"But—"

"You know, when you got to go, you got to go!" Mrs. Montgomery grabs her pocketbook and pulls her little plump body up by the seatback in front of her. "I'm sorry, Christopher, but I really need to get by. Thank you for everything, Christopher, you're a real sweetheart, someday . . ." she rattles on as he lets her into the aisle. Straightening her lavender floral dress and adjusting her hat, Mrs. Montgomery looks to the back of the plane. "Seems like a long way from here. But don't you worry, Christopher, I'll be fine. And you will too, dear." She gives him a wink, a gentle pat on the arm, and teeters down the aisle.

While he is standing up, Christopher decides to check on Rebecca and Ryan, who are still both fast asleep across the aisle. The doting father is still upset that he and the children are not seated together. *Apparently that seems to be the case for Mrs. Montgomery and her granddaughter too.* He shakes his head and settles back into his seat. Christopher rests his eyes for what seems like a moment. Yet thirty minutes later, he feels someone touching his shoulder.

"Excuse me, Mr. Dunn? Would you stand up for a moment please?" asks Sarakiel. "We need to use the empty seat next to you."

"Yeah, sure," he replies groggily, temporarily forgetting that Mrs. Montgomery is in the lavatory. He rises out of his seat and steps into the aisle only to come face to face with one of the most beautiful women he has ever seen. For a moment, he feels as if he might lose his balance. Discreetly leaning into the seatback in front of him, he allows the mysterious lady into the seat next to his. He takes a deep breath and stands still for a moment before sitting back down himself.

"Are you okay, Mr. Dunn?" asks Sarakiel.

"Yes . . . yes, everything is fine, thank you," he says, looking not at Sarakiel but at the gorgeous woman seated next to him. "Oh, what about Mrs. Montgom—" he starts to ask. "Oh, never . . . never mind."

"Hi, my name is Samantha. I'm really sorry to disturb you." Enthusiastically she puts out her hand to introduce herself. Christopher doesn't reciprocate. "Okay . . . I'm sorry. The flight attendant told me that this seat was available. I was stuck back there in 47E between two very large men. I mean, they were pouring over the armrests and onto me; and trust me, it didn't smell too pleasant either," she explains nervously, trying to be funny, but not wanting to be an intrusion.

"Oh . . . Samantha," replies Christopher knowingly. "I see . . . you must have traded seats with your grandmother."

Samantha gives him an odd stare.

"Mrs. Montgomery? The little old lady with the lavender dress, white lace collar, and an old-fashioned white velvet hat?" Christopher encourages her with a half smile.

Samantha's face turns white. "My grandmother had a dress like that. It was her favorite. As a matter of fact, I buried her in a dress like that—seven years ago.

Christopher face turns white, as if he has just seen a ghost. "Seven years ago?"

"Yes. One day while I was at school, Grandma wanted to prove to my parents that she wasn't too old drive . . . that she was still capable of driving. Although Mom and Dad tried to convince her to give up her driver's license and her car, my mother went with her. Well," chokes Samantha as she tries to continue, "they both died in a horrible crash that day when Grandma's old clunker of a car stalled on a railroad track."

Chapter 75

"Mr. Peterson . . . Martin, would you like to sit in your seat up in first class for a while?" asks Louis Bradley, noticing how cramped he is in the smaller coach seat. "My wife is sleeping soundly now. Please, go up there and stretch out. It's a long flight."

"No, no, Louis. I'm fine, really," replies Martin as he attempts to lean forward and speak to Louis over Father Knorosov, who has returned to his center seat. "Let Briggs sit up there with his mother. He is truly an amazing child. I know as a parent, you must be extremely proud of him."

Father Knorosov and Martin resume their conversation about the healing miracles that take place in Medjugorje while Louis wearily watches Jane from his seat.

"So you've really witnessed these so-called miracles?" Martin asks with some skepticism.

"Yes, many times." Father Knorosov smiles knowingly, nodding his head.

"Were you with Jane her first time to this Medjugorje place?" Martin inquires further.

"Yes, it was truly a miracle. Everything healed perfectly according to all the tests and lab results. The doctors were amazed but said little. Yet Jane never understood—no matter how many times I told her—that the medical problems were not happening to her. But, in fact, she had brought them to herself. Cancers and tumors protect people from the memory and painful feelings stored in there. If they don't resolve the emotional issues that bring them on, these cancers and tumors—no matter how many times you cut them out—will reappear at a later time."

"Miracles in Medjugorje?" Martin begs the question with upraised brows.

"Indeed. I've been going there now for a long time with many different families and groups. I have made it somewhat a habit of mine to record and study the miracles that I have seen take place, not only there but all over the world."

"Miracles . . . all over the world?" Martin continues to give the priest a doubtful look. "Why don't we hear about these things in the news if so many of these events are happening worldwide?"

"A very good question, Martin. And one that I plan to change," he adds with an air of confidence.

Nicole overhears Father Knorosov as he converses with Martin. Father Knorosov glances up at her, and their eyes lock. Nicole blushes as the priest stares longingly at her.

"You've seen miracles?" she asks him innocently. Noticing the strength of his jaw line and the magnificence of his smile, Nicole becomes completely mesmerized while staring at his full and perfectly shaped lips.

"Yes," he replies, swallowing hard. The thirty-two-year-old man happily gets out of his seat to stand in the aisle closer to the beauty before him.

"I have too." She smiles knowingly, oblivious to all the passengers that are watching them and those who are wanting her services.

Father Knorosov reaches into his pant pocket retrieving several items. He looks momentarily at an old ivory and onyx disc, still fascinated years later by its symbols from an ancient civilization. He realizes that Nicole is watching him as he turns it over and over. Father Knorosov quickly returns it to the safety of his pocket while a beautiful rosary remains in his hand. He gently takes Nicole's wrist and places it in her soft ivory palm. "Here's a miracle for you," he whispers, gazing adoringly at the flight attendant trainee. "Before I went to Medjugorje, the beads were stainless steel. While I was there, they turned to gold." He holds her hand tenderly as he points to each bead. Breathlessly Nicole watches as his strong long fingers hold hers.

Nicole clutches the beautiful string of prayer beads and holds it close to her heart. "Thank you, Father," she whispers back, staring deep into his eyes, deep down into his very soul. "This means the world to me."

He suddenly redirects his attention to Jane as he sees that everyone around them is watching, pointing, and whispering.

Chapter 76

Kent Phillips remains in a rather stunned and contemplative silence following Elizabeth's heart-wrenching confession. He wrinkles his brow in confusion and shakes his head gently as if he does not understand. *Why would she ask such a question about forgiveness? Doesn't she understand the depth of my heart?* He looks over at Elizabeth's face and the serenity that now seems to envelop her delicate features. Completely purged of her deepest darkest secret, relieved to have everything out in the open, she has fallen asleep on his shoulder.

"Liz, would you like some more of that champagne?" Kent asks quietly, nudging her awake. "I know I would. I want to make a toast." He breaks into a full grin, raking his long fingers through his graying blonde hair in a kind of nervous yet excited way.

"A toast?" Elizabeth asks groggily as she touches his arm. Tears well up in her eyes as she sees the look on Kent's face. Realizing that he still loves her and accepts her completely, she buries her face in his shoulder as he goes to ring his flight attendant call button for more champagne. Rochel immediately arrives with another bottle before he can utter the very words of his request.

Kent chuckles and then pulls his lost love closer. "To our future together," he replies proudly as he pours the champagne. Suddenly a very romantic notion comes to mind.

Standing up in the aisle, towering over Liz and everyone else, Kent raises his glass in the air and proclaims loudly, "For better or worse, I do take you, Elizabeth, as my beloved wife, to have and to hold from this day forward, promising to love and comfort you, honoring you, and forsaking all others, to care for you in sickness and in health so long as we both shall live. That is . . . if you'll have me?"

Everyone claps and cheers as Elizabeth accepts his marriage proposal. "I do, I do, I do," she repeats with tears streaming down her face.

"Champagne for everyone!" Kent announces to everyone in the area, inviting them to share in the celebration of his love.

The man seated next to Elizabeth is the first to happily accept the offer. "I certainly need one after all that!" he says jokingly. Elizabeth and Kent laugh together, toasting each other, vowing never to be apart again.

Elizabeth's guardian angel gives a high five to Kent's guardian angel. Both of them sit perched arm in arm on the back of Kent's seat, celebrating the long-awaited reunion.

 *Chapter 77*

Walking out of the first class lavatory, Martin notices William who is waiting at the end of line to use the facilities. He does a double take when he sees William's eyes. There's something vaguely familiar about them.

"Excuse me, I'm Martin Peterson. I think we must know each other from somewhere," he says to the same man that Father Knorosov had approached earlier.

"William Gladstone, if the name rings a bell." His fingers brush against his thick black hair, revealing his smooth broad forehead, thick shapely brows, and dark brown eyes.

"Uh . . . not really. What business are you in, son?"

"I'm a professional intuitive consultant," William replies quickly.

"Hmm, sounds interesting, but I guess I don't know you then. It's strange, you just seem so familiar to me. Maybe it will come to me later. Sorry to disturb you," Martin says apologetically.

"No problem," muses William, stepping closer toward the lavatory.

Martin glances across the cabin toward Jane as he returns to his seat. His heart tugs painfully when he notices Briggs wiping his eyes has tears stream down his cheeks. The young man sits mournfully next to his mother, stroking her frail, limp hand. Walking cautiously around the bulkhead wall and maneuvering past his briefcase on the floor, Martin lands back in the cramped coach seat. He looks in Louis's direction for conversation but notices that Father Knorosov is resting with his eyes closed.

Sitting quietly, different thoughts and emotions stir inside Martin. *This poor family has been through so much. All this talk with Louis reminds me of my own personal heartaches. I don't know why—especially with every thing else I need to work on—but somehow I have to help this family.*

In the center seat with his seatback fully reclined, Father Knorosov's mind begins to drift as thoughts of Nicole continue to flood his senses. His heartbeat quickens; his body begins to ache as the visions of touching her, stroking her face, and touching her skin replay again and again in his memory.

Nicole begrudgingly walks up the aisle from the back of the plane pushing the overloaded trash cart toward the row where Elizabeth and Kent are now kissing passionately. As passengers hand more and more trash and used newspapers to Nicole, she stares curiously at the reunited couple. She is mesmerized as their long, wet, deep kiss continues. The sexual desire, the passionate love—the eternal desire to be together forever that Elizabeth and Kent now feel for each other—flow into Nicole as she watches them intently. Consumed with a sexual longing, uncontrollably obsessed with desire for Father Knorosov, Nicole quickly pushes the cart to the front row of coach and approaches the sleeping priest, gently tapping him on the arm.

Father Knorosov suddenly snaps out of his trancelike state when Nicole asks nervously if there is anything that she can do to be of service. Staggered by her beauty and unassuming grace, he feels a sudden palpitation in his chest. Unconsciously his eyes, in a daze of passion, skim her gorgeous figure, bringing a wash of color to her already pink cheeks. Before he can respond, Nicole breathlessly says, "I really want to talk to you, Father. I need to talk with you." Feeling the same attraction for her, he discreetly follows her to the area next to the lavatory near the emergency exit door where they can talk privately.

Father Knorosov's heart feels as if it is on a roller coaster. He is incredibly happy to be with her yet anxious at the same time as an underlying fear holds him back. Thoughts of being with Nicole send him flying sky high. Making love to her is a scene that now plays over and over in his mind as she looks longingly into his eyes, innocently asking for more.

How can a woman consume my thoughts? he begs of himself in a silent confession. *It's not just that I've been alone so long; it's Nicole. This woman excites me in a way that I thought was not possible, but the timing seems so wrong. Yet I know she is the one for me. I feel it down in the very center of my being. God has somehow woven us together in a delicate, intricate web of destiny.*

Standing silently in the aisle are two faithful servants of the Lord. Both are crucial instruments of God's grace in the lives of the people they touch. The same but different. Somehow, somewhere in time, the remuneration for their service and dedication is about to be rewarded in a way neither dreamt possible.

Stepping out of the way, so Rochel can pass by with another cart, Nicole unexpectedly finds herself up against the wall with Father Knorosov. "Oh, I'm sorry. I—" she starts to say. Sudden surges of erotic passion from Father Knorosov consume her vibrations. He rolls his torso toward hers, propping his elbows and hands against the wall with his unseen muscles tight and taught. His groin pulsates as his body becomes a reservoir of swirling sexual energy.

Simon Knorosov has been blessed with the most incredible face. His brilliant smile can melt ice and over the years has certainly turned the heads of many a young lady. Under the priest's clothing, his body looks as if it has been chiseled out of marble, a sculptor's masterpiece of perfection, like Michelangelo's David. His personality is magnetic, attracting people of all ages, his voice absolutely captivating. His piercing gray eyes look straight to the heart.

The priest gazes steadily into Nicole's crystal blue eyes. "Ah, Nicole," he murmurs, his words are soft and hesitant, his manner somewhat uncertain. With his warm lips against her ear, no longer able to resist his carnal urges, he presses in even closer as if trying to absorb her into his being. Nicole's trembling hands find their way across the muscled span of his back. His embrace is masterful, sensually riveting. She feels a strange sense of homecoming.

An intense and unfamiliar pounding in her chest begins as she waits for him to speak. She studies his face intently, seeing something in his eyes, considering something, debating something very serious. Finally, his lips part for the deepest, the gentlest of voices. "Nicole, I need to—" he starts then stops abruptly. No longer able to control his urges, he kisses her soft and supple lips gently and then again, more deeply. His probing tongue intoxicates her so wildly that it takes her a minute to realize that his leg is also exploring the space between her thighs. The heat of her response and unbridled passions send him directly to cloud nine. He closes his eyes allowing the exhilaration of their union to penetrate his soul. He listens to the cadenced sound of their combined breathing that fills the pressurized air around them. As time and the miles fly by, on the threshold of sensual rhapsody, all of the priest's honorable intentions soar away into the ethers.

"Oh, God," Nicole slowly moans, lost in the heavenly depths of their indulgence. The taste of him is addictive. The angel from above needs his kiss again. Now even fuller, firmer, even deeper than before. She craves the physical sensation of the sexual earthiness of his kiss. Her ivory hands draw his face up to her mouth, where she lustfully indulges her physical desire, forgetting that she is an angel working on a crowded airplane at forty thousand feet above the Earth to help save humanity.

Mirroring the pulsating passion that has been awakened in the priest before her, Nicole's body is stimulated in the most unfathomable ways. The aching of his flesh is flowing energetically into her celestial body, stirring her into rhythmic throbbing sensations that overwhelm every part of her being. Rather than satisfying a hunger, his taste fills her with a desire for even more.

"I can't—" He tries to twist away, yet his lips close more firmly over hers, and the words are lost in the cavernous depths of his mouth. His warm, wet tongue meshes with hers; together their taste is like that of sweet, warm honey. He holds her silently while her hands tenderly cradle his face. Abruptly Father Knorosov clutches her shoulders as he musters a breathless plea. "We've got to stop, Nicole," he begs. He strokes the side of her cheek then pulls on the white collar of his clergy shirt to release the heat that is rapidly building inside. Looking around the cabin to see who may be looking, he forces a painful return of self-control.

Chapter 78

Nicole looks back longingly toward the coach cabin for a possible glimpse of Father Knorosov as she hands the Hamiltons another cocktail. She can't see him because the bulkhead, the partition between cabins, blocks her view. Yet she knows he's there.

"Ladies and gentlemen, this is Captain Smith," starts the announcement over the public-address system. "We have just been contacted by flight control. Apparently a major power outage has occurred in the Los Angeles area. The airport is closed, suspending all arrivals and departures at LAX indefinitely. Flight 555 is being diverted to Las Vegas, Nevada. We will be landing in one hour. Please understand . . ." The announcement is drowned out by the cries of frustration, disappointment, and the deluge of ringing passenger call bells throughout the plane. Many anxious passengers line up in the first class aisle to speak with Eve. First in line is Martin Peterson.

"I want to speak to the captain right now, Ms. Matrona. Something needs to be done about this situation. Jane Bradley and her family need to get home to Victorville and as quickly as possible!" Martin demands emphatically.

"Yes, Mr. Peterson, I understand." Eve is composed and very professional. "Our reservationists are already making arrangements. We are especially aware of Mrs. Bradley's situation."

"Look, I'm president and CEO of Peterson Properties. And I know people in high places, Ms. Matrona. It's not beyond my power to contact them if necessary!" Martin announces loudly so not only does Eve hear him but everyone else around. He wants it clearly understood that he carries the power, influence, and connections to make things happen, no matter where he is.

"Yes, sir. At Infinity, we also know people in very high places. And rest assured, Mr. Peterson, they're making all the arrangements necessary to take Mrs. Bradley home. Thank you for your continued thoughtfulness regarding her and her family. Please know that she is in good hands," Eve says calmly and reassuringly, even though there are now twenty passengers lined up behind him.

Although the anxiety, fear, and frustration are mounting in the passengers, the love Nicole now feels is maintaining a unique balance in her. Working in the aisles with the other flight attendants, she tries to be helpful, doing whatever she can to assist people with their questions; however, she is only willing to help those passengers who are seated within seven rows of Father Knorosov. Her mind spins as she happily tries to grasp the magnitude of her feelings for Father Knorosov. Recurring thoughts of their first kiss swirl in her mind. Nicole now understands why a kiss is the most powerful and universal expression of romantic love. The emissary from the heavens above now yearns for more.

The pilots signal that it is time to land. Eve taps Nicole on the shoulder and instructs her to return to first class. "Nicole, please help prepare the galleys, cabin, and passengers for landing. Los Angeles International Airport is still closed. Las Vegas is now our destination."

Chapter 79

The forward boarding door is opened. "Eve, everyone is ready. Let's get her home," instructs the gate agent. Several Infinity Airways representatives and emergency rescue technicians immediately come on board to secure the safe and expeditious removal of Jane Bradley. As the paramedics carefully prepare to carry the dying wife and mother off the plane, Nicole stands at the door with Eve and Sila. They watch as Louis, Briggs, Father Knorosov, and Martin Peterson follow the stretcher to the front of first class.

"Thank you, Mr. Peterson," exclaims Louis, shaking Martin's hand enthusiastically. "Thank you. This is truly a miracle. I don't know how I can ever repay you."

"What is he talking about, Eve?" begs Nicole as she observes the scene before her. Jane is secure on the gurney; an IV drip has been set up.

"While we were still in flight, Mr. Peterson used our onboard telephone service to make a call. In a divine moment of inspiration, he chartered a private emergency medical helicopter to transport the Bradleys back to Victorville in California, fulfilling Jane's wish to pass away at home." Eve explains further, a sense of satisfaction hangs on her words, "Apparently the helicopter and crew were being dispatched to leave for California anyway. Through some of his local contacts, Mr. Peterson arranged to have the Bradleys transported on the flight. Father Knorosov will be going as well. He is committed to seeing Jane—one of his former parishioners—pass away at home, administering her last rites, and honoring her request to have him perform the services at her funeral."

Sila and Eve step aside to make room for everyone to exit. The look of shock that covers Nicole's face speaks volumes. With eyes wide with surprise, Nicole remains at the door in disbelief, oblivious to what to going on around her. Father Knorosov stops in front of the door and looks painfully at Nicole. Sensing that everyone is watching Nicole and him, he fights back his tears, his pain, and struggles to smile.

Seeking to rein in her own emotions, Nicole forces herself to remain composed as she stands at the boarding door. Her manner is subdued, mirroring that of the priest before her. Everyone waits for him to leave with the Bradleys. Nicole senses a secret in his smile.

Sila whispers to Eve, "Are you seeing what I'm seeing, Eve? She's an angel, yet the passion, the heartache, the undeniable love between them seems to exceed all boundaries. Standing there at the threshold of timelessness are two divine servants of The Creator; nevertheless, two lovers—one mortal and one immortal—who cannot come together."

Father Knorosov tries to smile. The man of the cloth is eminently grateful for the time he has had with Nicole yet feels naggingly empty. "Maybe another time, another place," he whispers to her. As he speaks from the heart, he gently squeezes her hand as he tucks a piece of paper firmly between her fingers. "Thank you for sharing a miracle with me. A miracle I will never forget."

As his words trail off, Nicole's thoughts return to the hour earlier, to their intimate encounter, their passion, and desire—their first kiss. She stares at his mouth, transfixed on the masculine firmness of his lips, recalling their warm persuasion. Even now at the boarding door, she craves the same deepening sensation. Knowing that it is impossible, she struggles to smile instead.

"For the first time, Nicole looks empty," Sila says sympathetically as Eve signs some paperwork from the gate agent.

Michael steps out of the cockpit and joins Eve and Sila. "Is everything okay, ladies?"

Sila points toward Nicole and continues. "Just look at her. Numb from the pain and anguish, the poor thing is speechless, unable to put together the words to convey the hurt, torment, and loss she feels. She's still standing there at the door trying to smile as the other passengers wait restlessly to deplane. Yet I sense that Nicole feels as if a large part of her has been ripped away, never to be seen or experienced again. It's my guess that unknowingly Simon Knorosov has captured the heart of an angel." Eve smiles in agreement. Michael stands stoically silent.

Out of the corner of his eye, Father Knorosov sees that Michael is watching him closely. He glances briefly over to the airline captain then looks ahead as Louis and Briggs wait for him. *I had it all mapped out! Now, all of a sudden my life, my heart are swirling. My God, she is in my every thought. I truly believed that I had everything all worked out,* he says to himself as he walks painfully away from Nicole.

Heartbroken and confused, the priest reluctantly continues down the jetway toward the arrival gate, forcing himself to take one step and then another. *The timing seems so wrong. How can it be that I would meet someone now, Lord, after all these years? Is this some kind of curse—or a blessing?"* He demands an answer as his frustration grows. *I have come so far, given up so much, to be where I am now. My life, my beliefs mirror the very sacrifices I've made.*

Tears emerge from the corners of his eyes. *Maybe it's time to enrich my solitary existence and stave off my loneliness. However, I know I will lose myself in the passion of her love if I turn around now.* Mustering his last remnants for reason, he forces himself to retreat and proceed to the gate. *Presently, my devotion to Jane Bradley has to override any of my personal desires.*

Chapter 80

As Martin Peterson settles into the front row of the passenger bus heading to the hotel for the stopover in Las Vegas, he struggles to understand the rapid change of events. *Dammit! I can't figure out what is going on. Here I was able to get a helicopter for the Bradleys, yet I'm unable to get a plane or helicopter for myself. Today, someone else seems to be in control.* He takes a long deep, breath then turns to his seatmate.

"So, William, please tell me again what it is that you do for a living?" Martin asks, somehow feeling compelled to make small talk with his fellow inconvenienced passenger.

"A professional intuitive, a researcher, primarily a researcher of metaphysics," William replies casually while staring at the dazzling Las Vegas billboards out of the bus window. "I've been on numerous television and radio talk shows. As a matter of fact, I was on my way to Los Angeles for a live in-studio interview with George Noory of the *Coast to Coast AM* radio show."

"Is that the one that comes on really late at night? The one about ETs, crop circles, and ghosts?" asks Martin, halfway listening as he puts away his cell phone. "Damn! Still can't seem to get a hold of anyone."

"Los Angeles was hit hard," William says knowingly as he rubs his forehead. "I'd hoped to warn everyone again. But no one wants to listen," reflects the slender twenty-three-year-old researcher, clutching his worn leather briefcase. "The power outage at LAX was caused by an earthquake, Mr. Peterson."

"And how do you know this?" Martin asks curiously, wondering where he is getting his information.

Distracted with his thoughts and visions, William absentmindedly turns the conversation back to the accomplished architect and real-estate developer. "So, Mr. Peterson, what do you do for a living?"

"Real estate, young man. Design, development, and land acquisitions," replies Martin proudly, looking out the front windshield at the hotels and casinos along the Las Vegas Strip. "Still seems strange how you seem so familiar to me, yet obviously we are in completely different businesses."

"Egypt," states William.

"Egypt?" questions Martin.

"Egypt. We know each other from ancient Egypt, and we are going there now," William declares very matter-of-factly. Just as the words leave his mouth, the Infinity Airways representative on the bus announces that the hotel accommodations have just changed because of the size of their group. They are now heading for the Luxor Hotel & Casino.

"Well, now. Isn't it a small world!" exclaims Martin with a certain level of intrigue and anticipation.

"Yes, in some ways you can say that," remarks William as he closes his eyes.

"I was a partner in the building of the Luxor back in the early nineties. Funny thing is . . . I've actually never stayed there," Martin replies as they drive on the south end of the Strip toward the thirty-story black glass pyramid. The bus pulls into the parking area for guest registration. The passengers in the bus are so loud in their excitement that Martin and William can barely hear each other. Looking at the captivating resort, William suddenly feels dizzy, swept away by the mystique of ancient Egypt replicated by the luxurious hotel.

"Yeah, if I remember correctly, this baby features over forty-four-hundred custom-designed guest rooms and suites located in the pyramid and a pair of stepped-pyramid towers. Each room is decorated with an Egyptian motif featuring wooden furniture etched with hieroglyphics, making this place unlike any other hotel on Earth," boasts Martin. "Pretty amazing architecture, don't you think, son? With slanting walls and elevators called inclinators that move at a thirty-nine-degree angle, we had a hell of a time figuring some of the internal structural engineering." He laughs heartily as he looks directly at his seatmate. "But I guess it is mere child's play compared to the actual design and construction of the Great Pyramid of Giza. Although the ancient Egyptians didn't have to worry about interior lighting, climate control, or valet parking. Nonetheless, that Great Pyramid is an unrivaled feat of engineering and craftsmanship, son. Do you know that those blocks weigh over twenty tons each? Now you tell me how they did that back then. I certainly don't buy that stupid asinine theory about ramps and pulleys."

"Levitation."

"Levitation? Okay," Martin repeats doubtfully.

"Yes. You asked how they moved the blocks—levitation," remarks William as he rubs his throbbing forehead. Visions, thoughts, premonitions, and memories come flooding in. Los Angeles, ancient Egypt, earth changes, akashic records, Atlantis, earthquakes, and pyramids whirl in William's mind like a desert sandstorm. He continues to explain, "The blocks are alive. They have a consciousness, a type of intelligence. When one speaks to that intelligence, a request may be given."

"Well, never heard that one before," says Martin amusingly. "Although it's funny you mention Egypt—that's why I got involved in this project—something just seems familiar about it. Always had an interest in those burial chambers for the pharaohs since I was a young kid," rambles Martin as he looks excitedly over at the sphinx replica in front of the hotel, sitting right along the Strip.

"Sorry, Martin. That's a common misconception. The Pyramid of Giza was built as an energy device used for initiation rituals for those wishing to enter the priesthood. I suppose three days lying in a sarcophagus in the pitch dark could initiate anyone, assuming they survived the madness first!"

"Well, this pyramid won't drive you to madness and certainly not into priesthood, but you will love the inside of this place," Martin boasts proudly. "Hey, William, since we're both traveling alone, let's have dinner together in the Isis Restaurant—great food, beautiful decor. Around six o'clock? That's of course if we haven't gone back to the airport before then."

"Six, six will be fine. I should be ready by then," William answers automatically, still dazed, processing the events of the last five hours.

As the airline representative exits the bus Martin leans over the handle railing and instructs her to make dinner reservations for William and him. With one waiting stretch limousine and eight buses parked side by side, the Infinity representatives proceed quickly to the Luxor registration desk to check in almost four hundred passengers.

Chapter 81

In the bus seated three rows behind William and Martin are Samantha and Christopher, with his two children seated behind them. Christopher cranes his neck between the upholstered seatbacks. "Let me see how Ryan and Rebecca are doing—how they are adjusting to the sudden change in plans." He steals another quick glance at the beauty sitting next to him. Samantha catches his roving eyes.

"Christopher, does it seem strange to you how we have been drawn together in these most unusual of circumstances?" Samantha asks inquisitively as she searches his eyes for an explanation. "How we somehow feel this sense of familiarity between us and that now this place feels familiar too, like home? Yet we've never met before today, and neither one of us has been to Las Vegas before, much less to this hotel."

"Yes, it is perplexing yet exciting. I look forward to spending more time getting to know you and hearing about the plans for your art gallery. Hmm, I wonder if this pyramid, I mean, this hotel offers childcare," Christopher says nervously, surprised by his own suggestions. *Strange. Childcare is something that I've never considered until today. Hell, I never even thought of being with another woman until now.* He inwardly pushes aside his disgust at his wandering thoughts and yearnings to be with a stranger he just met on the flight. He pushes aside the feeling that he is somehow cheating on his deceased wife. Mysteriously, almost obsessively his thoughts change directions. *Who cares what is happening in California? My focus is being with Samantha. I feel that I just need to spend more time to be with her . . . alone. Right now, I don't care if we ever get to LA!*

Christopher chooses his words carefully. "Samantha, since we are all stuck here for a while, would you like to join me for a drink, say around five o'clock?"

"Are you sure, Christopher? What about the children?" she asks, nervously crinkling her nose. She looks back to check on Ryan and Rebecca as the chatter on the bus grows louder and louder. Christopher is unable to pull his gaze away from her graceful movements, from the way her jeans hug her hips, the way her pink thong is revealed as she stretches over the back of the seat, the way her top stretches across the fullness of her breasts.

"Oh, no problem," he replies nonchalantly. Looking out the window in the other direction, Samantha excitedly nudges his arm, pointing to the sphinx replica. "Is five okay for you?" he asks sheepishly as Samantha drives his senses crazy without even knowing it.

Christopher begins to think about the future again. For the first time since Kim's passing, he feels his unending nightmare of loss and despair may actually be over. He thinks about what the future could be like with Samantha at his side as the dark cloud of grief starts to float away in the dry desert winds of Las Vegas. *I have lived my life for the last several years just day to day, not allowing myself any thoughts about what the future might hold for me, especially about loving someone again. I thought Kim was the only one for me. Now there is Samantha Montgomery.* He sits quietly in his seat amid the excitement, confusion, anxiety, frustration, panic, and fear that are reigning as news of what has happened in California spreads like wildfire among the waiting passengers in the buses. Text messaging, cell phone conversations, and radio broadcasts are consuming the attention of most every passenger. Worried about friends and family, worrying curiously about their homes and property, they wait anxiously, trying to figure out what will happen next. The Ricardo family sits quietly in the back of the bus, feeling tired, lost and confused by the chain of events in their attempt to get to California. Mrs. Ricardo looks curiously out the window to a white stretch limousine parked alongside with its engine idling in the hot, scorching desert sun.

Inside the air-conditioned limo parked next to the passenger buses is the Hamilton family. The children are standing on the seats with their heads popping in and out of the open sunroof as they wait to hear when they will be able to get home to LA. Charles pours another drink while Catherine is on the phone making arrangements to meet a high-society friend who resides in the Las Vegas area. She opens the window when Michael approaches.

"Captain, is it really true Los Angeles encountered a severe earthquake?" Catherine asks in a dramatically engaging manner, outwardly flirting with the pilot in command.

"Yes, Mrs. Hamilton. We were just notified that the power is back on at LAX. After inspecting the runways and taxiways, the authorities have announced that they are going to resume flight operations as soon as possible. Our flight has been rescheduled to depart tonight at eleven o'clock. The buses are scheduled to leave the hotel at nine o'clock sharp. Please be ready to leave by then as well."

"We're thinking about having the driver take us to Los Angeles now. Can we—" Catherine starts to ask when the children scream loudly, interrupting their conversation. Charles quickly downs his drink as Catherine decides what they're going to do next. As the children scream louder and louder, Rosa frantically tries to control the boisterous brood.

Michael continues, "Mrs. Hamilton, according to everything I've heard, all the highways into southern California are either damaged by the quakes, threatened by raging wildfires, or so backed up with motorists that it will take you all night to get there." The limo driver quickly nods in agreement. "I would highly recommend that you and your family enjoy yourselves here in Las Vegas for a few hours. And let us fly you there safely later tonight."

Looking over the roof of the limo Michael sees the passengers pouring off the buses, grabbing their baggage, and proceeding to the hotel. Glancing farther over, he notices that Nicole is still in the van sitting alone, while the rest of the crew is out in the hot desert sun assisting hundreds of passengers into the hotel lobby.

With the rosary in one hand and the piece of paper in the other, Nicole looks at Father Knorosov's scribbled phone number as she sits alone in the crew transportation van. While the rest of the crew continues to help direct everyone to the hotel, she closes her eyes to block out the reality of her existence, trying desperately to visualize Father Knorosov's face, trying to remember the details of what he looks like, what he tastes like. Slowly she glides the paper under her nose, inhaling the remainder of his scent. A little tremor shivers inside as she recalls the warmth of his handshake. The man whose life has now become an obsession for Nicole is the very same man whose sensual kiss has set her soul on fire. The remnant of that life-changing moment still lingers in the depths of her consciousness. She awakens into the here and now from her daydream in sudden desperation when the piece of paper begins to slip out of her hand. Grabbing it quickly, she holds the paper and the rosary closely to her breast as looks out the van window with a bewildered daze.

"Where are you, Father?" she begs prayerfully, looking toward the heavenly skies, wondering where he is, wondering when she will see him again. Heartbroken and distraught over his departure to California, she weeps silently, holding her pain, wondering how she can think of anyone else ever again.

Chapter 82

After an hour in the sweltering heat checking all the passengers into the hotel, Michael returns calm, cool, and collected to the crew van with room keys and the layover expense allowance for his flight crew. With luggage already unloaded, the Infinity Airways crew heads to the main entrance of the Luxor Hotel. Michael and Eve walk slowly together behind Nicole.

"I think we should try to help her—" starts Eve as they pass through the enormous lobby across its sleek marble floor. She glances up at the towering palm trees in voluminous ivory pots that line the walls of the hollowed pyramid.

Michael interrupts her abruptly, his eyes betraying restrained emotion. "I appreciate your concern, Eve. But Nicole is on her own. There's nothing—" Michael begins when Nicole suddenly comes to a halt. A frown momentarily creases his brow.

Where the rendition of the Great Temple of Ramesses II, rising thirty-five feet into the world's largest atrium, captures the attention of most visitors, it is the casino entrance that has captured Nicole's. She stands still and stares obsessively. The roll of dice, the shuffle of cards, and the spin of the roulette wheel from the lively gaming floor call incessantly to her.

Michael and Eve continue to walk toward the elevators, leaving Nicole behind while the energies from the opulent 120,000-square-foot casino with everything from slots and video poker, to baccarat, blackjack, craps, keno, and roulette overpoweringly consumes the last of her angelic vibrations. The untrained angel easily succumbs to its irresistible invitation to try her luck.

"But, Michael, she's falling, and she doesn't even know it—soon to be completely human in every way," declares Eve. "She is passing through the Veil of Forgetting. I know she'll remember that she's a flight attendant in training, but she'll have no memory that we're angels. She won't remember who she is, and why she's here on Earth."

While the magnificent colossal statues of Ramesses II, wearing the double crown of Upper and Lower Egypt, watch over Nicole, the elevator chimes its arrival. Eve and Michael walk in and stand side by side facing the doors of the inclinator.

"She'll be like the others—lost forever," Michael acquiesces quietly, concealing his forlorn disappointment.

As the inclinator doors begin to close, Eve smiles.

Chapter 83

Nicole accidentally bumps into a retired couple, passengers from the flight, when she rushes excitedly out of her hotel room into the hallway. Having changed out of her uniform into her new clothes from Saks and grabbing all her expense money for the layover, Nicole is definitely ready to make something happen for herself.

"C'mon Fred, let's make the most this. Let's go downstairs to the casino right now. I'm feeling lucky!" yells Shirley. The heavy-set sixty-five-year-old woman is pulling her overweight husband by the hand. Quickly Nicole and the old couple enter the inclinator. Already inside the lift are Elizabeth Walters and Kent Phillips, who are dressed to the nines. As Elizabeth and Kent kiss and hug, excited about their plans for the day, Nicole once again gets a glimpse of one of their deeper, more passionate kisses. Nicole mournfully reflects back on her kiss with Father Knorosov. The passionate desire of love from Elizabeth and Kent and the excitement of gambling in Las Vegas from Shirley and Fred begin to consume Nicole within the confines of the elevator as they approach the hotel lobby.

When Nicole enters the casino, she turns many a head as she strolls in wearing the latest fashions from New York City. A handsome tall blonde bachelor in particular notices her immeasurable beauty. Surrounded by sexy, adoring women near the blackjack tables, he seductively blows a ring of smoke into the air. With style and a hint of arrogance, he holds his cigarette in a sterling silver holder close to his lips as he watches Nicole closely. His grooming is impeccable and his manner fastidious.

Strolling down one of the aisles, Nicole finds herself surrounded by frenzied gamblers partially obscured by plumes of cigarette smoke mixed with the overpowering smell of cheap booze and even cheaper cologne. Ready to gamble in the casino that is as wide as the Nile, overwhelmed by the razzle-dazzle and clanking of coins, Nicole impulsively decides to play the slot machines where several excited gamblers are winning. She decides to sit on the end stool by the aisle when the retired couple that followed her in proceeds to sit next to her, happily offering to teach *their* flight attendant how to play the slot machine. "You should always play full coins on these machines, honey. They always give out big jackpots for doing so," advises Shirley, the self-appointed gambling expert.

"Really?" asks Nicole excitedly.

Following the woman's counsel, Nicole begins to load the machine full of coins on each turn, quickly blowing her layover allowance. Fred and Shirley encourage her to slow down and enjoy the experience, but Nicole has no control over the obsessive energies that now engulf her. While she searches her purse for more money, Nicole somehow senses a stranger's seductive gaze. She discreetly looks his way when the cocktail waitress offers to take her drink order. The mysterious man smiles in a way that conveys his interest in her is more than casual. She turns away from his provocative stare with a pang of guilt but feels his eyes as they slowly follow every curve and contour of her superbly sculpted body, undressing her with his penetrating eyes.

Nicole is surprised when she feels a warm yearning envelop her, rising upward, aching from the center of her being. Although she finds him physically attractive, she attempts to regain her composure by thinking about Father Knorosov. She remains seated squarely in front of the *one-armed bandit* ready to play some more. Shifting anxiously on the stool as she tries to focus, she momentarily forgets about her open purse resting on her lap only to see its contents spill out over the floor and under the feet of several other gamblers. Not being one to miss an opportunity, the man of mystery appears next to Nicole as she slides off the stool to retrieve her bag and what's left of its now-scattered contents.

While picking up her makeup and room key lying on the carpet, their eyes lock as they simultaneously reach for a lone coin. Nicole smiles hesitantly when his warm hand suddenly holds hers. The coin slowly slides between her fingers into her palm as he returns her smile. Quick to return to her seat to play her very last coin, the gentleman leans on the side of the machine with his arms crossed observing the beauty before him. Nicole nervously takes in his perfectly tanned skin and chiseled features as the very suave and debonair bachelor continues to smile at her knowingly.

Obsessed with hopes of winning like those feverishly playing around her, Nicole looks back at the machine that takes the last of her money. Suddenly, the winning line changes before her eyes. As Lady Luck would have it, the numbers roll over, paying out the grand prize of $100,000. Nicole jumps for joy as she looks at the handsome stranger. Shirley and Fred jump off their seats to celebrate her beginner's luck.

On a whisper of excitement, Nicole catches her breath. "I won! I won!" In her exuberance and celebration, she hugs the neck of the man of mystery.

Chapter 84

Leaving his children with a sitter for the first time in their lives, Christopher sits in the hotel bar, waiting excitedly for his date with Samantha. After an hour of twisting and pulling at the cocktail napkin underneath his vodka and tonic, he begins to shred it into smaller pieces. He dejectedly glances at his watch. "It's already six o'clock. She's not coming."

William meanders into the bar dressed in a shirt and jacket. The end of a tie that he squashed into his coat pocket reveals itself.

"You look so familiar. Do I know you from somewhere?" The conversation starts.

"I think I've heard that line several times today," William remarks while he orders a sparkling water with lemon, no ice, from the bartender.

"You look so familiar. I mean besides being on the bus and all," Christopher professes, shaking his head trying to remember from when or where.

"Seems like everyone on that flight thinks they know me from somewhere." William looks blankly down at his glass, watching the bubbles rise to the surface. Strangely, at the same time, he begins to feel something bubbling inside, rising to the surface as well.

Sitting one seat over from William at the bar, Christopher is sure that he and William have met before. Striking up a casual conversation, Christopher states that he has no recollection of when or where they may have met but that William definitely looks familiar. After talking generally about their lives and careers, they exchange business cards.

"Hey, you look familiar!" comes a voice from behind.

"Hey, you do too!" Christopher jokes nervously, as he recognizes Samantha's voice. She has entered the bar without his realizing it. He immediately turns to his right pulling back the barstool, expecting her to sit on that side of him. Startled that her comment is directed toward William and not him, Christopher quickly spins his head around to the left as Samantha sits down enthusiastically in the empty seat between the two surprised men. Her perfume arouses both Christopher and William, a scent that seems so familiar yet nothing like they have ever smelled before. Spellbound by his presence, Samantha unexpectedly gives William her undivided attention.

Realizing that Samantha is ignoring the desperate attempts of Christopher, who is trying to get into the conversation, William encouragingly remarks, "Hey, Samantha, did you know that Christopher here is a successful accountant getting ready to relocate to southern California?" She shakes her head, her full attention directed to William. Sensing how hurt Christopher feels with the recent turn of events, William works diligently to pull him into the discussion. Yet despite William's concerted efforts to get the two together, Samantha is only interested in him.

"Hey, Martin, what's up?" the young researcher asks when he answers his cell phone. "Yeah, sure, no problem. Another fifteen minutes?" His anxiety shows on his face and carries in his voice as he looks back to Christopher and Samantha. "Well . . . okay. Yes, I have a coat and tie. I'll meet you there."

"You're not going anywhere, are you?" begs Samantha as she moves her seat closer to William's. She seductively rubs her leg next to his while placing her hand across his forearm. Leaning in his direction, William can't help but notice her heaving breasts that are barely covered by her very low-cut red silk top.

"No . . . unfortunately . . . no," he mumbles uncomfortably under his breath as he checks his watch again.

Christopher stares intently at William and Samantha. He does not like the direction that any of this is taking. Samantha observes the very intense expression on Christopher's face, noting the way his intelligent dark brown eyes seem to be searching inside her.

Without warning, like a knee-jerk reaction, William's hand flies up to his forehead. Something overwhelmingly powerful is moving him. He feels a tight band of pressure around his head as awesome forces stretch his memory to the utmost. Uncontrollably, as if someone is turning his head for him, he looks directly into Samantha's eyes and then quickly diverts his attention to the eyes of Christopher sitting next to her. His attitude softens as his gaze darts back and forth between Samantha and Christopher and finally settles on Samantha. Instantly, in a spiraling vortex through boundless depths of insight, traveling along the twists and turns of a tangled knot that has wound itself around their hearts karmically, William releases a heartache of the past, from their past that the three shared together—a lifetime 12,500 years ago.

Chapter 85

"Look, there she is!" exclaims Shirley. "One hundred thousand dollars! Must be nice winning all that money," the retired woman screams enviously across the crowded hotel lobby. Arriving guests in the lobby look toward Nicole.

"Yes, ma'am, and it's all mine!" Nicole boasts as she walks toward the hotel entrance in search of a taxi.

"Yes, indeed, it must be your lucky day, my dear!" says Ashton Olivier in an Oxford English accent as he walks briskly alongside Nicole. Again she is surprised and delighted with all the attention she is receiving. "There's nothing like the feeling of having money and the feeling of power it can give you, the freedom it can buy you. Don't you agree?"

"Yes, it's wonderful. Do you know where I can go shopping around here?" Nicole asks excitedly, as she continues toward the hotel entrance. "Uh, do you work here or something, mister?"

Ashton stops and takes Nicole's hand. "I beg your pardon, my lady. Please forgive me, Nicole." He bows respectfully and kisses her hand. "Ashton Olivier at your service."

"Uh, how do you know my name, Mr. Olivier?" asks Nicole innocently, embarrassed by his sudden and overt interest. She nervously glances away yet takes in his firm bronzed body. She senses an air of refinement when she notices his very stylish custom-tailored clothing and expensive Italian leather shoes. His clothes shows off his physique of perfection, making him look distinguished and yet mysterious at the same time.

"It's my business to know the name of the absolutely most beautiful woman in Las Vegas," he goes on, his voice silky smooth. Ashton, gushing with worldly charm, smiles while still holding her hand, kissing it once again. His handsomely chiseled features capture her attention while his deep green eyes stare seductively into hers. "It would be my honor and greatest pleasure if you would allow me to escort you to the finest designer stores our city has to offer."

"Really!" exclaims Nicole.

Excited, overwhelmed, thrilled, and confused, Nicole graciously agrees. Drawn to his power and style, his good looks, and sense of fashion, she happily gets into his black stretch Rolls Royce limousine that is waiting by the front entrance of the hotel. As Nicole gets in, her gaze darts around the plush, well-appointed interior of the most luxurious limo ever designed. Taking in everything including the fully stocked bar, she says under her breath, "No more basement bargains for me!"

# Chapter 86

"Wait, you can't leave!" William pleads.

"I think I've had enough; thank you very much." Christopher tosses a crisp twenty-dollar bill on the bar. He puts forth a silent question by cocking his head and raising an eyebrow.

"Please stay, Christopher. I want to explain everything. I now understand what is going on here. Please, just for a few minutes," begs William as he guides him back to his seat.

Feeling totally rejected and humiliated after several attempts to get Samantha's attention, the only thing Christopher wants desperately is to return to his room. Varied emotions mixed with vodka now churn in the pit of his stomach. He wants to check on his children, to go back to the safety of what he knows, to be with those who love him. William again encourages him to wait, to be patient.

Committed to his truth, to what he knows, William feels that he has to tell Samantha that despite the feelings and undeniable attraction she feels for him and he feels for her at some level, he is not interested in having a relationship with her. Nevertheless, a hint of romantic anticipation tingles inside Samantha.

After nervously shifting his weight from one foot to the other, William takes a deep breath and begins the explanation of what has just been psychically revealed to him. "Unbeknownst to you both, we have all had a past life together in ancient Egypt, and the Law of Karma is now in effect. Now I know you are going to think that I'm out of my mind but please listen. Maybe something I say will resonate with you at some level."

"What?" asks Christopher, completely bewildered by William's verbiage. The power of William's stare causes a tremor of apprehension to shiver up his spine. Apprehension of what? Christopher does not know. The conversation begins to take a strange turn.

"I am the reincarnation of the High Priest Ra, also known as the Sun God from ancient Egypt. And, Samantha, you are the reincarnation of Priestess Tarello, his or should I say my last wife and the one true love during my . . . his thousand-year life," explains William as he talks over the music playing in the background. Surrounded in the Egyptian motif of the lounge, Samantha and Christopher stare blankly at William as he carefully unravels the intricate web of their destiny.

"Look, all I know is that RA is the name of some nightclub in this place," exclaims Christopher as he looks around to see who else may be listening to the most bizarre story he has ever heard.

Samantha finishes her margarita and motions to the bartender for another one. In tight faded jeans that encase her long legs, she shifts her weight uncomfortably as she settles onto the barstool. As she returns her attention to William, a frown wrinkles across her brow as she narrows her eyes. He notices her uneasiness, the way she glances away when he looks at her.

"Before his departure from Earth, Ra instructed Tarello to marry his trusted friend and devoted servant, Exderenemus, who is now you, Christopher." William points to the incredulous man as he continues. "Look, I know this all sounds bizarre, but things on this planet are moving faster and faster; time is accelerating. I have to explain this to you so you understand and are able to process what is going on right now between the three of us."

"Look, man, you can have the girl. Really!" Christopher spits out angrily, his patience totally exhausted. "I have enough drama in my life right now. I don't need this," he retorts defensively as he gets up to leave again.

"Then tell me this, Christopher; why do I seem so familiar to you? Why were you so instantly attracted to Samantha?" William shouts, "Please, just hear me out!"

Christopher stops reluctantly and turns. He takes a calming breath and tries to force his doubts away. "Samantha, what do you think about this? What do you think about what this guy is saying?" asks Christopher, still overwhelmed, and confused. His features soften from the hard look that was there just a moment earlier as he waits for her reply.

Samantha takes a gulp of her margarita and looks at Christopher, slowly shaking her head, contemplating several thoughts in her mind. "Look, it all sounds a little crazy . . . but after your seeing my grandmother on the airplane today . . . well . . . maybe we should listen to what else the guy has to say. Can't really hurt, can it?" asks Samantha, shrugging her shoulders. She too tries to shake the ever-present skepticism and the disturbing feeling that things are not as they appear. Seeing that Christopher is already impatient with the turn of events, she doesn't want to say anything that may exacerbate the situation further, even though she has no clue about what is really happening. She pats the seat of his barstool and smiles.

William sighs in relief when Christopher sits down. "Okay, as I was saying, to maintain his influence with the people of Egypt and the temple activities, Ra asked Exderenemus, to marry his wife, Tarello, after he leaves the planet," William carefully measures his words as he continues. "Heartbroken and distraught, she . . . Samantha, keeps the commands of her husband, Ra . . . me, and continues his work with Exderenemus, you, Christopher. Can you see? Karma is balancing between the three of us. But this time, things are meant to work out differently. We never come into a life to learn the same lessons again. We move on, trying different scenarios, sometimes switching roles. The familiarity between us is undeniable. And being in this hotel that is in the middle of the desert, resembling the very place where we were together before, 12,500 years ago, is just escalating the whole thing more quickly and more intensely."

"You're right, William," affirms Samantha unexpectedly.

"I am? I mean, yes, I am," confirms William, surprised by how easily Samantha is processing his explanation. "Look, I'm a professional intuitive. I've known things since I was a kid—things that no one else can see, hear, or understand. I have spent my entire life in rigorous scientific and metaphysical research. This is what I do for a living for God's sake! I help others with health issues, give them information about their past lives, and share information about the future."

"Well, let me share information with you both about what I know about the future," says Samantha as she stands up, facing both William and Christopher, husbands from her distant past, men she once passionately loved and cared for thousands upon thousands of years ago.

William smiles knowingly. Christopher is excitedly optimistic. And Samantha is determined and focused.

"Well, here's what I know about the future. Or at least, my future," she begins to explain, speaking loudly and clearly over the din of dozens of people who have entered the lounge. "Now, William, you tell me if this is a good karma or not. But according to what you're telling us, I've had you both before, right?"

"Excuse me?" asks William, quickly trying to follow her line of thinking.

"Didn't you say that things are meant to work out differently—that we never come into life to learn the same lessons again, that we move on, trying different scenarios—sometimes switching roles? So maybe it's time for me to create some new karma. You know, like with some new man for me in this lifetime. Not you old guys from some thousands of years ago." She points across the room. "You know, like with that guy over there!"

And with that Samantha turns on her heel, swinging her luscious long auburn hair over her shoulders and walks seductively over to a table where a young good-looking muscle-bound man with a shaved head and tattoos on his forearms has been sitting alone.

William laughs. "Now, Christopher, that's some serious karma in action!"

Chapter 87

Nicole looks at their reflection in the mirror as Ashton stands closely behind her. Dozens of Dior evening gowns surround them. He takes a step even closer, speaking more softly, almost intimately.

"The red one, Nicole, definitely the red one," he whispers warmly in her ear. Together in the fitting room, standing behind her, with his body ever so close to hers, Ashton slowly and seductively pulls the zipper of the shimmering strapless flame red satin evening gown that hugs every one of her curves. She feels his hot breath on her neck as he pulls the zipper up to the top and gently pulls the hook into place. He whispers again, "Let me purchase this gown for you, Nicole. Seeing you in this tonight is worth more than the $60,000 it costs." His hot hands glide slowly down the back of her exquisite long bare arms.

"Oh, well, thank you, but I have enough money now to pay for it myself," Nicole replies proudly as she steps away, moving closer to the mirror. His advances make her feel uncomfortable. Suddenly, she looks shyly apprehensive as Father Knorosov's face emerges in the mirror.

"It's a small price to pay if you will have dinner with me tonight, Nicole," Ashton says enticingly.

Nicole is oblivious to Ashton's comment as she stares in the triple-sided mirror. "Do you really like it?" she asks Father Knorosov as she stares into his eyes. "Is it too revealing?" she asks bashfully as she pulls the dress up higher trying to cover her chest. The plunging neckline of the shimmering gown reveals her celestial beauty and a heavenly body with breasts that were sculpted by perfection itself.

Nicole jumps when suddenly Ashton's body presses firmly into the curves of hers, pulling her waist close into his. She stares blankly at their reflection together. Unexpectedly sensations race through her body, blood pulsing through her veins, the aches and yearnings of her new human body confuse her so.

"Oh, Father, help me," she begs softly. Her heart belongs to Father Knorosov, yet she finds it hard to resist Ashton's very seductive advances. In her confusion, she quickly moves away to admire more gowns hanging in the store.

KNOCK! KNOCK! KNOCK! The Dior store manager rushes to the locked glass door where two women are knocking and banging impatiently on the storefront window.

"Sorry, ladies, the store has been closed temporarily for a private shopping excursion for one of our most important clients," informs the manager as he points to the "SORRY, WE'RE CLOSED" sign in the window.

Curious to see which famous celebrity may be inside, one of the women, Catherine Hamilton, nosily peers through the window. At the same time Nicole happens to glance over as she looks at gowns by the store's front window.

"What!" Catherine screams incredulously. Opening the door slightly, the Dior manager asks the ladies to please leave quietly. "That damned flight attendant! Oh, please don't tell me you closed my favorite store for a goddamned flight attendant! She's nothing more than a glorified waitress!" Catherine Hamilton is stunned as she tries to enter the store again only to be ushered out immediately. Outraged by this unexpected turn of events, she again demands to be let in. Catherine's friend frantically encourages her to refrain from any more outbursts as she sees several large security officers, with their hands on the holsters, rapidly approaching the store.

Ashton brings his cigarette holder to his lips and begins to snap his fingers. Instantly the manager returns to light it. Ashton is an enigma in Las Vegas, a mysterious puzzle with many layers and facets, even to his closest friends and business associates. The store manager has serviced Ashton and his female friends on more than one occasion in the past. He knows that Mr. Olivier is a very wealthy and powerful man who will stop at nothing to get what he wants. Well aware of Ashton's impatience, he discreetly yet urgently signals his staff. Instantaneously the store's fashion consultants return to the fitting area where Nicole now has the entire staff exclusively at her beckon call. As always, Ashton's every request is granted immediately, no questions asked.

With words that carry of absolute authority, Ashton tells the manager in a clear, firm voice, "We'll need a diamond necklace for her gown. Go over to Tiffany's—" Ashton pauses to laugh as he looks down at Nicole's stocking feet.

The Dior manager exclaims, "And we can't forget the shoes!" He motions for the clerks to measure Nicole's feet.

"Oh, Ashton, this is like a dream come true. I can't believe I was just shopping in New York City this morning; and now, here I am in Las Vegas trying on the most fabulous designer evening gowns." She smiles, enthralled in the moment as she twirls around admiring the dress, surrounded by a staff waiting anxiously to offer her evening shoes, purses, and accessories to match.

"Nicole, there is more—much, much more," he whispers slowly, breathing heavily with each word, sending chills down her legs. His hand snakes out to snag her waist and draw her nearer to him. "You can have it all. With a body and looks like yours, Nicole, you can have it all." Excitedly she turns to hug him to show her appreciation and excitement. Suddenly her head begins to spin, feeling as though she is going faint. Pulling away, Nicole looks at him straight in his face, sensing that something is wrong—very wrong.

Chapter 88

Sitting in the plush upholstered booth in the Luxor's renowned Isis Restaurant surrounded in the décor of ancient Egyptian artifacts, William looks around at the familiar images of times past while Martin gives the waiter their dinner order. They resume their earlier conversation.

"Sorry about the delay," Martin apologizes. "I had to work out the particulars to reschedule the board of directors meeting that was planned for tomorrow. Guess you heard the details about what happened in LA? Some kind of earthquake knocked the power out for several hours. Apparently the damage was limited mostly to property with limited injuries and fatalities. Definitely could have been worse."

"Well, those days are coming sooner than most realize," states William knowingly. Turning his dinner knife over and over repeatedly on the white linen tablecloth, he looks up at the circular vaulted ceiling. Above the restaurant, a field of deep blue is accentuated by hundreds of golden stars. William humbly feels he is about to dine with the pharaohs as he awkwardly adjusts his wrinkled tie. Looking at the surrounding patrons and at Martin, dressed in one of his thousand-dollar suits, William realizes that he is about to dine in a manner befitting royalty.

"So you're a professional intuitive . . . a psychic, right?" asks Martin as he grabs a warm roll from the breadbasket.

"Yes, sir. And you want to know about psychic abilities because this is something that you, a successful and powerful businessman, are unable to talk to anyone about. Because of the limitations of society that you have chosen to live within, you are worried about what your colleagues would think if they found out," William explains as he divulges his psychic understanding of the man seated next to him. Taking a sip of water, he looks directly at Martin for a reaction. "Yet the metaphysical realm truly interests you, sir. However—because of business, the wounds of your past, and your fear of the future—you have not taken the time to explore what is beyond the scope of your apparent reality. And this has brought you to ask me to dinner. Am I close, Mr. Peterson?"

"Well, yes," chokes Martin as he tries to swallow his piece of bread. "I would say that's close."

"Since we have a few hours before the buses reload to go back to the airport, Mr. Peterson, you may have my undivided attention. Where do you want to start?"

Suddenly Martin's feelings from his past come flooding in. Overwhelmingly compelled to give William some background information on himself, Martin begins with the death of his father.

With tears welling up in his eyes, Martin quickly condenses his story as the emotions are too intense. "My dad was a sort of Renaissance man, great at a lot of things. Yet there was one world that truly captivated his dreams, and that was flying. He was obsessed with aviation. All he wanted to do was fly—and fly he did," reflects Martin, trying to keep things light as they wait for their salads. "After retiring my dad bought an old two-seater airplane, giving lessons to anyone who wanted to fly. Very soon, with all his experience as a pilot, he became rated as an instructor. He was living his lifelong dream as his passion had become his reality." Martin pauses momentarily, finishing his scotch on the rocks. "And it also became the reason he is no longer here. One day while flying, the wing of his plane tore off as a result of metal fatigue. He had talked Mom into flying with him that day. I lost both my parents in that fiery crash after his spiraling plane plummeted to the ground."

"Oh, I'm so sorry," William says respectfully.

"In the months after the crash, there were many tearful phone calls, empty family gatherings, and, eventually for me, depression. Something was ripped out from under me, just like the wing of that damn old plane. Sure, there was the support of friends and family, medication, therapy, even support groups. The clergy were of little help. I found out that faith is a great concept until you need to rely on it. For me, it seemed there was no way out of the painful downward spiral, no way out of the nightmare."

"I know that must have been difficult for you," William says emphatically. Sensing there is a lot more to come, William encourages Martin to continue as the waiter lays down their salads.

The pain was more than I could have ever imagined possible. I missed my father and mother. I woke up angry every day, angry at the world, angry at God, even angry at my parents. I became more isolated. I wanted to die too."

"Pain and anger are natural in situations like that, Mr. Peterson," William says reassuringly.

"Please, call me Martin. So one day, one of my secretaries gave me a book, a book that had helped her. Several years earlier, she had lost her son in a tragic school bus accident and had been devastated for some time. I picked it up and could not put it down until I finished it the next day. Apparently, the author is a *spirit medium*. At that time, the term spirit medium was a new one for me, a concept I had never considered. He recounted incidents in which he could communicate with a stranger's lost loved ones and could verify this communication with incredibly private and undisclosed details. I realized that if this book was true, if there were spirit mediums, I was reading about miracles. His book left me with lots of questions like 'Why hadn't I heard about this before? Why wasn't this made known to me through our church? How can I communicate with my father? With my mother?' This new awakening was sort of the beginning of the end."

William reaches over to Mr. Peterson to reassure him. Placing his hand on Martin's forearm, William begins to see and feel something very deep yet personal.

"I'm so sorry about what happened with your wife, Mr. Peterson. You didn't deserve that," remarks William sympathetically.

"What are you talking about?" he asks defensively pulling his arm back. A certain level of anxiety jitters inside of him, not too intense but anxiety nonetheless.

"I picked up on your wife just now when I put my hand on your arm," explains William apologetically.

"Well, I don't know what to say except that sounds pretty incredible. And please, William, call me Martin," he implores. "At that point in my life, young man, I felt that there were very few things that could surprise me. My wife—my ex-wife to be more precise—was the thing that really just about did me in. In the weeks after reading that book, my mind and thoughts were consumed with this whole concept. Although filled with questions and doubts, I tried to keep an open mind. What if this concept of talking with the dead was true? And if it was true, shouldn't everyone know about it!" he exclaims.

Martin's spiritual revelations from the past continue. "So one evening after a long day at the office, this secretary told me about a local spirit medium named Florence. Her story was compelling. A story that convinced me that a connection between this world and the next really exists. That was all I needed. I had to try it for myself, even though I had some reservations and fears. I needed something, anything. So very apprehensively, I had my secretary make an appointment under a fictitious name. And as you already know, William, being in the more conservative, traditional corporate business environment, I prayed that no one would catch wind of what I was doing," continues Martin, as he unknowingly looks around to see if anyone seated around them can hear the conversation.

"You don't have to explain, Martin. I know this is very painful for you, sir."

"Thank you, but I really need to get this out. Do you realize that I have never been able to talk about this to anyone? A corporate executive of one of the largest commercial real-estate companies in the country seeing a spirit medium! I was putting my entire professional reputation on the line."

"I understand, sir."

"Now, don't laugh, William. But initially, I guess I was expecting something like black curtains and burning incense with sounds of chanting in the background. However, it was nothing like that. Florence was this warm and beautiful mature woman, a mother of three children, and grandmother of five. We sat down in her kitchen together, ate homemade cookies, and my life changed forever. My dad was there, talking to me through her. She revealed minute details of things that no one else could know, even my mother. Things that a father only shares with his son—privately. As I drove away from Florence's house, I felt like the weight of the world had been lifted off my shoulders. My mind was spinning, and my heart was smiling, something that I hadn't felt for years. I felt a sense hope for the first time, a sense that it was time to get back to living, to move forward with my life."

"Mr. Peterson, really, you don't have to say anything more," says William, sensing that what he is about to hear is unbearably painful for the man.

"Thank you, but I must. Although you're young, you seem to have a wisdom, a knowing, well beyond your years. I feel that you are the only one, William, because of your gifts, your abilities that I can confide in."

"I'm honored, sir, that you feel that way," William replies graciously.

"Like I was saying, I was feeling great. My father and mother were . . . are still alive. They gave Florence the exact messages I needed to hear. Although there was one that I wasn't sure what it was about—something about the new house my wife and I were building—I knew I had witnessed something special, a miracle. Florence had shown me without a shadow of a doubt that my father and my mother and other loved ones are with me every day. Anyway, I was too excited to go back to my office, so I went home to tell my wife this extraordinary news. I wanted her to know that they were okay and that I was going to be okay; our family was going to be okay. My pain had lifted, and I was ready to live again, no longer mourning the loss of my parents.

"Carol wasn't home. Most of her days were filled busily picking out wallpaper, carpet, light fixtures, etcetera. So I headed over to our new house, where her car was out front. The timing was perfect because I had some things to go over with our builder who was also there. He was someone in the company that I had worked with on several residential projects years before. Anyway—" Martin stops himself as the waiter arrives to clear the salad plates as they finish, placing their entrees before them. He is impressed with the impeccable service then glances over at William as he thinks to himself. *Mysteriously I feel so comfortable sharing my greatest heartaches with a virtual stranger I met on a flight. This day is truly like no other.* Martin shakes his head then continues with his story.

"Apparently they didn't hear me walk in," says Martin as he aggressively slices into his rare, slightly grilled tenderloin. "Once again, my world came crashing in on me. I found the two of them naked, having sex on the floor of what was to be our master bedroom. The happiest day that I had in years also ended up being one of the worst. I left there in shock. Thoughts of suicide came flooding in. Although I knew my parents were okay, I still felt the loss, and now I had lost my wife as well. I didn't think I could handle another minute on this Earth as I sat in my car, crying like I had never cried before. I couldn't understand why this was happening to me." Martin asks rhetorically in a moment of personal reflection, "What had I ever done to deserve this?"

"Nothing—absolutely nothing." William mumbles, "Not in this lifetime, anyway."

Martin sits quietly for several minutes. A sigh of resignation escapes his lips as he leans back against the plush bench seat. He folds his arms across his chest. "It seems over the years I've hardened my heart to so much, William. Although my children remain the highlight in my life, I bury myself in work to numb the pain of Carol's betrayal. My business is very successful, but I no longer have a personal life." He concludes mournfully, "Afraid to love again, I guess in many ways, Martin Peterson has become the classic workaholic."

# Chapter 89

Dressed in the most elegant evening gown, shoes, and shawl, graced with a stunning diamond necklace and drop earrings, Nicole half smiles as Ashton and the Dior staff proudly offer applause to the stunning beauty that stands before them. Flashbacks of Father Knorosov stir her heart, memories of passion, memories of the insatiable desire to be one with him, and memories to be united in body, mind and spirit. Again, she smiles weakly while her heart breaks inside.

"Divine, absolutely divine!" says Ashton, encouraging more applause as he steps up to raise Nicole's arm. He twirls her around adoringly. Nicole struggles to smile, feeling strangely self-conscious as the store staff looks on.

"Don't seem fair that one person can have so much," comments one of the onlooking clerks to her coworker. "She gorgeous with a perfect figure, just won all that money, and has the attention of Ashton Olivier, the most eligible and richest bachelor in Las Vegas, not to mention the best-looking one as well. They look like Barbie and Ken, a match made in heaven."

"Yeah, some girls have all the luck, don't they?" the other clerk asks casually, gathering up some of the shoe boxes as she gawks. "Never have I seen such beauty in one person. From head to toe, she is more beautiful than any model or movie star that has ever entered the doors of this boutique. But have you noticed that she doesn't really look that happy?"

Watching how devoted Ashton is to Nicole's every need, to her every desire, the coworkers continue to put away the remaining shoes. "Yeah, I did. Wonder what that's about. Maybe her life isn't so totally perfect after all," jeers the envious clerk.

Nicole goes back to the fitting room to admire herself. *Looks like I have to make a decision.* She twirls around, looking at the fabulous gown in the mirror. *Do I stay in Las Vegas with lots of money, glamorous clothes, and a gorgeous, wealthy man? Or do I get back on board Infinity to wait on four hundred irritable, obnoxious, hungry passengers? Hmmm.* Nicole laughs aloud. "Tough decision!"

Chapter 90

"Now that I've gotten all that out of the way, William, tell me please, what in the hell is really going on around here?" asks Martin sipping his after-dinner coffee. His voice is calm, his tone firm, conveying the fact that he has regained control of his emotions. He searches William's eyes and face for some sort of truth. "Let's just cut to the chase. Sorry to have spent so much time on my past. But I thought it might help give you some background of my limited experience with psychic phenomenon."

"What do you mean, Martin?" probes William, wondering just how much to share with the man, wondering how much he can really handle.

"Strange things are happening. That priest fellow, Father Simon Knorosov, that was sitting next to me on the flight, told me that there is some type of quickening or rapture that is about to occur. For almost five hours, he talked about the increasing miracles over the world. About how most of them are not disclosed to the public and that a lot of information is being suppressed. Is that true? What do your abilities, your intuition, or even your research, tell you, William? There is this incredible restlessness stirring inside me—an unexplainable kind of anxiety—one that goes beyond the craziness of today."

A withering sigh of resignation escapes William's throat. "I can only tell you what I know. I'm sure that this Simon fellow has his information from a good source. Although frankly, I can't say I trust anyone associated with the Catholic Church. They certainly have a history and a track record a mile long on withholding and manipulating information," William retorts as he stirs his herbal licorice tea. Looking straight at Martin, he begins to disclose what he knows.

"The earthquakes in southern California and around the world are increasing. They are mere ripples on the surface of the ocean of evolutionary change—an evolutionary change of the planet, an evolutionary change in consciousness. One you will not hear about on the six o'clock news or from any church," William explains deprecatingly.

"How do you know this?" questions Martin as he twists and folds his napkin. William senses the uncertainty in Martin's words. He sees the wariness in his eyes.

William chooses his words carefully trying to put as much clarity into them as he can. "Just as there are sounds of frequency that not everyone can hear, there are cycles of time with frequencies that are so high most modern human beings have difficulty noticing them. Our senses have been dulled by living in a society and environment that do not encourage our sensitivity to the divine flow of time," William continues, looking at Martin intently.

"Do not our moods change with the seasons? Are we not influenced by the full moon, like the one out tonight?" William is persistent and very clever.

"Okay, I'm with you. Please continue."

"If today we are to embrace a worldview in which consciousness is more important than matter, we need to base our timekeeping on the nonphysical, invisible reality rather than on the physical," continues William, as he checks to see how much time he has before they have to check out of the hotel. "See what I mean!" He laughs jokingly, pointing to his watch.

"According to my research, every thing in our solar system is changing drastically, faster and more intensely, including Earth. We are currently undergoing profound, never-before-seen physical changes. I have written papers on this, addressing, and scientifically documenting a wide variety of significant examples, drawing from a host of published mainstream sources," continues William as Martin orders his second cup of coffee. "And there are even greater anomalies to come."

"For example?" inquires Martin, his curiosity peaked.

"Okay, the Sun. There has been more activity since 1940 than in the previous 1,150 years combined. On Mercury, an unexpected polar ice cap was discovered, along with a surprisingly strong, intrinsic magnetic field for a supposedly *dead* planet. Venus is experiencing a 2500 percent increase in auroral brightness and substantive global atmospheric changes in less than thirty years. And Pluto, recently categorized as a dwarf planet, has a 300 percent increase in atmospheric pressure, even as it recedes farther from the Sun. Martin, none of these statistics are from fringe scientists. My report's scientific data is from a variety of highly credible institutions including NASA itself. What I have just told you is all very, very real and only a fraction of what is happening!"

"Well, William, this all sounds interesting. But what does that have to do with being psychic; sounds more like astronomy to me, son?" questions Martin as he tries to understand where William is going with this information.

"We are experiencing substantial and obvious worldwide weather and geophysical changes. Weather patterns, in fact, will be a thing of the past as there will be no discernible patterns to follow. Public awareness of the realities of climate change is increasing considerably, and people aren't laughing anymore. Dramatic shifts are occurring just like today in Los Angeles; and everyone, no matter where they are, should prepare for more. It's also a matter of public record that weird things are happening to our planet's magnetic field. Airport runways designated by degrees from magnetic north are having to be recalibrated and renumbered."

"Yes, what a coincidence! One of our corporate pilots was just discussing that several weeks ago." Martin winks at William as he says, "My father wasn't the only one interested in aviation. I just leave the piloting to the professionals."

"Good idea," William affirms with a wink.

"My pilot was saying something about the fact that atmospheric disturbances—beyond those normally encountered and watched for by pilots—are occurring everywhere. What he called *microbursts* are increasingly being reported, and downed planes blamed on this phenomenon. Since airplanes use satellites and magnetic orientation to guide them, these will either fail on occasion or give invalid readings. These global positioning systems, directed by satellite, are used more often than the increasingly unreliable compasses. My God, when you think about all this stuff, William, it really is amazing that anyone is flying!"

"Exactly, that is why I have published a very compelling scientific case for what some call the *Dimensional Shift* or *Ascension* that is now underway. This shift is not detectable by scientific instruments because they too are made of matter and no instrument can detect frequencies higher than the frequency from which it is made," William explains. "When this solar-system-wide process is complete, estimated to be within the timeframe of 2010-2013, we can expect an event that is literally beyond our wildest dreams. The changes in the solar system are only the more obvious and physical result of these changes. You see, where the energy of consciousness itself is being upgraded, it causes mass evolution to occur." William slowly sips his tea to give Martin a moment to allow these revelations to seep in. "Earth and our own solar system will soon come into galactic synchronization with the rest of the universe."

Martin questions William. "Galactic synchronization?"

"We are all part of The One—The All of All. We are made up of the very material, the same elements the Earth is made of. What happens to her happens to us—on many levels besides physically. So-called modern science has separated our existence into supposedly unrelated areas of study—especially in this country. For example, we see a doctor for physical ailments, a minister for spiritual guidance, and a shrink for our emotional problems. Yet one cannot separate the mind/body/spirit complexes that we all are. Your emotional or spiritual problems will cause your physical disease; what do you think cancer is!" William apologizes, "Sorry, that's a topic for another day."

"Okay, I get your point. Where are you heading with this?" asks Martin as he now looks at his watch. "And why aren't we being told about this through the news or our government?"

"Martin, I would think that would be obvious. The predicted changes are not in our future. They are here now," William states very matter-of-factly. "Our scientific and governmental communities know what is happening. In their desire to maintain control, they are choosing to divert our attentions to less important things like the fairy-tale wedding of Tom Cruise and Katie Holmes in Italy or the supposed *hunt* for Osama Bin Laden rather than reveal the truth. Just like the magician whose art of entertaining is to perform illusions that dazzle and amaze, distracting the audience's attention, giving the impression nothing else is going on behind the scenes; the magician has to keep them mesmerized while somewhere else the deception is carried out."

"Like smoke and mirrors," adds Martin.

"Yes. Yet despite their efforts to distract our attentions, what is happening now is no mystery. It is exactly as it was meant to be—as foreseen by the Mayan, Hopi, and other seers of the past with their calendars, legends, and assorted prophecies. Even the readings of Nostradamus and Edgar Cayce, the Book of Revelation, and cryptograms contain prophetic messages—all targeting the same moment in time, and it is right on schedule."

"I never thought about it that way," reflects Martin feeling uninformed and ignorant for not having looked outside the box of his reality.

"We all are getting information from different sources," William continues. "Call it channeling, spiritual or psychic guidance, meditation, a hunch, or whatever. For the first time in human history, we know what the schedule is. The Mayan Sacred Calendar gives us that. In our modern world, we have never before had a verifiable, unambiguous timeline. We no longer have to rely on hope, blind faith, or guessing. Yet this message is so important that there are beings and entities on the Other Side, like your parents for example who are trying to help us. We need to start listening.

What's ahead is wonderful from the divine cosmic side of things, but I—we—need to wake people up as to what is really going on. Hence, my broadcast on *Coast to Coast AM*. Which, by the way, I called George earlier while I was in my room. They're going to broadcast the interview we did on the phone, tonight over the air as scheduled. People need to understand what is happening now because there's more to come."

"Like what William? Get to the point, dammit!" demands Martin anxiously, sensing that things don't look good. "My whole life revolves around real estate. Especially in California. What do you know?"

"Your best investments are going to be in spirituality—not materiality or physicality. I would recommend selling what you've got—and quickly. Put your money into gold and silver coins. Lighten your load, Martin. Your *stuff* is not going to take you where you'll ultimately want to go."

"Tell me what you've seen, William," insists Martin, pushing harder for more information. Questions without answers continue to plague Martin with each succeeding twist and turn of William's revelations.

"In the bus, on the way over here, I saw—psychically, that is—a 7.2 magnitude earthquake that will rock the Gulf of Alaska. The resulting shockwave will travel as far as Mount St. Helen's, and the volcano will erupt causing tremendous strain on the Juan de Fuca tectonic plate. This event may also awaken other cascade volcanoes along the western coast. The Juan de Fuca Plate will shift and cause movement, possibly a slight rotation, of the Pacific Plate. The movement of the Pacific Plate will cause movement of all adjacent plates resulting in major quakes along the Pacific Rim and the San Andreas fault line. The resulting 8.4 megaquake will alter the western coastline of the United States permanently."

Martin clears his throat. "Okay, you have my attention."

"Three major cities in California will sustain the highest casualties due to their proximity to the fault, the effects of which will be felt worldwide due to rising tides and climate changes. As a result, many U.S. military bases will be destroyed, leaving the country vulnerable to invasion. And, no, I don't know when! Time is very fluid," exclaims the young researcher, overwhelmed with the visions, with what he knows, and trying to find people to listen. "There, Mr. Peterson. That is the tip of the iceberg of what I see and know each and every day. Call it the rapture or a rupture, but something big is about to happen!"

Chapter 91

"Michael, Nicole is not in her room, and the buses will be loading soon," reports Eve as they observe the rest of crew and Infinity Airways representatives assisting the frenzied passengers and their baggage back into the buses for their nine o'clock departure. "I think we should—"

"She's fallen completely," Michael interrupts, his voice holding no emotion.

"But, Michael, we have to—" Her words end abruptly when a man's hand suddenly grabs Michael's shoulder from behind. Hanging on heavily, Charles stumbles around to speak with the chief pilot. Charles is very intoxicated and slurring his words.

"Captain, is everything oper . . . operational at LAX? Catherine wants me to check our li . . . limo. Sorry . . . any trouble. My wife would rather be caught *dead* than be seen riding in a b . . . bus," Charles stammers, hanging onto Michael's shoulder so he can stand up. The wealthy alcoholic starts to chuckle loudly. "Maybe you could help me with that one?"

Michael has a good laugh with Charles. "Well, maybe I could, Mr. Hamilton. But let's have some strong, black coffee first before we work out the details." Michael signals for one of the bellmen to take Charles inside the café for a cup of coffee.

Rochel joins the conversation with Eve and Michael as a white stretch limousine drives up to the hotel entrance. "Well, there they are! Returning from the Chapels of Love are the newly married Elizabeth and Kent Phillips," announces Rochel joyfully. "Kent sought out one of Las Vegas' quickie marriage chapels to officially unite them forever. After twenty years of separation and not wanting to wait another minute, they said 'I do' at the drive-thru window where the ceremony was performed in the limo. Looks like they now want to be alone in their *matrimonial bliss* as humans call it."

Eve points and laughs incredulously. "Look, their guardian angels are riding together on the roof!" Elizabeth and Kent's angels wave, cheer, and laugh in their merriment to all the other angels surrounding the hotel.

"Yes, they are having a splendid celestial celebration after getting those two back together," Rochel boasts. "Love from the highest levels is penetrating the planetary veils as the karma between them is finally balanced. Their union has already lifted the load on the planet. Elizabeth's fear, shame, and heartache and Kent's heartache, loss, and loneliness are released not only from themselves but now from their Mother Earth."

Michael smiles in agreement. "The Love between them brings forth a Light that is greater than a thousand suns to awaken their hearts and illuminate their path to the next dimension, rich in rewards, abundance, blessings, and every goodness."

"Look, Kent just instructed their limousine driver to pull up next to the Hamilton's limo to await their return." Rochel exclaims proudly, "Isn't it wonderful to see how excited they are about going upstairs to their room to consummate their marriage vows!"

"You did a great job, Rochel, helping to get them back together," Eve says encouragingly.

Rochel chuckles. "I'll admit there were moments when I wondered if they would ever come together."

The crew of pilots and flight attendants continues to wait patiently as everyone checks out of the hotel. Sarakiel and Dina are inside the crowded lobby, ready to be of service.

"Seems that our passengers certainly made the most of this diversion." Sarakiel smiles happily as several of their passengers walk by. "According to the Infinity representatives, over three hundred of them dined in Pharaoh's Pheast Buffet, and over a hundred of our passengers enjoyed the Oasis Spa. I guess a little aromatherapy, massage, sauna, and relaxing in the whirlpools helped to make this day a little more peaceful after such a hectic start."

"Yes, although Christopher Dunn looks a little haggard and bewildered at how his day unfolded, don't you think, Sarakiel?" asks Dina, noting Christopher's darkened hazel eyes, clenched jaw, and slumped shoulders. "Maybe he should have headed to the Oasis as well. Instead he came down with Rebecca and Ryan to have pizza at the Pyramid Café before taking them to visit the Tomb and Museum of King Tutankhamen."

Christopher heads directly over to the Infinity representatives to make sure they have seats together on the bus and on the plane. Dina watches him while Sarakiel keeps an eye on Ryan and Rebecca as they play hide and seek in the hotel lobby containing the largest atrium in the world. Since the children want to go outside and look at the sphinx replica, the family of three head for the hotel door. Christopher allows Rebecca and Ryan look around outside by themselves while he waits by the door in case there are any last minute changes or announcements regarding their ride back to the airport.

The children are amused by the colorful statue with the face of a man and the body of a lion that looks as though it is guarding the pyramid-shaped resort. Ryan points excitedly to the pyramid's edges illuminated with thousands of strobe lights and the world's brightest beacon of light that erupts at the apex of the Luxor, shining high up into the desert sky above. An ancient Egyptian belief was that the human soul travels to Heaven in a beam of light. Although Ryan is captivated by the ten-story replica, it's the 191-foot, four-sided obelisk standing in front of the second largest hotel in the world that has captured his sister's imagination. Rebecca studies its ancient hieroglyphs where the text reads vertically from top to bottom. She straightens her posture and smoothes the wrinkles out of her dress when she looks at the erect Egyptian statuary adorning the base of the obelisk.

Suddenly Dina and Sarakiel's attention is drawn back to Christopher. "Oh, this is really going to hurt," says Sarakiel as she shakes her head. "Christopher will see a loud, flashy fly yellow Ferrari drive up to the hotel. This is where he sees Samantha kissing that young guy she picked up from the bar. Her new love interest will race off as she dashes back upstairs to retrieve her luggage. Heartbroken and confused, Christopher will look once again to this magnificent full moon shining over the sphinx, like he did so many times 12,500 years ago, and wonder what twist of fate awaits him in the days ahead."

Chapter 92

"So, Martin, what other explanation fits for our whole solar system going through this metamorphosis while similarly huge events are happening at an accelerating rate in Earth's society? How about including the fact that almost every established body of historical spiritual teaching, from all cultures, has some form of prediction about this event that is now coming true?" William replies defensively.

"I believe you, William, all of it," Martin replies sympathetically. He shifts uncomfortably in his chair while trying to project a casual exterior. However, the tension coursing through his body will not allow him to sit still. "What I didn't tell you is that before dinner, while you were waiting for me in the bar, I was also checking your credentials on line and with a private detective I use occasionally."

Martin pulls a folded paper out of his shirt pocket and begins to read aloud. "'William Douglas Gladstone intensively researches ancient civilizations, UFOs, and new paradigms in the science of matter and energy. Gladstone has appeared on television, lectured throughout the United States, Japan, Canada and Europe, written a variety of magazine articles, and has appeared on numerous radio shows. He is fluent in four languages and is the author of critically acclaimed scientific research giving definitive support to the idea that a transformation in matter, energy, and consciousness is now occurring on Earth and throughout the solar system. Gladstone is divorced with no children. Currently lives in New Jersey and lacks funding for further research.' Am I close?" Martin winks as he folds the paper and puts it back in his pocket. "I may not be psychic like you, but I too do my research and have my sources. I wasn't about to share my information with an unqualified self-professed psychic. There is too much at stake."

Slightly irritated by the invasion of privacy, William looks around in disbelief. The surroundings again feel like a glance back in time. In his agitation, he quickly returns his focus to his watch. "We've got to leave in forty-five minutes."

"What I didn't tell you earlier, William, is that I have had *visitors* for years," whispers Martin, once again looking around to see if anyone is eavesdropping. "A small golden rectangle appears on the wall of my study. It then grows bigger and bigger, expanding in all directions, becoming some kind of dimensional portal, I guess. From where—I don't know. These beings come in the room and walk around doing things, showing me things. They don't hurt me, but I can't understand what they are saying." He moves in even closer to William.

"Are they ETs of some sort like what you've seen on TV or in the movies?" asks William inquisitively, feeling as though the conversation is about to get more interesting.

"Oh, no! Interestingly enough, they are Egyptians. Last time a beautiful woman with straight black hair, just like the pictures in this restaurant, came through while I had a golf buddy of mine over to the house. She was wearing ancient Egyptian robes like those right off the temple walls. Of course, I was freaking out 'cause I thought he might see or hear her or that he would think I was crazy if I asked him if he could. This full-bodied apparition was as solid as this." Martin knocks on the linen-covered table. "She walked around jabbering in some strange tongue for ten minutes or so. Thank God he never saw her, or at least he didn't say anything if he did. You gotta understand, William, something like this gets out about someone like me. Well you know—"

"Yes, sir, I understand."

"I know this sounds unbelievable, but I can't see through these visitors like one can see through ghosts. However, with my architect eye and my builder mindset, I can study them intently. I've noticed that light reflects off the metallic foil of their robes and the gold and silver in their headdresses. Yet I remain confused because they show me things, like some sort of plans or calendars or sometimes what look like blueprints. I don't know . . . something about buildings, temples, priests . . . about some kind of beacon. Some of it looks like the same stuff at this hotel. I sense that somehow they want me to help them, or they have some kind of job for me to do," explains Martin, obviously disturbed by the visits. "What do you think, William? Have you ever seen or heard of such a thing? God knows, some days me and my poor linear brain think we're going absolutely crazy!"

"You're not crazy, Martin; I promise," encourages William. "Look, didn't I just say that there are beings on the Other Side who are trying to help us? Well, they are. And apparently they do want you to wake up and figure out what your real purpose is for this lifetime. Apparently, it's pretty important! You are interacting directly with some kind of multidimensional, extraterrestrial intelligence, Martin, like ambassadors from another world or even a parallel universe."

Martin pulls out the piece of paper with William's bio and sketches an emblem on the back. William casually watches as he draws. Martin explains as he finishes the illustration, "This disk has overlapping glyphs of the Alpha and Omega inside a moon gate, like the ones you see in Bermuda. The Alpha part of what my visitors show me glows with a soft golden white sheen, and the Omega has more of a dark luster like that of black onyx. What do you make of this, William?"

William is stunned beyond silence as he looks at the sketch. He slowly reaches into his pant pocket and slides something covered by his hand across the white linen tablecloth toward Martin. "There is more I need to tell you, Martin. I wasn't sure earlier if you can handle this; but obviously, you are much farther along—because of your visitors—than I thought you were," William confesses mysteriously as he slowly lifts his long, slender fingers one by one. Martin also sits in stunned silence as he stares at the very same disk that his Egyptian visitors have shown him. William states simply, "It was a gift from a close friend, an archeologist and an Egyptologist, who happens to live in the Los Angeles area. He said the symbol has something to do with the emergence from duality and the homecoming to unity." Martin shoots a questioning glance at William.

"Okay. Wait just a minute. I'm going to order another coffee. Do you want anything, William?" asks Martin, as he motions for the waitress. "Sounds like it's going to be a long night."

Chapter 93

"Ashton, this has been the best day of my life," Nicole exclaims in the limo as she downs another flute of champagne. She inhales deeply on a long cigarette in a sterling silver holder as she enjoys the ride inside the magnificent one-of-a-kind hand-crafted limousine that Ashton had specifically built. She runs her hand down the smooth inlayed wood panel while Ashton reaches for another champagne bottle from the fully stocked, carved stone bar. Under the champagne's influence, and well past the Veil of Forgetting, Nicole unknowingly repeats herself. "Oh, Ashton, this has been the best day of my life! Funny thing is . . . right now I can't remember much else!" She giggles as Ashton refills her crystal flute.

"Here's to you, Nicole. To the most beautiful woman in Las Vegas," announces Ashton. He shows her how to intertwine their arms before they drink from their glasses. Nicole laughs hysterically when she spills some of her champagne on Ashton's lap. Shopping bags from Yves Saint Laurent, Chanel, Gucci, Tiffany & Co., Dior, and other packages from the most expensive stores in Vegas surround their feet. Nicole kicks off her sandals and wiggles her bare toes into the fine black wool carpeting.

"Oh, Ashton, how did you manage it—my own private shopping spree in every world-renowned store in the most prestigious shopping area of Las Vegas?" Nicole giggles cheerfully.

Ashton smiles proudly then inhales deeply on his cigarette as he watches Nicole drink even more champagne. "I'll do anything to have you in my life, Nicole."

Nicole smiles halfheartedly as she leans back into the plush leather seat. Exhausted from her afternoon of shopping, she is glad that Ashton's chauffeur is heading back to the Luxor. The driver carefully maneuvers the elongated Rolls Royce down Flamingo Road past Caesar's Palace, turning onto the Strip in front of the dancing Fountains of Bellagio.

"Look over there, Nicole. The fountains of water and light are dancing to the music," explains Ashton as he opens the limo window. "Listen closely; it's a choreography of movement, light, and water, springing to life with the some of the world's most beautiful music. Isn't it magnificent, Nicole?"

"Oh, yes, Ashton. It's absolutely breathtaking—like nothing I've ever seen before," she exclaims excitedly.

"But it's nothing compared to the beauty that is sitting next to me," Ashton admits. As the window goes up Nicole suddenly hears the same music playing in the car, at the same time as the music playing in the famous fountains. She looks to Ashton in amazement. "It's all for you, Nicole." Ashton smiles as he gently squeezes her hand. "Like I just said, there isn't anything I wouldn't do for you, my dear."

Playing tour guide, Ashton, in his debonair style and regal Oxford English accent, points to all the fabulous hotels, casinos, and shows along the way. Nicole, still innocent and childlike, presses her face against the glass, looking through the tinted windows at the sights and sounds of America's adult amusement center. Slowly the limousine proceeds through the crowded Las Vegas Strip, heading to the Luxor Hotel and Casino.

"Look, Nicole, that's Bally's, next to that is Paris Las Vegas, a very romantic, lavish hotel with a distinctly European flair. The hotel has amazing replicas of the Eiffel Tower and the Arc de Triomphe," Ashton continues proudly.

"Wow, this place is truly amazing. And what did you say you do for a living Mr. Ashton Olivier?" inquires Nicole as she turns her head from side to side attempting to take in all the sights and sounds of Vegas. "Have you lived here for a long time?"

"Well, on most days, it seems like I've been here forever. And as far as what I do for a living, well, you could say I own this place. I have vested interests in everything you see here," Ashton explains while placing a call on the car phone.

Ashton points to the Aladdin while waiting for his call to go through. "This is a Sin City odyssey, my dear. Just feast your eyes on all the excitement and opportunities that abound. Further down is the Monte Carlo," Ashton continues. "Anywhere, anytime, any show you want to see, you just let me know and it's yours, my dear. It's all yours."

"Look, it's New York City! In Las Vegas?" Nicole asks inquisitively. "I'm a little confused, Ashton. Why is New York in Las Vegas?" she asks, not realizing he's on the phone. As the alcohol settles in, she lets out a huge yawn. Her mind wanders back to her time with Father Knorosov. She replays

GINA E. JONES

their first kiss over and over in her memory. Intoxicated previously on the plane with passionate love, she now slowly finds herself intoxicated with the finest champagne ever produced on Earth.

With his phone call complete, Ashton is quick to answer her question. "Many of the hotels here resemble buildings, monuments, or structures from other cities and countries. Look, Nicole, that's the MGM Grand Hotel and Casino with over five thousand guest rooms, making it one of the largest hotels in the world. Coming up will be the infamous Tropicana Hotel, and the Excalibur is coming up on your right; then we will be back to the mystical and mysterious Luxor, where I met the mystical and mysterious Nicole," says Ashton with his sensually alluring voice.

Nicole looks softly and in silence at Ashton, gazing at his lips, his nose, and then slowly into his eyes. He returns her gaze, bringing his face closer to hers. Suddenly, she bursts out laughing, spewing champagne mixed with saliva all over his face. "Did you see the look on that woman's face?"

Put off by her abrupt, unsophisticated, and rather disgusting outburst, Ashton wipes his face with his monogrammed silk handkerchief. "Whose face?" he asks. A tone of agitation blankets his words.

"Mrs. Catherine Hamilton." Nicole giggles, as she slowly closes her eyes, resting her head heavily on Ashton's shoulder.

# Chapter 94

"Before you begin, William, I was wondering what you picked up on that priest because he thought you looked very familiar to him as well," inquires Martin as he twists and folds his napkin again.

"Good man, dedicated, yet not all about the church as he may appear. There's something secretive about him. I really didn't spend much time thinking about him, although he is passionately in love with that flight attendant trainee that was working first class. But you didn't have to be psychic to figure that one out!" William laughs as he nervously twists his napkin as well. Thoughts and images wrapped in words suddenly come to him. "This man takes his spirituality very seriously. He's a man of truth who is compelled internally, almost driven somehow, to simply seek and know, to truly understand the truth."

"My God, you're right! Although he was traveling with the Bradleys as their former family priest—being with Jane on her second trip to that place called Medjugorje—officially he is no longer with the church. He was only dressed that way, you know, with the white collar, black shirt, and all, to fulfill the dying wishes of Jane. Guess she likes a man in uniform!" Martin jokes before continuing. "He has dedicated his whole life to be of service, not only to the church, but to help people heal miraculously. People like Jane Bradley. Let me tell you, I think Knorosov was doing more than praying over her," Martin discloses.

"Yes, I saw that—and I could feel it—energetically speaking, that is," adds William as he settles into his seat.

"This is between you and me; but Simon Knorosov, although ordained in the Catholic Church and a believer at some level, I guess, has been using his position to get into places that the average person would never have access to. Apparently, the church has information about people, places, and things where miracles occur that are hidden from the public. Interesting, huh, William?"

"I'd say," affirms William.

"What's interesting is he too is a researcher of sorts, a researcher of miracles. Apparently, he has studied and seen many of the miracles that have taken place throughout the world. Now get this; his studies also include the Mayan Sacred Calendar. His travels have taken him to Central and South America and Mexico where he has studied with shamans from various indigenous cultures."

"Well, now, I like him even more," chuckles William as he leans back into the upholstered booth. Martin can see the fire in William's eyes and knows that he has captured the brilliant young researcher's attention.

"He told me that his Russian grandfather was a young soldier for the Red Army during World War II. While he was in Berlin during the death throes of the Third Reich in 1945, he was able save one book, only one book, from the National Library that was completely ablaze. And it was one that later lead him to cracking the Mayan code."

"This is amazing and certainly more than a coincidence. The Mayan Sacred Calendar is one of the subjects I discuss in great depth at my lectures and on my website. I'm curious, Martin, what else did he tell you?"

"Well, something like the central message of the Mayan Calendar is that we are living in some kind of exact divine time plan that has a higher purpose in store for humanity at the completion of linear time—whatever that means. He said that he and others are trying to make this time plan known to broader groups of people. Yet, he stated, in many parts of the world numerous groups of people are being blocked from this knowledge about a time plan."

"He certainly would know about that since he was a priest in the Catholic Church!" William smirks irreverently. "It was the Spanish bishops who burned all the books they could find that had been written by the Maya back in the early 1500-1600s. The Maya were a people that were alone in the western hemisphere in possessing a written language. At the hands of the conquistadors and the friars, their culture was destroyed. Today only four books remain. And get this, Martin—they are all calendars!"

"Well, you two obviously know a lot more about this calendar stuff than I do. I don't know, William, it's really strange. But for some reason, he and I just clicked while on that plane, although sitting in that coach seat was about more than I could bear. I can't explain it, William. Knorosov just opened up about all this stuff. He wants to build a center, now get this, a center for spiritual, metaphysical healing, and psychic study and training. Can you believe it? What a coincidence!" Martin says excitedly.

"There are no coincidences, Martin." William smiles knowingly. "Please go on."

"Let me share with you some of the details of his desire to open this facility to educate people about the Mayan Sacred Calendar and train people to heal through prayer, psychic abilities, the paranormal, and even through miracles." Martin divulges what he knows and then enthusiastically adds, "I believe that the three of us should combine our efforts to build a pyramid-shaped building together, similar to the Luxor Hotel—only smaller. Look, the main architect for this hotel is a very close friend and one who owes me several favors." Martin winks as he checks his Blackberry for the phone number.

"Martin, do you have any idea why you think this is such a great idea? Or why you want to put together three virtual strangers together on an obviously very expensive and challenging project like this center you're talking about?"

"It's hard to explain. I don't know, son; it just feels right," explains Martin. He casually looks around the restaurant as he reflects on all the dynamics involved.

"It's because we—you, Simon, and I—have done this before! It just came to me, through some kind of nonlinear cosmic language while you were talking. The three of us were involved personally with the Great Pyramid of Giza," reports William. "I already know that I am the reincarnation of Ra, the Sun God of ancient Egypt." Martin raises his eyebrow with a doubting look. "I know, I know, Martin." William raises his hand to stop Martin's next comment. "That's a long story, which we can talk about some other time. But it did just come to me that you two were priests of the pharaoh who selfishly kept secret the miraculous healing powers of the pyramid from the people of Egypt. See any similarities here, Martin?" asks William.

"My God, reincarnation! Yes, that certainly explains the instant attraction, the familiarity among so-called strangers. Now I'm a builder, developer, and architectural partner in the Luxor Hotel. Simon is a priest; yet instead of hiding the secrets of miracles like in his previous life, he's trying to bring forth the information from the ones who are now hiding it. Damn, that's very interesting! And you, William?" Martin inquires. "What about you?"

"I guess I'm still trying to bring information to help people, to share information about The Law of One, where we are all part of The One Infinite Creator and that there is more than what we see. Throughout history, the true messages of all the masters seem to be withheld, misunderstood, manipulated, and even destroyed. So I'm back again, this time as a regular guy who lives in an apartment in New Jersey, to help wake people up through radio and television interviews, lectures, street corners—basically where anyone will listen!" He laughs humbly. "Not through building temples and pyramids, like before. That obviously didn't work."

"But wait, William, don't you see it? A center like the one Simon proposes would be a great place for you to operate out of, not some apartment in Jersey. Some place grand, like this place. You and Simon will be the architects for the brave new world. We tried it before—but didn't succeed. We get the chance to do it again—and this time succeed!" Martin enthusiastically pats William on the back as the check for dinner arrives. "My treat, son."

"Martin, we're not quite finished," William confesses. "There's more."

Chapter 95

The limousine cruises up to the hotel in front of the Anubis statue near the main entrance of the Luxor. Nicole glances over at the black jackal-headed funerary god of Egypt while she searches anxiously through her purse. "Where in the world did I put that room key?" she mumbles, looking through the Lauren Wellington purse she bought in New York.

"Here you are, Nicole." She looks curiously at Ashton's hand. "It's the key to your penthouse suite. I called and had your things moved to the suite on the top floor of one of the towers. The closet in those regular guestrooms certainly can't handle all these fabulous new clothes. Plus, you're a winner now, Nicole. You have to live like one." Ashton slides over to kiss her on the cheek. Still uneasy with his forward romantic gestures, Nicole leans over, quickly grabbing one of the bags to look at some of her new things.

"You think of everything, don't you?" exclaims Nicole.

"Yes, you could say I like to plan ahead," he muses as the limousine parks in front of the hotel entrance. "Don't worry about your bags. The bellmen will take everything. We'll take the private elevator."

"I feel so special and important with all this attention. You're amazing, Ashton." Nicole notices the onlookers outside the hotel lobby. Many of them are admiring the car's dramatic-flowing body line, soft esthetics, its rich exterior detail, and elegant accessories. The chauffeur opens the oversized passenger door for Nicole and Ashton. The Infinity crew and several passengers look on as Nicole enters the hotel lobby with Ashton. Four men of his employ dressed in coal-black Armani suits quickly walk up to escort them to the penthouse elevator. Nicole gives the crew a casual wave as they walk by. She is perplexed when she notices that the captain is staring intently at Ashton.

Eve speaks up, "Aren't you going to do something, Michael? I know she's unique, but she's never been trained for this dimension. She won't be able to—"

"Training or no training, Eve, she has Free Will. We have to honor the Law of Noninterference. No matter what we say, she won't understand." He shakes his head in frustration. "She's human now. Like so many who have come here, Nicole has fallen, becoming entangled in the denser, lower vibrations of the Third Dimension. There is nothing that you or I can do. She is on her own now."

"But, Michael, she's wi—" starts Eve.

"I said there's nothing we can do," he states firmly.

Dissatisfied with Michael's position and his sudden refusal to intervene on Nicole's behalf, Eve follows behind Ashton's entourage. She waits patiently for her golden opportunity, then rushes over to speak with Nicole. As she approaches, several of Ashton's men block her from getting close. However, Eve is able to overhear Ashton's dinner invitation to Nicole. "Don't forget, nine o'clock in my private dining room. I can hardly wait to see you in that luscious red . . ." says Ashton with a very provocatively suggestive tone. Eve is aghast as she watches Nicole happily enter the private penthouse elevator with Ashton.

Chapter 96

"Martin, something very interesting just came to me about this flight, about all of us being here at the Luxor, and why you and so many others think I look familiar. I couldn't say anything before," explains William mysteriously, leaning closer toward Martin. "But after what happened earlier in the bar and what came to me about our past life connection, I'm sure I've got most of this figured out," William says excitedly, ready to share his latest psychic impressions.

"Just give it to me straight, William. We don't have much more time." Martin furrows his brow.

"Every one of us on that flight—all the passengers, that is—were all in Atlantis together and later reincarnated in Egypt. We're like a large traveling cast of characters that has been called to play out certain dramas written for this planet." William quickly glances over to read the expression on Martin's face. "We each had some role to play in those scenes that were scripted for this planet back then and have come forward again in this lifetime to play out this particular closing scene. It may seem hard for all of us to comprehend; but the time of Revelation, if you want to call it that, has come. We are living out the defining moment in the history of this planet."

"Okay." Martin listens patiently.

"It seems hard to think that we are the generation meant to experience the culmination of a sixteen-billion-yearlong plan, to experience the end of time—the end of duality. It feels as though this last act should be still for some time to come or maybe played out by some more fully aware generation. You know, like individuals that are willing to live outside the limitations of conflict and killing. Or maybe a generation of liberated beings that are comfortable with the true nature of consciousness. But what I'm gathering from all my sources, in fact, is that you and I and everyone on that flight and everyone on this planet are actors of an enormous cast in this most riveting dramatic play down here on Earth. And this is the final act. Some could even say that this is the final curtain call of God's judgment of humanity."

"Okay, so where are we going, William?" demands Martin quite emphatically, feeling the intensity and uncertainty of life is increasing. "If this is the final act, then where in the hell are we going?"

"I don't know if there is any way to explain it. No one here has the answers in a way that most people can understand. We have been held in the dark so long—in a cave without light—that I'm afraid that when we do finally come out, we are going to be totally blinded by the reality of what is to come. Most are so unaware, yet it can only help to know that something is coming. This process is so vast in its infiniteness that it boggles the imagination to even begin to conceive of it," William utters reflectively.

William stretches out his legs under the table and casually crosses his ankles. Half-slouched in the booth while propped up on his elbows, he is the epitome of confidence. "Maybe this analogy will help answer your question, Martin. It's the old story of a turtle and a fish. The turtle lived on land as well as in the water while the fish only lived in the water. One day, when the turtle had returned from a visit to the land, he told the fish of his experiences. He explained that creatures walked rather than swam. That they breathed air, not water. The fish refused to believe that dry land really existed because that was something beyond his own experience. In the same way, people may deny that there is a dimensional shift or planetary ascension about to occur, but it does not mean that the dimensional shift is not possible," says William, his eyes almost as expressive as the words he speaks.

"Martin, we need to help others to see, with the relaxation of knowing, that this is but a very small planet; and the dramas that we create among ourselves can seem quite impressive for one within the illusion. But as soon as we step outside of it, into the mystery of infinity, we will realize how much the world is gradually slipping farther and farther into insanity, creating magnificent dramas for ourselves within our own complex minds along the way. Everyone needs to be committed to being conscious witnesses of their lives—individually and collectively—before it's too late."

"Okay," remarks Martin quizzically, unsure how to implement such a tall order for all of humanity.

"Regardless of what it looks like from our focus, from our perspective, a divine plan is in the works and is playing itself out now. There is perfection in the design, so much so that it inspires communication and confidence from beings on the Other Side of the Veil, like your parents or the visitors in your study. It need not be any worse than it is right now; and many will figure this out much later, although probably after the fact," William muses.

"There is so much to learn and so little time," Martin reflects. He looks intently at William, with a new respect for the young researcher, about his dedication to serve, to help enlighten humanity. "We have to build the facility for you and Simon as soon as possible. As this scientific evidence converges with these ancient prophesies, it seems to me that we, as human beings, are going to find ourselves at the ultimate crossroad. Together, we and this center, will serve as a beacon of power and knowledge to help prepare as many as possible that will listen." Martin feels alive and rejuvenated by the revelations he has just heard. Somehow William's words have activated a dormant life mission within Martin. "As way showers, you, Simon, and I have the opportunity and responsibility to share this vital information with everyone we meet. William, when I get back to my office, I'm clearing my schedule and my investments to sponsor you and your efforts. I truly feel that this is what my *visitors* have been trying to tell me. That this is my real job for this lifetime."

"I don't know what to say, Martin. Although I know and see a lot, I'm touched and honored by the very thought that you would do that for me, for humanity," says William most graciously. "However, as much as I think I know about what is going on, there is something about this flight, especially about this airline, that seems to be very surreal. I don't know or understand exactly what it is. It's like nothing I have ever seen or experienced before." William reflects thoughtfully. "And it is something very special."

Chapter 97

"Come in, Eve. How are you? Haven't you had fun today in this marvelous city?" asks Nicole as she frolics around the penthouse suite with a lighted cigarette in her hand. Eve walks in and leans over to smell the fragrant red roses in the beautiful crystal vase on the foyer table of Nicole's luxuriously decorated penthouse suite.

"Nicole, what has happened to you? Don't you remember we're leaving in a few minutes? The buses are loading now." Eve looks around the room where shopping bags and clothes are strewn all over the furniture.

"Fix yourself a drink, Eve!" Nicole shouts as she walks into another room. "There's a fully stocked bar over there in the corner. And there's some champagne already open on the counter. I'll be out in a minute."

"Nicole, we need to go—now!" Eve exclaims matter-of-factly.

Nicole shouts back from the master bedroom, "I'll be right there!"

"Nicole!" With her mouth agape, Eve watches in disbelief as Nicole models her new very revealing, very low cut shimmering red evening gown. "Where is your uniform?"

"Oh, that old thing! I won't be needing it anymore, Eve. I've decided to stay here in Las Vegas. During our stopover here, I've won lots of money and met Ashton Olivier, a wonderful, good-looking guy with lots of money. And he wants me too." Nicole twirls in delight. "And Ashton is certainly more generous than that penny-pinching Captain Smith. Look, he even bought me this $60,000 Dior gown! And what about this stunning necklace with matching diamond earrings from Tiffany's! Can you believe it?"

"So you're quitting?" asks Eve in her stern yet motherly manner.

"Well, yes, I guess so." Eve notices the hesitation in Nicole's voice. "I mean—yes!" confesses Nicole as she clutches more of her shopping treasures to her breast.

"It's your choice, Nicole. I wish you the best. Just remember, it is always better to love people and use things, not love things and use people," says Eve, sharing a spark of her knowledge, wisdom, and love as she gives Nicole a warm hug. Eve walks back to the penthouse door and turns around, looking at Nicole imploringly. "If you change your mind, the buses are leaving at nine o'clock sharp. I hope to see you there, Nicole. If not, I truly hope you find what makes you happy—inside."

"Goodbye, Eve. Have a nice flight back to LA!" Nicole lifts her champagne flute to bid her farewell.

"Goodbye, Nicole," says Eve as she walks into the hallway shaking her head in disbelief. She leans against the penthouse door for a moment to collect her thoughts then sighs deeply. A proud smile crosses her face.

Chapter 98

Nicole plops down on the sofa, putting her stockinged feet on the coffee table and fully opens the remote-controlled drapes covering the floor-to-ceiling windows to expand her view of Las Vegas. She notices a local newspaper that lies atop a stack of Las Vegas and Nevada tourism magazines. In picking up the evening edition of the *Las Vegas Sun*, Nicole reads, "An emergency medical helicopter crashes in the San Gabriel Mountains, one hundred miles northeast of Los Angeles." Staring her in the face is a photograph of the downed helicopter. Reading further, the article lists Father Knorosov's name, as well as the rest of the Bradley family, among the fatalities.

"No, Father! It can't be!" she screams desperately. She looks again, rereading every word of the article to see if there has been some mistake. It clearly explains every detail of the crash. Father Simon Knorosov is dead.

Nicole pulls her knees up under the gown and bands them together with her arms in an attempt of self-preservation. Tears of pain and disbelief stream down her face, dropping down onto her bare chest. The room suddenly begins to spin as the walls of the penthouse turn to black ink, slowly pouring down into a pool of despair, a pool of deep dark emotion right in the middle of the living room floor. A bottomless pool in which Nicole suddenly feels she is drowning. No longer able to focus on anything, she runs past the bedroom furniture etched with hieroglyphics and dives deep into the bed. Surrounded by reproductions of ancient times past, she cries uncontrollably while presently her heart breaks. The pain of her loss is excruciatingly overwhelming.

The penthouse doorbell suddenly chimes. *Ding-dong! Ding-dong!*

"Go away!" she cries.

A deep voice comes from the other side of the door. "Miss Nicole! Mr. Olivier has sent me to escort you. Are you ready, miss?" It's Ashton's right-hand man.

Wiping away her tears, trying to collect herself, she reluctantly shouts back, "I'll be there in a minute!"

Nicole quickly fluffs her mass of tumbling blonde hair with an upward stroke of her slender fingers. Mesmerized by her reflection in the mirror, she remembers how Ashton had made her feel special too. Thoughts of his persistent efforts to make sure she was taken care of—buying her so many beautiful things, filling her penthouse suite with flowers—all flow through her mind. Her hand glides gently over the magnificent glittering diamond necklace. *It's beautiful. Everything seems so beautiful, yet something is missing. Someone is missing—gone forever.*

Ding-dong! Ding-dong! The penthouse door chimes again.

"I'm on my way!" Nicole calls out, grabbing the new shawl and purse as she heads to the door. Suddenly she stops dead in her tracks. Frantically she runs back into the bedroom. Standing in the closet, she searches feverishly for the rosary that Father Knorosov had given her on the plane. Calmness comes immediately when she touches the beads in her uniform pocket.

A piece of paper falls on the carpet. While she hurriedly wraps the rosary around her wrist, hastily tying it into a bracelet, she sees Father Knorosov's phone number scribbled on the paper. In an almost trancelike state, she picks it up. Slowly she puts it under her nose, hoping to smell something of him again. There's nothing.

Ding-dong! Ding-dong! The penthouse door chimes followed by a loud pounding on the door.

A gasp escapes her throat as the bold knock startles her, quickening her already racing pulse. "Hold on! I'm coming." Nicole scrunches the paper, tossing it in the trash as she goes to open the door.

Chapter 99

Having sat deep in conversation for several hours in the Isis Restaurant, sharing their private, spiritual, and professional lives, Martin and William remain engaged in conversation. Martin begins to feel the same enthusiasm that he sees on William's face and hears in his voice. The information that had at first startled him and filled him with fearful trepidation of the future is now turning into brilliant rays of hope.

"This entire day I've felt like Alice in Wonderland falling through the rabbit hole, and everything is getting *curiouser and curiouser*, especially since I've been sitting here with you!" jokes Martin, patting William firmly on the back with his large hand.

"Well, it's about time! And everything we've discussed is about exactly that—time." William smiles before continuing. "I know that time is speeding up. The days seem shorter—that time is just flying by, going faster and faster—because it is. Everyone comments on that one. But it seems like today our karmic balancing or karmic relationships are being pushed along faster than normal as well, somehow invisibly guided or even orchestrated. Everyone in the right seat at the right time. It's not the *Oh, it must be a coincidence!* excuse that everyone uses who has no understanding of how life really works," William rambles. "Today has been more intense and more karmically balancing than any one day I have ever experienced."

"Well, speaking of the right seat at the right time, we need to be moving out of here if we are to get to LA tonight!" laughs Martin, as he slides across the booth bench to get out. "We definitely need to meet with that Egyptologist friend of yours tomorrow and locate that Simon Knorosov fellow as soon as possible."

"Wait, Martin, there's still more!" William quickly grabs Martin's arm, pulling him back into the booth. "Just one more minute . . . please. Our crew, the pilots and flight attendants, did you notice anything unusual about them?" asks William raising his brows as he holds Martin's forearm firmly. "Did they seem different to you? Maybe something like your guests in your study? Except they are not Egyptian, of course."

"No, I guess I didn't notice. They seemed very dedicated to passenger service and helping people out, like Mrs. Bradley. No other airline would have taken her like that. I'll have to admit that was a miracle in itself," replies Martin, perplexed by William's question. "Why do you ask?"

"They don't have the typical kind of aura around them. I see auras, and what I saw around them was not—"

"Auras?" interrupts Martin.

"Yes, it's kind of like an energy field, one that encapsulates animate and inanimate objects; everyone and everything has one. Looks like a luminous body that surrounds and interpenetrates the physical body. And what I saw around that airline crew, Martin, is not of this world. I really don't know what to make of it." He laughs nervously. "I'm just glad I got an involuntary upgrade to First Class. Since they were overbooked in the back, they moved me up front at the last minute before I boarded the plane."

Momentarily stunned, Martin looks at William with disdain. "Involuntary upgrade! I gave up my full-fare seat in First Class while you sat up there the entire flight on an involuntary upgrade! You have got to be kidding me!" He laughs out loud, shaking his head as they leave the table. "Karma!"

Chapter 100

"Never have I ever seen anyone more beautiful, more exquisite, or more stunning than you, Nicole. Just let me look at you, my dear." Ashton twirls her again, this time twisting her back into his arms. Nicole suddenly finds herself face-to-face with Ashton. Music plays in the background as his personal wine steward opens Ashton's favorite from his private collection. The staff of servers lines the wall, awaiting instruction from the maître d'hôtel.

While Nicole lays her shawl and purse on the table, Ashton's arm circles her back, holding her snugly; his other hand rises through her long hair to cup her head. He pulls Nicole even closer as he dances with her slowly around the room. He motions for everyone to disappear as the lights dim, leaving them dancing alone by candlelight. He is so close, so virile, that Nicole has to catch her breath. His fingers weave into the thickness of her hair as he holds her head in place.

"Ahh, my beautiful Nicole. Since I first laid eyes on you, I find that there is so much I want to tell you. There are so many places I want to take you. There is so much I want to do with you. There are so many things I want to share with you," whispers Ashton breathlessly on her neck, sending chills down her body. "I want to look into your eyes, to let you know that I am here. When I look at you, Nicole, I realize exactly how much I—"

On a stroke of resistance, Nicole stops Ashton's confession of affection abruptly. "Shh," she murmurs, murmuring softly enough to hide the unsteadiness she feels. Nicole places her finger over his lips to silence his words that remind her of the painful longing she feels to be with Father Knorosov. With their faces almost touching, her insides begin to tremble, a strange and unfamiliar sensation caused by the unsettling anxiety that is welling up inside her. The makeshift rosary bracelet slides down her arm. Nicole lowers her gaze, breaking eye contact with Ashton. There is an awkward moment of silence as she stares at the beads of gold, lost deep in thought.

Nicole confesses, *Somehow, on some level, I feel like I'm betraying him.* She feels a twinge of guilt when she turns back to look at Ashton. *Yet Father Knorosov is gone—killed in a helicopter crash just hours ago.* Overwhelmed with emotion, Nicole's tears of pain blend with her tears of joy as she looks around at the elegant surroundings.

Ashton notices the bracelet and slides it off her wrist. "It doesn't go with the gown and your necklace." He grimaces as he places it in her hand.

Agreeing with Ashton's sense of fashion and style, she slowly walks over to the dinner table. As she puts the rosary in her purse, Nicole confesses, *That was then.* She looks pensively back at Ashton. *And this is now.*

Ashton gently takes her hand and pulls her in closely. Dancing around the room, captivated by everything around her, Nicole looks longingly into Ashton's eyes, sensing that he truly adores her. The unnerving sensual pull of the man in front of her refuses to go away. Ashton stops and looks deeply into her eyes. With eyes closed, she opens to him, letting him explore her mouth with his tongue, joining him in its intoxicating rhythm. Thrusting and sweeping, lips open wide, her breath mixes with his in heated gasps. Somehow she knew it would be like this. It is what she'd feared. Inexplicably drawn to him, she senses that he has some kind of power over her. Power than no other man has.

When he speaks again—his eyes ablaze with mesmerizing passion—she listens as he touches her soul with his words. "I can't hold it back any longer. I have to tell you that I have never felt this way before. Nicole, I'm in—"

"Boss! Boss! You have to come downstairs right now!" demands his right-hand man as he bursts into the dining room. A despairing sense of urgency rings through his words. "All hell is breaking loose! You need to get down there now, Mr. Olivier!"

Ashton recoils as his attention is diverted momentarily from the exquisiteness he was dancing with. He looks remorsefully back to Nicole. "I beg your kind indulgence, Nicole, for their discourtesy which must be appropriate," says Ashton while raising his voice, "although I cannot imagine why!" He shoots a penetrating glare across the room as if looks could really kill.

"Sorry, boss, but you have to see this for yourself!"

Returning his gaze to the beauty that stands before him, Ashton says with sincere apologies, "I'm sorry, my dearest Nicole. Please forgive me; obviously I must go, but I will be back shortly." He bows courteously, gently kissing her hand. "Make yourself at home. My staff will get you anything you ask for. Again, I am truly sorry."

Father Simon Knorosov! Will your staff bring back to me the love of my life? Nicole screams silently, then smiles with grace as she replies, "Go ahead, Ashton. I'll wait for you."

Cigarette smokes furls in front of the tinted window where Nicole reflects on the dramatic turn of events that have occurred since her layover in New York City. Looking out from Ashton's penthouse suite, she sees the buses lined up to take the Infinity passengers back to the airport. She takes a long, deep drag from the last of her cigarette. At a loss, no longer sure of her decision to quit flying, Nicole tries to envision what her life is going to be like in Las Vegas, what life is going to be like with Ashton, not Father Knorosov.

As dusk eases into night, Nicole watches below. She is momentarily amused when she sees Samantha running to the bus, and her suitcase pops open, throwing all her clothes across the hotel driveway. Nicole quietly observes Rochel as she helps Samantha pick up her things. *Rochel is so sweet. She's always helping people find the things they've lost.* Nicole's attention shifts when she sees Eve waving at the bus driver, motioning to him to open the bus door. *And there's Sarakiel walking slowly to help that old women board the bus.* Nicole squints to get a closer look. *Wait! It's Mrs. Montgomery. I guess she will still be counseling her granddaughter about the direction of her life on the flight to Los Angeles.*

Nicole sighs deeply and turns away from the window, her heart heavy with sorrow. Her situation feels very confusing, very unsettled. Glancing back around at the extravagantly elegant dining room, Nicole notices the open bottle of Bordeaux on the table. The wine steward approaches.

"Yes, please." Nicole smiles weakly.

After he pours the wine into the exquisitely cut crystal goblet, Nicole inhales the bouquet briefly then quickly gulps it all at once. Feeling the warm stimulating sensations flow through her body, she quickly motions for him to refill her glass, higher than before.

Chapter 101

"Oh, my God! Oh, my God! Look, Fred, I won the grand prize—the $1,000,000 jackpot! Oh, my God! I can't believe it!" screams Shirley. The old, retired woman has been sitting in the casino with her husband all day compulsively playing away the remainder of their meager life savings. All around them are screams of joy as every machine and every table pay out their grand prizes at the same time.

Ashton arrives with his right-hand man and observes the pandemonium that surrounds them. Gamblers everywhere in the casino laugh and cry in celebration. "It's a gift from the ancient gods of Egypt!" one gambler screams exuberantly.

"What the hell?" exclaims Ashton loudly, trying to talk above the sound of ring bells and clanking machines as he looks around.

"What in hell is going on, boss?" begs the right-hand man as he looks to his employer. Several more of Ashton's strong-arm underlings come rushing up to help handle the situation.

Ashton replies with a long, deep sigh, "Oh, you really wouldn't understand." He looks toward the lobby and sees the Infinity Airways chief pilot starting to walk out of the hotel, tipping his pilot hat to the doorman. Capt. Smith turns on his heel and gives the scurrying hotel staff standing near the casino entrance an exaggerated salute. Michael soon joins his crew in the awaiting van to head back to Las Vegas' McCarran International Airport. Ashton and his men shake their heads at the mayhem that surrounds them. Suddenly, Ashton panics as he races back upstairs. "Nicole!"

Returning to his private dining room, Ashton finds a sight to behold. The tall tapered black candles continue to burn, and the aroma of Coquilles Saint-Jacques that his chef has specially prepared permeates the room. Soft music still plays in the background. And Nicole is passed out on the table, her face flat in the sterling silver platter of hors d'oeuvres. An empty bottle of Château Margaux 1961 lies on the white tablecloth next to her head.

Chapter 102

The first faint glow of morning light streaks through the window, casting long, narrow rays across the room. A smile creeps across Ashton's face as he feels deeply satisfied and very pleased with himself. He yawns while quietly savoring the first moments of being awake. With his hands clasped together behind his head, he stretches his perfectly sculpted long, firm nude body before he gets out of bed. The sunshine highlights the bronze tan that covers his well-toned torso, his strong arms, hard chest, and flat abdomen. Ashton smiles happily again when he hears the penthouse doorbell chime. After reaching for his silver lighter next to the clock on the nightstand, he lights a cigarette and takes his time to put on his red silk robe. He strolls casually out of the bedroom to answer the door when the bell chimes again.

Nicole struggles to awaken. She squints and then quickly attempts to cover her eyes as the Sun shines in across her face. She slowly raises her head with effort. Momentarily disoriented, she looks around anxiously at the unfamiliar surroundings. Nicole hears the sounds outside the window and looks for the remote to close the drapes. Quickly rising to sit up, she lifts her shaky hands to grab her head in an attempt to stop the spinning and the throbbing pain inside.

"Oh, my God, my head," croaks Nicole, her sleepiness hangs in her throat. "Is this some kind of wrath of grapes from drinking so much wine?"

she whispers quietly, no longer able to stand any loud sounds from herself or anywhere else. As she tries to orient herself in the bedroom, she sees the red Dior gown in a heap on the bedroom floor staring her in the face. The feeling of nausea and thoughts of regret now churn in her stomach.

Nicole suddenly sits bolt upright and grabs the black satin sheets to cover her bare breasts when she hears someone open the door. A waiter in a black tuxedo enters the room, pushing a room service table. Ashton stands smiling proudly beside the man.

"It's time to rise and shine," Ashton announces happily. Her head spins frantically out of control when she realizes that she is in Ashton's bedroom. Under Ashton's direction, the waiter moves the elaborate breakfast presentation in even closer to the bed. When Nicole gets a whiff of the Eggs Benedict, she begins to heave.

Their day together starts out fast and furious as Ashton shows Nicole all around the glitzy resorts of Las Vegas. In total defiance of a normal relationship, Nicole feels the mesmerizing pull of Ashton's presence. The tingling sensations of excitement and power permeate every minute she spends with him. Consumed by obsessive thoughts of how she can spend even more time with Ashton, she is unable to shake the feelings for him that circulate in her mind. Yet in some ways, she is surprised by her unexpected attraction to him. Her instincts are engaged in an internal battle with her external reality.

Visiting all the famous tourist spots, Nicole and Ashton laugh cozily, holding hands and kissing each other passionately throughout the day. Ashton teaches Nicole how to play the tables at the most posh casinos. While enjoying the best cuisine in town, Ashton spoon feeds Nicole in very sensual and seductive ways. The finest wines further intoxicate Nicole as everything with Ashton is romantic yet very provocative, even smoking together. All the while, Nicole notices that everywhere they go women seem to know Ashton in a way that seems to be more than that of just friends. He is quick to dismiss them, focusing his attention exclusively on Nicole.

Drawn to the excitement and thrill of gambling, Nicole tries to win yet loses more chips, losing more of her own money. The more she loses, the more she drinks. During the afternoon, she notices that Ashton is nodding to the dealers, encouraging them to give her more chips even though she is on a tough losing streak. Eventually everything in her world is swirling around, completely out of control. Dragging Ashton from casino to casino, Nicole desperately tries to win back her money. Although she now owes more than she can ever repay, Nicole compulsively continues to gamble as Ashton waits quietly by her side. By the end of the day, Nicole is drunk, exhausted, and looks like a tramp. The very clingy low-cut black dress hangs disheveled on her slumped shoulders as she gambles, yells, smokes cigarettes, and downs free cocktails left and right, compulsively trying—obsessively hoping—to win a jackpot again. To passers-by she doesn't seem to be paying with a full deck.

"Put six hundred on red!" shouts Nicole as she slides her next wager across the green felt roulette table. She nervously eyes the few remaining chips in her pile. The brief excitement of being up is now heavily outweighed by the numerous times of being down. "Come on, baby, show me red!"

Again, she loses. Her winnings are quickly evaporating. The last twenty-four hours of shopping and gambling have depleted whatever sense of power she initially felt by having money.

"Nicole, are you ready?" Ashton remarks impatiently, "The car is waiting."

"Just one more, Ashton. I really think this is going to be the big one. This baby is going to pay off any minute. I can just feel it. I'll be right there; let me try just one more time," exclaims Nicole. Inside the smoke-filled casino, desperation hangs heavily in her voice. Distracted by the intensity of the game and the small amount of remaining chips, she does not really know what to feel anymore. Her entire existence has turned into an emotional roller-coaster ride. Every time she thinks she might win big, that the nightmare ride is about to end, she loses again, taking another death-defying plunge into overwhelming loss, sinking deeper and deeper into debt.

"Look, Nicole, it's just not in the cards for you to win tonight!" he quips sarcastically as he winks at the passing cocktail waitress.

"Just hold on, Ash—" Nicole argues defensively.

"Nicole, please! We need to go. We're supposed to have dinner with Steve Wynn and his wife at Wynn Las Vegas in a few minutes. Now, get your things, and let's get out of here. You're not exactly winning!"

"Don't be so impatient. Just one more—"

Ashton grabs her arm, forcefully pulling her away from the table, through the crowded lobby, and out to his awaiting limousine.

Nicole digs feverishly in her purse. "Where did it go!" she exclaims. Nicole panics as she counts the money left in her wallet. "I've been robbed. Almost all my money is gone!"

"There's more where that came from," Ashton retorts condescendingly. "Now fix your hair and makeup, Nicole. I don't want to be embarrassed by the way you look when we meet the Wynns. They are most influential in this town."

"I'm sorry, Ashton. I don't want to embarrass you. Do you really think I need more makeup?" she asks, turning her face toward his.

Grabbing the lipstick from her purse, Ashton applies another heavy coat of the "Firehouse Red" to her already very red lips. "Put on some more of that black eyeliner, Nicole. You need more blush as well."

Nicole looks in the limousine's drop-down vanity mirror. *Just how much more makeup can I put on and still look like me?* Stroking her cheek gently with the blush applicator, she sees a side of herself that she does not recognize. Something seems wrong, very wrong. Nicole stops and stares blankly at herself as the car races quickly down the Las Vegas Strip.

"Ashton?" begs Nicole, seeking reassurance from the man in her life.

Ashton blatantly ignores her as he discusses business on the phone along the way. Looking deeper and deeper, beyond her reflection, beyond the gnawing emptiness, a voice within hauntingly asks, *Who are you? Why you're here? Is this really what you came here for? Is this what your life is supposed to be about?* A tear moistens the corner of her eye as her confusion and emotions mixed with the alcohol she's consumed come pouring out.

"Ashton?" she asks again politely.

"I'm on the phone god damn it!" he yells.

"Sorry." Nicole sinks down in the seat repulsed by everything that is happening with her and with Ashton. The desert sun blazes low in shades of orange and varying degrees of gold, accenting Ashton's tanned facial features, imbuing them with a more dramatic edge. The heat of the evening only intensifies her world of despair and heartache. Nicole stares upward through the open sunroof as the last streaks of sunset fade from the sky. *Where are you, Father? In heaven?* She sighs heavily. *Why on Earth have you left me?*

Chapter 103

Returning from their evening out, Ashton lays two crystal brandy snifters on the black marble counter of his fully stocked wet bar. In his attempt to expose Nicole to the finer things in life, he asks, "Would you like to taste the world's most expensive cognac? It's called *timeless,* and it was made by Hennessy from a blend of eleven cognacs dating from 1900 to 1990. Only two thousand bottles were produced, Nicole, and I own most of them," he boasts, demonstrating his passion for elegance and sophistication. He cradles the glass in his hand, and warms the luminous golden-colored brandy to help release the delightful aromatic bouquet. Ashton confidently swirls and aerates the perfectly aged cognac before nosing the spirit. He proudly offers the snifter to Nicole.

"You gotta be kidding. I'll throw up if I have another hors d'oeuvre or glass of anything!" exclaims Nicole as she begins her tirade. She is losing control having drank and eaten too much. Her weariness, a result of the late hour and the long day of sightseeing and gambling, is now reflecting in her voice. "I'm tired, Ashton, and I owe money to practically every damn casino in Vegas! Never in my life have I had so much and yet have so little." Nicole grabs her thighs. "Look at me. In just two days, I'm already getting fat!"

Ashton lashes out, "You ungrateful little bitch!" His unexpected anger frightens Nicole as he throws the snifter her way, flying straight toward her face. She just barely steps out of the way when the glass hurtles past her cheek. Ashton's reaction to her comment is chilling in its malevolence, and his once-pleasant appearance twists repulsively with anger. As glass and cognac splatter all over the wall, Nicole quickly grabs her purse and rushes over to the door.

"Wait!" Ashton extends an apologetic smile, waving her back into his suite. Pausing momentarily, Ashton inhales the aromatic scent of his favorite cognac and slowly takes a sip while collecting himself. He attempts a casual manner, mustering all his reserve composure in order to maintain control.

"Excuse me?" asks Nicole incredulously. Her brow furrows deeply, confused by the drastic change in his demeanor.

"Nicole, I'm sorry," Ashton replies remorsefully as he sets his glass down on the coffee table. He tries to offer what he hopes is a plausible explanation. "Forgive me for losing my temper. It's just that I have given you so much. Yet you don't seem to really appreciate all I have done for you, all I have given you. I know our time together has been short; but it seems that no matter what I do for you, you're never really happy."

Ashton consciously unclenches his fists, suppressing his building anger as he looks at her in a way that she has never seen before. Suddenly Ashton smiles as he motions for Nicole to return, to sit with him on the sofa. With great trepidation, she slowly walks back into the room. She smiles back halfheartedly as she remains standing.

Caressing her left hand gently and tenderly, he sensually strokes her ring finger. "There's something that I want to ask you, Nicole. Your answer can change everything—for both us."

"Oh, Ashton, I don't know what to say." Despite his attempted assault, Nicole decides to sit next to Ashton. Suddenly visions of trying on beautiful white wedding dresses in the most expensive bridal boutiques race through her mind. A scene of walking down a church aisle flashes past her. "After the way you've been acting in this evening, this is the last thing I expected."

"Just say yes, Nicole," he begs as he slides off the edge of the sofa. He crouches down closely beside her, one knee on the floor.

"I don't know what to say. I have so many questions, like when and where?" Nicole dismisses her skepticism, turning her attention to Ashton, who now kneels before her. In her surprise, she looks into the warm depths of his green-eyed gaze.

"Tomorrow night. The way I see it, there's no need to waste time." Ashton's voice is as deep and as warm as his gaze.

"What! Tomorrow night?" Nicole begins to think something is amiss, but she is still in the dark.

Answering Nicole's questioning look, Ashton begins to explain. His face very close to hers, their lips almost touching, his voice a mere whisper, "You said you're broke, right?"

"Uh, yes, but what does that have to do—" Without giving Nicole the opportunity to finish her question, Ashton delivers his mouth to hers and envelops her in a kiss of uncontrolled passion. She slips her arms around his neck and runs her fingers through his thick blonde hair while returning his kiss. Wildly her own heated passion mirrors the fervor that radiates from Ashton. Yet unanswered questions run through her mind. Nicole breaks off the succulent kiss that fans her burning desire for more. Thrusting herself away from his embrace, Nicole begins to ask again, "But, Ashton, what—"

Ashton places his finger over her luscious lips. "Shh. I've already got the night all lined up for you." He licks his lips slowly and sensually as he traces the outline of her lips with his middle finger.

"What are you talking about, Ashton? You have me totally confused!" Her voice quavers slightly as she tries to project a calmer, more controlled demeanor.

"You said you're broke, right?" he explains simply.

"Uh, yes, but what does that have to do with—" Again Ashton places his finger firmly over Nicole's lips. Something about his manner touches a note of uneasiness and suspicion deep inside her.

"The night is already lined up," he continues.

"What are you talking about, Ashton?" begs Nicole as she looks to him with bemused concern as she tries desperately to understand. The situation grows more intense by the moment. She searches the intensity of his eyes, trying to read his mood, trying to calculate the severity of her predicament. Nicole studies Ashton's face for a moment longer, not quite sure what to do or what to say. He is successful in masking whatever is going on inside him. Nicole sees nothing in his expression; nothing reflected in his eyes.

"You're broke, right? You're beautiful and have the most amazing and delicious body." Ashton looks her over with his eyes resting on her breasts. "Nicole, I'm offering you a job."

"What!" exclaims Nicole as she cocks her head. She gives Ashton a questioning look, not certain of what it is that he is alluding to.

"A call girl, Nicole. With your expensive tastes, your insatiable desire to gamble, and that killer body of yours," Ashton rises and waves his arm slowly across the room while he continues, "you can have it all. You just have to make a few men happy—if you know what I mean. It's the perfect job for you, Nicole. You'll be able to shop to your heart's content."

The silence of shock meets Ashton's words, and Nicole waits with what seems to be an eternity. The total realization of what is happening explodes in her mind with amazing clarity. Suddenly everything makes sense. Yet Nicole still finds it inconceivable that Ashton could ever make such a proposal.

"Ashton, I thought you cared about me," cries Nicole as she shakes her head in her hands.

"Don't you see that I do? Where in the world do you think you can make that kind of money, Nicole?" Ashton asks casually as he picks up his cognac. "Do you have any idea how many women would kill to be in your shoes?"

"Then they can have these damn shoes!" she screams as she removes the black Chanel evening sandals, throwing them at Ashton as she marches toward the door.

"Stop right there, you miserable little—" he starts. Ashton quickly reaches her in four long strides before he forcefully grabs her arm, pulling her back to prevent her from leaving.

"You're hurting me!" shouts Nicole staring at Ashton with genuine fear for the first time. Her insides tremble with every quaking breath that she draws. The intense pounding of her heart reverberates in her ears and scares her right down to her toes.

Ashton squeezes harder, pulling her in, face to face. "Don't be stupid, Nicole. You're just another dumb blonde who is totally clueless! You don't have a college education, and you can't even remember going to high school," he teases. "So where in hell do you think you would be able get a job to pay off your kind of debts?"

With her free hand, she tugs at his fingers, prying as hard as she can to loosen his fierce grip. Mustering every bit of muscle and strength within, Nicole successfully peels his penetrating fingers off her arm as she boldly looks straight into his eyes, trying to put some sense and logic to all of what is happening. She rubs the spot where his fingers had squeezed into her arm as she takes a couple of steps away from him. As she begins to run to the door, Ashton laughs cynically at her feeble attempt to get away from his clutches of control, and his rule of influence.

Chapter 104

Surrounded by piles and piles of glamorous designer clothing and accessories on the penthouse sofas, Nicole cries as she picks up each item. Stroking the fabrics, rubbing the silk scarves against her cheek, and smelling her new perfumes, Nicole replays the day's scenes over and over in her mind. She touches the shimmering diamond necklace that Ashton generously gave her. Holding the clothes in front of herself, Nicole looks painfully in the mirror. She feels weak and disoriented, no longer able to cope with the harsh reality that surrounds her, that completely envelops her. Nicole closes her heart as she throws everything down on the floor in abhorrent disgust.

Retreating to the master bedroom only worsens her despair as she looks at the plush bed where Ashton suggested that she make her living. She cries out in anguish. "What happened? How did I end up like this?" Nicole asks over and over. Her confusion is complicated by the fact that she somehow feels helplessly bound to Ashton by her present circumstances—chained, handcuffed, and the key thrown away forever.

Her pain and despair increase as she walks around the luxurious penthouse. Exquisite crystal vases of red roses grace every tabletop and counter. Nicole stops to smell the roses; their fragrance intoxicates her senses. When she pulls one of the long-stem roses out of the vase, a thorn pricks her finger; and red blood flows forth. The sweet scent of their beauty quickly disappears from her memory as she feels the painful sting of life. The spectacular view of the night lights of Las Vegas from the window beckons to her. Looking out, an unbearable revelation occurs to her. *Everything here is connected to Ashton in some way.*

Unable to think clearly, unable to truly understand the scope of her situation, Nicole wanders to the bathroom. Next to the solid marble steam room, she places some lavender sea salts into the raised Jacuzzi tub. The fallen angel surrenders deeply into the echoing silence of her circumstances. Her body trembles as flashes of memory parade through her mind's eye. Unable to bear another moment of her own existence, Nicole strips naked; her sleek black satin dress, silk bra, and red lace thong drop to the cold marble floor. Looking deeply into the mirror as the bathwater rises, she slowly caresses her nude body with the prayer beads from Father Knorosov. Caressing the very same places that he had touched—places had that stimulated her into the rapturous ecstasy of Seventh Heaven.

Like a bolt of lightning searing through her heart, repulsive visions of Ashton touching her breasts and body suddenly haunt Nicole. She begins to rub her boobs vigorously with the gold-beaded rosary. She feels compulsively drawn to try to erase the places where Ashton's hands have been. Rubbing harder and harder, while tearing at her flesh with her nails and the chain of the rosary, blood begins to flow. She now hates the very body that attracted someone like Ashton. Nicole rips her nails into the hands that had held him so close. The pain of the memory is more painful than the pain of shredding her own flesh. Feeling tainted and tarnished, she loses sight of herself as steam slowly fogs the mirror, clouding her reflection. Her bloody hands slam against the mirrored reflection that once was.

Lost in a turbulent ocean of emotion, she slowly slides her beautiful, yet bloodied body from Heaven into the scalding hot waters of the marble tub. Sinking deeper and deeper into her heartache and painful sorrow, Nicole closes her eyes, praying silently in the gray shadows of her existence. Completely distraught, she begs to understand the purpose of her life. *Lord, I'm so physically weary, spiritually defeated. I feel so small and insignificant, drained of every joy. Why do I feel so incapable of living or even loving? Giving up my job at Infinity has somehow left me wallowing in the cesspool of wretchedness of what life has offered me.* Nicole sobs, "Why am I so tortured and tormented by the thought of walking through life less than ordinary . . . feeling so alone, different . . . disgraced, disheartened, and somehow . . . exiled from all that is?"

Nicole slides lower and lower into the steamy waters that surround her. Her salty tears flow down her cheeks, merging with the bloody bathwater, as thoughts of suicide flow endlessly through her mind. *There is one way to escape this pain . . . to no longer be aware of anything . . . or anyone.* She slides further and further into the deep scorching waters of death.

Confusion consumes and eats away the very core of her being, leaving her nothing but disillusioned in a dreadful dark pit of doom. Lost in her weariness, Nicole's voice no longer holds the energy to fight or even live.

"Lord, I'm so tired. Please help me . . . please forgive me." She drops the blood-covered rosary beads on the cold hard floor.

Taking one last deep breath, Nicole exhales deeply, slowly submerging her entire body into the bath's alluring water. As suddenly as her life had begun, it now is about to end. She does not move, preferring instead to allow her mind and body to drift away into the mysterious abyss of death. Nicole settles into an unusual tranquility with a body that is no longer weighed down by pain and fear. There is a comforting stillness. In the submerged silence she longs for her nonexistence.

Gentle waves of eternity and uncertainty crest together as unfathomable visions of the strange unknown swim by, one after another. Beneath the waters of consciousness that cover her head, Nicole peacefully soaks in the solitude of absolute nothingness. Serenity surrounds her. As the light grows dimmer and dimmer in her mind's eye, drowning in a sea of desperation, her essence merges with the never-ending darkness in the spiraling black pool of all infinity.

Chapter 105

"And where in the hell do you think you are going?" demands Ashton as he storms around the end table, knocking over the lamp. "And dressed like that?"

While lying in her depthless burning tomb, beyond the reach of all emotion, as desperation had dug its fated grave, a sudden blinding flash of intense light violently startled Nicole back to life. In her last moment of consciousness, an answer to her cries of despair came from deep within. An answer that was gently whispered by the voice of All That Is. Now dressed in her flight attendant uniform, Nicole has returned to Ashton's suite, her thoughts coming together with remarkable clarity.

"I'm going to work, Ashton. But definitely not for you. Not as some pitiful call girl who sells her body for money, for things," Nicole retorts as she thrusts all the possessions he has bought for her up against his chest. Her uniform blazer opens slightly revealing the white embroidered Infinity Airways logo on the white cotton uniform blouse underneath. However, it doesn't reveal the painful scratches and bloodied markings from her nails and the rosary that now cover her chest and arms.

Ashton pushes back, refusing to take anything. He laughs at her tauntingly. "Ha! Catherine Hamilton was right, Nicole. You're nothing more than a glorified waitress!" he screams. The veins on his neck begin to protrude as she drops all the clothes and jewelry at his feet. "You think that working for some wing and a prayer airline is going to provide you the income to afford all this. You must be dumber than you look!"

"Say what you want, Ashton. I've made up my mind! And this is the smartest decision I have ever made." Gaining strength in the fight with

Ashton, Nicole lashes out partly against her own inability to deny his claim and in part against the very strength that inexplicably draws her to him.

As Nicole heads for the door, Ashton grabs her arm and face, painfully forcing her to look into his eyes. He forces himself right into her face, breathing deeply as sweat glistens across his face, his fingers pushing harder and harder into her jaw and cheeks. Ashton is not sure what he is seeing. It appears to be a combination of apprehension, guilt, and maybe a small hint of panic; but it is definitely not fear. Beyond the face that no longer bares makeup, there is a confidence in Nicole that he has never seen before—a look of self-assurance, even composure.

Ashton tries to intimidate her further. "You have no idea who you are dealing with, Nicole. I suggest you change your mind if you know what's good for you, for your safety, if you know what I mean!"

Two of his men dressed in black suits promptly enter the room. "Everything okay, boss?" they ask as a look of concern quickly darts across their faces.

"I'll handle her, boys," Ashton replies, his voice hollow, devoid of all emotion. After a long pause, he releases her from his grasp. Ashton signals them to wait outside the room.

"Look, Ashton, this is obviously not going to work. You've got your things back. What do you want from me anyway? Why don't you go find one of those women that would *kill to be in my shoes* to fill your wonderful employment opportunity?" exclaims Nicole as she tries to leave.

Without warning, Ashton instantly steps into her path, as quickly and quietly as thought itself, to intercept her departure. A shiver of anxiety suddenly quivers through her as he blocks her way. "I never lose anything that I want, Nicole." He gently strokes the soft skin of her cheek, noting the red marks left behind by his firm hold. He continues to slowly caress the smoothness of her complexion with his fingertips. "And that includes you." Ashton senses her introspection and smiles as they pause at the penthouse door.

Her anxieties lessen, but she remains alert and does not move away from her avenue of escape. "The only thing I wanted from you, Ashton, was love and respect. At first, I really thought you were in—" starts Nicole as she tries to sound casual in her expression.

"In love? With you?" he laughs devilishly, his sarcasm unmistakable. "Oh, please, Nicole. What a pathetic little human emotion! The whole love concept is a grand illusion that gives people some kind of false hope. Let me tell you a fact about that elusive emotion called love. It can be bought and sold anytime. And everyone has his or her price." Ashton pushes her blazer aside and gropes her breasts, breathing harder and harder as he unbuttons her blouse. "So why not use what you have, my dear, to make the most of love, to really profit in the game of love?"

Suddenly he notices the torn flesh and the scratches on her chest as he fondles her breasts and begins to snicker darkly. Looking closer, Ashton begins to see that Nicole is somehow different from the way she was just an hour earlier. Beside the fact that she is no longer wearing makeup, there is a certain glow of self-satisfaction about her. Peering into the window of her soul he sees an unbridled passion, an uninhibited sense of excitement, an overflowing power of sexual energy and a renewed fervor. He likes what he sees. *A beautiful woman who has a taste for sadomasochistic masturbation—my dream come true!*

Roaring louder and louder with approving laughter, Ashton's appearance seems to change in front of her very eyes. Shaking her head from side to side, Nicole tries to awaken from the nightmare around her. She powerfully grabs Ashton's wrists in an effort to push his hands away from her wounded chest. Her muscles tense along her shoulders and arms as pain shoots through her hands and throughout her body. She looks down and sees blood coming through her blouse, staining the purity of the white Infinity logo over her left breast—the logo directly over her pounding heart—the logo of limitless time, space, distance, and love. Looking straight into his eyes, in a moment of pure inspiration, Nicole tells Ashton, "And you have no idea who you are dealing with!"

"You're really going to give up all this, to wait on people at forty thousand feet? To serve disgusting, sniveling, whining passengers—demanding this, that, and the other—never thanking you, never giving you anything for your thoughtfulness or consideration? You're giving up all of *this* for *that*, Nicole?" Ashton asks caustically in a state of disbelief. Sensing that he is losing Nicole forever, Ashton continues his tirade in belittling flight attendants in an effort to get her to change her mind. "You mean that slinging hash in jam-packed cattle cars is better than *this*?" he asks, waving his arm, highlighting the luxury that surrounds them. "You mean you—"

"Yes! I mean I would rather be of service—even without a single thanks—than to have all this!" she protests emphatically, mocking his arm-waving gesture as blood drips from her hand. "And let me tell you a few other things about my job. We are on board for passenger safety. And safety, these days, means far more than demonstrating oxygen masks, securing the overhead compartments, and checking seat belts."

Ashton looks at his watch and then yawns in total disrespect.

Nicole decides to set her anger and anxieties aside, realizing they will only cloud her thinking. "And furthermore, we are on board for safety. Flight attendants are the first line of defense while the plane is in the air," says Nicole as she tries to force a confident tone to her words. "While we may be serving drinks, peanuts, or *slinging hash* to those *disgusting, sniveling, whining passengers,* we're taking care of hundreds of people on just one flight—giving them whatever they want without judgment—we're also there to guide them to safety in the event of an emergency—to show them the way. Flight attendants are like angels in the sky. They are constantly on watch for any kind of threats—protecting their passengers from takeoff to touchdown. Sounds like more than a glorified waitress job to me!"

Ashton shakes his head; his disapproval surrounds every word. "You can't really think that you could be all that important, do you?" he jeers, his lips thinning in sarcasm.

"Yes, I do. I can't really explain it, Ashton. All I know is that I just want to fly. I just want to help people," Nicole says knowingly. Her answer overflows with strength and affirmation.

"You don't even have any wings. You're just some insignificant little trainee," remarks Ashton as he pours himself another cognac. "And one that was left behind. Just how many of them came to you to change your mind before they left the hotel? One? Ha! Doesn't sound like you are very important to anyone at Infinity Airways. Flight attendants are nothing more than flying whores, Nicole. They are a dime a dozen."

"They are not! God, you are so vile and despicable, Ashton. And certainly an expert on whores. You can say what whatever you want . . . but I will get my wings and a whole lot more. You just watch, *Mr. Ashton Olivier*," exclaims Nicole as she buttons her white blazer. Anger quickly replaces her earlier fear. "Flight attendants work three hundred sixty-five days a year, twenty-four hours a day—even on holidays and weekends. They are always available to serve, no matter what. They give so much to make sure that their passengers are comfortable and safe along their journey. It's what they chose to do, Ashton—to serve others! And it's what I chose to do too."

"You better think twice, Nicole. The whole airline industry is going to hell and soon there won't be a flying job left to apply for," declares Ashton with his very arrogant, holier-than-thou attitude. "I'm finding this conversation to be absolutely boring."

Nicole grips the door handle tightly—her blood smearing across its shiny finish—desperately not wanting to believe what her eyes and ears are telling to her. Yet she stays committed to her call. "Well, I know one way to take care of that!" Nicole weeps, still hurt by Ashton's derogatory comments and depraved behavior. Rushing through the door, she hesitates momentarily—for some reason wanting, even needing, to look back at Ashton once more. Nicole now clearly sees the man before her. She leaves in tears, disgusted not only with him, but also with herself. "How could I have been involved with someone so cruel, so heartless?"

Chapter 106

"No red, no blue, and definitely not black!" exclaims Nicole, sobbing through her tears, as she sorts through her new clothes, many still with tags on them. Memories of Ashton cling to the black satin dress she has just worn that evening. She tosses it to the corner of the bedroom floor with abhorrent disgust. Grabbing her suitcase out of the closet, Nicole tries feverishly to cram as much as she can into it.

Nicole shakes all the contents of her designer purses into the suitcase realizing that very little will fit in her white uniform purse. With mounting frustration, she cries even harder realizing that nothing will fit in the small company-issued crew luggage. Nicole angrily dumps it over on the bed to start packing again. Out of corner of her eye, she notices the shimmering long white feather sticking up out of the corner of the suitcase.

"What is this?" Nicole gently glides the feather through her fingertips admiring its glistening, almost luminescent, pure white appearance. "I don't remember this being in there." Instantly, the full gamut of human emotion explodes inside of her. The faces of the taxi driver, Nancy Westman, Senator Stevens, the young harried mother, Jane Bradley, Catherine Hamilton, and every person she has encountered since her arrival on Earth flash in front of her while simultaneously all their emotions, pain, and suffering erupt inside her.

So many emotions, so few explanations. Nicole runs to the mirror in tears to see what she must look like. Her reflection reveals that her blood, sweat and tears have defaced the very fabric of Infinity Airways. The fallen angel from above—still behind the Veil of Forgetting—feels as though she is going to implode and explode simultaneously as the tumultuous feelings wrestle around inside. Using the feather in her hand, Nicole wipes away her last tear. A sense of peace suddenly overcomes her.

Nicole slowly and calmly buttons the top button on her blazer then glides her finger over her trainee nametag. "My name is Nicole. Hmm, N-I-C-O-L-E." She smiles, standing straighter, and then self-assuredly steps into her uniform shoes. Nicole, feeling proud about her decision to return to Infinity, looks around and decides to leave everything behind.

"Now, in my clearest moment of understanding, I realize that I must cut the tethers that have anchored me to the world of materiality," she announces proudly. "If I am to soar above my misery, there must not be all this baggage—the very baggage that was created in the ambiance, in the very vibrations, of my own self-condemnation."

As she looks around the room, Nicole proudly proclaims, "It's time to fly!" Miraculously she transforms back into an angel, although her wings are a dingy yellowish color—stains from the pollution and the negative energies of being human—and seem so much heavier than she remembers. Her feathers are ruffled, and her wing is still bent on its side. Looking back in the mirror, she laughs joyfully—suddenly remembering who she really is—although she remains perplexed by the color and heaviness of her angel wings. She looks curiously at the wounds that continue to bleed through her uniform and onto her feathers, yet she no longer feels the pain.

Tap! Tap! Tap! A startling sound comes from outside the penthouse window. Nicole runs awkwardly in her high-heeled uniform shoes to the window and sees her two faithful white doves waiting outside on the penthouse window. They flap their wings, ready to escort their angel home.

"Yes, you are right. It is time to fly. But this time with these wings." Nicole curiously looks over her shoulder as she attempts to extend her wings fully. She chuckles as she prepares for flight.

The divine messenger and her escorts rise up swiftly, ready to fly through the ethers above the wake of the world. Pumping her wings powerfully, Nicole pushes skyward like a rising phoenix—the ancient mythical Egyptian sacred firebird that symbolizes immortality, resurrection and life after death—flying upwards inside the spectacular beacon of light rising out of the Luxor Hotel toward outer space. Like the phoenix, with its beautiful gold and red plumage, rising from the ashes, Nicole, with her dingy yellow wings tainted with streaks of red blood pouring from her wounds, rises above the burning embers of her painful experiences on Earth.

"I guess I'll make it back to the Celestial City," Nicole exclaims to her feathered friends. She giggles joyfully. "If not, I'll just have to wing it!"

Chapter 107

"As this world continues to reel from an endless series of seemingly chaotic global events politically, financially, spiritually, energetically, and physically, more ominous signs of imminent, cataclysmic events will occur. A tsunami kills three hundred thousand after an undersea quake of a 9.0 magnitude of intensity in the Indian Ocean, followed by an 8.5 quake. A new ocean is forming with staggering speed, causing Africa to eventually lose its horn." Michael continues with his presentation. Riveting scenes of earthquakes creating the new ocean in the northeast region of Ethiopia are seen and experienced by members of The Council of Saturn and the gallery of guests through the holograms.

"These earthquakes are one way of releasing pressure at various stress points that have built up. It is also another way of alignment. In order for the planetary energies to align within, sometimes there is a breakaway in the land. Disruption in the world—not just one event, but perpetual negative, discordant influences throughout the years—can cause a breakaway, a type of splicing, a splintering of the balanced energy within Earth herself. There exists a great split in the consciousness. This planet is pulsing with microchips, radio, television, and satellite signals, electromagnetic noise from telephones, PEDs, and the like, resulting in distortions in the vibrations of Earth herself. And we haven't even touched on the impact of their underground nuclear testing yet. As you can see—"

"We get the picture!" shouts Semyaza impatiently. "What's your point, flyboy? Can't you see you're losing everyone here, Michael—just like you are on Earth." He continues to callously scold Michael in front of everyone present. "Did you forget to tell our guests and The Confederation of Planets about the *loser layover* you had in New York City, my dear pathetic Archangel Michael, Leader of the Losers!"

"As you can see, the Earth's changes are increasing more dramatically than previously expected," the archangel continues on. "We have placed the Wanderers, our intergalactic volunteers, in every country to assist with the increasing changes. These benevolent beings won't rescue humanity. They are only there as midwives to help in delivering Earth and its humanity in the ascension process through sharing their love and an understanding of genuine unity."

"Oh, please!" exclaims Semyaza as he looks to the other council members for support in his objection.

"If you look closely at the holographic display, you can see many of them already at work . . ." Michael trails off, realizing that he may, in fact, be explaining too much. He remains silent as everyone views the volcanic eruptions occurring in Hawaii and the northwestern portions of the United States stimulating tremors and quakes down the west coast of California, following the San Andres Fault. They watch as large portions of California are shaken and cities destroyed. As the council members look on, Michael walks confidently around the conference table past the invisible gateway of the Celestial Corridor ready to conclude the emergency session of the Council of Saturn. Suddenly a slight movement catches his attention from the corner of his eye.

"Excuse me, Captain Smith . . . uh . . . Michael . . . whatever!" A female hand taps impatiently on his shoulder. "What happened to my wings?" demands Nicole breathlessly, having returned to the Eighth Dimension through the portal of Light. She notices that the blood has disappeared, that her wounds have miraculously healed, and that her uniform must have returned to pure white while she was inside the Celestial Corridor. However, her wings remain dingy yellow and are sparsely covered with feathers. "Why are they so heavy? I mean—" Nicole pauses for a moment to catch her breath. The exhausted messenger is anxiously seeking answers from the Infinity Airways chief pilot. "I could hardly fly back! Look, I know I blew it down there on Earth . . . sir. I'm very sorry. I know that I'm out of the flight attendant training program, but I don't understand what is happening to these wings of mine. Look at me! I'm losing feathers every time I move," pleads Nicole. She grabs his arm, unaware that there are other beings still in the room. "You have to tell me what's wrong, Michael, please!"

He turns, standing in silence, looking deeply into her eyes. The intensity of his gaze is more than she can handle as she senses some very troubling news is forthcoming. Remaining motionless, with what feels like forever, Michael smiles at the exasperated angel. "Apparently, many of your human qualities remain, Nicole, woven into the very fabric of your angelic being. Interesting, very interesting."

"You mean that I'm a *human* being? Is that why I'm losing my wings?" Nicole desperately seeks an answer from the leader of archangels.

"Oh, please! Can we just get on with this bloody meeting?" demands Semyaza with an Oxford English accent from the council table.

Nicole turns around with a start. A sick sinking feeling overcomes every part of her being. Semyaza conceals himself from her view behind the statuesque shoulders of Ra.

"I had no idea!" exclaims Nicole as she turns to The Council of Saturn and the audience of beings in the gallery. "I just can't seem to do anything right!" Embarrassed and humiliated, she tries to fly away back toward the portal. Her energy is low, and her sparse wings are strangely too heavy. Her loose feathers float around briefly then become lost as they drift slowly into the heavenly mists.

Silence fills the chamber as brilliant Light of the highest divine radiance penetrates the room and descends on Nicole, swirling to hold her up. "Nicole, do you know who you are? Do you know what you have done?" booms the voice of The One Infinite Creator.

Michael speaks up. "Nicole, because of your actions, emotions, and loss of your angelic vibrations—by becoming fully human—we have had to carefully reconsider your application for flight attendant."

Nicole, stunned in her own silence, is only able to remain upright because of the intensive healing white Light that surrounds her. The weight of her still-human emotions of grief, humiliation, disappointment, and embarrassment are pulling her down. To her horror, a fast-forward holographic review from her three-day experience on Earth is being shown to everyone.

"Please, I can explain," begs Nicole ruefully as she looks on, stricken with shame at the scenes of herself in New York and Las Vegas. "I can't bear to relive that again," she whispers, watching herself in the store fighting with the shopper over the aqua silk pants. Members of the gallery whisper, some point, and others just sit staring as more and more is revealed. Nicole hangs her head in humiliation. Suddenly a loving voice speaks to her again. *Remember, Nicole, trust your heavenly instincts—and trust your wings of divinity—as they will always guide you where you need to go.* As Nicole hears the familiar words she looks up and sees her friend, Alexis, poking her head inside the Council Chamber doors. A smile crosses their faces, each for a different reason.

"You don't know what it's like!" Nicole lashes out angrily in her own defense. She sees Eve sitting smugly in the front row of the galley of guests as she marches around the council table. "You don't know just how hard it is to be human! How could you know? You are all masters, ascended beings, lords, and ladies from the higher dimensions. How could you ever know? You're not there, not now, not at this time on Earth." Several council members sit quietly looking on while others are aghast, some smirk and some smile as Nicole points to the holographic display. "You must forgive me, Lord, but this is too hard. And quite honestly from my brief and limited experience there, helping humanity seems quite hopeless," cries Nicole.

Exhausted and defeated, she reluctantly looks back to Michael. She gasps in the struggle to catch her breath. "May I please go now?" She barely finishes her question when intensely brilliant Light fills the chamber.

"No, Nicole, you may not," answers The One Infinite Creator. The swirling Light around her disappears. Barely able to stand, her wings begin to quiver, buckling under their weight and the weight of her emotions.

"Continue, Michael. Time is of the essence," instructs The Creator.

"Nicole, because of your unusual angelic vibrational composition combined with your denser human vibrations and because of the things you did while there, you have put yourself and everyone here in a daunting and most extraordinary position," Michael explains compassionately. "You are being assigned to return to Earth."

Totally devastated and distraught, no longer able to contain herself, Nicole crumbles to the mist-covered floor. Her heart now weighs heavy like her wings. "No, you cannot make me go back! It's too painfully hard. Please don't punish me for my mistakes," she begs tearfully. "I was never trained; you just sent me there totally unprepared. How can you do this to me!" she pleads desperately in a quiet anger. "I did my best; that's all I know how to do! Isn't that good enough?"

The only thing that can be heard throughout the Celestial City is a deafening silence. The angelic choirs no longer sing; the celestial music no longer plays. Time and space stand still as everyone looks at Nicole, kneeling pathetically in the heavenly mists, brokenhearted again. After an infinite span of time, after the unseen silence is heard, Nicole slowly and somberly looks up at Michael.

"Yes, it is true. You did your best, Nicole, and it is good enough. Isn't that right, Semyaza?" Nicole follows Michael's gaze to the crystalline council table. She sees the beaming, smiling faces of Buddha, Quetzalcoatl, Mother Mary, Immanuel, and Ra. "Isn't that right, Semyaza?" Michael asks again, even louder. Slowly, the face of the black-haired angel slowly emerges. Nicole gasps and nearly faints as she looks into the deep green eyes of Ashton Olivier.

"Ashton?" questions Nicole incredulously.

"Nicole, the man that nearly destroyed you, the man who tried unmercifully to destroy your divinity, is none other than the Lord of

Darkness himself." Michael announces to everyone, "Let it be known throughout The Cosmos that against all temptations Semyaza could offer, against all the suffering, heartache, disappointment, and pain, you chose to rise above all your human weaknesses and shortcomings and ascend on the third day of your earthly existence, returning to the Celestial City, back to where your journey began."

As more of Nicole's feathers fall to the floor, she suddenly is propelled through a celestial vortex to a clearer understanding who she is, and why she is there. It is all part of the divine plan. Looking inside herself for all the strength contained within, Nicole, a glowing vibration of divine, angelic proportions, now stands under her own power. Michael smiles as she stands proudly next to him.

"Thank you, Michael." Nicole smiles sweetly. "However, I'm not going back. Understanding that I have Free Will, like all the manifestations of our One Infinite Creator, I will do whatever I can to assist humanity through their remaining days of Earth's dimensional transition but from here, within the harmonious surroundings of the heavenly Celestial City," she says firmly.

Semyaza coughs and then beams proudly at Michael and Nicole. "Well, well, Michael, I guess you can't have everything now, can you?" A sense of satisfaction resides deep inside the Lord of Darkness for his undying dedication in attempting to destroy the angelic vibrations within Nicole while she was on Earth, especially in his strongholds of New York City and Las Vegas. And yet, even now, in the safety of the Celestial City's surroundings, her fears are still holding her back.

Michael is quick to respond, his voice calm yet compelling. "This is not over, my friend." He turns and looks proudly at Nicole, raising her arm up high.

"Nicole, it is with great honor and pleasure, as Vice President of Operations for Infinity Airways, to offer you the newly created position of Vice President of Inflight Service, overseeing all flight attendant training programs and all onboard passenger services for Infinity Airways," Michael announces proudly. "You have earned your golden wings and more!" The shimmering sound of angelic choirs can be heard again throughout the Celestial City. "It's time to leave your pain and suffering behind, Nicole. Allow your destiny to unfold by spreading your wings; fly with courage and love, on a wing and a prayer."

Eve sits silent and unbelieving. *What! Nicole has just defiantly refused to return to Earth; and yet Michael still offers her, a trainee, one of the top management positions in the airline? A position that will work side by side with him for the rest of eternity!* Eve is stunned as she watches Michael walk toward the gallery, stopping directly in front of her. He reassuringly pats her hand and then continues to speak to everyone as he looks at Eve. "Your passion, Nicole, your unique ways of working with our passengers, and now your inherent understanding of humanity, can bring forth the very understanding our airline needs to help calm the fear that permeates humanity."

Eve stares back at Michael, shocked and bewildered by his decision to choose Nicole over her for the job. He turns his back to Eve to address Nicole and The Council.

"I don't understand!" exclaims Nicole. Waves of sorrow, joy, pain, elation, and regret sweep over her with his announcement.

Michael resumes his presentation of the final phase of Earth's dimensional shift with images of changes occurring on Earth as he walks once again around the council table. "The timeline has been moved forward, my friends. Indeed, we are no longer looking to Earth's year-end of 2012 for its ascension into the Fourth Dimension, as reflected in the Mayan Sacred Calendar. Most of humanity's understanding about their future is still in the dark, if you will pardon the pun, Semyaza," says Michael, staring at his old friend and foe intently to make his point. "Their original wound of separation from our Infinite Creator, their fear, humanity's resistance to unconditional love, and their negative feelings about the planet's changes are increasing and intensifying the very situations they fear most. Mother Earth can no longer absorb their slower, denser negative vibrations." A sense of urgency permeates the words in his message; a hint of warning carries in his voice. "She is moving forward with her ascension, with her divine cosmic plan. With the constant bombardment and intensity of fear, wars, pollution, and the unceasing low levels of consciousness emanating from our human friends, Earth will not tolerate any more. We are now looking at 2011 or even sooner. Therefore, our efforts have to be stepped up to awaken those who chose to be awake!"

Michael presses on to provide more information. He turns to address everyone in the gallery. "Our angels are working with The Ascended Masters and The Intergalactic Ambassadors to assist with The Council of Saturn and Infinity Airways in speeding up the karmic balancing among the souls on Earth. We are working in an unprecedented universal effort to release some of the negativity, to balance the karmic scales of a few, and to educate them to the truths that are so obvious to us, yet blinded from humanity. Working together, we can help ease the pressure and difficulty of the Earth's birthing process, to reduce the pain and suffering caused by humanity's misunderstanding of the ascension process. Their planet is not dying; humanity is not dying. Indeed, together, they are giving birth to the new, lighter, and brighter generation—the Fourth Dimension of Consciousness."

The hologram emanating from *The Book of Life* displays further portions of Washington, Oregon, and California sliding into the Pacific Ocean after a polar shift. Hurricanes, droughts, wildfires, flooding, tsunamis, and earthquakes continue to increase around the globe while volcanic ash blackens the skies from the dramatic rise in volcanic eruptions. Record amounts of snow, wind, and rains continue with expansive storms moving across all landmasses. Energies throughout the solar system and galaxy are shown to be increasing, along with unprecedented solar activity and accelerating speeds of change in the Sun's magnetic field. The atmospheric changes and polar shifts on the other planets are also displayed.

Nicole quietly interrupts. "Excuse me, please. But how can an airline, Infinity Airways, help when we are looking at major cataclysmic events like these? Like I said to you before, Michael, it all seems somewhat hopeless. No disrespect is intended; however, I was just there. I was just completely human. How can we really make a difference?" Her voice holds all the weariness of someone who has reached the end and no longer has the energy to fight. Lowering her eyes, she timidly asks, "How can I make a difference?"

"Yeah, Michael. Really! Someone like her, an angelic human mutt, is going to make a difference? Oh, please!" Mother Mary, Archangel Metatron, and Buddha give Semyaza the look. Semyaza forces his gaze elsewhere, rebelliously ignoring their glare, as he continues with his outburst. "You are really wasting my time and that of everyone here."

Sacred silence is heard as the brilliant white Light fills the room once more. Immediately the voice of The One Infinite Creator comes forth. "Because of her unparalleled understanding of humans and her experience as one of them qualifies her to make a difference. Nicole, not only have you brought a little of Heaven to Earth, you have brought a little of Earth to Heaven. And what you can do for just one passenger, you do for all. There is no separation, Nicole. All are Part of The One. To serve One is to serve All. That is the message. That is The Law of One."

Nicole stands quietly, pondering the divine words of The Creator. "Dear One Infinite Creator, may I come before Thee with a most humble question?" Nicole's voice quivers nervously as she tries to sound most reverent. "Please?"

"Yes," The Creator responds.

"What is the purpose of the Third Dimension? I mean, I'm not questioning your divine authority or your plan. I'm ... uh ... I'm just trying to understand more fully what we are there to do?" asks Nicole, feeling so small and so humbled to be in the presence of The Creator of All That Is.

Michael walks around the room, looking at everyone in the gallery. Quietly, he stops directly in front of Nicole. Eve watches sadly as Michael looks intensely at Nicole and smiles. "The purpose of incarnation in the Third Dimension is to learn the ways of Love. That is its only purpose."

Everyone turns as the giant alien in the gallery stands. "What is the experience in the Fourth Dimension for this category of planet and its inhabitants?"

Michael addresses his question. "The Fourth Dimension is not of words. One is aware of the thoughts and vibrations of others. Primarily, it's a plane of compassion and understanding of the sorrows of those in the Third Dimen—"

"No one is going to make it! You're just wasting your time!" Semyaza cries out in complete exasperation. He violently slams both his fists down on the council table as he rises from his seat, knocking his council chair to the floor. Reverberations are felt throughout the Council Chamber as his anger grows. "They're all going to be stuck in their miserable little third-dimensional existence for another tortuous and tormented seventy-five thousand years if I have anything to say about it!"

Michael smiles slightly, waiting for Semyaza to finish his tirade and be reseated. "The Fourth Dimension abounds in compassion. There is no experience of disharmony within the self or within other peoples. Perfectly designed by our Creator, it is not within the limits of possibility to cause disharmony in any way." Michael walks to the table and pats Semyaza heartily on the shoulder. "Sorry, Semyaza, not much fun for you and your Legions of Darkness since this cycle lasts approximately thirty million of Earth's years."

Nicole boldly speaks up, "Creator, may I ask one more question of Thee?" Feeling more confident, she doesn't wait for an answer. Nicole points directly at Semyaza and demands, "Why is he here?"

"My lovely expression of The Divine, Semyaza is part of All That Is. In the third-dimensional experience of duality, you cannot have the Light without the Dark; you cannot have good if there is no bad; there is no short if you do not have tall; there can be no right if you do not have wrong. Do you see? Evil serves as a very crucial and necessary part in the lower vibrations so one can learn what one is, by what one is not. It is all about choice, and there are many. Semyaza is an honored and faithful servant of The One Infinite Creator, taking on a role that most are not powerful or dedicated enough to perform. Look closely, Nicole. Look very closely at what he did for you."

While staring fiercely at the Lord of Darkness, Nicole notices the *Las Vegas Sun* newspaper in his hand. As a sudden surge of panic jabs her, she begins to tremble when she sees the photograph of crashed emergency medical helicopter on the front page. To her shock and amazement, Semyaza is holding the very newspaper that was in her penthouse suite, the very newspaper that reported Father Knorosov's death. Overwhelmed and confused, Nicole reflects quietly on the difficult trials and tribulations that occurred during her time on the Earth. Everyone in the Council Chamber sits patiently. Michael stands quietly next to her. Nicole is terribly confused and lost in deep thought trying to digest the significance of all that has happened.

Michael breaks the protracted silence and startles her with a question. "Do you know why your name is Nicole?"

Nicole looks bewildered and shrugs her heavy shoulders.

Michael allows a serious expression to cross his face as he explains, "The name Nicole comes from the Greek root words, *nike* and *laos*, respectively meaning *victory* and *people*."

Nicole begins to cry, her body trembles and more feathers drop. Her voice quivers, "Must I go back?" She weeps uncontrollably with warm human tears streaming down her angelic face. She glances at the hologram of devastating earthquakes tearing away landmasses in southern California. "It's just too painful. It's just so dense. It's just so hope—"

The face of Simon Knorosov suddenly comes across the holographic display. She looks on, watching him closely. His face is weary and saddened as he watches Jane take her last breath. In their family home, Briggs, Louis, and other family members around the deathbed console each other and pray for Jane to pass on peacefully to the Other Side after the long journey back to their hometown.

"Father! You're still alive!" exclaims Nicole, quickly trying to comprehend the consequences of this discovery.

As she and everyone else continue to watch the hologram, Rochel and Dina come into view wearing their Infinity Airways uniforms. Nicole looks quizzically to Eve then returns her attention to the images where Rochel and Dina assist Jane's guardian angel in freeing Jane from her diseased body. As family and friends begin to weep and mourn Jane's passing, the house begins to rumble, and walls break apart as another intense aftershock reverberates through their town. Nicole watches anxiously as Father Knorosov suffers minor injuries during his heroic efforts to get everyone out. He stands outside the Bradley house in the sweltering heat and looks around. His vestment is torn. His face dirty, and blood from the gash above his eyebrow drips down his cheek. The priest looks up with tears in his eyes to the heavens above and faithfully gives thanks to God.

As blood, sweat and tears blend together and stream down his face, he notices an Infinity Airways plane flying high overhead. The world suddenly seems to stand still. In an instant he surrenders his heart in confession, dropping to his knees in prayer. Everyone in the Council Chamber hears him whisper, "Where are you my beloved, Nicole? God knows I would give my very soul to find you again." Everyone present can feel his love, his pain, his heartache, and his passion for Nicole. Through the hologram, they can smell his sweat and the unsettled air around him. They experience his fatigue and his injuries. They feel the intense summer heat and feel the turbulent shifting vibrations emitting from the Earth below his feet.

With the sudden realization that she had been maliciously deceived by Semyaza, Nicole stares fiercely at him as she marches toward the council table. Nicole's blazing eyes glare past the other council members, seeing only the one who had defiled her.

Semyaza snickers darkly, raising the *Las Vegas Sun* newspaper to cover his smiling face. "Oops!"

Nicole violently rips the newspaper from Semyaza's hands. "Is there no limit to the depths of your despicable deceptions and evil lies!" Her voice becomes louder as her anger rises. "Well, Mr. Olivier, Semyaza, or whatever the hell your name is, you are not going to mess with me again! I will go above and beyond, returning to Earth not only to help humanity and Infinity Airways, but also to find my real true love—again!" The power of the moment permeates Nicole to her soul as she points to Father Knorosov's image on holographic display. With defiance in her eyes, she announces boldly to everyone present. "I will return to Earth . . . but only as Eve's assistant."

Nicole turns and glares carefully at Michael. She then marches over to Eve as she continues with her announcement. Everyone is murmuring as they wonder what she will say next. "Eve Matrona has a wisdom that is hard to find. One that cannot be found in some training program, dug up from some old book, or from some angel who has never had an assignment before. In fact, it cannot be found at all. Her irreplaceable wisdom comes from within, from eons of experience, fortitude, and understanding. Her wisdom and expertise are always there, even at forty-one thousand feet in a crowded airplane heading to New York City. And with that kind of wisdom comes the power to fly higher. But sometimes wisdom's power has to come through pain and sometimes pleasure, sometimes both." Nicole half-smiles at Eve before continuing, speaking words that seem beyond herself. "As a seeker of wisdom, one must be honest with herself. For hiding from one's weaknesses only brings about inertia. It requires very little for one to sit and pretend to be something she is not. And little will be the reward."

Nicole stares scornfully at the most senior of angels and then winks. "Human beings are not the only ones that need to transcend their ways. There are beings around here that need to shift out of their comfort zones as well, to move forward to the next level." Her words open the hearts of many in the gallery. As Nicole turns back to face The Council of Saturn, she suddenly collapses to the floor, powerless to get up. Staring back in disbelief, Nicole watches as all her remaining dingy yellowed feathers fall into the mists. Slowly her wings begin to morph before her very eyes and that of everyone else. Miraculously out of nowhere, a brilliant golden light emerges from the most beautiful of feathers ever created. Nicole looks back questioningly to the leader of archangels.

Michael stands motionlessly looking into her eyes with praise and adoration. Glowing into higher and higher frequencies, his pilot uniform drops to the floor, disappearing into the mist-shrouded floor. Nicole gasps as she looks on. As he transforms into his natural angelic form, enormously magnificent wings appear behind him. Raising his arms full and wide, the archangel's glorious golden wingspan spreads beyond the infinite boundaries of her view. With his golden hair, gilded wings, and flowing ivory robes, the archangel beams victoriously as he looks over to Semyaza.

"How can this be?" Nicole cries in humbled bewilderment as she looks back to her own wings that now glow brightly. She comes to understand that every pain, every heartache, every disappointment was deliberately laid out for her to experience—to bring her to this magnificent point in her journey. "My wings . . . my wings look like yours."

With his deeply penetrating eyes still locked onto Nicole, Michael extends his power and glory to her with his outstretched arm. Lifting a shaky hand toward his with all the strength that remains, Michael pulls Nicole up from the floor. Everyone watches in awe, as the newest of archangels takes her rightful position next to Michael. As the only fallen angel to ever ascend back to its Source, Nicole is honored and rewarded for her epic triumph. The whispering and pointing from the gallery begins again. Eve allows a bittersweet smile, everything now making sense. Nicole not only passed the test on Earth but has also passed the test in Heaven.

Archangels Metatron and Michael along with every member of the council nod and smile proudly at the Lord of Darkness. Out of the blue, Nicole abruptly marches over to the back of Semyaza's chair. Confidently standing behind the endarkened angel of the highest order, Nicole suddenly points to the revered members of The Council of Saturn. "Are you just going to sit there staring and grinning, feeling proud of yourselves, or are you going to do something?"

Semyaza laughs as Nicole stares audaciously at his fellow council members. Shifting her intense, chastising gaze from one member to the next, Nicole spreads her contagious determination and commitment to everyone. An urgent message is conveyed through her eyes from the depths of her half-angel, half-human being. As her eyes meet with those of Ra, she notices something vaguely familiar about them. *Can it be possible?* Before the meeting, she had never seen of anyone on The Council up close before. She quickly shakes off the feeling of familiarity as she looks next to Kuan Yin. Nicole begins to understand on some psychic level who Kuan Yin is in the astral world. Nicole ponders the possibilities of what the Bodhisattva of Compassion can do on Earth in the remaining years of the planet's third-dimensional existence.

As Nicole's eyes rest on the last of the ascended masters, she begins to get a queasy feeling in her abdomen and a faint swirling sensation in her head. She looks closely at Quetzalcoatl. His penetrating amber eyes beg to join her in her enthusiastic quest to help humanity. Nicole feels a sense of familiarity there too. However, it feels more intimate, more personal, than that of Ra. As their eyes lock for what seems like forever, Semyaza begins to stir in his seat then lets out an unnerving guffaw. Mother Mary and others shift awkwardly then offer Michael a questioning look.

Nicole concludes her admonishment of The Council. "We need to get back to Earth as soon as possible. On the cusp of massive shifts, humanity needs all of you saints, holy people, masters, avatars, adepts, prophets, yogis, and saviors or whatever else you call yourselves, more than ever!"

A chilling silence overtakes the gallery as the Lord of Darkness grins haughtily, reveling in the fact that Nicole is using his very own words to address the rest of The Council. Satisfaction fills him, understanding that there is still some part of him that remains with her. As Semyaza anticipates his forthcoming defeat of The Council and The Confederation of Planets in their efforts, he simultaneously tries to understand what Nicole is up to—to understand her motivations. *Does she belong to me now?* He begins to wonder.

Semyaza's thoughts are suddenly disrupted when Nicole unexpectedly grabs his chair and powerfully spins him around. Fearlessly, she points her finger in his bewildered evil face. "And let's first start with you!" Like the phoenix bird—a symbol of fire and divinity that is said to regenerate when hurt or wounded by a foe, and thus being almost immortal and invincible—Nicole challenges Semyaza. In front of everyone present, the newest of archangels challenges her fiendish foe to go to Earth to help save humanity as well, shrewdly understanding what he did for her, he can do for others.

Chapter 108

Dressed proudly in her crisp white uniform, wearing her new gold Infinity Airways flight attendant wings, Nicole explains the boarding process to several new flight attendant trainees. Eve smiles as she walks by the boarding door with makeup on, her hair down, and with an open blouse.

Saint Pete walks on board and hands Nicole the passenger manifest with a wink and a smile. She picks up the aircraft handset to make an onboard announcement. "Welcome aboard Infinity Airways flight 666 to Washington DC. It is a pleasure to have you with us this morning. Please place all your heavy baggage . . ." Nicole begins enthusiastically. As she smoothes the front of her uniform blazer with her hand, the gold-beaded rosary that Father Knorosov had previously given her slides down to her wrist.

The Mayan Sacred Calendar

The Maya, once occupying what are today southern Mexico, Belize, and Guatemala, are shrouded in mystery. Archeologists believe that they crossed the dry Bering land bridge, while others (including Edgar Cayce) claim they were emigrants from Atlantis. For reasons which are still much debated, in the eighth and ninth centuries, the Maya culture went into decline. Detailed monumental inscriptions all but disappeared. Many great cities were abandoned, some just left half-built for the jungle to reclaim. Warfare, ecological depletion of croplands, and drought or some combination of those factors are usually suggested as reasons for the decline.

When Hernán Cortés, along with his host of conquistadors and the attending Catholic friars, landed on the east coast of Mexico in 1519, the total population of Mesoamerica was an estimated twenty-five million people. A century later, it fell drastically to about one million. Exactly how and why this happened is not fully known because Spanish missionaries destroyed all but a handful of the Mayan books. It took less than a century for a prominent and ancient civilization to be decimated and the calendar that had served as their compass guide for thousands of years to be driven into near obscurity.

The Maya accomplishments were legion. They were brilliant mathematicians who used a sophisticated numbering system with which they calculated the distance to the Sun to three decimals and predicted eclipses. Their greatest achievement was the famous Mayan Sacred Calendar, not based on astronomical movements, but on the rhythm in which divine creation unfolds. It is a scientifically specific and an unambiguously true timeline for the evolution of consciousness. The sacred calendar of the

Maya is above all a prophetic calendar that may help us today to understand the past and foresee the future.

This calendar used by the Maya is actually two in one. The mundane calendar, the Haab, governed daily life, especially crop planting, and was more accurate than our Gregorian calendar. Their year had eighteen months of twenty days plus five "unlucky" days at the end to make up the 365 days. The Tzolkin or sacred calendar used two cycles. Twenty named days repeated thirteen times gave each day a special meaning, making for a 260-day sacred year that governed rituals and ceremonies. Thus, every day had two meanings—its Haab meaning and its Tzolkin meaning—and any particular day took fifty-two years to come around again.

The calendar also features a great cycle of 5,125 years, five of which incidentally yield 25,625 years, which is their calculation for the precession of the equinoxes. Since the Mayan Calendar began with the start of the current great cycle in 3113 BCE, the 5,125 period gives us the year 2012 as its close—December 21, to be precise.

However, like everything else in the world, there are different opinions as to the actual start date. Dates, when plotted according to one calendar method, do not always line up exactly when translated to another calendar. One may be accurate in calculating the number of days, months, and years between events; but unless the starting point is *precisely known*, the end point remains questionable. To others, it will happen sooner. To others, it will happen later. To some, it is happening now. But all agree—it will happen.

So what is significant about the close of a great cycle? It points to a tremendous shift in human consciousness that will synchronize us with much larger cosmic patterns. Esoteric researchers have always known that the Mayan Calendar was aligned with something far larger than just our tiny planet, but whether this signals full-blown ascension into the Fourth Dimension remains to be seen. For now, in the last katun, or twenty-year cycle of the calendar (1992-2012), we are seeing unparalleled frequency shifts as more light pours onto the planet. Those who chose to jump aboard will enjoy immense transformation amidst the chaotic collapse of old outworn systems. Those who rigidly hang on to those old systems will perish along with them.

Keep in mind that many who have studied the Mayan Sacred Calendar are focusing on the end date—overlooking the transformation of consciousness that is occurring slowly day by day. With this narrow perspective, the path to enlightenment is lost. Therefore, we have to remember it's about the journey, not just the destination.

What else can we expect? The falling away from duality, increasingly direct experience of who we are as spirit, the speeding up of time, synchronicity, and paranormal experiences becoming commonplace and a grand sense of completion. We can also expect to see the UFO cover-up collapse as more countries join France, Belgium, and Brazil in full disclosure to their citizens. The Internet will continue to grow as people find access to information increasingly empowering and education reforms as the school system is confronted by Indigo children who demand more control of their lives.

And beyond 2012? What can we expect as we enter a new twenty-six-thousand-year cycle? The Mayan Calendar is silent on this, but the current cycle is all about preparation for synchronizing with a much larger cosmic game plan. Will there be an end to death at the end of time? Will we exist as part of the timeless, enlightened cosmic consciousness? Will life truly begin? Can we expect full, open contact with our extraterrestrial neighbors, already gathered around the planet for the celebration? Will human beings then be considered a fellow citizen of the galactic community?

We will soon find out as the last few years of the great cycle of this fascinating blueprint should prove to be very interesting indeed. Are you ready?

For more information on the Mayan Sacred Calendar, go to these web addresses:

www.MayanSacredCalendar.com
www.calleman.com
www.Mayan-Calendar-Code.com

My Recommended Reading List

McCarty, James Allen and Elkins, Don, and Rueckert, Carla, *The RA Material: The Law of One: Books I-V,* Whitford Press, Atglen, PA (1984)
http://www.llresearch.org

Free, Wynn and Wilcock, David, *The Reincarnation of Edgar Cayce? Interdimensional Communication & Global Transformation,* Frog, Ltd. Berkeley, CA (2004)
http://www.ascension2000.com
http://www.divinecosmos.com

Calleman, Ph.D., Carl Johan, *The Mayan Calendar and the Transformation of Consciousness,* Bear & Company, Rochester, VT (2004)
http://www.calleman.com

Mac, Andi, *5 Astonishing Revelations Found in the Mayan Calendar Code,* (an e-book) Mayan Calendar Code/FreshAir Enterprises (2006)
http://www.mayan-calendar-code.com/

Koven, Jean-Claude, *Going Deeper: How to Make Sense of Your Life When Your Life Makes No Sense,* Prism House Press (2004) Rancho Mirage, CA
http://www.goingdeeper.org

Argüelles, José, *The Mayan Factor: Path Beyond Technology*, Bear & Company, Rochester, VT (1987)

Begich, Nick and Jeanne Manning, *Angels Don't Play This HAARP*, Earthpulse Press, Anchorage, AK (1995)

Brinkley, Dannion, *Saved by the Light*, Harper Collins, New York, NY (1995)
http://www.dannion.com

Camp, Robert Lee, *Destiny Cards*, Sourcebooks, Inc., Naperville, IL (1998)
————*Love Cards*, Sourcebooks, Inc., Naperville, IL (1998)
http://www.7thunders.com

Cayce, Edgar: many books have been written about the sleeping prophet. The Association for Research and Enlightenment (A.R.E.) in Virginia Beach, VA is a voluminous source of spiritual, metaphysical, and historical books and material.
http://www.edgarcayce.org

Coe, Michael D., *Breaking the Maya Code*, Thames & Hudson Inc., New York, NY (1992)

Davidson, Gustav, *A Dictionary of Angels: Including the Fallen Angels*, The Free Press, New York, NY (1967)

Dougherty, Ned, *Fast Lane to Heaven*, Hampton Roads Publishing Co., Inc., Charlottesville, VA (2001)
http://www.fastlanetoheaven.com

Dyer, Wayne W., *There Is a Spiritual Solution to Every Problem*, HarperCollins Publishers, New York, NY (2001)

Goldberg, Dr. Bruce, *Past Lives Future Lives*, Ballantine Books, New York, NY (1982)

Hawkins M.D., Ph.D, David, *Power vs. Force: The Hidden Determinants of Human Behavior*, Hay House, Inc., Carlsbad, CA (2002)

Hicks, Jerry & Esther, *A New Beginning II: A Personal Handbook to Enhance Your Life, Liberty and Pursuit of Happiness*, Abraham-Hicks Publications, San Antonio, TX (2001)
http://www.abraham-hicks.com

Ingram, Julia and Hardin, G.W., *The Messengers: A True Story of Angelic Presence and the Return to the Age of Miracles*, Pocket Books, New York, NY (1996)

Kenyon, Tom and Essene, Virginia, *The Hathor Material: Messages from an Ascended Civilization*, S.E.E. Publishing Co. (1996)

Melchizedek, Drunvalo, *The Ancient Secret of the Flower of Life*, Volumes 1&2, Light Technology Publishing, Flagstaff, AZ (1990 & 2000)
http://www.floweroflife.org

Moody Jr., M.D., Raymond, *Life after Life: The Investigation of a Phenomenon—Survival of Bodily Death*, HarperSanFranscisco, New York, NY (2001)
http://www.lifeafterlife.com/

Newton, Ph.D., Michael, *Journey of Souls*, Llewellyn Publications, St. Paul, MN (1994)
————*Destiny of Souls*, Llewellyn Publications, St. Paul, MN (2000)

Perala, Robert and Stubbs, Tony, *The Divine Blueprint: Roadmap for the New Millennium*, United Light Publishing, Campbell, CA (1998)
————*The Divine Architect: The Art of Living and Beyond*, United Light Publishing, Scotts Valley, CA (2002)

Robbins, John, *Diet for a New America*, H J Kramer, Inc. and New World Library Novato, CA (1987)
http://www.foodrevolution.org

Van Praagh, James, *Talking to Heaven: A Medium's Message of Life after Death*, New American Library, New York, NY (1997)

Walsch, Neale Donald, *Conversations with God: an Uncommon Dialogue*, Books 1-5 G.P. Putnam's Sons, New York, NY (1995)
————*The New Revelations*, Atria Books, New York, NY (2002)

Weiss, M.D., Brian L. *Many Masters, Many Lives,* A Fireside Book, a division of Simon & Schuster Inc. New York, NY (1988)
————*Only Love Is Real,* Warner Books, New York, NY (1996)

Whitton, Dr. Joel & Fisher, Joe, *Life between Life: Scientific Explorations into the Void Separating One Incarnation from the Next,* Warner Books, New York, NY (1986)